SONGS

OF THE

EARTH

SONGS OF THE EARTH

THE WILD HUNT
BOOK ONE

&

ELSPETH COOPER

GOLLANCZ
LONDON

First published in Great Britain in 2011 by Gollancz
An imprint of the Orion Publishing Group
Orion House, 5 Upper St Martin's Lane, London WC2H 9EA
An Hachette UK Company

A CIP catalogue record for this book is available
from the British Library

ISBN 978 0 575 09614 1 (Cased)
ISBN 978 0 575 09615 8 (Trade Paperback)

1 3 5 7 9 10 8 6 4 2

Typeset at the Spartan Press Ltd,
Lymington, Hants

Printed and bound in Australia by Griffin Press

The Orion Publishing Group's policy is to use papers that
are natural, renewable and recyclable products and made
from wood grown in sustainable forests. The logging and
manufacturing processes are expected to conform to the
environmental regulations of the country of origin.

www.elspethcooper.com
www.orionbooks.co.uk

For my parents, who set the seed.
I hope it was worth the wait.

1

CONDEMNED

❧

The magic was breaking free again.

Its music sang along Gair's nerves as if they were harp-strings, a promise of power thrumming through his fingers. All he had to do was embrace it, if he dared. He pressed his face into his knees and prayed. 'Hail, Mother, full of grace, light and life of all the world. Blessed are the meek, for they shall find strength in you. Blessed are the merciful, for they shall find justice in you. Blessed are the lost, for they shall find salvation in you. Amen.'

Line by line, verse by verse, the devotion tumbled from his cracked lips. His fingers twitched for the familiar shapes of rosary beads to keep the count, but he had lost his place long ago. When the words faltered, he hugged his knees tighter to his chest and began again.

'Now I am lost in a place of darkness O Mother I am fallen from thy path guide me once more . . .'

Music still whispered seductively in his ears. Nothing drowned it out, not prayers, not pleas, not even the few hymns he could still remember. It was everywhere: in the rusted iron walls of his cell, in the rank sweat on his skin, in the colours he saw in the dark. With every breath he took, it grew a little louder.

Silvery chimes rang in the air. Gair opened his eyes and they were seared by a light so bright, so white, he had to shield his face with his hands. Through his fingers he saw two figures, clothed in brilliance. Angels. Holy Mother, angels sent to carry him home.

'. . . bless me now and take me to your side let me be forgiven of all my sins . . .'

On his knees, Gair waited for the blessing. A backhanded blow across his face sent him sprawling.

'Save your chants, hidderling!'

Another blow flung him hard against the iron-plate wall. Pain exploded in his temple and the music shivered into silence.

'Gently, now. He has no power to harm you here.'

No. He had no power. The magic was too wild, too unpredictable to belong to anyone for long. He didn't need iron walls to be helpless. Slumped on the floor, Gair clutched his pounding head. *Blessed are the lost.*

Silver-spurred boots crossed his line of sight, rowels chiming. Not bells. No robes of light, just the white wool surcoats of the Lord Provost's marshals. Iron manacles snicked round Gair's wrists and the marshals hauled him up by the chains.

He fell back to his knees as the cell wheeled crazily around him. Cursing, a marshal drove his boot into Gair's rump.

The other marshal clicked his tongue. 'It's a sin to take Her name in vain, you know that.'

'Heh. You swore yourself to the wrong House, my friend. You preach like a lector.' Another kick. 'Up, witch! Walk to your judgement, or we'll drag you!'

Gair lurched to his feet. Out in the stone-flagged corridor, sunlight lancing through high windows blinded him again. The marshals took position either side of him with their hands under his arms, half steering him, half supporting him when he stumbled. Scabbards slapped and spurs rang as more marshals fell in step behind.

Endless blurry corridors. Stairs that tripped him and tore at his bare toes. No time to rest or catch his breath; he had to walk or fall, and he had fallen so far already. Out of the Goddess' grace, out of Her hearing, no matter how many fragments of prayers still skittered through the void the magic had left inside him.

'. . . be a light and comfort to me now and in the hour of my death . . .'

'Quiet!'

A gauntleted hand cuffed the side of Gair's head and a yank on his chains pulled him on. Wider hallways now, panelled in wood. Marble tiles underfoot instead of bare dressed stone, and hangings on the walls. One final turn and the marshals halted. Dark doors towered ahead, flanked by smudgy figures carrying long banners. A breath of air stirred the fabric, and Holy Oaks flamed as thread of gold embroidery caught the sun.

Recognition sank like a stone into Gair's gut. Those doors led to the Rede Hall, where the Knights held their councils and ceremonies . . . where the Order gave its judgements. His knees buckled, and chains clattered as he put out his hands to stop himself sprawling on the polished floor. Inside him, a whisper of music stirred and was still.

Judgement. Too late to hope he might be spared; too late to hope for anything but forgiveness.

Oh Goddess, look kindly on me now.

Ahead, the massive doors swung noiselessly inwards.

꙰

From the curtained alcove above the doors Alderan could see the length of the Rede Hall, from surcoated sentries to the many-leaved bronze Oak above the Preceptor's chair, glowing in the sun that was streaming through the tall windows. His perch was high enough above everyone's eyeline to be safe, provided he did nothing to attract attention to himself, but it was still a risk being there.

The benches either side of the hall were crowded with hier-archs, magnificent in their formal scarlet – a full house, as close as he could count, full of rosy cheeks and well-padded arses, gossip-ing and nodding and fluffing their feathers.

Alderan's lip curled. *These are the inheritors of Endirion? The First Knight must be weeping in his grave.*

From a side door came a pair of clerks, sober as ravens in their black robes. They took their seats at desks facing each other across the hall before the Preceptor's chair on its dais, the prosecutor sorting his papers, the scribe setting out pens and ink to record the day's proceedings for the archives. A moment later, the Preceptor himself entered the hall.

Ansel's angular frame was as upright as ever, but his thick hair matched his white robes, and the hand that held his staff of office was knobbed and twisted by arthritis.

So at last he's met a foe he cannot vanquish. The hero of Samarak, finally brought low by time.

At Ansel's side, the Chaplain was unchanged, if a little greyer than when Alderan had last seen him. Leonine head bent to whisper a word for Ansel's ear alone, Danilar frowned at the response, then folded his massive hands in his sleeves and walked to his seat on the front row of benches. Ansel squared his shoul-ders, then climbed the steps onto the dais and turned to face the hall. The hierarchs fell silent.

'I call this Rede to order,' he announced. 'Let us begin.'

A twitch of Ansel's fingers signalled the sentries to open the doors. Every hierarch leaned forward, the better to watch the entrance of the accused. In his lap, Alderan's fists clenched. These were the Order's most senior officers, subservient only to the Preceptor, himself second only to the Lector of Dremen.

And yet look at them! Gawking like yokels at the fair, waiting for the showman to bring out his painted lady or a two-headed calf. I hope the Goddess is watching what Her anointed few are about to do in Her name.

Through the doors came a pair of marshals, their prisoner stumbling between them. Long lank hair and many days' growth of beard hid the captive's face, but nothing hid what had been done to him. His naked body was patterned with bruises. Scabs from the lash crusted his back, and one foot left bloody smears on the black and white floor with each step. When the marshals chained him to the mahogany rail of the witness stand he crashed to his knees, too weak to stand.

As one, the Curia caught their breath. Some of the hierarchs made a show of holding handkerchiefs to their faces as they stared.

Was this how far the Suvaeon had fallen from the tenets of Diamondhelm? Returning to the question and the tawse, that had been outlawed for centuries? Anger uncoiled in Alderan's belly like a serpent rearing to strike. Was this what they called justice?

&

Pain stabbed Gair's foot as he fell. Buzzing darkness swarmed into his vision from all sides and the Rede Hall became a vortex of scarlet and sunlight, sucking him down to the chequered floor.

His stomach clenched to spew. He swallowed the nausea down hard and shut his eyes until the dizziness passed. The hierarchs were staring at him. Their revulsion, their awful fascination, prickled over the back of his neck. Their silence rang as loud as a shout.

Apostate! Unbeliever!
He had no answer for them. How could he deny the truth? His skin crawled with guilt.
Stand up, novice. Whatever comes, face it on your feet.
Selenas, the Master of Swords, hard brown hand extended to help a boy up from the dirt of a sun-soaked practice yard, what felt like a century ago. Helping him up to fight again.
Gair opened his eyes. Black and white tiles under him. Smells of floor polish and incense and – merciful Mother! – his own unwashed body. On the periphery of his vision, dark wood, red robes. Let the Curia stare. They would not see him mewling on the floor like a pup.

Slowly, chains heavy on his wrists, he took hold of the mahogany rail and pulled himself to his feet.

❧

Alderan let out a breath he had not even realised he held. They had not broken him. The boy was unsteady, but he was standing, head up to meet the Preceptor's gaze full on. Exultation punched up from Alderan's gut. There was hope yet.

The Preceptor raised his steel-shod staff and struck the dais three times, measured as a heartbeat. Around the hall, the hierarchs stilled. Motes flared in the sunlight from the long windows. The sun had moved westwards; now the dais lay in shadow and the witness stand stood full in the glare.

'Who stands before the Rede?' Ansel's voice was worn thin by the years, but still it had a snap to it.

'One who stands accused,' responded the prosecutor, warrant in his hands. He did not look at the prisoner.

'Of what is he accused?'

'My lord, he is charged with foully desecrating the house of the Goddess, sinning against Her commandments and violating the sternest precepts of our faith.'

'By what means?'

'Witchcraft.'

A hiss of indrawn breath rippled through the crowded benches. Just the word was enough to have them reaching for their rosaries. Alderan's fists clenched again; he made himself fold his hands in his lap. He was not there to tear the Rede Hall apart brick by brick. Not today.

'Why does he stand here?'

'To receive the judgement of the Rede.'

Silence, apart from the scritch of the scribe's quill, then even that ceased. Despite the weight of the stares on him the lad held his head up, kept his eyes fixed on the place in the shadows where Ansel's face should be. He did not squint, though his eyes must

6

surely be watering. The sun cut through his overgrown beard, revealing the hard angles of the face beneath. Typical Leahn, from the ruler-level brows and long straight nose to the set of his jaw. Not even a hint that he was perturbed to stand in front of the Rede in naught but his own sweat. Or if he was, he would damned well not let it show.

Oh, he's going to be a handful.

In the hall below, the silence grew heavier. The prosecutor shuffled his paperwork irritably, stealing a glance at the Preceptor. Even the dust in the air seemed to pause, suspended like flies in amber. On the benches, hierarchs leaned forward.

Ansel stepped into the light. His pale hair flared halo-like around his head as he took the charge sheet from the prosecutor. The Curia stood up with a creak of benches and a rustle of robes.

'You have been charged with numerous acts of witchcraft, the details of which have been discussed at length by this assembly,' Ansel said, glancing at the parchment in his hand. 'The Rede has heard the evidence presented to it, including the sworn statement lodged by Elder Goran. We have also heard the testimony of other witnesses, given under oath in this chamber, and the reports concerning your confession.'

He looked straight at Gair. To his credit, the lad did not flinch.

'The Rede has reached a verdict. Are you prepared to hear our judgement, my son?'

'I am, my lord.'

Alderan shook his head. *Goddess love the boy, he stares damnation in the eye!*

The Preceptor paused, the attention of the room locked upon him.

'Hear now the judgement of the Rede.' Ansel's words were flat and cold as stone. 'We find the accused guilty of all charges. The sentence is death by burning.'

Gair gripped the railing tight and locked his knees. He would not go down again. He would not! But still the verdict roared in his ears.

Be a light and comfort to me now and in the hour of my death oh Mother if You can still hear me I don't want to die.

'However.'

Ansel crumpled the parchment between his hands. The prosecutor blinked; opposite him, Brother Chronicler goggled up at the Preceptor, wet lips slack as the ball of paper dropped onto his desk and pattered across it to the floor.

'An appeal for clemency has been entered into the record, citing your previous good character and conduct. The Rede must take this into account, therefore the sentence will be commuted to branding, excommunication from the Eadorian faith and banishment from this parish on pain of death. You have until dusk today to comply. May the Goddess have mercy on your soul.'

Ansel's staff struck the dais three times.

Gair stared. Reprieve? How? Surely he had misheard, his ears still filled with the sizzle of flames.

'Preposterous!' Elder Goran strode down the tiers from the upper benches on the left side of the hall. Angry purple suffused his meaty face. 'This is outrageous, Ansel! I demand to know who entered this plea!'

'I cannot tell you, Goran, you know that. It was entered as a sealed plea and as such is anonymous. Consistorial law is quite clear on the point.'

'The punishment for witchcraft is death,' Goran insisted. 'There can be no commuting it, no appeal. It is stated in the Book of Eador: "Suffer ye not the life of a witch and shun ye all works of evil lest they imperil thy soul." This is not *justice*. This is an insult to the Goddess Herself!'

'Peace, Goran.' Ansel lifted his hand as angry mutters of support rose from the benches. 'All of you. We have argued this out before. It serves no purpose to do so again. This Rede is concluded.'

'I must protest, Preceptor! This creature has turned his face from the one true Goddess. He has besmirched the sanctity of the Suvaeon Order, instigated who knows what corruption and depravity amongst us. He has performed acts of witchcraft here, on holy ground. He must be punished!'

The sun was too hot on Gair's face. His head spun and he clung to the wooden railing for support.

Across the chamber, Danilar leaned forward from his seat. 'Don't you think the boy is being punished enough, Goran?' the Chaplain asked mildly. 'He will never be welcome in a place of worship again once he wears a witchmark. Never be able to wed, never have his children blessed and taken into the faith. It will go with him to his grave, along with the hatred and suspicion of his neighbours. Is that not enough?'

'The punishment for witchcraft is death.' Goran smacked one plump fist into his other hand to mark out the words. 'We cannot flinch from it because the accused comes from our own ranks. Whosoever commits Corlainn's sin shares Corlainn's punishment. He must be burned.'

Angry voices shouted support for Goran. Hands waved and faces twisted into ugliness. Hate-filled words stabbed at Gair's ears, but he kept his eyes fixed on the Preceptor. His intervention was all that kept him from the fire.

Please don't let me die.

Ansel raised his hand for silence and was ignored. Demands tossed down from the benches to either side of the hall thickened the air. Frowning, he drove the heel of his staff onto the dais so hard it rang like the Sacristy bell.

'I have passed sentence!' he barked. 'It is the task of the Rede to determine a verdict. It is mine to set the sentence and I have set it. Now that is *enough*!'

The Curia subsided into vengeful muttering and finally a silence of vast disapproval. Goran remained in front of the lowest tier, glaring.

'Goddess in glory.' Ansel planted his staff between his feet. 'You are disciples of Endirion, my brothers, not a pack of unruly schoolboys. Now go with the Goddess. The Rede is over.'

A few stubborn murmurs of protest caused the Preceptor to lean forward, into the sunlight. His lips thinned and his blue eyes flashed. 'No more, I tell you!'

'This is not the end, Ansel.' Goran levelled a finger at Gair. 'You will hear of this again.' He stalked away towards the doors, his supporters clustered around him. Rustling and shuffling, the remainder of the hierarchs descended from their benches and followed.

Gair sagged against the railing. It was over, and he still had his life. Somehow. Before he had had more than a moment to savour it, the marshals had unchained him and were marching him across the marble-tiled floor. He looked back over his shoulder, but Ansel had already turned away.

Out in the vestibule, his escort prodded him through a side door and down a sloping windowless corridor. It opened onto a circular, chimney-like courtyard floored with cracked and blackened stones around the deep socket for the stake: Traitor's Court, where Corlainn the heretic had paid for his sins in the Founding Wars, and where the citizens of Dremen would have come tomorrow to see another witch burn. The tiers of galleries stood empty, looking down on nothing more than a scarred wooden block with leather straps nailed to it. A brazier stood next to it, tended by a squat, shirtless man in a farrier's apron. Above the brazier the air danced with heat. The iron pushed deep into the coals was cherry-red halfway to the handle. Despair yawned in Gair's belly as he was shoved out into the sun.

A few feet from the farrier stood a slim, upright figure in marshal's mail and surcoat. Gold thread outlined the gauntlet badge on his breast and he wore the golden cords of Provost on his upper arm.

The marshals stamped to attention. Bredon acknowledged their salutes with a nod. Dark, hooded eyes looked Gair over without emotion.

'Please, my lord . . .' *Don't do this.*

The lines that ran from hooked nose to mouth deepened a fraction. 'Is the prisoner fit to stand sentence?' Bredon asked.

The farrier grasped Gair's head between callused hands to thumb back his eyelids. He jerked his head away as the sunlight stung his eyes. Then the farrier pinched up the skin on his upper arm, hard enough to hurt.

'Seen better,' the man grunted. 'But he's got the will.'

'Proceed.'

Gair's escort dragged him towards the block. A kick in the back of his knees forced him to kneel whilst the manacle on his left wrist was unlocked. Desperately he lashed out with the dangling chain and missed. The butt of a marshal's mace connected with the side of his head.

'Be still, hidderling,' the marshal snarled. 'Face your punishment like a man, if not a Knight!'

The noon sun was too bright, its shadows black and sharp as daggers, pounding into Gair's skull. He couldn't focus, had no strength to resist as his left arm was forced onto the block, the other twisted up tight between his shoulder-blades by the chain. His fingers were shoved under a broad iron staple and leather straps hauled tight around his elbow and wrist. Blood dripped from his face, pocking the dusty stones like summer rain.

At the brazier, the farrier wrapped a scrap of leather around the iron's handle and lifted it from the coals. The straw-coloured heel of the branding-iron smoked, the air around it roiling.

Oh Goddess no. Gair struggled to tug his hand free, but the straps held him fast.

'No,' he managed. His breath whistled through clenched teeth. 'Goddess, please! No!'

The throbbing heat of the iron struck like a blow as it was aligned carefully, almost delicately, above the centre of his palm. Sweat burst from his skin. The farrier's eyes slid briefly in Bredon's direction, seeking approval. Then the brand pressed down.

2

SHADOWKIN

&

Wind swept down from the snow-cap with a keenness that cut the breath from Gair's lungs. He had climbed as high as he dared this time, to a rocky spur far above the tree line where the air was so thin and cold it burned. This was where he belonged. Up here he could be himself, with none to watch him but the sky.

He stepped towards the edge of the rock. The wind swirled boisterously there, fiercer, colder, eager to be gone, like him. Below his perch lay the Laraig Anor range, a maze of black granite and blue snow-shadows, awaiting the sun. Soon it would crest the ridge behind him. Already the sky above was brightening, the last stars long since faded. Simiel Dawnbringer was a mere ghost in the west, yellow as old bones.

He took another step. The wind snatched at him; he stretched his arms wide and embraced it. Sunrise struck the shoulder of Tir Breann opposite, turning the snows bright as steel fresh from the forge. One last step and his toes gripped the very edge of the rock. Almost time. Now he leaned out into the void, only the wind between him and a slow fall into nothing, but he trusted it. The wind would carry him; it always had. As long as he lived, it would not let him fall.

His pulse quickened in anticipation. The new day was close,

sizzling just out of sight. Below, the valley held its breath. A moment more, a blink, a heartbeat. *Now.* He leapt.

For an instant he hung suspended, neither rising nor descending, neither flying nor falling, captured as surely as a charm in a sphere of finest Isles crystal. Muscles moved, slid over and against each other, shifting bone and sinew in the complex dance that enabled him to ride the wind. Perfect. Pinions thrummed, whispering their song around him. Sunlight across his shoulders turned his flesh to gold and fire. *Perfect.*

And then he fell.

Gair jerked awake. His breath whooshed out of him, stomach yawning away, still falling into the ringing silence of the mountains – except he wasn't in the mountains any more. Dogs barked in the distance, wagons rumbled over cobbles. In the city? Not the Motherhouse; the bed under him was too soft and the linens too fine. Where was he?

He pushed himself up into a sitting position and his left palm blossomed into fire. 'Holy Mother!' Clutching his hand to his chest, he fell back onto the pillows. A blank white shriek filled his head. *Holy Mother dear Goddess above it hurts.* He squeezed his wrist tightly to distract himself until the pain began to ebb.

'Drink this. It'll help with the pain.'

A hand held a pottery beaker towards him. Beyond it, Gair saw only a vague shape in the shadows where the speaker must be.

'Where is this place?'

'We're at an inn called the Oak and Eagle, off Copper Chare on the west side of Dremen. I brought you here from Traitor's Gate.'

'Are you a physician?'

'A hedge-doctor, no more.' The man nodded towards the cup. 'That'll do you more good if you swallow it. It tastes foul, but trust me, you'll feel better for it.'

Gair took the cup. 'What's in it?'

'Athalin, with a little willow-bark, and white mallow for your bruises. Nothing that will cause you harm.'

The man's rounded baritone was soothing, but still. 'I don't know you.'

'I didn't bring you here just so I could poison you in private, lad. Drink up.'

Gair looked at the milky stuff in the cup. Well, he had nothing left to lose. As promised, it tasted dreadful. Holding his breath, he downed it in three swallows.

The man took the empty cup from him and set it aside. 'Now, a little light so we can see what we're about.'

He folded back one of the window shutters. Afternoon spilled into the room, bright as a banner. It illuminated a large-boned fellow with fierce blue eyes framed between a short pepper-and-salt beard and bristling brows. Thick, wavy hair matched the beard for colour and curled around the man's ears like the mane on a stone lion.

'Is that too much?'

'No, it's fine.' Gair still had to squint, but his eyes were stronger than before.

The man pulled up a chair, reversed it and sat down, his arms folded across the back. Ropy muscle corded forearms the colour of teak under a scurf of silver hair. 'How are you feeling?' he asked.

'Well enough. Sore.'

'The athalin should take the edge off it soon. Ironhand's a good man, but some of his marshals are a little too fond of their maces.'

'You know Bredon?'

'By reputation.'

Gair's left hand lay in his lap, curled like the claws of a dead bird. The gauzy dressing wrapped around it gave a prickly herbal smell. Branded. What did it look like? Angry and bloated, blisters rising out of his flesh like bubbles in a pot of stew? *Goddess forgive me.* He rubbed his eyes wearily.

'Try to keep that hand still if you can. Considering what they did it's not too bad. It should heal well, although you'll always have a scar.'

A witchmark. A slanted, scowling eye staring out of his palm to remind him of his sin, and to warn others against him. He could wear gloves; keep his hands dirty. Keep it hidden. His stomach coiled into a sour knot. Being outcast was nothing new, after all.

Saints, his head hurt. 'Why did you bring me here?'

'You needed somewhere to be. This was as good a place as any.'

'You could have left me.'

'No, I couldn't. There was a mob waiting for you at the gates, ready to finish what the Motherhouse started. I was not prepared to stand by and let murder be done.'

'But you know what I am.'

A smile twitched the man's beard. 'I know what the Church thinks you are, which isn't quite the same thing.' He extended a square hand. 'My name is Alderan.'

Gair stared at him. Who was this man? Why did he want to help a stranger, when he could easily have crossed the square and gone on with his day? Why store up trouble for himself? Alderan's mild, open expression did not change a whit and his hand remained extended towards the bed. Slowly, Gair accepted the clasp.

'Gair.'

'No family name?'

'No family.'

'A man's friends make the best family, my mother used to say. At least he can choose them.' The chair creaked as Alderan stood up. 'Rest there for a while, let that athalin get to work. We'll talk more when you're feeling better. There'll be time enough tomorrow.'

You have until dusk today to comply. 'What time is it?'

'Gone three hours after noon. High rang whilst you were asleep.'

16

Fear became an icy grip on Gair's spine. 'I have to be out of the parish by dusk.'

'There's plenty of time.'

'You don't understand. I have to go, now.'

He swung his legs over the edge of the bed and sat up, but the room wheeled around him. That had been a mistake. But time was passing, time of which he had too little to waste. Lightning-flashes of sickly yellow lit up the dull red throb behind his eyes, but he gritted his teeth and tried to stand.

Alderan's hand pressed on his shoulder. 'Wait.'

'I appreciate what you've done for me, but I have to get moving.'

The hand pressed down more firmly. 'Just wait.'

'Damn it, Alderan, I've got to go!' Gair struggled to rise, but was kept seated with distressingly little effort. He should have been able to put the old man on his backside but he couldn't even get up from the bed. He kicked out in frustration.

Alderan sidestepped, smooth as a dancer. 'Goddess' golden apples, boy!' he exclaimed. 'Must you make everything hard work?'

Strength draining from him like water from a holed bucket, Gair sagged onto the pillows. His head thudded. Waves of nausea rose and fell, leaving a sour taste in the back of his throat.

The old man blew out his moustaches and dropped back into his chair. 'Let me help you. I've got a spare horse in the stables; we can be over the border well before dusk with no one the wiser. You'd never reach the boundary in time if you went on foot – the marshals saw to that when they knocked your wits into next week. Besides, you need a bath and a shave and you haven't a stitch to wear. Now we can fight about it if you want, or you can sit still and recognise good sense when it's poured in your ear. What's it going to be?'

'You're only making trouble for yourself. I can get a horse if I need one.'

17

'By thieving? And what about clothes? Would you steal those too?'

'If I had to.'

Alderan shook his head. 'I don't think so. You haven't got the time, nor, dare I say it, the temperament to be skulking about the city in your skin stealing what you need.' The lines around his eyes softened and his voice gentled. 'I mean you no harm, Gair, truly. Please, trust me.'

If only he didn't feel so helpless. He needed to get moving, get out of the city without a moment's more delay, but he could hardly stir. The bed was comfortable, the sheets soft on his skin and his battered body wanted to curl up in them and sleep. Saints, yes, sleep. It had been so long. His eyes closed as drowsiness pawed at his mind. 'I need to get out of here.'

'Then let me help you.'

'If they take me again, they'll burn me for sure.'

'We'll just have to make sure we stay a few steps ahead of them,' Alderan said lightly. 'For the record, I don't think you are a witch. All I can see is a lad in deep trouble and I'm in a position to help. If you don't want me to, that's your choice. I'm not holding you here. You can leave right now, but believe me, your chances are less than poor. If the Knights don't take you the townsfolk certainly will.'

After ten years in Dremen, Gair didn't need to be told what would happen to an excommunicate under sentence of death in the Holy City. Whether he liked it or not, he needed Alderan. He made himself look squarely at him. 'I was rude. I'm sorry. Thank you for your help.'

'You're welcome.' There was no rancour in Alderan's voice. 'There's a warm bath through that door over there; I suggest you use it. I can take care of the rest.'

'What are we going to do?'

'Get you out of the city for a start. After that we'll see. Are you always this full of questions?'

18

'How do you know I won't just turn you into a toad and take your horse?' Could he? Probably, if the magic didn't burn down the inn or blow off his head first. If the magic ever came back.

'I don't doubt you could, but I don't think you will.' The old man gave him a sidelong look full of twinkling amusement. 'Besides, who's to say I'm not a witch myself? Now for the love of Eador, go and wash. You stink.'

*

The bathroom was tiled with pretty blue and white Syfrian ceramic. Most of it was taken up by a large, deep bath better than half full of warm water. Folded towels and a cake of soap stood on a stool next to the washstand. Thoughtfully, someone had provided an array of sponges and washcloths and a long-handled brush on a shelf over the tub.

Gair clambered into the bath, careful to keep his burned hand elevated, then leaned right back until the water closed over his ears. Silence. Nothing but the whisper of blood in his veins and the slow throb of his injuries. The athalin had begun to work at last, lifting his headache. Even the pain in his hand had begun to recede. He knew it was there and what it was, but the sharpness had blurred, become as indistinct as a landscape retreating into mist.

The music was still absent. He probed the place it had been cautiously, feeling his way round the void as if it were the socket of a missing tooth. Nothing there. He thought he felt something once, a sense of presence as of another person behind him in a darkened room, but it was so fleeting he wasn't sure it'd been anything at all. Maybe it was gone for good now, and with it the temptation. And maybe he was as mad as a saint and would open his eyes in a moment to find this had all been another dream and he was back in his cell, waiting for the questioners to come.

No. He would not think about the iron room again, nor the events in the Rede Hall. He took a deep breath and slowly let it out. That was behind him. Muscle by muscle, he compelled himself to relax, closing doors on the memories as he went, locking them securely. The weight of them fell away with the sweat and filth dissolving from his skin. Good enough. That was good enough for now. It was time to get moving. Sitting up, he set to work with the soap to scour himself clean of the last traces of the Motherhouse.

When he was done, he towelled off as best he could and padded over to the washstand where a comb and razor had been left for him. As he tilted the looking-glass up it filled with colour. Bruises bloomed across his belly from breastbone to groin: violet-blue, mossbell-green, the purple-black of irises. He brushed away drops of water, remembering. The bruises should have hurt, so much he couldn't stand up straight, but he felt no pain. Maybe he had Alderan's medicine to thank, or maybe he'd locked the pain in a box with the other memories. No matter. He wouldn't think about it again. Getting out of the city was enough to worry about. Clumsily he managed to wind the damp towel around his waist and began to lather up his beard.

When Gair returned to the other room, wearing a linen robe he'd found behind the door, Alderan was seated at the table next to a large tray covered with a napkin. He looked up as Gair sat down. 'Feel better?'

Gair nodded. It had been awkward shaving with a new razor and only one good hand. His face and neck were as pink as a boy's.

Alderan pushed the tray across the table. 'I thought you might be hungry,' he said, flicking the cloth away. 'You look like you're missing a few pounds.'

Slabs of pork pie were piled on a plate. Fresh bread and a crock of butter. Roast meats and pickles and a bowl of fruit. A dewy pitcher of cold milk to wash it down. Gair's stomach growled. His left hand sketched the sign of blessing before he remembered. He hurried through his thanks for the Goddess' bounty and tucked the hand in his lap out of sight. 'Force of habit,' he said.

'If I'd been through what you've endured, I'd be giving thanks for a slice of pork pie too,' said Alderan, calmly quartering an apple. 'But go steady with it, or you'll make yourself ill. I take it you weren't fed too well recently?'

'I got food and water when they remembered. Neither was particularly fresh.' He bit into a slice of pie. Golden pastry melted on his tongue. Wonderful. Nothing in the Emperor's banquet hall could have tasted better.

'How long did they hold you?'

He shrugged. 'I was arrested on St Saren's Day, in the spring. What day is it now? I lost count.'

'It's four past midsummer.'

Gair stopped chewing. Three months, plus a bit. A hundred days – an eternity in that iron room. Gone. He swallowed hard.

Alderan watched him, bouncing his knife in his hand. 'It doesn't usually take the Curia that long to make up their minds. You must have presented them with quite a problem.'

'I suppose.' The question was plain enough, though Alderan had not asked it directly. Gair finished a glass of milk to chase the pie down and took his time pouring the next one. Then he helped himself to some roast beef, rolling it up with his fingers. Still warm, it dripped with rich juices. He reached for another slice.

'So how long have you been able to hear the music?'

'What music?' *He knew.*

'Rumour in the city was the Knights were trying a witch today. Only one person was thrown out of Traitor's Gate like an old carpet.' Alderan popped a piece of apple into his mouth. 'How long,' he asked, chewing, 'have you been able to hear the music?'

'I don't know what you mean.'

Another slice of apple went the way of the first. 'It usually starts about the age of ten or eleven, give or take a couple of years, though there're often signs before that. Round about the time a boy's voice breaks and his arms and legs start to sprout like weeds after rain, it becomes much more powerful. Then he learns to use

21

it, after a fashion. Little things at first, like lighting candles, but it grows with him and eventually he has to learn to control it, before it starts controlling him.' A third slice of fruit and Alderan smiled across the table. 'How am I doing so far?'

He *knew*. Gair had no idea how, or who this man was, but he had recounted events as if he'd seen them written in a book. He spread his good hand on the tabletop, pressed it down on the polished wood as if he would slide off his chair without it. The room had tilted on its axis and he did not know which way was down any more. 'Fairly close. How did you know?'

'It always happens the same way, more or less. I've seen others like you and their stories differ only in the details. Why don't you tell me what happened?'

'You already seem to know most of it.'

'Tell me anyway. It'll pass the time whilst we eat.' Alderan finished his apple. 'Is there any mustard? That beef looks good.'

How can he be so matter-of-fact? Magic is a mortal sin – I'm damned for all eternity, and he might as well be discussing the price of grain! How does he know so much about it, about my life?

Bewildered, nursing the embryo of a new headache, Gair told him. 'It began when I was a boy. Maybe five years old. I sneaked into the pantry after marchpane, but I was too small to reach the jar at the back of the shelf. I tried and tried, then eventually I held out my hands and willed the jar to move towards me. I ate so much I sicked up all over my foster-mother's best rug.'

'Did you tell her what had happened?'

'She didn't believe me. She thought one of the maids must have got the jar down for me, or left it out where I could reach it.' He'd insisted his story was the truth, not wanting to drop the maids into trouble for something they hadn't done, but it had done him no good. Nurse had still slippered him for telling lies.

'And then?'

Gair rubbed his forehead. The headache had settled in behind his eyes, not so much an ache as a buzzing discomfort, prickling at his brain. 'Oh, very much like you said. Little things. Simple things. I could make a light when I had no candle, start a fire without flint and steel. The music came later, the summer after I turned ten.' Having a secret no one else could know had been thrilling, at first. He'd spent hours in out-of-the-way places with a stub of candle filched from the chatelaine's pantry, practising even though he'd known there'd be worse consequences than a slippering if he was caught. After a time he had started to hear music, at first just when he touched the magic, then all the time, weaving through his consciousness every moment of the day. Later, flames had refused to come when called; candles had exploded in a shower of scalding wax. Then he had heard the music shriek.

'How did you come to be at the Motherhouse?'

Too old for the nursery by then, he had a room of his own, up under the roof. He'd grown accustomed to the privacy and thought nothing of conjuring a light when his candle had burned down so he could read past his bedtime. That night he'd had his nose buried in the pages of *Prince Corum and the Forty Knights* well past midnight and Chatelaine Kemerode had tapped on his door to remind him it was time to go to sleep. He hadn't noticed the knock, nor the door opening, but he'd heard her scream when she saw the light by which he read.

'*Hidderling!*' Her mouth a round red O of horror, her hand fumbled *through the sign of blessing over her breast.* '*Oh lady, fetch the lector, quickly! The boy is shadowkin!*'

And that had been that. His foster-mother had wept slow, silent tears whilst her husband raged at how Gair had repaid them for the roof over his head and the food on his plate. Then the lector had been summoned. Less than a day later Gair had been set on a horse and sent north, just a boy, clutching a too-long, too-heavy sword to his chest, who was grateful for the rain on his face so that the bony-arsed spindleshanks of a curate in the saddle behind him wouldn't see he was crying.

Rage and shame flickered again, humiliation glowing like a coal. All that time ago and it still had the power to hurt.

'Gair?'

'I was careless.' It came out more shortly than he'd intended. 'The housekeeper saw me with a conjured light, so the family couldn't foster me any longer. For want of anything better to do with me, they put me into the Church. Look how well that turned out.'

'How old were you then?'

'Eleven.' Gair dabbed some cheese crumbs from his plate with his fingertip and licked them off. 'So you were right about that, too.'

'And you managed to keep it a secret for, what, another ten years?'

'Until someone saw me when I thought I was alone. One of the other novices, I think. He ran to Elder Goran and Goran brought charges. The marshals came that night, at supper.' They'd dragged him from the refectory, past the shocked faces and dropped spoons of the entire novitiate, so that everyone could see what had been living amongst them. He'd felt his friends' eyes on him as he was marched past, but no one had spoken up.

The headache had worsened. It gnawed at the inside of his skull, preventing him thinking clearly. Gair kneaded his forehead again.

'I think you know the rest.'

'Enough of it, anyway. Are you feeling all right?'

'Just a headache. It's nothing.'

'Is the music there now?'

'No, not since this morning.' He pinched the bridge of his nose and pressed hard into his brows. 'Saints, it's like wasps.'

Alderan frowned. 'What?'

'That headache. It's like wasps under my skin.'

'How long have you been feeling that?'

'Not long, maybe ten minutes. Why?'

The older man pushed his plate to one side and stood up. 'We need to be somewhere else. Come on.'

'What is it?'

'Rumour has it Goran keeps a witchfinder,' Alderan said grimly.

'I think he might have just earned his pay.'

3

GORAN'S HOUND

જે

Panic fluttered a wing in Gair's chest. 'I'll need some clothes.'

'Already taken care of.' Alderan pointed at a bundle on the settle by the hearth. Wrapped up inside a stout winter cloak, Gair found several plain shirts, some breeches and a sheepskin jerkin, hardly new, but all neatly mended. They were also his.

'Where did you get these from?' he exclaimed. Everything was there, from smallclothes upwards. Even his boots.

'The Chaplain's poor-box. I reckoned the Order owed you a little charity. I think this is yours as well.' From the back of his chair, Alderan unhooked a broad baldric carrying a longsword in a simple leather scabbard. He laid it next to their plates.

Gair dropped his clothes and returned to the table. The sword was a plain soldier's weapon, ungilded, with only knot-shaped bosses on the cross-hilts and a moonstone set in the centre for ornamentation. The dark baldric was supple from use, worn shiny under the buckle. Of all the things confiscated by the Lord Provost's marshals when he was arrested, this was the only item he had really wanted back, though it was as shabby as the rest. He rubbed his fingers over the hilt. 'I never thought to see this again.'

'It's precious to you?'

'It's all I have that's really mine. The Church gave me everything else.'

'You can thank me later. We need to move.' Alderan pulled saddlebags and bedrolls from a closet, piling them on the floor. 'Hurry, Leahn!'

Gair eased the sword part-way from the scabbard. Heavy, double-edged steel gleamed at him under a thin sheen of oil. He heard his foster-father's voice again, harsh and bitter. *Take it. You might find a use for it in time. If the Goddess grants you the courage you'll fall on it.* Slowly he slid the blade home. 'Thank you, Alderan. I don't know where to begin to repay you for your kindness.'

The old man dismissed it with a wave and a shrug. 'It's not necessary. I wasn't prepared to leave you there and I'm sure if our roles were reversed you would do the same.'

'Until they are, I am in your debt.'

'Consider it a loan, then. When I think of something you can do for me, I'll ask, and then we'll be square. Done?'

'Done.'

'Now that honour is satisfied, will you for the love of the saints get dressed?' Camping gear joined the pile in a clatter of tin plates. 'Or were you planning on greeting the witchfinder in a robe that barely covers your stones?'

ॐ

Gair felt eyes on him the moment he left the stableyard. He caught no one looking, and from what Alderan had told him of events outside the Motherhouse gates, the shave and clothes should render him unrecognisable, but his spine crawled under the imagined scrutiny. He shifted in the saddle. 'Everyone's looking at me.'

'They're not, trust me,' the old man murmured. 'Relax. Try to look like you're enjoying the ride, and we'll be out of here in no time.'

'Easy for you to say,' Gair muttered. 'You're not under sentence

27

of death.' He scanned the crowd eddying around them as they picked their way across a busy junction. His borrowed horse tossed his head, fidgeting with his bit.

'It's just your imagination. Saints, lad, *breathe*! You're as tense as a nun in a bawdy-house.'

'I can't help it.'

'I know, but you're upsetting your horse. If he bolts you really will have every eye on you and we can do without that.'

Gair made himself sit still. His right hand, holding the reins, he rested loosely on his thigh and let his hips move with the rhythm of the horse's gait instead of fighting against it. By the time they had reached the far side of the Cornmarket and swung west towards the Anorien Gate the horse had settled into an easy walk.

Alderan gave him a nod. 'Much better. When you look as if you have every right to be there, everyone else will assume that you have. Generally, people believe what they see.'

'You sound like a slipocket.'

'But I don't look like one, do I? The best slipocket is the one who looks just like another ordinary citizen. Sneaking about is the fastest way to draw attention to yourself.'

'I still feel as if everyone's looking at us.'

The old man chuckled. 'Do you know how many people pass through these gates in a day? In an hour? Thousands. We'll be invisible in plain sight.'

If only I felt half that confident. Gair glanced around him, but casually this time, giving his gaze something to rest on other than his horse's ears. No one appeared to be paying any mind to him, but every time someone's eye caught his, however briefly, he felt uneasy.

'How far to the gate?'

'Less than a mile. Look, you can see the towers.'

He followed Alderan's gesture. Two square grey towers were just visible at the far end of the street, white banners curling like feathers against the sky. The sun sat a hand's breadth above them.

Plenty of time then, though he was sure he could see it sinking as he watched.

Ahead the crowds thickened and slowed to a crawl. Carters sat their wagons in ragged lines, laughing and calling to each other over the heads of those on foot. Sober-skirted Dremen goodwives in starched linen coifs stood elbow to elbow with Belisthan trappers in buckskins. Young nobles on fine-boned Sardauki saddle-horses were obliged to give way to a farmer in pursuit of a mud-spattered sow with no mind to be sold. Caged fowl squawked, pedlars flourished their boards of ribbons and lace and slowly everyone inched closer to the gates and the winding dusty ribbon of the Anorien Road.

By the time the gatehouse's shadow fell over him, Gair was nibbling his lip anxiously. The witchfinder's presence in his head had faded still further the closer they came to the gate; surely that meant the search had turned to one of the other four roads out of the Holy City. He hoped so. His nerves were stretched tight as lute-strings as it was.

At the gates themselves, a party of Church Knights stood guard, surcoats gleaming in spite of the dust. They watched the townsfolk going to and fro but made no effort to inspect the carts that plodded along the road. Gair imagined their eyes boring into his back the instant he rode past. He all but swallowed his tongue when one of them called: 'Halt!'

Alderan glanced back over his shoulder at the Knights. Though his expression was no more than idly curious, his eyes were sharp. Gair tried to emulate his casual attitude, but his heart was still leaping in his chest. A brewer's dray stood immediately behind them, drawn by a pair of towering Syfrian bays with scarlet ribbons woven through their manes. The drayman twisted round in his seat and tipped his hat back to watch the Knights push through the throng. Gair looked forward again. The crowd was funnelling into the gate ahead, with barely a scrap of daylight to be seen. Men and horses shuffled either side of him; no room to

29

dismount. His mouth dried even as fresh sweat broke out across his back.

'Come on, come on,' he muttered. The chestnut danced from foot to foot, unhappy with the close quarters.

Alderan laid a hand on his arm. 'Easy. I don't think they're coming for us.'

'Are you sure?'

'Not entirely, no, so stay alert. Can you still hear our friend?'

'Not as close as he was, but he's still there.' Gair stood in his stirrups to look round behind him, but the arched necks of the dray horses and the rampart of barrels blocked his view. Nothing to see but sweating men and restive animals. Somewhere up ahead an ox-team lifted their tails and added a bovine tang to the fug.

'Smell that fresh country air,' said Alderan.

Gair looked across at him. The confined quarters and soupy air made him uneasy and every minute he waited plucked more spiky, staccato notes from his overstretched nerves. Yet the old man appeared completely unmoved, sat in his saddle like a sack of turnips and picked at his teeth.

'How can you be so calm? It's like a cattle-crush under here. We'll never get away,' Gair said, peering behind him again. The guards were closer; he heard them shout at a carter to clear the way.

Alderan flicked away whatever he'd extracted from his teeth. 'I'm not, but fretting won't make the crowd disappear. We just have to wait it out. Yes, it's taking a bit longer to get out of the city than I would have liked, but there's nothing we can do about it. There are things in this life we cannot change, we must simply accept. Death. Taxes. Queues.' He grinned suddenly, like a fox. 'Look at you. Anyone would think you had something to hide.'

Gair said a word that would have earned him a birching from the Master of Novices and sat down.

Alderan's laugh rang out, rich as port wine.

At last the guards came round the dray. Quickly Gair faced

forwards and gathered up his reins in anticipation. He couldn't bear much more. If the Knights were coming for him, he had no idea what he would do. He had no room to even draw his sword, much less turn to face them. He chewed his lip and tried to work some moisture into his mouth, but he had no spit to spare.

'Ho, master drayman!' a guard shouted. 'One of your barrels is leaking!'

Merciful Mother, thank you. Weak with relief, Gair leaned on the saddle-horn and let out a shaky breath.

Alderan grinned again, but not unkindly.

Ahead of them the crowd began to move. The press diminished, at last disgorging them into the evening sunshine. Once past the last sprawl of houses clustered against the city wall, Alderan reined his horse onto the verge and halted in the shade of a copse.

'Now that wasn't so bad, was it?' he said. 'You're safe until dusk and even then they're going to be looking for a fugitive, not some arrogant young lordling out for a ride in the country.' Gair bridled at the description. 'Forgive me the choice of words, but you have that look about you. It's the way you carry yourself, as if you own the space you occupy. I don't think anyone would ever suspect you'd been beaten senseless a few hours ago.'

'Arrogant?' Gair repeated.

'Perhaps it's a family trait.'

'I have no family. I was found on the chapel porch a few days after I was born.'

'You know, that has the ring of a story to it,' Alderan said. 'The orphaned boy with the crown-shaped birthmark that identifies him as the lost heir to the kingdom, and so forth.'

Gair shook his head. 'No crowns. No kingdoms. Just a soldier's brat put out to charity.' He had worked that out long ago. His name-day, the one he'd been given, was close to Eventide; assuming a normal confinement that meant his mother had conceived early in the spring, round about the time the local levies were coming through on their way to Leahaven to take ship for Zhiman-dar, where the army staged for the final push against the Cult. It took little imagination to work out the rest.

Perhaps his father had been a braveheart, one of the thousands lost to the bloody sands of Samarak. Or perhaps the truth was more prosaic, some country girl played false by a liegeman, too poor or too ashamed to keep the child she found herself with when the soldier was long gone.

Lips pursed, Alderan watched him a moment, then squinted along the dusty road on the south bank of the Awen towards the settling sun. 'We should keep moving. I reckon there's two hours of good daylight left. Do you feel up to a canter?'

Gair shifted in his saddle. His bruises ached steadily now as the motion of the horse stretched his muscles. Scabs snagged on his clothes and pricked at him all over his back and legs, but his belly was where the questioners had worked the hardest. 'I can try.'

'Then let's put some distance behind us.'

The road followed the course of the river west and south, up the flank of the valley and onto the moors, where it forked. Gair reined up, twisting in the saddle to look back. From this distance Dremen was a jumble of blue slate roofs, church spires thrusting through the evening haze. It looked just what it was, a provincial capital humming with ordinary people living out ordinary lives, but for the city within a city that occupied a slight rise somewhat to the north of the centre. Pale walls girdled a glorious confection of domes and gilded cupolas where sunlight flashed on window-panes and pennons streamed from every graceful spire. Tallest of them all were the twin towers of the Sacristy, soaring heaven-wards as if to touch the glory of the Goddess Herself.

Rising almost as high behind the Citadel was the Motherhouse. A grim, unlovely construction of grey Dremenirian granite, it stood four-square to the north and wrapped its massive walls around the inner city like a mailed arm. Its towers were blunt and regular, its windows mere watchful slits. The Suvaeon Order had guarded the Church for more than two thousand years, defending

32

her against unbelievers with armour of righteousness and shields of faith, backed up with good Syfrian steel. Its uncompromising bulk straddling the neck of land between city and river loomed ready for two thousand more.

'There's still a way to go, Gair,' Alderan called from further ahead, but Gair barely heard him, caught up in memories. He'd first seen the Holy City, ten years ago, from almost this exact spot. Now it, like his foster home, had turned its back on him.

Hoofbeats sounded as the old man nudged his horse up beside him. 'Even from here it looks a hard place,' he said.

'It's all I've known since I was eleven years old.' Gair fingered the bandage on his left hand. For better or for worse, the Mother-house had left its mark on him, as surely as his magic had. He would never be the same again.

'The border's not far to the south,' said Alderan. 'You could be in Leah in a few days.'

'What for?'

'You have no kin at all there? No one who would take you in for a day or two?'

'I told you, I have no one.'

'Have you thought where you might go?'

'Where can I go, with this?' He held up his left hand. *Damn it, I don't want to talk about it. I just want to get away, as far away as possible.* Jerking the chestnut's head around Gair urged him along the right-hand fork of the road. It led southwest over the heathery uplands towards the mountains and Belistha beyond. The road was good, beaten smooth by centuries of travellers, so he let the horse have his head. A few paces behind, he heard Alderan shout after him, then the sound of hooves as the old man spurred his mount up to a gallop. He did not look back again.

A league or more passed as the sun settled lower in the sky, flushing the moor with red-gold warmth. As the road drew nearer the foothills it dipped into a winding glen. Shadows threw parts of the trail into gloom, so Gair slowed his horse to a walk. He was too close to the parish boundary now to throw his liberty away by breaking his mount's leg in a hole in the road.

If circumstances had been better, it would have been a pleasant place to stop. Kingfishers quartered the river pools beneath thickets of blackthorn and ash where sparrows bickered. Telltale circles broke under the clouds of insects, hinting at larger fish to be had — trout, most likely, and a summer's evening was about the best time to catch them.

Steel glittered in the sun as lances rose above the road ahead. They were followed by a row of shining helms, white plumes nodding. Gair reined back as Church Knights trotted out of a fold in the ground and formed in a line across the road. Five matched greys tossed their heads, silver curb chains jingling, and five silk pennons fluttered in the breeze. Cursing, Gair swung the horse round to look for Alderan. The old man sat his mount quietly some forty yards back, with five more Knights behind him.

The trail was blocked. To his right was the river, thirty yards across and Goddess knew how deep. To his left, a steep slope scarred with scree and boulders. Probably just about climbable, if he led his horse, but there was no way to know what lay at the top. The Dremenirian moors were rumpled like an old blanket, criss-crossed with streams and dells where armed men could be waiting. The only other way out of the trap was to go straight through the line. He swung his horse back round.

'In the name of the Goddess, stand fast!' bellowed a Knight with the red cord of captain round his arm.

Five men, armed and armoured. Heavy cavalry, the Church's finest, and a world apart from quintains and straw-stuffed dummies, but Gair had done little else for the past ten years. The longsword hissed out of its sheath.

'What do you think you're doing?' Alderan demanded, urging his horse alongside. 'Do you see the red rose badge on their shields? They're Goran's men.'

'Goran wanted to see me roasted. If he can keep me in this parish until dusk, he'll get his wish.'

A movement behind the captain caught Gair's eye. Another man, with a shabby hide jerkin, on a dun-coloured pony. His watery blue eyes slid around the scene like a couple of raw eggs in a skillet, but they kept coming back to him.

'Who's that?'

Alderan followed Gair's gaze and grunted. 'Witchfinder.'

'I thought we'd slipped past him.'

'So did I. Either I was wrong, or he made a really good guess which of the five gates we'd take.'

Gair stared at the man as that underdone gaze slid off him then pulled back. The prickle behind his forehead intensified. 'How does he *do* that?' He scrubbed his face with the back of his hand, but it was useless. The witchfinder made his brain itch. 'I've got to get past them.'

'Gair, there's no point. They can track you across a hundred miles with him. Leave it.'

'No.' His horse shifted under him, tossed his head. 'I can't let them take me. I've got to get past.'

The chestnut was no war-horse, but he was steady and strong. Gair started him forward. Alderan's voice calling his name was left behind. He was not going to go back.

'Stand fast, in the name of the Goddess!' the captain shouted again.

Ignoring him, Gair touched his heels to the horse's ribs and brought his weight forward, holding the sword across his body. He had only one chance to get this right. If he failed, he would die, spitted on a lance or bound to a stake, it made no nevermind.

Ahead of him, the Knights sat their horses uncertainly. There were too few of them to effectively block the road and too many to get out of the way. As the captain bawled at him to stand, Gair heeled the chestnut to a dead run and aimed for the gap between the second and third Knights. Lances wavered halfway to the couch and gauntleted hands sawed at reins, but by then it was too late. Yelling ferociously, he charged through the line and on down the road. He was through!

More mailed Knights rounded the next bend at a trot. Their lances were already couched. Gair hauled on the reins so hard the chestnut almost sat down in the road, then urged him back the way they had come. *Holy Mother, I don't want to die.* A spur of rock ran down to the road, fractured into a crude staircase. He set the horse at it and dug in his heels. The chestnut scrambled up the first step, then another; Gair lifted his weight out of the saddle to help him. Another leap, steel shoes skidding, gorse clawing at Gair's boots. He looked up at the ridge-top and saw more Knights.

A sick dread sat on Gair's stomach. He had nowhere to go. The Knights were advancing, the trap Goran's hound had set closing around him. Ansel's reprieve had risked the Curia's wrath for nothing.

Then his ears began to ring with a keening note.

36

4

GATEKEEPER

ༀ

Masen breathed out slowly. His breath curled into steam on the frosty air and disappeared into the bare branches of the trees around him. He had to be careful now, not make the slightest sound, or his quarry would hear him, despite the chatter of the stony river. The stag's hearing was exceptional, even for one of its kind. No wonder it had been hunted so unsuccessfully for so long.

He watched it pace through the trees ahead, a flicker of white amongst the winter-black trunks. The beast was a long way from home. This forest stretched the length of the Brindling Mountains from the an-Archen south to Astolar and they were well above the plains, almost to the snowline. No country for deer, especially one carrying such a magnificent rack of antlers. Deer lived on their wits and their speed; they did not willingly choose terrain that could foul their heads or break their legs. Something had brought it here, something it feared enough to overcome its instincts.

Masen shifted position a fraction, transferring his weight smoothly from one foot to the other. He would have sworn he made no sound, but the stag heard him and bounded ahead. Hooves clattered on stone, splashed through water. Well, if it knew he was here, he could afford a little less caution. Shaking out his net, he moved towards the river.

The stag stood four-square on a gravel-spit out in the rushing water. Its pelt glowed in the thin sunshine, each of the twenty points of its antlers shining silver. Wide blue-black eyes fixed on him and wet nostrils flared as it sifted out his scent.

A few more steps brought Masen to the water's edge. He kept his net loose in his right hand. The stag's head jerked warningly, antlers flashing – nineteen points, not twenty; one was broken and the rest furrowed and scarred from many battles. A wily one, this. It had chosen to face him across the deepest part of the river channel, where the water flowed fast and dark and ice sparkled on the stones. Behind it lay the shallows on the outside of the bend, ready for a swift escape. Masen grinned. Wily indeed.

Close to, it truly was magnificent. Finer-boned than a highland stag, but no less strong, with a deep chest – big lungs, for long running – and powerful haunches to drive it forward. Head up, its ears swept the air for the slightest sound. Every muscle under that snowy pelt was bunched and ready to run hard. He could take no chances here.

Slowly, Masen transferred his net to his other hand so he could shrug off his bow and quiver. The stag snorted and stamped a foot, scattering gravel into the water. With great care, he hung his weapons from a branch on the nearest tree and held up his hand, moving away from them. Its head turned to keep him in focus, ears flicking back and forth warily. A Kingdom boar had taught Masen not to underestimate these creatures. Seeing the scar on his thigh each time he undressed made sure he didn't forget.

A breeze brought the scent of it across the river to him. He smelled the musk of the rut, rank sweat in its coat, the sour edge of fear. Pitching his voice low and soft, he began to speak. It didn't matter what he said, for the stag had no language, but the tone was important. Masen murmured nonsense, hummed snatches of lullabies, anything he could think of that was soothing to the ear. Some of the tension drained from the stag. Its fixed stare shifted for a fraction of a second, then again as it dared to look around.

Masen hunkered down to make himself smaller and less threatening, but he kept the net ready. The stag dipped its head towards the water and he saw a flash of its dark, purplish tongue. It was thirsty, and the smell of the water was overcoming its caution.

When it leaned down to drink, Masen lunged. Straightening his legs he thrust himself up and flung his arms wide. The invisible Song-woven net soared out over the river, spreading, falling, powered by his will. The stag's head jerked up, but too late. The net coiled around it; in moments the Song had tangled the proud antlers and hobbled the stag's legs. It crashed down on its side in the gravel and bleated frantically. Panicked eyes rolled in its head.

Masen hopped onto a rock in the middle of the water and then onto the spit, crouching beside his captive.

'Hush, hush now,' he murmured. 'I mean you no harm. I'm here to take you home.' He stroked its shoulder, the net prickling as his hand passed through it. He had to be careful not to leave his hand in one place for too long; the stag's flesh was as cold as the snows. It panted and strained against the mesh, silvery hooves thrashing in the gravel.

'Rest, my prince. All will be well.'

The inky eyes closed. It laid its head on the stones, breath huffing through flared nostrils.

'There now, see? All will be well, I promise.'

Masen felt the hunter's approach as a shiver in the air, not unlike someone close behind him calling the Song. He heard no sound but the river, no footfalls on the leaf-litter, but the world had changed its shape behind him and he knew the hunter was there.

Readying a defensive shield just in case, Masen pushed himself to his feet.

I see you, human.

He turned round. A hornbow was levelled at his heart, the arrow-point glistening like ice. The hunter himself stood half-hidden in shadows that fell the wrong way for the direction of the

39

sun, the shadows themselves cast by massive trees that resembled none in the surrounding forest.

'My lord.' Masen bowed. 'Well met.'

You have something of mine. Return it to me.

'I will return it to its kingdom, for it does not belong here, but I will not hand it over to you. I will not break the law.'

Give it to me! The hunter took a half-step forward into a shaft of sunlight. Fierce green eyes sighted along the arrow-shaft, a breeze stirring his braided hair around his shoulders. Masen met his stare.

'You must follow the law of the hunt, my lord.'

Give me the stag, human, or I will strike you down.

'No, my lord, I will not. Your arrow will not pass the border of your kingdom.'

The stag passed.

'The stag found a Gate and blundered through. There is no Gate here.'

With a silent curse, the hunter lowered his bow, easing the strain off the string. His stare remained forbidding. *I have hunted the stag for many days. I had it at bay by the waterfall, within my grasp.*

'Then you must hunt it again, bring it to bay again. I will not gift you your prize.'

It would earn you much favour with the Queen.

'I do not seek the favour of your Queen. I seek only to see the laws of the hunt upheld. I am bound by them, just as you are.'

At Masen's feet the stag tossed its head. The Song's shimmering, half-unseen mesh pressed into the winter-thick pelt. It knew that death was close at hand and its every fibre strained for flight.

Dropping the arrow back into the leather quiver at his shoulder, the hunter relaxed. His ragged, forest-coloured clothing blurred into the shadows around him. *Very well, gatekeeper. I accede. But the Queen shall hear of this.*

'I'm sure she will,' Masen said. 'This is a royal stag, one of her pets. Greater hunters than you have sought to capture it and failed. You stand in exalted company, my lord.'

The hunter snarled. His hand dropped to his waist and a knife flashed into flight towards Masen's chest. It shuddered to a halt just short with a flash of blue-white light like a spark from the Goddess' own anvil. The hunter bared his teeth, then whirled and vanished into his forest.

Masen reached out towards the knife suspended in mid-air and laid his hand flat against the invisible barrier. The knife-point grazed his palm, not sharp enough to break the skin but firm as a bodkin through a blanket. He frowned. He should not have been able to feel anything at all. The knife should have bounced back at the hunter's feet, not stuck there. That could mean only one thing. The boundary was weakening.

A chill slithered into the pit of his stomach. The Veil had not weakened like this in many years, not since the reiver. Oh, there had been tears in places, small rips that spilled a little of the Hidden Kingdom into the world the way an old sack spilled a few grains of wheat onto the floor, but that was easily swept up, easily mended. Since he had become Gatekeeper he had seen nothing to compare with this. In this place, the very fabric of the Veil was wearing thin.

He studied the hunter's dagger. Long and flat, the blade was fashioned from icy blue light and etched with sigils. As he watched they faded into illegibility and the knife itself dissolved into smoke. The pressure against his palm was gone.

With the Song, Masen felt the slippery fabric of the boundary for a tear. No threads were snapped, but there was a distortion where the knife-point had pulled it askew, like a bramble-thorn on the weave of a shirt. Slowly, carefully, he wove together gossamer strands of the Song and eased the fabric smooth again. Its dancing light faded as he withdrew.

The stag stirred by his feet. Its breathing was more measured now, but its eyes were open, staring at the shore. Deftly Masen unpicked the net around it and rewove it as a leash. The stag scrambled to its feet and bolted, only to be fetched up short on its hind legs, cloven hooves pawing at the air.

'Easy, my prince.' He raised a hand to stroke its face and antlers lunged towards him. 'I understand, I understand,' he soothed. 'You don't want to be here. You're frightened and alone and you can't find your way back. You can't feel the Gate from this side, can you? Not this far away.'

The stag snorted, saliva dripping from its jaws. Its pelt twitched and trembled with the urge to flee. With the leash still held tight, Masen began to sing in his throat, more than a hum, but not as articulate as speech, and the melody spread out and twined amongst the winter-bare trees as if it was a living thing, which in a way it was. Its rhythm obeyed no formal musical convention. Instead it resembled the flow of water or leaves in a breeze, constantly changing without ever repeating yet always, somehow, the same. Years of practice had been required to perfect the necessary breathing techniques, yet in its kingdom of origin that complex melody was a lullaby such as a mother might sing over a cradle.

The stag's ears flicked upright, curved round to capture the sound. Blue-black eyes fixed on Masen's and it ceased straining against his hand.

'There now, that's better. Let's send you home, my prince. The Queen will be pining for you.' He stepped onto the rock midstream, paying out some leash behind him. The stag leapt clean over the water to the shore where it looked back at him as if to ask why he was taking so long. Laughing, Masen jumped to the bank and, side by side, they set off into the forest.

The Gate was not far. The threshold tickled at Masen's awareness, tugging at the nail in his pocket. Several Gates existed in this region; he had mapped them long ago. This was one of the highest, on the shoulder of the Brindling Mountains. He had seen no reason to seal them yet, not this far out. Though the lowland soil was fertile and well watered, few people had settled this region, and the ruined farmsteads of those who had tried scattered the plain below.

Too many ghosts. Ghosts of dead kingdoms, ancient battles,

leached out of the soil like firedamp. Treachery and despair hung in the air, and spoiled a man's sleep and greyed his hair until one day he piled everything he owned into his wagon and left his fields to return to the wild. Those plains were fertile because they were soaked in centuries of blood.

First Slaine, if legend was to be believed, then the city-state of Milanthor, had tried to claim the whole of the northern plains for itself. Its hundred towers were crow-eyries now. And then Gwlach's army, east and south of here. At Riannen Cut the Knights had finally broken them, then driven them into bloody retreat through Whistler's Pass. The night air was thick with their shades.

Masen scrambled up the steepening slope, using protruding roots and dangling branches to pull himself along. He envied the stag's nimbleness; its dainty hooves found footing amongst the rocks where his clumsy boots could never fit. A tired grin split his face. 'Have some patience with an old man, my prince!'

The stag snorted. Now who was the quarry and who the hunter?

At the top of the slope the thin scrub pine fell away entirely to leave the ridge-line bald. To the left the mountains continued to rise towards the high peaks and the Fjordain beyond, with their white heads in the clouds and their feet in the sea. To the right the knobby spine of the ridge sank back into the forest and the distant plains. The wind, sharp with snows to come, brought the thunderous boom of falling water.

Beside Masen, the stag strained forward, the leash carving a furrow in its pelt.

'This is where you came through, eh?' he asked. He paid out a little more slack and the creature shuffled forward as far as it could, eyes fixed on the unseen waterfall.

He'd have to seal the Gate behind it. He couldn't take the risk that it would remember this world as a refuge when the hunt began. It could not be allowed to return at will. The balance would

43

be upset, unless something from here passed through to the Hidden Kingdom in exchange, and that was precious risky at best. Small things, inert objects such as pebbles and twigs, could pass back and forth without harm, but a large animal was a different matter.

Besides, the stag was a creature of power. Its presence weighed on the world the way Masen felt stones in his pockets. Looked at with the Song, it was sculpted of blue-white light, cold and tumultuous music, a frozen river of energy that distorted everything around it. It did not belong here, and never could.

He walked to the edge and peered over at the roaring river. It had no name that he knew; if it had ever had, it had gone to dust with the cartographer who had plotted its course. Grey-white water boiled down a narrow defile, its steep walls gleaming with a sheath of ice. A path of sorts, where the rock had fractured into a series of shallow steps, led down the gorge to where it ended, maybe a hundred yards away. There it simply opened into space and the river poured out in a foaming mare's tail that the wind would fray into rain long before it ever reached the ground.

The hunter's waterfall, at a guess. It was rare that the landscapes of the Hidden Kingdom coincided with the daylight world. Usually it was an echo, distorted by time and distance until it was barely recognisable as what it had been. Forests were older, or younger, or had other features subtly rearranged to be more pleasing to the creatures that inhabited them. Rivers changed their course or became lakes, even dried up altogether. Occasionally there were points of congruence, places such as this where the two kingdoms could intersect, and there were the Gates.

Masen started carefully down the path with the stag clattering behind him. He would have to get closer to the falls to find the Gate. This looked to be the only way, and the wet ice was unforgiving. Make haste slowly, then. One cautious step at a time, he descended into the cleft.

The noise of the river pummelled at his ears, confined and amplified by the rocky walls. Needle-sharp spray stung his face,

44

soaked his clothes. Behind him he heard the stag huff excitedly and risked a glance over his shoulder. Spray turned its antlers to liquid silver and beaded its coat like seed-pearls, so lovely it made Masen's heart ache to see it, but the glamour of the Hidden's creatures was treacherous. He turned his back again and with clenched teeth edged further along the path.

The threshold pulled more strongly now. The stag sensed something too, tugging on the leash to dart ahead, its silvery hooves ringing on the rock. It snorted, eager to be gone. It had the scent of home in its nostrils, undetectable to Masen amongst the smells of water and pine and cold wet rock. They were almost above the falls now; the wind whirled around them, reminding him that he stood perilously close to the void. From his pocket he pulled a horseshoe nail and held it up by the thread tied to it. It swung instantly to point towards the waterfall. He'd reached the right place. There was a Gate above the falls, still open to the Hidden Kingdom.

He dropped the nail back into his pocket, where it pressed insistently at the fabric of his coat. Then he slipped the leash on the stag with a thought and released his hold on the Song.

'Time to go home,' he said.

The stag threw back its head and belled. Its cry was more tenor than the bass bellow of a bull elk, less raw than a red deer, but just as unearthly. Its hindquarters bunched and it launched itself down the precipitous slope towards the waterfall. One bound, then another, somehow finding footholds on the ice-covered rock, then it soared out into the gorge. Brilliant spangles surrounded it as if the sun had lanced through the clouds and refracted from every single droplet of water on its pelt. In a blink it was gone.

'Goddess speed you, my prince,' Masen murmured, gazing after it. Even after all this time, it unnerved him to see one of the Kingdom's creatures disappear without a track through a Gate, especially ones that seemed to open into plain air. He should have become accustomed to it, but it still lifted the hairs on the back of his neck.

He picked his way back along the path to the rim of the gorge and started down the slope. His spray-damp clothes clung uncomfortably to his limbs; by the time he reached his camp he'd be thoroughly chilled. Sealing the Gate would have to wait for another day. Even with ropes and climbing irons it would be next to impossible to reach alone. Easier by far would be to destroy the lintel-stone, assuming he could find it, though that would leave an ugly tear in the Veil that was in its own way just as dangerous as an unprotected Gate and would take twice as long to stitch up as simply sealing it properly in the first place.

But for now it would have to keep. He had a far more pressing task at hand. Masen slid and skidded down through the trees. The Order had to be warned. It was twenty days' hard riding down the Greenway to the upper arm of the Great River, where he could transfer to a ship. Astolar was closer, but with the High Seats in turmoil they might close their borders. He could not afford to spend weeks wandering in the Astolan Hills, unable to find a route out, should the White Court move to isolate itself. The journey would be long and arduous enough as it was.

No, the Greenway it had to be, then south. He was sure to be able to find a ship of some kind – hells, he'd earn his passage as deckhand if he had to; it wouldn't be the first time – anything that would send him on his way to Fleet. If the Veil was failing, he had no time to waste.

5

MAGIC

ಅಾ

Magic, rising, swelling into many voices. It filled the air around Gair and time slowed. Tiny details became sharply, painfully clear. Gorse-flowers blazed bright as flames on the viridian bushes. A billion motes of dust spangled the air. Hooves rose and fell as if through treacle and each hoof-beat boomed round his head like the fall of empires.

Oh Goddess, help me. Sunset burned his eyes. All he could see through it was red – red as roses, red as blood, drenching the Knights and tipping their lances with gore. Goran's captain swung his arm to urge his men forward and the cords flew like spatter from an opened vein.

Alderan opened his mouth to yell, but there were no words. There was no sound at all now but the song inside him and the tingling rush of it along his limbs.

Hail, Mother, full of grace, light and life of all the world. Blessed are the meek, for they shall find strength in you. Blessed are the merciful, for they shall find justice in you. Blessed are the lost, for they shall find salvation in you. Amen.

Sparks spat from the chestnut's shoes as Gair wheeled him round to face the way he had come. Muscles bunched in his hind-quarters and his ears snapped back; the granite stair was steep, but the horse leapt forward. The landing jolted Gair in the saddle but he kept his seat and somehow the chestnut gathered himself for another leap.

Trust the horse. He had to trust the horse. Trust the horse *Holy Mother Goddess I don't want to die.* One more leap and Gair was back on the road. Dust swirled around him. Sensation thrilled along every nerve. The magic filled his entire being; he was bloated, potent with it, an overfilled wineskin about to burst. And it sang to him. Everything he'd been taught shrieked out the wrongness of it, but it was too late to fight: he was helpless in its grip. He had to use it before it consumed him. He would fly apart, explode into lightning and—

It was gone. Normality crashed back down on him, hard enough to knock the breath from his body. Slumped over the horse's neck, he sucked air into his lungs and broke out coughing with the dust. He smelled sweat, heard jingling harness and restive horses and, oddly, a skylark, sweetly clear from invisibly far above, but the music was gone. It had never done that before. Dazed, he spat on the road to clear his mouth and straightened up.

Alderan seized his shoulder. 'What in all hells did you think you were doing?' he hissed.

'I don't want to die, Alderan. I won't let them take me back.'

The old man leaned forward until his face was level with Gair's. His fearsome brows knotted and he spoke quickly as the Knights gathered in, his voice pitched low. His grip did not relent. 'Listen to me. No one is taking you anywhere today, do you understand? You have my word on it. Now stay calm, stay quiet and for the love of the Goddess keep a check on it. Do you understand?' He shook Gair's shoulder. 'Gair, do you understand me?'

Gair nodded, spat again. The music was gone, but dread still had his heart clenched in a mailed fist. The grip on his shoulder became a pat.

'How long until sunset?' he asked.

'A little under an hour. The parish boundary's only a mile or so from here. We've ample time.'

Knights formed a ring around them, lances at the ready. Gair dropped his sword back into its scabbard and became aware of just how much his branded hand hurt. Bloody fluid stained the bandage and pain stabbed through his palm. He let it rest upturned on his thigh as the captain took off his helm and nudged his horse closer.

'By order of Elder Goran, I am placing you under arrest,' he declared. 'Throw down your weapons.'

The witchfinder's face appeared between the captain and the Knight next to him, pale eyes swimming from one captive to the other. His features sharpened into a grin, all narrow jaw and pointed teeth like the skull of a fox.

'Arrested? On what charge?' asked Alderan.

'Trespass and theft.'

'Trespass?' The old man's brows lifted. 'This is a public thoroughfare.'

'I did not say you were trespassing now.' The Knight smiled, or at least showed his teeth. 'You trespassed on Elder Goran's private estate, five miles back.'

'We went ten yards off the road to water the horses!' Gair protested. 'You can't call that trespassing!'

The Knight gathered up his squad with a look. 'I rather think I can call it what I like.'

'And I suppose the theft relates to the water the horses drank?'

'Of course not. Water is the Goddess' bounty, freely given to all men and beasts.'

'Then to what does the charge relate?' Alderan's tone was short.

'I presume you are going to tell us?'

The sandy-haired captain bared his teeth again. 'The charge relates to the disappearance of a small object from the Elder's personal apartments. It is a trinket, nothing more, but one of immense sentimental value. We shall have to search your baggage.' He shrugged. 'It could take some time.'

'Would you mind telling us what this object is? Forgive me,' Alderan said, 'but I'd rather know now, before you find it in my saddlebags.'

'Confessing your guilt, old man?'

'Me?' Alderan spread his hands. 'I'm sorry, my friend. I've had a long and interesting life, in the course of which I have undoubtedly been guilty of many things, but sadly, none of what you think.'

Another of the Knights stared down his nose at them.

The captain frowned and motioned some of his men forward. 'Search them! Search everywhere!'

Five Knights dismounted. One held the horses whilst the others rifled through the saddlebags, clumsy in their thick gauntlets. Alderan watched the nearest Knight until the man became so perturbed that he glared back.

'What are you looking at?'

'I was wondering whether that was such a good idea.' Alderan nodded towards the man's arm, elbow-deep in spare clothes. 'I mean, you never know what you're going to find in a witch's pockets.'

The Knight scowled and turned back to his task. Abruptly he yelped and snatched his hand back. He stripped off his gauntlets and rubbed his fingers. A moment later, the other three Knights were doing the same.

Gair flashed a look at Alderan and saw the old man shortening up his reins.

'Ready?' Alderan never took his eyes off the captain, who was shouting shrilly and pushing his men back to their task. The remaining Knights watched them instead of their prisoners. It would take only a moment.

With a wild yell Alderan urged his horse towards the gap in the line left by the captain and his five men. Gair was only a second behind, the chestnut stretching into a gallop. As they broke the line Alderan laid about him with the flat of his hand on the rumps of the nearest horses, making them squeal and dance to add to the confusion.

'Stop them!' the captain bellowed. 'By the Goddess, I'll have your hides for boot leather! *Move!*'

Too late. Gair had clear road ahead of him to the crest of the rise. He dared a glance back over his shoulder. A handful of Knights had organised a pursuit, rowelling their greys ruthlessly, but they were a good way back. He bent low over the chestnut's neck and urged him on.

'A thousand yards!' Alderan pointed at the ridge ahead, where the road wound up out of the deepening shadows. A stubby stone marker stood silhouetted against the ruddy sky. Once past that they would be out of Goran's diocese, out of danger.

Gair set his heels and asked for one last effort from his mount.

Five hundred yards on, the horse was tiring. At a thousand, sweat and foam curdled on his coat. Each breath rasped through nostrils stretched wide, but he kept running, and every stride brought safety closer.

A hundred yards more, Gair whispered to the horse. Just a hundred yards, less than that now, barely fifty, good lad, just a little further, come on now, there's the stone, and then they were past. He sat up and reined the blowing horse to a halt, then swung down to walk the few yards back to the marker. Below the rise, the Knights milled around their captain, who crossed his forearms on his saddle-horn and glowered.

'Goran won't be pleased when he learns his hounds have failed,' said Alderan, leaning down from his saddle to catch the chestnut's reins. Gair plucked his shirt away from his sweaty back.

'There were forty of them, Alderan. That's a lot to send after just the two of us.'

'And a seeker too.'

'The witchfinder?'

'During the Inquisition, the Church called them seekers after truth. Most of the ones who call themselves witchfinders today are just prodnoses with nothing better to do than spy on their neighbours for a shilling, but there're a handful with a genuine talent, like that fellow there.'

The Knights on the road had formed up to ride back to Drennen. A few yards behind them, an unremarkable man sat his pony and stared up at the ridge. The prickling across Gair's forebrain was less intrusive now, but it lingered, even after the witchfinder swung his pony round and trotted after the retreating soldiers.

'I can still feel him, in my head. How does he do it?'

'Perhaps he has the ability to sense what you can do, somehow.' Alderan shrugged. 'I don't know. But I don't think we've seen the last of him, unless Goran does us all a favour and drops dead of an apoplexy – saints know, he's fat enough.'

Gair stared, startled by the old man's venom. 'What?'

'Let's just say I've heard a few stories about Elder Ignatio Goran. If even half of them are true he's not fit to wear the scarlet. Come on. We should find somewhere to rest up.'

'He believes what he's doing is for my own good.'

'Then Goddess spare us from believers like him! Preserving your eternal soul from damnation by purifying your body with fire? Do you really think She wants that?' Alderan handed Gair the reins to his horse.

'I was raised to believe that no one is so far gone that they cannot be redeemed.'

'But the same people who taught you that locked you in a cell for three months and put a red-hot iron to your hand.'

Other things had been done to him too, in the name of truth and redemption. Not all of them had been painful. Some had been designed instead to humiliate, to debase, to break his will. Alderan was right. It really did not make any kind of sense. Abruptly Gair felt exhausted, more utterly spent than he could ever recall being

52

in his life. 'I believe the Goddess forgives,' he said at last. 'It's just the Church that doesn't.'

Not far from the marker they found a hollow in the lee of a craggy tor where a stream danced down to the river below. After watering the horses, they stripped off the saddles and whilst the animals cropped, rubbed them down with handfuls of grass.

'Are you still sure you don't want to turn south a ways?' Alderan asked over his horse's back. 'It's not too late.'

'I'm sure. There's nothing there for me.'

'One day you might be surprised.'

'Maybe.' Enough had happened on that one day without looking for old wounds to pick at. 'Alderan, what did you have in your saddlebags?'

The old man straightened up, tossing the wad of grass to one side. 'Mouse traps,' he said.

'Mouse traps?'

'Have you not heard about the problems with slitpockets in the cities these days? You can't trust a soul.'

Supper was cold pork and pickles, washed down with hot sweet tea. Afterwards, Alderan produced a clay pipe and tobacco pouch and settled back against his saddle for a smoke. Stretched out on a blanket, Gair tried to sleep. In spite of his weariness, the heavy aching in his limbs, his eyes would not close. The stream chattered constantly. Small things scampered in the tussocky grass and night birds called to each other. Loudest of all was the sound he could not hear, the song of the magic within him.

Part of him wished it would never come back, even as his belly hollowed at the thought of never hearing the music again, never experiencing the sweet rush of its power. Not that it would make any difference if it did stay silent; he was already damned. He had spurned the Goddess' teachings the instant he had surrendered to temptation, and it had cost him everything except, somehow, his life.

He turned onto his back and folded his arm behind his head.

Above him, stars glittered like holes in the curtains of heaven. He counted the constellations he knew, from east to west: the Pilgrim, rising now – by midwinter he would be gone; the Chariot; Amarada on her throne; the Huntsman and his Three Hounds; Slaine's Sword with the Pole Star on the cross-hilts, bright as a diamond. The first moon, Miriel, fat and golden, hung low on the shoulder of the Archen Mountains. Behind her, the tail of the Dragon was just visible above the luminous peaks as he chased the remains of the day.

'Can't sleep?' Alderan asked from the far side of the fire.

'I can't hear the magic. It feels like something's missing.'

'That's a strange kind of a lullaby.'

'I've been hearing it for so long, I've got used to it being there. It's gone away before, but that felt different. Like it was sleeping. Now I can't hear it at all and that feels . . . wrong, even though it shouldn't.'

'Wrong?'

'I don't know how to describe it. Every sermon I've ever heard warned me against sin. Every prayer I've ever learned was meant to steer me away from it. But when I heard the music it felt so good, so right, I didn't fight it. I opened myself to it even though I knew it would cast me out of the Goddess' grace for ever.' He fingered his breastbone through his shirt, where the tiny silver St Agostin medallion had once rested on its chain, before the marshals snatched it away. Not even the Knights' patron saint had kept him in the light.

'You were a child then.'

'I was old enough to know the difference between sin and virtue,' said Gair, 'and I did it anyway.'

'Because you were curious?'

'At first, and then I couldn't help myself. Even though I knew it was forbidden, I had to let the music in. It was . . . glorious.'

'So what happened back there on the road? When you set my

54

poor horse at a pack of Suvaeon Knights and gave me a fright to take five years off my life?'

'I just had to get away. The magic was breaking free and I felt as if I had to do something with it or I would burst. I'm sorry about the horse.'

'Don't worry about it, he came to no harm. Does it often happen like that? Where the magic seems to take over?'

'Sometimes.' Talking in the dark was easier, like confession. 'More often than not, lately, although it wasn't like that at first. Each time I'm scared I won't be able to control it. That something awful is going to happen.'

'More awful than eternal damnation?'

'I meant something that might hurt other people.' It wasn't as if he could make it any worse for himself.

Across the fire, Alderan's pipe-bowl glowed as he drew on it. 'That is a danger faced by all who can touch the songs of the earth,' the old man said slowly. 'With guidance and strength of will, you can learn to control it. In time, you could ride your gift as a bird rides the wind.'

'But how? Who is going to guide me, show me how to master it?' A long moment of silence. 'Alderan?'

'There are people who could teach you,' he said at last. 'If you could find them, and if they were willing.'

'Who?'

'They call themselves Guardians of the Veil. There're few of them left now, thanks to the Church, but there are some. They could help you.'

A jolt of excitement ran through Gair and he sat up. To never again be alone with the magic, to never have to fear what it might become – could it be possible?

'Where can I find the Guardians? Do you know?' he asked, but Alderan shook his head almost before the words were out of Gair's mouth.

'I couldn't say. They keep themselves quietly, for fear of

attracting the wrong kind of attention. The Inquisition may be long gone, but there are still many in the Church who have the means and the will to do them harm.'

So he would be as alone as he had ever been. The brief hope that had kindled in Gair's heart dwindled to an ember, not extinguished, not entirely, but neither was it enough to keep him warm at night. He leaned back on his elbow as the breeze sighed over him. Overhead, the stars wheeled infinitesimally closer to dawn.

'I don't understand how you know so much, Alderan,' he said. 'I can do things that I've only read about in storybooks, children's tales, yet you talk about it as if it's something normal.'

'But it is normal. It's the most normal and natural thing in the world. The Song is part of the very fabric of creation. People have simply forgotten how to hear it.'

The red eye of the pipe sputtered and went dim. Alderan knocked it out on the heel of his boot, then scraped out the dottle with his belt-knife and repacked the bowl.

'I've made something of a study of the Song,' he said. 'It's a hobby of mine. It's quite well documented, if you look in the right books – the ones the Church did not destroy, at any rate.' He kindled a gorse-twig in the fire's coals and puffed his pipe back into life. 'Did you know that one of the greatest libraries in the Empire is locked away in the vaults below the Sacristy, never to see the light of day? Thousands upon thousands of books, lost to all knowledge save the keepers of the Index.'

'Aren't they heretical?'

'What is heresy but an alternative point of view? Books are meant to be shared, Gair. They should be open to all, not put away out of sight because they might, heaven forfend, encourage free thought.'

Gair frowned. 'But the Index was created to keep us from sin.'

'And what sin was that?' the old man retorted. 'The sin of philosophy, of astronomy, of medicine? No, the Index was drawn up to control knowledge and keep people in ignorance, keep them believing that the ague came about from an imbalance in the bodily humours, rather than from digging the latrine too close to the well.'

'That's not what I was taught.'

'And the Church taught you what it wanted you to know.' Alderan harrumphed and sucked fiercely on his pipe. 'You've been led around with blinkers on, lad. Trust me, you're better off out of that place. The Church still has the dead hand of the Inquisition on its shoulder.'

'What do you mean?'

'You know your history, yes? How the Empire was founded? A dozen petty dukedoms squabbling amongst themselves, too suspicious of each other to stand together but none of them strong enough to stand alone when the Nimrothi clans came down through the passes. It took the Church to forge them into something that could halt Gwlach's advance.'

'The Grand Rede declared a crisis of the faith. They had to fight together or face excommunication.'

'And afterwards, of course, Mother Church had the Emperor in her pocket. He ruled only at the whim of the lectors. Anyone who challenged the Church's sway or spoke the wrong word in the right ear found black robes at their door come the morning.'

'That's not how the Master of Novices tells it.'

The old man snorted. 'Well, he wouldn't, would he? The Church keeps too many secrets.' Alderan stretched his legs out towards the fire and crossed his ankles. 'We live now in an age of reason, with clocks and manufactories and broadsheets to tell us the news. But because of the legacy of the Inquisition, we have lost something extremely precious. We have almost no one left who can hear the songs of the earth.'

'Except me.'

'And the others like you, yes. I've met several in my travels, all over the Empire. Most were like you, misunderstood, confused, lost. I tried to help where I could.'

'Is that why you helped me get out of Dremen?' Gair looked across the fire at the other man's shadowy form. 'Who are you, Alderan? You know almost as much medicine as Brother Infirmarer, and more about this gift of mine than I do. What is it? Where does it come from? What am I going to do now, with my life? With this?' He held up his branded hand.

'So many questions, I hardly know where to start!' The old man chuckled. 'Well, what I am is a scholar, a collector of books, the older and rarer the better. There is much to be learned from the past that deserves not to be forgotten. As for where you can go, that's up to you. There are places where that scar won't be such an issue.'

'Where? The first lector who sees it will have me in irons.' When Alderan had cleaned and dressed the burn again after supper the shape of the witchmark had been clearly visible, even with the swelling and the blisters. When they were gone there would be a scar that would be hard to hide.

'Not necessarily. I know one or two who have a more flexible interpretation of the Book of Eador.'

'It's doctrine, Alderan. "Thou shalt not suffer a witch to live."' In his head Gair heard Elder Goran say those very words. The law was as black and white as the tiled floor of the Rede Hall. Panic stirred again.

'Doesn't that rather depend on your definition of witchcraft? I said before that I didn't think you were a witch. I don't think you have it in you to do that kind of harm.'

'Then what am I?'

'You're a young man who can make of himself whatever he chooses to be,' Alderan said. 'You're fit and healthy and good with a sword – they'd have sent you to the scriptorium if you weren't – so there're plenty of places you could make a living where that hand won't occasion anything more than a raised eyebrow. You could be a merchant's guard, or serve in the retinue of some landowner. The Imperial Army. You could even become a mercenary. It's an uncertain sort of existence, but I hear it pays well. Kasrin of the Glaive is supposed to live like a prince.'

It sounded straightforward, the way Alderan told it, but Gair could see only obstacles. No money, no family to fall back on – hells, he didn't even have his own horse. 'I wish it was that easy.'

Alderan sat quietly for some time. Then he took the pipe from between his teeth and blew a long stream of smoke up into the night sky. 'You could come back to the west, with me,' he said. 'I have a school on Penglas, in the Western Isles. You could study, maybe go on to be a teacher yourself, or learn a trade. You'd be free to come and go as you please. It would take you away from here, at the very least. I can't help but feel that the longer we spend in Dremenir the more likely we are to run up against Goran's men again, jurisdiction or no.'

'That's very kind of you, but with respect, I don't know you. You've gone out of your way to help me out of the city, but I couldn't ask you to do any more for me.'

'Nonsense. It's my duty as a good Eadorian to extend the hand of friendship to those less fortunate than myself and from where I'm sitting you still fall under that heading. I'd be glad to have you along, if only for the company. On a journey of a thousand miles, you quickly come to realise that horses are not great conversationalists.'

'A thousand miles? For old books?'

'I like to travel.' A flash of teeth around the pipe-stem. 'Besides, the rarer volumes are scattered across the twelve provinces and beyond. I've a hankering to visit Sardauk again next year. They have a fine library in Marsalis and their university is older than the Empire itself. For some reason the desert produces most excellent scholars – all that sand and heat concentrates the mind.'

Gair watched the ghostly shape of an owl drift overhead in pursuit of its supper. Alderan had done nothing but good by him since he had woken up in the inn and his suggestion of going out to the Isles appealed far more than the alternatives. He'd always loved reading, adventures, histories, even the epic poems of the Nordmen when the mood took him. The Motherhouse's library had inclined towards the more ecclesiastical texts, but some of the early monks had taken great pains to record the history of the lands from the Founding onwards and there had been plenty to divert him.

'What would I do, out there? In the Isles?'

'Whatever you like. You could follow your own course.'

'And what I am doesn't matter to you? The magic, I mean?'

'Not in the least. You and the others I've met have been almost without exception honest, decent folk who're better Eadorians than many of the lectors I've known, including our dear friend the Elder. I tread lightly around Churchmen, as I said, and there're only a few I'd choose to call friends.'

'Is your parish lector one of them?'

Alderan laughed heartily. 'He is indeed. A very fine fellow, who sends me a bottle of good Tylan goldwine every Eventide and doesn't frown at me if I don't go to confession. For the record, Gair, based on our short acquaintance, you would be welcome in my house.'

Welcome was a word he had heard all too infrequently. He had been sent out of Leah by the people who should have known him best and put out of the Motherhouse by those who should have forgiven him for his sins. The one person who had extended a sincere hand was the one he knew the least. He'd had his fill of being turned away. 'How long will it take to get there?'

'The rest of the summer, I'm afraid, but we can take a boat most of the way and spare our arses the saddle. Should I take it you've decided to come with me?'

'I like books.'

'I see. Well, there's a good few miles to Mesarild yet and you've already had quite a day. Try to get some sleep.'

Gair pulled his blanket up round his shoulders. West. A new

start, some kind of a life of his own, instead of one chosen for him. That could only be good, couldn't it? He closed his eyes. Besides, it wasn't as if he had anywhere else to go.

6

QUESTIONS

ත

The wooden chair was upright and unyielding as the black oak of Traitor's Gate. Gair shifted as best he could with his arms fastened behind the chair back, but it was no good. His backside had lost all feeling.

Sober and patient as crows on a fence, three questioners watched. Identical in their black robes, their masks of unglazed porcelain, nothing distinguished which one spoke.

'Are you uncomfortable?'

He nodded. His shoulders burned, neck aching with the effort of keeping his head up.

'This will all be over shortly, then you can rest.' The soft, mellifluous tones were more suited to the confessional than the stark whitewashed chamber where the questioners performed their work. 'Perhaps have a bath, a hot meal. Would you like that?'

Another nod. Hot water. Warm, fluffy towels to wrap him up, like snuggling into summer clouds. Yes.

'All we want is the truth.' Different voice this time, harsher, flat as stone. A proper questioner's voice.

'I've told you the truth.'

One mask turned away. One didn't move at all. The third, in the middle, tilted inquisitively.

'Have you? You cannot have done, or you would not be here. The questions are very simple. Why won't you answer them truthfully?'

'I've told you the truth.'

'Come now, Gair,' chided the smooth voice, a schoolmaster disappointed with a favoured pupil. 'You know that's not so. We have been patient with you – and it is such a little thing to ask. All we want is the truth. That is our task, to seek out the truth. All you have to do is tell us. It's really very easy.'

Always the same questions, and he had answered them more times than he could remember. He had given them the truth, over and over. He'd told them what he thought they wanted to hear, but untruth did not satisfy them either. They asked their questions again and were hurt when he had nothing new to say. And he was so tired of it.

'There's nothing more I can tell you.' He jerked at the restraints and the thick leather cuffs cut into his wrists. 'How many more times do you want to hear it?'

'Lying is a sin before the Goddess,' said the harsh voice abruptly. 'The world is as it is, and to say otherwise is to demean the perfection of Her creation. Answer the questions put to you, or face the penalty for your sin!'

'I have answered the questions.' Blood trickled over Gair's hands.

'Who is your demon?'
'I don't have a demon.'
'Who is your demon?'
'I don't have a demon! I've told you a thousand times!'
'*Who is your demon?*'

He shook his head. It was pointless. Same questions; the same answers, round and round for ever. A hundred years in that damned chair, with his arse numb and his legs twitching with cramps he couldn't ease because they were chained to the floor. A thousand

63

years in that dank little chamber breathing the acrid smoke of stale lamp oil and his own stink. Pointless.

'*WHO IS YOUR DEMON?*'

'You're wasting your time.'

'Speak, boy, and be saved! Who is your demon?'

'I don't have a demon! For the love of the Goddess, aren't you listening to me?' His voice cracked. 'I don't have a demon!'

'Blasphemer!'

'Blasphemy is a sin, Gair. Taking Her name in vain like that . . .' Smooth-voice shook his head slowly, sadly.

'Tell us what we want to know,' the other questioner snapped. 'Be truthful!'

'I don't know what you want me to say.' Gair's fists clenched and unclenched, fingers sliding greasily in his own blood. 'I've already told you the truth. I don't have a demon. I don't have a familiar. There is no coven.'

'Just answer the questions.'

'I've answered them. What more do you want?'

'We want the truth.'

Finally, the third questioner spoke. His voice was cultured, silky. Refined, even. 'You have not yet given us the truth. Therefore, you must be encouraged to be truthful.' One black glove emerged from a sleeve and made a small gesture.

Unseen hands slipped a bolt behind the chair and Gair's arms swung forward. At once a hot, prickling tide swept through them as circulation was restored, then they were jerked away from his sides by the ropes that led from the cuffs to iron rings in the walls and thence to the questioners' silent, soft-footed assistants.

'Please, no.'

Arms outstretched by the ropes, he was lifted out of the chair. His cramped legs howled. Higher. Returning blood stabbed him with tiny needles. Higher again. Hot-wire pain in every muscle. Sweat stung his bloody wrists.

64

'Goddess, please!'

Hemp creaked, taut as mast-shrouds. *O Mother be thou a light and comfort to me now and at the hour of my death.* Toes scrabbled for purchase on the floor. *I am a supplicant before thee—*

'Please!' Gair gritted his teeth against the pain *a light and comfort to me* if he could just straighten his legs, get the balls of his feet under him *now and at the hour of my death—* 'What do you want?'

'Just answers to our questions, Gair.' Smooth-voice sounded resigned. 'Tell us the names.'

'I don't know any names,' Gair gasped. Fresh sweat broke over his skin. Holy Mother his shoulders hurt. 'There is no one else.'

Behind him, he heard a serpentine slither; leather uncoiling on stone. His mouth dried. When he tried to swallow, his throat made a brittle click. 'I don't know what you want me to say!'

Then the tawse sang and licked his naked back with fire.

Gair flung himself awake, heart leaping in his throat. Merciful saints, he couldn't get his breath. Fear had his lungs in an iron grip, pounding its drums in his ears. A shadow moved beside him.

'Are you all right?' Alderan asked.

Gair nodded, not trusting himself to speak. The night breeze chilled his sweaty neck. Sitting up, he leaned on his knees and waited for his runaway pulse to slow.

Alderan fetched a water bottle from the packs and pushed it into Gair's hand. 'Here.'

'Thanks.' The water was flat and tasted of leather but it cleaned the stale taste from his mouth.

'I can give you something to let you sleep.'

Just leave me be. 'I'm all right.'

'You need rest, Gair. I saw your back – they'd striped you like a *qilim* rug.'

I know. 'I said I'm all right.' Gair drank some more water.

'The offer's there if you change your mind.'

I won't. 'Sorry if I woke you.'

'No matter. I had to be up anyway.' Alderan patted his shoulder and walked behind a gorse bush from where there shortly came the sound of a bladder being emptied. When he was done, he returned and rolled himself back in his blanket without another word.

Gair sipped water and stared out across the moor. Three days and a hundred miles between him and the Holy City, halfway to the Belisthan border, and he still couldn't leave it behind. He rubbed his eyes. No chance he'd get back to sleep now. It was the wrong time of the night. Lumiel, the second moon, had barely dipped towards dawn; the questioners had favoured this time, the small hours between Second and sun-up when the soul's waters were at their lowest ebb, when resistance was weakest. In this part of the night, dreams felt all too real.

He looked down at his still-swollen hand and tentatively flexed his fingers. The pain seemed a little reduced, but his hand had less strength than uncooked sausage. The ride to escape the Knights had done it no favours. Saints, he was tired – tired and sore and adrift in the dark, still waiting for the dawn.

'We should be in Belistha by the end of the week,' Alderan said the next morning, heaving the saddle onto the back of his bay. 'About three weeks from there to Mesarild, if the weather stays fair.'

Gair made a noncommittal sound, fumbling with his own saddle-girths. He could cinch it one-handed, once he got the strap through the buckle; it was feeding the strap through in the first place that was the problem. An insect tickled across his forehead. He dropped the girth and swatted it away, but the prickling intensified, the insects crawling inside his skin.

He swore. 'Alderan, I can feel the witchfinder.' Straightening up, Gair scanned the rumpled moor in the direction of Dremen. Red heather and clumps of gorse, and crusty tors poking through the thin soil like bones through a rotten blanket. No sign of a pursuit. 'I can't see anyone.'

'We're a long way from Goran's jurisdiction here.' Alderan sounded doubtful.

'So why's the witchfinder still looking?' Gair turned back to his patient horse and struggled with the girth-straps, swearing in frustration.

'Slow down, lad, slow down. Let me do that.'

'I can manage,' Gair growled and snicked the buckle-tongues into the holes on the third attempt. *Finally!* He gathered up the reins and mounted, glancing round their campsite to ensure they'd left as little trace as possible. Fire-stones were scattered, turf replaced. In a day or two the crushed grass would spring back. It was the best they could do.

'I want to get away from here, Alderan,' he said. 'As far away as possible.'

'All right, I understand,' the old man soothed, securing the last buckle on his bags. He swung up into the saddle. 'Can you still sense him?'

Gair nodded. 'It's faint, but it's there.'

'He's persistent, I'll give him that. Goran must have paid him well.'

&

A wind-scoured border stone at the side of the road four days later was the only indication that they had passed out of Dremenir and into the southernmost reaches of Belistha. The landscape reminded Gair of Leah, up near the foothills of the Laraig Anor. He had travelled league upon league up there, just a boy on a sturdy fell pony, watching the seasons turn from winter to spring, summer to autumn. He clamped down hard on those memories. No good would be had from letting them linger. There was nothing for him in Leah any more.

67

Now the main roads were choked with caravans, trailing huge dust clouds that coated everything within half a mile in fine grit. Alderan swung off the highway onto narrower roads that wound down through deer country to the greener, gentler lowlands. Three weeks after leaving Dremen, they joined the broad Imperial highway from Fleet in Arennor and turned south towards Mesarild. Two days down the highway, Gair felt the crawling, nettle-sting touch of the witchfinder again.

'He's closer,' he said.

Alderan glanced up from his cookfire where he stirred a pot of stew. He had proved to be a better than fair trail cook, conjuring hearty meals from whatever supplies he had, or could catch with a snare, like this rabbit, seasoned with a handful of herbs from the roadside.

'Our watery-eyed friend? Can you tell where he is?'

Gair got to his feet and turned slowly in a full circle, staring into the towering trunks of the beechwood surrounding their camp. The sensation intensified a little when he faced east of north. He pointed. 'That way.'

'Any idea how far?'

'No. He's closer, or trying harder.'

'How can you tell?'

'I can't. I'm guessing.' He looked round when the old man said nothing and found him studying the stew-pot as if the gravy had just curdled, spoon motionless in his hand. 'Alderan?'

'Supper's ready.'

'Alderan.'

A plate of stew was held out to him, with a hunk of bread. 'You just pointed at Dremen, true as an arrow,' the old man said. 'I'd love to know what you did to make Goran go to these lengths – catch him with his hand up a choirboy's cassock or something?'

Gair sat down with his supper. 'I hardly knew who he was until the charges were brought.' He pushed the meat around on his plate, searching for an appetite though his ears were full of the

68

sing of the tawse. The dreams had not relented. 'We got better acquainted later, when he oversaw my questioning.'

Alderan grunted. 'They were his questioners?'

'I think so.'

'I'm not surprised. Does Ansel know?'

'I've no idea.' *I don't want to talk about it.*

'Sing out if you hear it again.' Alderan pointed at Gair's untouched plate. 'Are you going to eat that?'

❧

In the morning, the witchfinder's presence was gone. Around noon they broke their journey in the shade of a copse. Gair hobbled the horses under a tree to graze and climbed up on the field-wall to sit next to Alderan. Summer had ripened towards autumn and harvest had begun. Sickles flashed in the fields and rows of stooks striped the hillsides, racing home ahead of the thunderheads piled along the rim of the valley.

'Have you ever been this far west, lad?' The old man handed him a water bottle.

'No. Never further than Dremen.' Gair yawned.

'Doesn't look much different, does it? A farm is still a farm, whether it's here or six hundred miles away. That's about how far we've come – maybe a bit more. The rest we'll do by boat. We can take a barge from Mesarild to the White Havens, then sail around to the Isles.'

'How long will it take?' Gair smothered another yawn.

'Should be there by St Simeon's. Tired?'

'A bit.'

'Sleeping all right?'

'Fine.'

Alderan looked sidelong at him. 'And the truth?'

In truth, he had dreamed again, as he did most nights. Sometimes those dreams wrenched him awake in a sweat, his body tensed for a blow. Occasionally, like last night, he dreamed of

Goran's piggy eyes glittering in anticipation as the heavy leather tawse reared up.

'Not good,' Gair admitted. 'Better than I was, but not good.'

'It'll take time.'

'Fresh air helps. Daylight.'

'They kept you in the dark?'

'The cell was lined with iron plate. I could barely see to avoid pissing on my feet.' Gair stoppered the bottle and handed it back. 'How far are we from Mesarild?'

'We'll be there in time for supper. It's in the next valley.'

An hour later, the road brought them to the rim of a broad, shallow valley, bisected by the shimmering expanse of the Great River. At its centre a wedge-shaped rocky outcrop rose above the confluence with the River Awen, upon which a huge fortress grew up from the cliff tops as if birthed from the belly of the earth. Cascading down the back slope of the outcrop lay the city itself, encircled by tier upon tier of walls, as if Mesarild in its expansion had been obliged to keep letting its belt out a notch.

Gair sat his horse in the road and stared in disbelief. 'It's huge!'

'And getting bigger.' Alderan pointed at tiny figures scrambling about the red-brown scar of fresh earthworks. 'Look, the outer wall is only a hundred years old and already they're digging foundations for a new one.'

'What for?'

'Goddess knows. There hasn't been a war in Elethrain in nine hundred years. Still, it keeps the stonemasons in business, I suppose. Are you ready to go?'

Gair nudged his horse on to catch up. 'Will we stay there overnight?'

'Probably. It depends on whether there's a place on the next barge. Why?'

'It's the capital city. I've never seen it before.'

'That's as good a reason as any. Come on.'

Where Mesarild truly began was difficult to say. The North

Road acquired a straggle of houses as it progressed southwards into the valley, then a few more, then side streets, inns, livery yards and stockpens. Soon it became impossible to see between the buildings to the surrounding farmland. Smoke and refuse became the dominant smells, instead of earth and new-mown hay. The houses crowded ever more thickly together were now three and even four storeys high. The more prosperous residents could afford to decorate their windows with panels of stained glass, something Gair had only ever seen in churches before. In Leah, windows were plain leaded casements, with stout shutters to keep out the storms. He had never thought of them being ornamental as well as functional.

Alderan was unmoved by all the wonderful strangeness of it, maintaining a confident, slightly bored air, whilst Gair could not help but stare like a bumpkin. He tried to match the old man's composure, but it was impossible when each turn of the road brought something new to his eyes. Colonnaded buildings framed wide, fountained squares swirling with crowds. Statues held their hands high in benediction, or gazed imperiously towards the horizon along avenues of broad-leaved trees underplanted with flowers in more colours than he could name. It was all he could do to keep his jaw from dropping.

By the time they reached the third city gate, a broad arch of ruddy Elethrainian granite, the afternoon was well on the wane and their pace had slowed to a crawl. The queue in front of them turned the jostle at the Anorien Gate in Dremen into something resembling the serving line at a bakery, but finally deposited them onto a square the size of a village green. The mass of people thinned as some went this way and some that, until all the backs with which Gair had become familiar during the long wait had been transformed into scurrying citizens and disappeared like raindrops into a running stream.

Alderan guided his horse left towards a side street and Gair followed.

'Where are we going?'

'There's no chance we'll find passage this afternoon, so we need somewhere to spend the night.'

'Up here? Why not closer to the docks?'

'Because I prefer not to share my bed with creatures that have more legs than I do. There're rats down there the size of terriers.'

Gair's belly hollowed. 'Rats?'

'They come off the grain barges, great big ones, full of fleas.'

'I see.' He felt queasy.

Alderan twisted round to look at him. 'Don't tell me you're afraid of rats.'

'Not afraid, exactly, but . . .' Gair swallowed. A memory loomed large, of dark, odd-smelling places and a small boy who had missed his footing and tumbled headlong into a nest of unseen furry somethings that squirmed and squealed and bit. He shuddered. 'I just don't like them.'

'So I see.' Alderan smiled. 'Come on. There's a good inn not far from here.'

Running parallel to the curve of the city wall, the street led through two more arched gateways into still older levels of the city, becoming successively steeper as it ascended the flank of the hill towards the looming rust-red Citadel.

At last Alderan turned his horse in through wide double gates beneath an overhanging timbered balcony. Blue shadows climbed the walls of the yard and suppertime smells wafted from the inn's door.

Gair's stomach grumbled that it had been a long time since he had eaten. Inside the large square common room, a counter ran the full width of the back wall between kitchen door and staircase, with a row of squat barrels behind it like hogs at a trough.

Alderan rapped on the counter. 'Landlord?'

A round man in a white apron emerged from the back room, drying his arms on a towel. 'What's your pleasure, sir?' he asked brightly, flipping the towel over his shoulder. 'Ale? Wine? We have some very fine Tylan goldwine, just in.'

'Rooms for myself and my squire, then some supper.' Alderan's tone was offhand, and he leaned on the counter as if it belonged to him. 'A private dining room, if you have such a thing.'

'But of course, my lord. A moment, please.' With a bob of his head, the landlord disappeared into the back room.

When he returned, he was ushering a maid in front of him. 'Maura will show you to your rooms, my lord. If there's anything lacking, she will fetch it for you.'

A cool stare assessed the maid's appearance from coif to shoes, lingering on the shape she made under her apron.

The maid coloured, and Gair frowned.

'Thank you,' the old man drawled. 'Shall we go?'

The maid dipped an uncomfortable curtsey and led the way to a suite of rooms on the second floor, high enough above the common room not to be bothered by any noise. She listened to Alderan's arrogant instructions concerning the disposition of baggage, bathwater and supper in that order, then bobbed her way out with the old man's hand cupped on her rump.

The instant the door shut Gair rounded on him. 'Do you always treat women like that? She's not your property!'

'You've got a witchfinder on your tail, remember? This way the landlord will remember me and not you, and with a bit of luck we'll slip through the city like fish,' Alderan told him. 'Now I've got to see about booking passage for us. I'll be back in a couple of hours.'

Without any further explanation, he left the room and Gair heard him stride back down the stairs. He plopped himself in a chair and frowned at the empty hearth, thoroughly puzzled. Something was going on and he was right in the middle of it, but he had not the faintest idea what it was. There appeared to be more layers to Alderan than there were to an onion, and like an onion it was making his eyes water, trying to fathom the old man out. With Alderan gone, there was nothing to do but wait and see if he was prepared to answer questions when he came back.

7

OLD FRIENDS

☙

Bathwater and supper came and went without a sign of Alderan. Bored, Gair prowled the room for as long as he could stand, then made for the door. The maid had mentioned a garden on the roof of the inn; a breath of air would do him good.

Two flights of stairs brought him to a low door onto the roof, where there was indeed a garden. The roof had been levelled and laid with square slate tiles, on which stood pots and barrels containing flowers and neatly clipped miniature trees. Scattered benches allowed the inn's patrons to take their ease. A breeze blew from the river, but enough heat struck up from the tiles underfoot to make it more than warm enough to sit out in shirt-sleeves.

Gair wandered amongst the plants, enjoying the fragrance and colour. The terrace overlooked a good two-thirds of the city, revealing a surprising number of other similar gardens, some even illuminated with coloured glass lanterns. Overhead, swallows screamed as they sliced the evening air.

'Lovely view, isn't it?' said a voice behind him.

Gair swung round.

A man lounged on a wooden bench by the wall, a silver goblet in his hand. Dark hair lay loose around the shoulders of a violet silk shirt, open at the neck. He raised his goblet in salute. 'Your health.'

'Forgive me, sir; I don't think we've met.' Gair gave him a formal bow.

'We have a mutual acquaintance in Alderan,' the man said. 'I was hoping to look him up whilst he's here in town.'

'He'll be back shortly, if you'd like me to carry a message.'

'Oh, it's not important.' The man waved his goblet airily. 'I just thought we might catch up on old times. I have some business interests in the capital. Rather tedious, most of it, but it pays the taxes.'

'I'll tell him you asked after him.' Gair paused, wondering how the fellow had known where to find the old man in all of Mesarild. 'Are you staying at the inn?'

'Alas, no. I have appointments elsewhere today. A pity, since the landlord here keeps quite a good cellar. Do tell Alderan Savin was here, though. Are you new?'

New? New to what? 'He and I are only recently acquainted, yes.'

'You seem very different to the strays he usually picks up. Gutter-sweepings, most of the time, I have to say, but you strike me as a cat of a different colour altogether.' Savin gestured to the bench beside him. 'Come and have some wine and tell me about yourself.'

Who was this fellow? For all he said he was acquainted with Alderan, his manner was off-putting. It set Gair in mind of someone who would squash a bee he found in his room, rather than open the window and let it out. 'Thank you, sir, but no.'

Savin picked up a bottle from the floor and refilled his goblet. 'Sure I can't offer you some? I won't bite.'

Gair remained where he was.

A flicker of irritation crossed Savin's immaculate features. 'As you wish.' He set the empty bottle on the tiles and snapped his fingers. It disappeared as completely as if the world had opened up and closed itself around it.

Gair was startled, but not really surprised; Alderan had mentioned knowing others with abilities like his own.

'I despise untidiness, don't you?' The man lounged against the arm of the bench, ankles crossed. His boots were black and glossy, quietly expensive. 'So, tell me how Alderan came to find you.'

'I doubt you'd find it interesting.'

'I am beset by a curious nature; I find all manner of things quite fascinating.' Savin savoured a mouthful of wine, then treated Gair to a disarming smile. 'Besides, I'd have thought you'd enjoy some conversation. You must be bored out of your mind, stuck with him every day of the week.'

'He's not so bad.'

'But it's hardly been exciting, though, has it? Alderan's such a stuffy old coot, although his heart is in the right place.'

'I've had enough excitement lately to last for a good while.' Savin rubbed across the grain. Just being next to him was enough to raise the hairs on Gair's arms.

'Really? Do tell me what happened.'

'I had a close call with some Church Knights.'

'How thrilling. What sort of trouble were you in?'

'It was fairly serious.'

'Well, I'd love to hear you tell the whole story, but alas, I have to go.' Draining his goblet, Savin stood up. 'I've enjoyed our chat, even if it was a little one-sided. Perhaps we can talk again sometime.'

He extended a hand on which winked a heavy silver and amethyst ring.

Gair gave another stiff bow. For no reason he could explain, he did not want to be any closer to the man in the violet shirt than he already was.

Disappointment tightened Savin's mouth, but he responded with a bow of his own, crisp and courtly. 'Perhaps you'll come to trust me eventually. Until then, let me just say that you'll do yourself a favour if you think hard about whatever Alderan tells you and take

77

it with a pinch of salt. He is not what he seems to be. Now I must take my leave. I think I have outstayed my welcome.'

'I'll be sure to tell Alderan that you called by.'

Footsteps sounded on the tiles behind Gair. He looked round to see Alderan striding through the potted shrubs towards him. When he looked back to Savin, the man was gone. 'You just missed a friend of yours,' he said.

Alderan stared at him as if he had declared the sky was green. 'What?'

'A man called Savin. He said he was a friend of yours – an acquaintance, anyway.'

The old man frowned. 'And his name was Savin?'

'He said he wanted to catch up on old times, hoped to find you here. I said I'd pass on the message.'

Alderan's face grew grim.

'Have I done something wrong?'

In a blink, the old man's expression shifted to geniality. 'No, not at all. I just wasn't expecting to run into him here, that's all. Well, well. I haven't seen Savin in a very long time.'

'He asked to be remembered to you.'

'I'm sure he did, lad. Now, did you leave me some supper?'

Back in their rooms, Alderan ate in silence. Gair sensed that something was wrong, but he could not tell whether it was connected to Savin's visit. He wandered the room, nibbling grapes and trying to puzzle out what it was about the elegantly dressed fellow that had sounded such an odd note in the otherwise tranquil garden.

'Did Savin say anything else?' Alderan asked abruptly, pushing away the tray.

'He said I was different to the others you picked up. What did he mean?'

The old man dabbed his mouth with a napkin. 'You're not the first who's come to the Western Isles with me. Some stay, some don't. They've all been people who needed to be somewhere else for a time, much like you. What did you tell him?'

'Nothing. I didn't care for his manner. Besides, if he'd come to see you, what did he need to know about me?'

With a harsh laugh, Alderan threw the napkin down onto the table. 'You have excellent instincts, my boy. Savin and I go back a long way, but I don't much care for him and I don't particularly want to spend the evening drinking and trading war stories with him. You've done me a favour, no mistake. By the way, you might like to know that I've booked passage for us, leaving first thing tomorrow. It's nothing luxurious, but it'll get us there, and the sooner we get there the better. These are troubled times and from what I heard down in the city, they're only getting worse.'

He tugged a crumpled paper from his pocket and tossed it on the table. Gair smoothed it out. It was a four-day-old broadsheet, the low-grade paper already yellowed, but the print was sharp. He read a few lines of a report of renewed banditry in the Arennorian Marches and the dispatch of five hundred men from the garrison at Fleet to deal with them.

'Bands of thieves roaming the highways, civil unrest – there was an apprentices' riot in Yelda last month, and rumours coming out of the desert too. All the broadsheets are full of it. According to the people I spoke to, we were lucky not to have had trouble with brigands on our way south. The Imperial patrols scour them away every few months, but they creep back. All the merchants are forming up into caravans and hiring mercenaries for protection.'

'So why aren't we travelling with one of the caravans?'

'I don't fancy waiting two days for the next south-bound one,' Alderan told him. 'The convoys are slower than molasses at mid-winter, anyway. I'd rather be on my way quickly and round the Horn of Bregorin before the autumn gales. The bargees at the docks said there are fewer brigands along the waterways, although there are still some.'

'That's not very comforting.'

'Oh, I think you and I can handle a few ruffians with rusty knives, don't you? After seeing off a troop of the Church's finest?'

Grudgingly, Gair surrendered to the old man's humour and smiled. 'I suppose we can,' he said. 'When do we sail?'

'Dawn, so you'll need to be early to bed. Did you leave me any bathwater?'

The *Trader Rose* was a two-masted lugger carrying grain down-river to the White Havens. There was room on board for two passengers, provided they did not mind sleeping on deck and helping with the rigging if called upon. The horses, however, had to be sold. Gair had grown fond of the chestnut and stood stroking his long nose and tugging his ears whilst Alderan negotiated a price with the liveryman at the inn. Then they shouldered their saddlebags and made their way down to the docks in the rosy early light.

The *Rose's* bargee was a villainous-looking creature with only one eye and a stubby clay pipe clamped in the corner of his mouth. For company he had a black and white dog of indeterminate parentage, and a cat to keep down the rats.

'Rats?' Gair echoed, glancing around the neatly painted deck.

'She's a grain ship; the buggers is attracted to it.' The swarthy bargee cackled. 'Don't you be worryin' yourself, though. I ain't seen one in three days and old Reuben is just as fat as butter!'

Scratching his rump, he ambled back to the wheelhouse and produced a black leather bottle from which he took a long pull.

Gair eyed the man's stained clothing and stubbled chin. 'Is he reliable?' he asked Alderan as they stowed their belongings against the bulwark.

'Skeff? More or less. I've travelled with him before. Besides, he was the best I could do at short notice.'

'What if we're robbed?'

'Unlikely. The brigands generally leave Skeff alone – they know there's slim pickings to be had from him. Whatever he earns he drinks away.'

'This is not doing much to increase my confidence.'

A dockhand cast off the ropes and tossed them onto the *Rose's* deck. Toby the dog barked excitedly at the mongrels on the other barges as wind and current took hold, and once she started downstream, he took up station in the bows like a figurehead, grinning and panting. Reuben eyed him disparagingly from the top of the rope locker, and tucked his tail round his nose.

The cat certainly seemed to be a competent ratter, as the first night on board was undisturbed by so much as a squeak. His night's work over, he sat up in the bows performing his morning ablutions. He was a large orange tabby, with white paws which he washed carefully, back and front, before swiping them around his ears. Occasionally he paused to stare at Gair with slitted yellow eyes before returning to his toilet.

'Breakfast is served.' Alderan emerged from the tiny galley below deck and set two plates on the hatch-cover next to Gair. They were piled with steaming bacon and fresh bread from the stores.

'Looks like it's going to be another fine day,' he added, squinting at the pale sky. The sun was a bright golden disc in the haze and skeins of mist lay across the water in front of the barge. Where the sunlight penetrated, dew sparkled on the grasses on either bank. The air smelled of damp earth and freshly mown fields. 'Did you sleep well?'

'Very.' Gair helped himself from a plate. 'Better than I've slept in a while.'

'No bad dreams?'

He shook his head. There had been some, if he was honest, but none to wake him in a rank sweat the way he had the first few nights out of the Motherhouse.

'The music?'

'I can't hear it.'

Alderan produced a clay pot of relish from his saddlebags and began spreading it liberally on his bacon. He had an apparently inexhaustible supply of condiments. 'What about our friend over yonder?' He gestured roughly north of east.

'Nothing. Do you think he's lost the trail?'

Alderan looked thoughtful. 'Maybe, maybe not. Time will tell. Let me know if you sense him.'

Whilst he ate, Gair attempted to bribe Reuben with a sliver of bacon, but the cat was too engrossed in grooming his belly fur. Toby, however, skidded to a halt at Gair's feet, tail wagging.

'All right, then,' he laughed, and tossed him the scrap. The dog wolfed it down, then begged for more.

'I'm sorry, that's it.'

Toby whined, so Gair bent down and ruffled his fur, and was rewarded with an enthusiastic face-wash. From the top of the locker, Reuben favoured them with a yellow-eyed look, then curled up with his back to them.

Time passed slowly on the barge. The late summer heat was pleasantly languorous and the gurgle of the water soothing. Alderan stretched out with his saddlebags for a pillow and quickly fell into a doze, but Gair grew restive. Over the after-deck a breeze freshened the air, so he sat there for a while and watched the beasts and waterfowl that patrolled the Great River until even that palled. Rhythmic snores from the vicinity of the bulkhead told him he'd be short of conversation from Alderan, so he quietly fetched his sword from the baggage and took himself back to the after-deck for a little practice.

Ten years of discipline could not be unlearned in a hundred days, although Gair's body was not quite so sure. The iron room had robbed his skin of colour and his muscles of much of their tone, but the exercises came back quickly. Stripped down to bare feet and breeches, he swung his way through the forms until his shoulders burned and sweat ran down the hollow of his spine.

It felt good to be doing something physical again. The patterns of the solo sword-forms had a grace and rhythm to them that was almost like dancing and he knew the steps so well that he could concentrate on each move without worrying about what came next. With every step he grew more aware of how he was breathing, the ways his muscles were bunching and sliding as the longsword flashed silver under the sun. He did not have to think, and, most importantly, he did not have to remember.

When his shadow reached the foot of the port bulwark, he noticed Alderan leaning against the mast, watching him. He finished the form and stepped back, bringing his feet together and raising the blade to the salute. The old man acknowledged it with a dip of his head, then threw him a towel.

Next morning, Gair was as stiff as if he'd been beaten with staves, and every muscle protested when he moved. Selenas would surely laugh at how unfit he had become, if he could but see him. After breakfast, though, he was back on the after-deck, a scrap of bandage protecting his scarred hand, shaking off the rustiness of a night's sleep.

They discovered early on in their voyage that Skeff subsisted almost entirely on bacon and cheap brandy, with only a little bread or a few beans for variety. Alderan muttered something about nutritional values and on the evening of the second day waded ashore to cut a whippy sapling for a fishing pole. With the aid of a hook and line from his saddlebags, he trawled the barge's wake for alternative fare. His efforts had not yielded anything much bigger than a fingerling so far, but he had hopes. Anything, he said, was better than more bacon, even with Syfrian hot mustard.

The third day on the barge was much the same as the first and second. Towards the end of the afternoon, Alderan came up with a towel before Gair had finished his exercises.

'I'm not done yet,' he panted, mopping his face.

'I know. Keep practising, but I thought I should let you know that we're not alone.'

'What do you mean?'

Alderan's head inclined fractionally towards the starboard railing. 'Under the trees, over there. Someone's taking an interest.'

Gair glanced at the far bank. A large shadow flickered through the trees, pacing the ponderous barge. 'Looks like a man on horseback. A traveller?'

'Maybe, but the highway is three miles from the river, hereabouts. There're just farms for leagues in all directions.'

'Could be a farmer?'

'How many farmers do you know who carry swords?'

'How can you see that from here? He must be a quarter of a mile away.'

'Every once in a while the hilt flashes. There's probably a chunk of glass in the pommel, cut to look like a gemstone. It's the sort of thing footpads and the like are impressed by.'

'Brigands?'

The old man shrugged. 'Haven't a clue. But he's been pacing us for the last couple of miles, so it will do us no harm to be cautious. I'll warn Skeff.'

Nothing happened for the rest of that day and their night's sleep, with the *Rose* moored to a tree, was undisturbed. In the morning Gair resumed his practice. Both he and Alderan kept a discreet eye on the bank, but their shadow did not reappear.

That night brought a sprinkling of rain, but it was barely enough to dampen the decking and dried quickly with the breeze. Gair fell asleep not long after. He was woken by the firm pressure of a finger in his ribs. He opened his eyes and saw Alderan watching him from his blankets, his face illuminated by the faintest hazy moonlight. The old man slowly raised the finger to his lips for silence, then pointed towards the bank on the starboard side. His movements were so lazy and unobtrusive that they could have been made by a man stirring in his sleep.

84

Gair let his eyes drift almost closed and looked at the near bank. Men moved amongst the trees. If he listened closely he could hear the creak of saddle-harness above the slap and gurgle of the river. He counted the indistinct shapes, then carefully extended eight fingers. Alderan gave him a barely perceptible nod.

Eight brigands, probably armed, against two men and a drunk. And Toby. The dog was asleep, pressed into the back of Gair's legs. It could be worse. He cocked an ear to the rasping snores coming from the wheelhouse and wondered how much worse was worse.

And then he felt it: a brief, buzzing discord that swept over him like the brush of a nettle against bare skin, hardly a touch at all, but leaving his magic prickling in its wake. He flinched before he could stop himself. Alderan frowned. All Gair could do was tilt up his branded palm and hope the old man knew what he meant.

On the bank the furtive movements continued, followed by the sounds of at least one person wading carefully into the river. It was not especially deep here; the *Trader Rose* was broad, but she had a shallow draught like most river craft, and was moored only about fifteen yards from the bank. Gair, concentrating on listening to the brigands' progress, barely heard Alderan whisper to close his eyes.

A few seconds later a sulphurous flare arced up from the mainmast head to flood the deck, river and forested bank with harsh yellow light. Bowstrings twanged and arrows sprouted from the furled mainsail and the wheelhouse roof. Toby leapt to his feet, barking furiously.

'Fetch Skeff!' Alderan shouted. 'I'll try to distract them!'

Gair scuttled along the deck, keeping close to the cover of the bulwark, and entered the wheelhouse where Skeff was still snoring, wrapped in greasy blankets. Gair grabbed the bargee's shoulder and shook him hard. He surfaced groggily, belching a foul fug into Gair's face, his leather bottle tumbling to the deck with a slosh. He understood the word 'attack' only at the third attempt, then he staggered up and groped under his bunk. When he produced a worn bow and quiver of plain arrows, Gair offered up a small prayer; there was no way, soused as he was, Skeff would ever be able to shoot straight.

'Thank you,' he said, and snatched them from him.

He took cover behind the wheelhouse and quickly strung the bow. It was decent enough yew, if poorly cared for, and shorter than the bows to which he was accustomed, so he could draw it without difficulty, even with a less than perfect hand. Nocking an arrow, he leaned round the edge of the wheelhouse to pick his first mark. The flare was drifting slowly downwards, but it illuminated the figures wading out from the bank surprisingly well. They made perfect targets.

Gair swallowed as he drew the string back. He had never fired at any living thing bigger than woodcock before, and he was loath to start now. He aimed for the clear water between the legs of one of the men to give him a fright and loosed. His aim was off, or the shaft was crooked; the arrow buried itself in the meat of the man's thigh and he went down, floundering and choking in the water. His companion turned to see what was happening and Gair's next arrow whipped past his cheek. With a yelp the man clapped a hand to his face. As Gair stooped for another shaft, an arrow struck splinters from the edge of the wheelhouse right in front of him. Now he had become a target.

Two more men waded into the river, long knives glinting, as the more severely wounded of the first two hobbled ashore. They advanced purposefully towards the mainmast shrouds amidships.

Gair caught a glimpse of a pale, foxy face, hiding back in the trees. 'The witchfinder!'

'You sure?'

Aiming quickly, Gair loosed another arrow towards where he'd seen the seeker. The face disappeared, but he couldn't be sure he'd hit anything. 'I'm sure!'

Alderan swore. 'Get some way on her!' he yelled. 'Don't let them aboard!'

Skeff had found an axe and as he reeled towards the stern anchor arrows sprouted at his feet.

Darting back behind the wheelhouse, Gair turned his aim on the archers on the shore. He could not see much amongst the trees, but he let fly and his second shaft resulted in a cry of pain, confirming he had found a target. In fact, he had possibly killed a man. A Leahn longbow could put an arrow through plate-armour at two hundred paces; this was shorter by a foot or more, but even a shortbow was deadly at a range of no more than twenty-five yards. He nocked, drew and let fly again. He had no time to dwell on it.

The bargee had reached the stern rail and was hacking at the tough hemp of the anchor rope. On the riverbank, the archer shifted his aim again, this time to Alderan, but the feathered shafts missed, burying their heads in the far bulwark instead. Gair aimed for the source and loosed three arrows in quick succession. None came in reply.

In the water, the three men had reached the shrouds. The bow would be next to useless at close quarters, so Gair dropped it and ran for his sword. It was unsheathed and in his hand as the first arm appeared over the bulwark. He brought the flat of the heavy blade down hard.

Bone snapped.

The man fell back shrieking, but two others were already climbing over the bulwark. Gair was joined by Alderan, and a few solid blows from the stout oak belaying pin he was wielding soon persuaded the remaining brigands that the *Rose* had thorns.

Astern, Skeff finally succeeded in severing the anchor rope and as the barge drifted into the current Alderan ran to the halyards to raise the mainsail. Behind him, Skeff weaved over to let out the boom and catch the wind, then the stubby little barge was under way. A few desultory curses and a stray arrow followed her, but as the flare finally hit the surface of the river and fizzled out, there was nothing to be seen of the remaining brigands.

'That was close.' Alderan drew a deep breath and raked his hair back off his face.

'Do you think it was the same band who had a man watching us the other day?' Gair asked.

'Probably. They've been known to scout the river, looking for prey.' Alderan tossed the belaying pin up, caught it and dropped it back into the pinrail. 'But then there's the seeker to consider. Are you absolutely sure that was who you saw?'

'I'm positive. I felt him before they tried to come aboard. He's gone now.'

'Or dead – though that may be too much to hope for.' The old man blew out a sigh and scratched at his beard. Something caught his eye in the scuppers and he picked up a worn washleather purse.

Gair heard the distinctive chink of coin. 'What's that?'

'I think one of those fellows dropped it when we were helping them back over the side.'

Alderan loosened the strings and poured some coins into his palm. Fat silver marks, the Holy Oak stamped into each one, winked at him. His eyebrows rose. 'Well. That fair sours the cream, now, doesn't it?' he said. 'I wouldn't have expected to see that many oakmarks this far from Dremen.' He tipped the coins back and fastened the purse. 'So Goran's little pet is off the leash, with a pocketful of coin to ensure he can complete his task. I'm guessing he hired those thugs so that when our corpses floated downstream we'd look like two more unfortunates who'd fallen victim to bandits. Nasty business.'

He sucked his teeth, bouncing the leather bag in his palm. Then he held it out. 'Here. A man should always have some coin in his pockets. Besides, I reckon you'll put it to better use than he would have.'

Gair took the purse. The weight surprised him.

The old man gave him a wolfish grin. 'Just as well you never got round to swearing the vow of poverty, eh?'

'Do you think they'll come after us again?'

'No, this was their last chance. We're too close to the bigger towns; it's not good country for footpads. Too great a risk of being observed the further south we head.'

Gair realised he was still holding his sword and slid it back into its scabbard. He felt a little sick now, and the wind made him shiver.

'I hope so. I don't really enjoy hurting people.'

'That's odd, coming from someone who's spent the last decade learning how to chop them into little pieces.'

Gair folded his arms over his queasy stomach. 'Quintains don't scream.'

Skeff trudged towards them, plucking at the ragged end of the anchor rope.

'Cost me forty shillin', that anchor,' he mumbled, hiccoughing. 'Now I'll have to buy 'un all over again.'

8

A GATHERING STORM

❧

The *Rose* stopped for half a day in Yelda to take on two wooden crates which Skeff lashed to the foredeck. The crates were branded on the outside with a sigil above a design of crossed swords.

'The mark of a master armourer,' said Alderan. He pointed beyond the city's jumbled rooftops, where smoke stained the sky. 'See over there? That's the smelters. Some of the finest steel in the world comes out of those furnaces, and the craftsmen of Yelda turn it into swords. About the only place that makes better is Gimrael.'

He offered his belt knife to Gair. It was halfway between dagger and poniard, with a slightly curved hilt and a tapering blade.

Gair tested the edge with his thumb and almost cut himself. He whistled in appreciation.

'It's an absolute bugger to sharpen, but I don't have to do it very often because it holds an edge like nothing else. I've even used it as a razor once or twice, when there was nothing better to hand.' Alderan tucked it back into its sheath. 'I always wanted a *qatan*, but I had to make do with this.'

'The Master of Swords had a *qatan*. He ran rings around us in the yard with it.' Selenas could flick that blade through a student's guard like a striking adder when he chose. It had taken quick wrists and quicker feet to match it.

'Soul-swords, the Gimraelis call them. The craftsmanship is breathtaking – those swords are possibly the most beautiful made things I have ever seen. The curve of the blade is supposed to fit the outside of a woman's thigh.' Alderan's fingers sketched a graceful arc in the air and his expression grew distant. Then his hand dropped back into his lap.

'The Gimraelis have a tradition that a sword, once blooded, represents a warrior's honour. If it breaks, their honour is diminished and they have to perform some great feat in order to restore it and earn a new *qatan* from their chief. They will die before giving the sword up. It's a subject they get quite passionate about.'

'Have you been there?'

'A few times. It's a desolate, desolate place, the deep desert especially, but it's also beautiful – seductive, even – and dangerous as a snake.'

Gair watched the stone jetties of Yelda's docks slipping past, the bustle of the city giving way to rich farmland. He imagined rolling dunes, a searing silver-blue sky and robed warriors with deadly curved swords. 'I think I'd like to see Gimrael one day.'

'Don't let the poetry fool you, my lad, all silk tents and sloe-eyed girls in veils,' Alderan said. 'Once, maybe, when al-Jofar was writing his songs of gardens in the wilderness. These days, the desert is full of fundamentalists.'

'I thought Eadorians were respectful of other faiths?'

'When it comes to them I'm prepared to make an exception. The Cult is utterly convinced that the Sun God gave them Eadorians for kindling, and they like nothing better than a big bonfire.'

'That's appalling!'

'Isn't it, though? And they seemed like such a nice people when we converted them, too. You mark my words, there'll be another desert war, and soon. Kierim's a good man, and loyal to the Emperor, but there're clans out there in the deep desert near the Sardauki border that he has only a fingernail's hold on, and that's where the Cult is strongest.'

Alderan stretched, eyeing the slow-moving river. Clouds of tiny brown flies danced above the surface, which every now and then broke into a pattern of spreading rings.

'Anyway, haven't you got a sword to practise with? I'm getting tired of bacon again.'

◦◦

After a week afloat, even on an old barge, the stout cobbles of the White Havens' deepwater dock bobbed and swayed alarmingly under Gair's feet. If he closed his eyes and stood still, the sensation lessened, but standing still on the wharf invited being bundled aboard the next ship as cargo, so he wove a careful path through the teams of stevedores, the weighty saddlebags over his shoulder growing heavier by the minute, and wished he could find a place in the shade to sit down.

Saints, it was hot. His clothes stuck to him as if he had taken a bath in them. If Alderan was lucky and found a ship quickly, they could be away on the evening tide, which was due about supper-time. If he wasn't, they would have to find somewhere to spend the night, and the sullen thunder-heads building along the inland horizon promised that it would not be a comfortable one.

They had parted company with Skeff that morning at the northside docks and hired a waterman to ferry them through the Havens' maze of canals to the bustling deepwater wharves on the south side of the city to begin the final leg of their journey to the Isles. The White Havens had acquired its name not from the colour of the rock walls of the harbour, which were the same rusty red as the earth, but from the buildings, for every structure from the meanest waterfront tavern to the Governor's mansion was covered in a thick white plaster that reflected the mid-afternoon sun with painful intensity.

Against this dazzling backdrop the city itself was a riot of colour. Gaily painted shutters and doors clashed cheerfully with the rainbow-coloured flowers spilling from every window box. Equally gaudy was the populace, who to a man had a magpie's taste for things that shone or sparkled. Even the canal-boats were decorated with scraps of bronze and glass; it looked as if the whole place was decked out in its feast-day best. It was enough to give a man a headache.

Gair hitched the saddlebags higher onto his shoulder and wondered how much longer Alderan would be. His boots felt a size too small for his throbbing feet, his eyes ached from squinting and his forehead was sunburned. The Havens was the busiest port on the north shore of the Inner Sea and from the number of times he had been barged into, trodden on and cursed he had begun to feel like flotsam on the tide of commerce. *Saints*, it was hot.

A hand clapped Gair between the shoulder-blades. He turned, and there was Alderan, still looking as if his shirt was fresh from the press. How did he manage it?

'We're in luck,' the old man announced. 'The *Kittiwake*'s in and she sails tonight. Captain Dail is an old friend of mine; he assures me we'll be in Pencruik by the end of next week.'

'Is there anyone in the world that you don't know?'

'I've covered a lot of miles over the years, that's all, and I remember my friends.' Alderan began to walk along the dock, Gair trudging after him. 'Come on, she's tied up at the next wharf.'

'Does that mean we can finally get out of the sun? My feet are melting!'

'Can't you take the heat?'

'I'm a northman, I'm not used to it. Where I come from, there's snow on the mountains all year long.' Gair pulled a face. 'I miss the snow.'

'It'll be cooler once we're away from land, you'll see.'

'I hope so. I'm getting blisters on my blisters.'

The *Kittiwake* turned out to be rather larger than her name suggested. She was smartly painted in blue and white, and sported three masts and a short row of portholes, which suggested she regularly carried paying passengers as well as cargo. Dockside

93

cranes swung back and forth with nets and barrels, teams of seamen guiding them down through the gaping deck hatches. In the bows the bosun was supervising the repair of a worn sail, and aft on the small quarterdeck a sturdy brown man was haggling with the harbour-master.

Alderan strode up the gangway, one arm raised. 'Ahoy, Captain Dail! Two to come aboard!'

The man on the quarterdeck waved his acknowledgement, then turned back to the portly harbour-master. A purse changed hands, a receipt was signed and the harbour-master was escorted to the dockside.

With his business concluded, the captain strode over to greet his passengers. He had the easy, rolling gait of a lifetime spent at sea, and ruddy, weatherbeaten features in which pale blue eyes gleamed like eggs in a nest of fine lines.

Alderan made the introductions, naming Gair as a new student for the library.

Dail looked him up and down as if to assess the set of his rigging, and then stuck out a hand. 'Have you sailed before, lad?' he asked. His accent was broad Syfrian and his grip that of a bear-trap.

'A bit. Up and down the coast from Leahaven.'

'Then you'll have few problems. 'Tis like a millpond, this time of year.' Whistling one of the sailors over, he pointed to the ladder leading below decks. 'Get your gear squared away – any cabin you like. We sail on the tide.'

Below decks a short, panelled passageway ran aft to the stern cabin, with three doors either side for passenger accommodations. All were empty, so they had a cabin apiece. The bunks built against the bulkheads were made for men shorter than Gair, but the mattress felt comfortable enough. After he'd stowed his baggage in the under-bunk lockers he climbed back up on deck to rejoin Alderan, just in time to hear Dail calling for the sailors to cast off. Within the hour the *Kittiwake* had slipped away from the Havens.

As the coast of Syfria disappeared behind them, Gair and Alderan dined with the captain. Dail had a fund of sea-stories to while away the evening, accompanied by quantities of rich red port. Gair had not much taste for the drink and drowsed over a brandy whilst the others reminisced and the level in the decanter sank. He was jolted awake by a change in the ship's motion as it started to pitch more steeply.

Dail cocked an eye at the deck planking overhead. 'Wind's freshening,' he said. 'Might have a bit of a blow later.' He drained his glass and set it down.

'I thought you said it was like a millpond at this time of year,' Gair mumbled, hiding a yawn in his hand.

'It is, don't you fret. Now if you'll excuse me, I'll just have a word with the bosun before I turn in.'

Gair bid Alderan good night and followed the captain out, then made his way to his own bunk. As he tumbled into his blankets, his last coherent thought was that sea air always did this to him.

෧

He was woken later by the ship's motion when it threw him halfway out of his bunk. He didn't need to be a sailor to realise that all was not well; he had to brace his feet against the bulkhead and his elbows against the cot sides to keep from being pitched fully onto the deck. *Kittiwake* was no longer rolling easily over the waves. Now she lurched down from one crest and staggered up to the next with her timbers groaning in protest. Above all that came the sound of someone pounding on the door.

'I'm coming!' He kicked off his blankets and struggled to his feet. Almost at once he was flung back across the bunk. By the time he had found his boots in the dark he had bounced off what felt like every exposed beam and jutting corner in the cabin. Somewhere above an alarm bell clanged, three quick strokes, a pause for a beat, and then repeated. Shouts were sharp over the rising wind and feet pounded across the deck.

Alderan waited in the passageway, brawny arms braced against the panelled walls as seawater smashed its way aft and sluiced around, seeking a way over the high door-sills. The old man's clothing was drenched dark and clung to his skin, and he had a long line tied around his waist. With his dripping beard and streaming hair, illuminated by a solitary lantern swinging crazily in its gimbals overhead, he resembled a sea-god from a Nordman saga. His face was grim. 'Come on, lad, I need you!'

'How bad is it?'

'Bad enough.'

The *Kittiwake* heaved up the side of the next wave, forcing Gair to pull himself along the steepening passage by the handrails. Then with a sickening roll she pitched over and he and Alderan were flung against the companionway ladder. Each wave was the same, a staggering ascent, followed by a wild corkscrewing down into the following trough. Cold salt water was dumped down the ladder every few seconds and by the time he scrambled onto the deck after Alderan Gair was soaked through.

Conditions weren't much better up there. The wind drove rain across the deck in sheets that rivalled the stinging spray flung back from the bow, and the storm shrieked and shook the rigging like a madman in his chains.

'Damn thing came out of nowhere!' Captain Dail reeled across the sloping deck from the wheel, where two steersmen were lashed in place, fighting to keep the *Kittiwake*'s course. 'The wind backed so fast it nearly caught us broadside – all I could do was reef down and run. She's shaking apart!'

Alderan hauled Gair to the mainmast and tied a rope around his waist. Around them the heaving sea was dark as ink. Clouds stretched long fingers out of the east to smother the last of the daylight. Rigging thrummed and seawater sheeted across the deck with every wave.

'Never seen anything like it,' Dail bellowed, 'not in thirty years on these waters! Wrong direction, wrong time of year, and five hundred mile too far east!'

Water smashed into Gair and took his feet out from under him. His legs braced, Alderan rode it out, then helped him back up. The old man kept a hand firm on his shoulder, and once he could stand, fixed his gaze on his face.

'I need your help, Gair.' Urgency gave his voice an edge that cut through the keening of wind and water and timber in distress.

'What can I do?'

'Help me turn the ship. The storm is driving her too far south and there're shoals off the Maling Islands that'll smash her to kindling.'

'How? I'm no sailor—'

'The Song.' The old man's eyes gleamed in the fading light. 'There's something wrong with this storm, something that says it's not natural, and it'll be the end of this ship if we don't do something about it. It's too much for me alone, but with your help we can fight back. I know you can do it.'

Stunned, Gair put up a hand to push his sodden hair off his face. He must have misheard. 'I don't know how to use it like that,' he started, 'and besides, I can't hear it. It's been quiet for days.'

The old man's grip tightened on his shoulder. 'It's still there, Gair. It never leaves you, never for a minute. It's a part of you that no one can ever take from you.'

'What if it gets away from me? I can't control it, Alderan!'

'Don't worry about that. I'll do the weaving; I just need your strength.'

Oh Goddess, he couldn't do this. Too many times simple things had come unravelled in his hands – a roaring furnace in the grate, instead of a warming fire on a cold night, and dry wood that exploded into needle-sharp splinters. Conjured lights that wavered, went out and couldn't be called again. It was too unpredictable, too wild; he did not know what to do – and now his life, and that of everyone on board, might depend on him. Dread rose up in his throat, threatening to choke him.

Alderan's gaze gripped him as if he could see the thoughts written on the inside of Gair's skull.

He could not look away.

'You can do this, Gair.'

That deep, mellow voice filled his ears, louder than the storm, soft as a whisper. Huge waves were slamming into the *Kittiwake's* hull and boiling over the tilting deck, trying to scour it of men and gear. Surf crashed around their feet. Above their heads an over-stressed rope snapped with a whip-crack report.

Gair hesitated. 'I— I don't think I can. It's too strong!'

'Don't think; just believe. Believe in the Song. Trust yourself.'

With Alderan's words, a fluttering surrounded his mind, like the beating of strong wings. In response, a shimmering note sounded where previously there had been silence. Pale and fragile at first, it strengthened with every beat of his heart. More notes rang out, weaving around the first in a complex harmony that swelled and grew and pressed up against his will. All he had to do was reach out to it.

He couldn't.

Don't be afraid. It will not harm you.

Alderan's voice sounded as clear and close as if the words were spoken inside his head. Gair was astonished. The next wave nearly felled him and it was only the older man's strong arm that kept him upright. Seawater stung him, momentarily blinding him; he blinked his eyes clear and found Alderan watching him steadily, intently.

Touch it. Embrace it. It is part of you, Gair. It is yours.

'I'm scared,' he whispered, and let the magic in.

It flooded through him. The storm, the sea, the ship around him, all became secondary. He was still aware of them, but dimly, like a conversation in another room. What filled his senses now was soaring, thrilling music.

Instinctively Gair flinched from it. He could not do this! Any second now the magic would turn on him and rend him to pieces. Alderan had made a mistake. He had opened the stable door and instead of a stocky little barrel of a Barrowshire pony, there was a war-horse inside, nineteen hands of fire-eyed, battle-trained muscle, tossing its head and snorting in anticipation. Merciful Mother, it would trample him under its steel-shod hooves with no more thought than for the dung in its straw. How on earth was he supposed to rein in that behemoth? It would kill him for sure—

But there wasn't anyone else, just him and Alderan. Rope and sinews could endure only so much, and there was no chance that the storm would break before the *Kittiwake* and her crew did. If there was a chance that the ship could be saved, there was no one else but him to take it. Steeling himself, he reached for the Song.

To his amazement, it came to him like a plough-horse to its master. It leaned into his will as the animal would lean into its harness, and he felt its strength, a sense of massive might shifting under that glossy hide, but restrained, tempered with something like respect.

He touched it wonderingly. The magic had never felt like this before, and he did not know how it could be possible. It had to be Alderan's doing.

'Are you ready? You've not got much time!'

The *Kittiwake* lurched again, falling away into a trough with stomach-turning suddenness. As she hit the face of the next wave, sharp reports punctuated the harp-like thrum of the rigging and the fore topmast sheared.

''Ware below!' shouted sailors running from the fo'c'sle as, above their heads, the broken topmast plunged towards the port rail, sodden canvases flailing. Severed stays lashed the deck. Another wave snapped more shrouds; the sails slapped into the sea and began to fill with water. In moments *Kittiwake* was down by the head and ploughing deeper into each successive wave.

'Hands forrard!' the captain bellowed. 'Cut it free or she'll founder!'

Gair swept his streaming hair out of his eyes. He had to do *something* – it would take time for the crew to hack through the tangled tarry web that tied the ship to the great sea-anchor of the topmast, time *Kittiwake* didn't have. The power waiting within him could scour his mind away in the time it took for *now* to become *then*. It had bitten and burned and scorned him often enough in the past . . . but now it was rising to his bidding, and he wanted to know what it would be like to ride that power.

He gulped. 'I'm ready.' He braced himself against the quivering trunk of the mainmast as the ship shuddered again. 'Do it!'

Nothing could have prepared him for the sensation of another mind entering his. It enfolded his entire consciousness like a blanket and the Song leapt joyously in response. When Gair closed his eyes he could see the threads of Alderan's weaving. The pattern was vast as the sky; following the warp and weft of it made him dizzy. Yet at the same time it was stunningly, beautifully logical, and there he was, at the centre, anchoring it. It was all so clear he wanted to laugh out loud.

In a matter of seconds the weave was complete, a web of force as bright as the refractions from a jewel. Around them the storm continued to rage, and the ship to suffer, then Alderan spoke.

Now.

Gair gripped the mast with all his strength and released his hold on the Song. It washed through him, out into Alderan's web, and slammed into the storm like a fist. *Kittiwake* staggered. Gair was flung back hard against the mast, but there was no diminution in the flow of power Alderan drew from him. Storm winds swirled in confusion, giving the seamen a breather in which to scramble aloft to begin cutting the shattered mast free. It splashed into the sea, and as the loose canvas ballooned and bubbled as the waves battered the air out of it, so the *Kittiwake's* head came up at last. At the helm, the seamen gasped with relief as she pulled away, her motion instantly easier, and they regained a little control. Slowly, slowly, the ship began to come round.

Then the storm struck again. It hammered into the starboard beam, sending the ship lurching across the waves. Alderan swore and reinforced his weaving, but it was not enough. The advantage they had won was being eroded, and under his feet Gair felt the *Kittiwake* pay off again as the storm harried her round. If she turned broadside to the waves she was done for.

He embraced more of the Song, even before Alderan asked for it. The flow through him was breathtaking, far greater than anything he had ever handled before, but the old man's weaving simply soaked it up, shaped it and channelled it out into the teeth of the tempest. Degree by degree, the winds backed, forced round to a more easterly point by Alderan's will, so that the battered *Kittiwake* could catch them and run northwestwards, instead of being driven relentlessly south towards the reefs off the Maling Islands.

Gair had not paid much attention to the chart on the wall of Dail's cabin, and he could not visualise the reefs, but when he turned his head and squinted through the spray at the sea tossing beyond the port rail, the boiling white foam was unmistakable.

He swore, and shouted, 'The rocks! We're too close!'

Alderan did not even look round, but he redoubled his efforts. The weaving consumed more and more of Gair's strength, and each point they forced the wind round demanded ever greater efforts, making each tiny gain all the harder. Overhead, the *Kittiwake*'s single reefed topsail strained and over-stressed timbers groaned with each wave that slammed into them, but now she was gaining, turning her quarter to the driving sea and picking up speed.

'West-nor'west!' Dail bellowed, his face eerie in the light from the binnacle lamp. 'Give her her head!'

The bosun nodded and bawled for his maintopmen. 'Aloft! Cut the reefs! Get some way on her!'

The drenched seamen climbed the corkscrewing mast and scrambled out along the footrope. One by one the reefs were sliced through and the full weight of the sodden canvas boomed to the wind. Down on deck, the teams at the halyards skidded and swore and hauled till their hands bled, edging the yards round to capture as much of the wind as possible. Slowly at first, then with increasing sureness, the angle of the *Kittiwake*'s deck changed.

'She's comin' round! We've done it!' The bosun's face was split by a huge grin of disbelief. 'We've done it!'

'We're not out of the woods yet, man!' The captain hauled himself hand over hand along the railing towards Alderan. 'Can you get us clear of the islands?'

The old man's face was taut with strain, his teeth clenched. 'The lad has power and to spare. We can do it.'

In Gair's mind he heard Alderan's voice. *One more push to keep us clear of the rocks and then it's finished.* His tone was gentle, but his voice resonated with all the power of the Song he commanded. *You've done well.*

Gair felt an upsurge of power within him and let it go. He was no more than a conduit now, a channel through which it could run. He had no control other than what was needed to focus that tremendous energy. His eyes were tightly shut, his head bent, and nausea swilled around his stomach, but he clung to the mainmast and fought it down.

It had become difficult to judge the passage of time. He had no idea how long he had been on deck; all he could feel was the ship, every shudder and groan of the *Kittiwake* transmitted to him through the thick wood under his hands and feet. The steersmen had brought her head round and she was running flat-out. Gair felt the rush of water under her keel as she hauled away from the islands towards the safety of open water.

As the ship's motion steadied, still fast but smoother now, Alderan's grip on his mind relaxed at last. The Song drained away. It left behind a ringing emptiness in which his ears buzzed.

He lifted his head slowly. Already the storm clouds had broken up, and tentative fingers of morning sunlight were poking through the rents. The sea was still a heaving, malignant grey, but the waves had slowed and the wind had dropped to little more than a stiff breeze. All around him were bruised, tired faces, dripping wet, and a couple of men were clutching broken limbs, but somehow they were managing to smile. The bosun grinned like a monkey and Captain Dail, clasping Gair's hand, pumped his arm fit to break it off.

Then the nausea caught up with him.

9

ⱸ

Gair opened his eyes. He was back in his bunk. Someone had stripped off his wet clothes and dried him, but his mouth tasted foul and his head was ringing. Alderan sat on the bunk opposite with his back resting against the bulkhead. A book lay open on his lap. Bright sunshine spilled in through the porthole to pool on the deck.

'Welcome back.' The old man put his book aside. 'Would you like some water?'

'Please. What happened?'

'You threw up all over Captain Dail's boots and then passed out cold. We fetched you down here to rest.'

'I think my head is going to fall off.'

'If it's any consolation, it gets easier with practice. It won't be so bad next time.' Alderan filled a cup from a wooden jug and held it out.

Gair shoved himself up into a sitting position and took a long drink. The water tasted sweet after the sourness in his mouth. 'I've known about the magic for years, but I've never felt anything like this before,' he said after a moment.

'Did the Master of Swords never work you so hard that you sicked up? It's exactly the same thing. Drawing deeply on the Song is demanding, and last night you drew more than I had any right to expect from you. I wish I'd had time to prepare you better for it.'

'I think I'll survive the experience. Barely.' He kneaded his forehead. 'Saints, that *hurts*. Was there much damage?'

'Surprisingly little. The mast is being repaired, and apart from a sprung plank or two where it hit the fo'c'sle, the ship took no serious harm. Do you need something for your head?'

'Yes, please.'

'It'll be worse in the sun. I'll fetch my scrip.'

Whilst the old man went to his cabin, Gair leaned back against the bulkhead and tried to relax. A pump clanked dully nearby, and overhead the ship's carpenters hammered and sawed in time with the hammering in his skull.

When Alderan returned, he was rummaging about in his leather satchel. He produced a small porcelain vial and pulled the cork, which he sniffed. 'That's the one. Athalin again, I'm afraid, but it does work.'

He tipped some white powder into his hand, added a couple of pinches to Gair's cup, then topped it up with water. He poured the rest of the powder back into the little bottle and stowed it away.

'Drink up. By the time you've got yourself washed and dressed, you should be feeling more like yourself.'

Gair swallowed the bitter drink, grimacing at the gritty feeling it left around his teeth. 'You said the storm wasn't natural. How did you know?'

'Dail's an experienced seaman. I trusted his instincts.'

'That's not the real reason. You didn't tell me you knew about the magic, either. The Song?' He looked up from the empty cup. 'That you could use it.'

'True, I didn't. I owe you an apology for that as well. There didn't seem to be any time to tell you.'

'We've only been travelling together for two months. Hardly any time at all.'

Alderan smiled thinly at the reproof. 'Very well, then, there didn't seem to be a *right* time.'

'So what else haven't you told me? There's more to you than just a simple scholar, Alderan.'

Amusement quirked the fearsome brows and the older man dropped his satchel on the opposite bunk. He sat down and planted his hands on his knees, as if bracing himself for unpleasantness. 'All right, lad,' he said. 'You've caught my foot in a snare, good and proper. What do you want to know?'

'Everything, I suppose.'

'That could be a long conversation – it's a big world! Start small.'

Where should he start? Gair had so many questions: where had the Song gone since that day on the road, and why had it come back just when Alderan needed it? He had his suspicions the old man had had some hand in that. Was it really like he'd said: that it never actually went away? Who *was* Alderan anyway? Holy Mother, his head was booming. But he had to start somewhere . . .

'The Song – why haven't I heard of it before?'

'You probably have and just don't know it,' Alderan said, 'or you've heard of it under a different name. You'll find it in all kinds of legends and stories. The Nordmen, for instance, say it is the song the Lord-Fatherer sang as He worked at His forge, and a fragment of it is captured in everything He made. In other places they say it is the lullaby the Creator sang to Her daughter the World, echoing down through time, which I think is a lovely story and is quite as good an explanation as any other.'

'Is it magic?'

'Define magic.' The old man's shoulder lifted in a shrug. 'If you define it as a natural force or energy that is an intrinsic part of every living thing and the world around you, then yes, the Song is magic. It's an ugly label, though, don't you think? It has too many connotations.'

Gair remembered the shrillness of Kemerode's shriek, the way her face had been leached of all colour by the light he had made. 'At the Motherhouse they called me hidderling,' he said, 'and back home, the housekeeper thought I was shadowkin – half-human, half— Well, something other. She said the feylings had left me on the chapel porch as a trick.'

Alderan pursed his lips. 'The Hidden Kingdom is a mutable, treacherous place, and its denizens are devious, but leaving half-blood babies to be taken in as foundlings? No, that's the stuff of storybooks. The creatures beyond the Veil live long and they breed rarely. Their seed is far too precious to them to spend on idle mischief.' Looking at Gair, he asked shrewdly, 'Did you believe it? That you were not entirely of this world?'

'I didn't know what to believe. I knew I was different, and I knew why, but I didn't know whether it was the magic that made me different, or the other way about. Then I was sent to the Motherhouse, where everything I was taught came straight from the Book of Eador.'

'"Thou shalt not suffer a witch to live"', Alderan said. 'That's a harsh lesson to teach a boy.'

'They didn't know what else to do with me. They were raised in the faith – chapel every Sunday and twice on saints' days. I learned my letters copying out psalms for Father Drumheller. Where else were they going to turn?'

That drew a grunt. 'We should keep churchmen well away from the education of children. They shut young minds up in a box like veal-calves, then when they're let out, they keep the shape of the box.'

Though he had not parted from his foster-parents on the best of terms, Gair felt obliged to defend them. 'They thought they were doing the best they could for me, Alderan.'

The old man grimaced down at his hands, rubbing his fingers together as if they were dirty, or itching. A long pause was filled with the slap of water on wood and the sound of carpentry.

Behind it Gair heard the Song itself, melodious as distant singing, rhythmic as the purr of a contented cat, yet rippling and changing like a running stream.

'Once, they would have known,' said Alderan quietly. 'Your gift would have been recognised for what it was and instead of being punished for it you would have been given the opportunity to develop it. You would have been respected instead of reviled.' He looked down at his hands again. 'You were born a thousand years too late, I think.'

Too late for what?' 'I don't understand.'

'Throughout the First Empire, the Guardians of the Veil were accorded the respect they deserved. They maintained colleges in all the great cities, and no talent was lost that did not have to be. If you'd been born then, you would have found high honour in their Order. After the Founding, though, everything changed. In the space of fifteen years, the Guardians were persecuted almost to extinction, and their names were even erased from the histories, thanks to the Inquisitors.' Alderan's lips twisted sourly. 'Not Mother Church's finest hour.'

Shocked, Gair asked, 'Because they thought these Guardians were using magic? But you said the Song was part of the world around us, a natural thing. Why would the Church think it was so wrong?'

'They didn't understand it, and folk always fear what they don't understand. They couldn't see the difference between what the Guardians did and what was done by Gwlach's sorcerers. To them, it was all one.'

Fragments of Father Drumheller's lessons surfaced in Gair's mind, and snatches of booming, spittle-flecked sermons echoed down the years, reminding him of the secrets he had fought to keep. 'Doctrine teaches that the only power in the universe devolves from the Goddess and Her Grace,' he said. 'Doesn't that mean that the Song devolves from Her as well?'

'The lectors don't see it that way. They cannot accept that there can be any force at work other than the divine, so anything else must be by definition diabolical.'

'Evil.'

'Yes, in a word – to them, anyway. Why don't the stars fall down, you ask, and the lector replies, because the Goddess put them there. Why does a stone hit the ground if I drop it? Because the Goddess wills it to fall. Why can a woman lay her hands on a sick man and see that man rise up healed? Because she is a witch.' Alderan pulled a face.

'But she's just using the Song to make him well again?'

'Actually, she's using the Song to make the man make himself well again, but you'll have to ask someone more gifted than me to explain the finer points of Healing. I can draw a splinter and stop the bleeding if you've cut yourself, but that's about the limit of my skill. My talents lie in other directions.'

When the realisation struck him, Gair could only wonder why it had taken him so long to see. A school on the Isles. Old books. All the pieces clicked into place. 'You're one of the Guardians,' he breathed.

Smiling, his hand pressed over his heart, Alderan gave a little bow. 'You could say I am *the* Guardian. It has been my life's work to try to rebuild our Order and safeguard what knowledge of the Song remains. It is all that preserves the Veil between the worlds.'

This was beyond incredible. The ember of hope burst back into flame. '*That's* how you know so much,' Gair exclaimed, 'and all this time, you let me believe it was just a hobby, something that interested you! You devious old—' He bit back on the word he was about to say. 'Is that why you were waiting for me in Dremen? You want me to join your Order—'

But Alderan was already shaking his head. 'Nothing would give me greater pleasure than if you joined us, but that is a decision which only you can make. A gift not given freely is no gift at all. No, I was in Dremen because an old friend asked me to help you because he knew no one else could. I was happy to do so.'

'Was it Ansel?'

'No, and don't ask who it was, because I can't tell you. I gave my word and that I don't break.'

Gair took a deep breath. This might be his only chance, and if he did not ask now, he would never know. 'Could you teach me?'

'That depends on why you want to learn.'

'I don't want to be afraid of it any more.'

'And knowledge equals power. Good answer.' Alderan pushed himself to his feet and paced across the cabin, his arms folded across his chest. 'If I choose to take you as a student, Gair, there is something I must make clear to you at the outset. You are one of an increasingly rare breed. You can hear the songs of the earth, touch a power so great it can raise mountains, yet so subtle it can furl a thousand petals into a chrysanthemum bud the size of your thumbnail. That is a gift beyond measure, and access to that kind of power comes with a price. That price is restraint.'

The old man swung round on his heels. 'What you do with the Song *counts*, and *why* you do it counts even more. You must take responsibility for the results, whatever they may be. Sometimes the difference between acting and not acting is the difference between folly and wisdom. Knowing how to use power is meaningless without also knowing when and how *not* to use it. That's the first lesson I teach.'

Gair blinked. He had never heard Alderan speak like this before. He had grown accustomed to the man's easy humour; this side of him, so steely and commanding, came as a shock. After a moment, he said, 'I understand.'

'I was sure you would. If you had not, or I had any doubts whatsoever, I would have refused to teach you anything more than just enough to stop you tearing yourself apart. I have no use for people consumed with arrogance or greed, or obsessed with their own aggrandisement. The Song does not exist to serve you, although it will. Anyone with the gift can shape it to whatever purpose they choose, therefore those who can use it have an obligation to ensure it is used wisely.'

Alderan paused, his mouth shaping words as if he had more to say, then he changed his mind.

Gair wondered what had been left unsaid. Just for an instant, before Alderan's expression smoothed, he had glimpsed an old pain, but in a blink it was gone and the old man was scratching vigorously at his beard, chin stuck out like a dog pursuing a troublesome flea.

'So,' he declared, brisk again, 'what can you do already? Can you do this?'

No sooner had Gair felt a tickle in the back of his mind than a pearly-white globe the size of a walnut appeared in the air between the two bunks. It cast a gentle, silvery light: Lumiel in miniature. Inside him, the Song leapt. Concentrating, Gair made a globe of his own. It was more blue than white, and it swirled as if filled with smoke, but it was equally bright. That was the second thing he had learned how to do, after exploding a lot of candles.

Alderan nodded approvingly. 'Neatly done. That's called a glim. Ordinarily it would have been my next lesson, but you are not exactly an ordinary pupil, are you?' A wry smile split the pepper-and-salt beard. 'What else did you master?'

'I can make fire, move air – mostly simple things, like you said. When I tried for anything more, it usually went wrong.'

'You're not the first person to call the Song and have it bite him. With time, you'll learn how to avoid the teeth.'

'How long will that take?'

'How far do you want to go?'

'I don't know . . .'

'Then I can't say how long the journey will be. I've been a student of the Song since I was in swaddling; now I'm an old man with aching joints and a bladder that gets me up in the night, and I still don't know everything it can do. I don't even know if there are any limits to it. Who knows – you might be the one to find them, if you apply yourself.'

Reaching out a finger, Gair touched the surface of his glim. Colours swirled around his fingertip and made his skin tingle and fizz like sherbet on his tongue. 'You called it a gift,' he said, feeling his way to the root of what he really wanted to know. 'Is it a gift from the Goddess?'

'I'd like to think so. Not everyone is born with it, but neither is everyone born with the ability to sing. If you believe the Goddess grants some of us a tin ear and blesses others with perfect pitch, I think you have your answer.'

'It's not a sin, then.'

Alderan didn't respond immediately. 'There are things that are right, and things that are wrong, fundamentally so, some of which the Church calls sins,' he said at last. 'We don't always agree on the definitions.'

'That's not a straight answer.'

'It's not a straightforward question.'

Gair frowned. 'It sounds like you're saying it's only a sin if I believe it to be.'

'Maybe I am,' said Alderan lightly. 'Only you can decide what you believe, Gair.'

What *did* he believe? That was a question so huge he could hardly see the edges of it, and put it aside for now.

'Where does the power come from? Inside me, or somewhere else?'

'Both,' said Alderan, and grinned at Gair's surprised expression. 'It is a part of us, our environment, even the earth and the air. Eventually, you'll be able to hear its echo in whatever you touch. In some things, like a wild bird or an animal, it's very strong. In others, made things usually, it's barely there at all, just a remembrance, and the further removed from its origins, the fainter it grows. The truly gifted could take a handful of ash from a fireplace and hear the Song of the trees from which the wood was cut, maybe even go back far enough to hear the germ of the Song in the acorns that sprouted them.'

Now Gair was astonished. He'd had no idea that the simple magics he could perform barely broke the surface of what the Song was, what it could achieve. *Start small*, the old man had said; *it's a big world*. All of a sudden it was bigger than he had ever dreamed. The magnitude of what he had asked of Alderan staggered him.

'It looks like there's a lot for me to learn,' he said. His glim bobbed in the draught.

Alderan stood up and his own glim vanished as softly as a dandelion clock. 'More than you could imagine,' he said, shouldering his scrip. He reached for the door handle to let himself out. 'You have tremendous potential, Gair, but there is work to do to unlock it. Tomorrow, when you are rested, we can begin.'

'There never were any mouse-traps in your saddlebags, were there?' Gair asked.

Alderan showed his teeth. 'A simple trigger-ward – tiny little thing, yet it stings like an adder-bite. I'll show you how to make one sometime, if you like. You never know when it might come in handy.'

'And on the barge? The flare? I meant to ask you about it, but everything happened so fast it slipped my mind. That was the Song too?'

'No, that was Skeff's distress flare. Most of the bargees carry them these days. Some of the river routes aren't as safe as they used to be. I just didn't have time to wait for the fuse to burn through.' He opened the door. 'Come up on deck. Fresh air will do you good.'

When Alderan had gone, Gair lay back down on his bunk. He was not sure if the conversation had answered any of his questions or just created a dozen more. There was so much he wanted to ask that he hardly knew where to start, and so much to learn that what little he had so far grasped did not feel like a beginning; it simply highlighted the vastness of his ignorance, the way a candle-flame in the night did little more than reveal the depth of the dark.

His glim had drifted back to him, its surface shimmering in restless, perpetual motion with a thousand shades of blue. Glims had become so easy for him that he had grown careless – and that had been his undoing back in Leah. Then he had made the same mistake in Dremen. Not any more, though: in future he would be much more careful. But oh, the way the Song made him feel when he let it fill him! So vital, so charged with possibility that anything he could dream felt within his reach.

The glim hung above him, turning gently on its axis. He touched the Song and let the globe grow to the size of a honey-melon, then the size of his head. Inside him, a vast potential waited for him to bend his will to it. He felt none of the white-water wildness of which he had grown so fearful, though something told him it was still there, and would come if he called. Equally carefully, he shrank the glim until it was no larger than a marble, then let it go.

❧

Up on deck, the *Kittiwake* resembled a cross between a laundry and a lumberyard. Sailors' gear was hanging out to dry on the rigging, everything from hammocks to spare stockings, whilst the carpenter and his mates shaped a jury-mast from a spare mainyard. A pitch-boiler was set up on the fo'c'sle, where two men were tarring down new rigging. Sea and sky were midsummer blue, and a school of porpoises cavorted a few yards off the bow. Of the storm itself, there was no sign.

Alderan stood by the stern rail with Captain Dail. When he saw Gair, he beckoned him over.

'I'm sorry about your boots,' Gair said, embarrassed.

Dail laughed. 'Don't trouble yourself. After what you did for us last night, I don't reckon a pair of boots amounts to much.'

Gair flushed. 'It was mostly Alderan's work.'

'Not so.' The old man laid a hand firmly on his shoulder. 'I couldn't have done it without you. It was too much for me on my own.'

A seaman ran up and knuckled his forehead to Dail. 'Bosun's compliments, sir. He's about to sound the well.'

Dail nodded. 'Forgive me, gentlemen, but I am needed below.' With that, he strode towards the main hatch.

Apart from the steersman, Gair and Alderan had the stern deck to themselves. 'Captain Dail knows what we are,' Gair said quietly, a statement, not a question.

Alderan smiled. 'He's been running the trade routes from the Havens to Penglas since before you were born, and in that time he's seen quite a few of us come and go. He knows the sort of things of which we are capable – so do a few of his men, but most of them do not. We don't exactly keep it a secret, but we don't shout about it either. There are people who are uncomfortable around our kind, and some of them can let their prejudices get the better of them. One accusation of witchcraft in your life is quite enough for any man.'

That was another thing; now was as good a time as any to ask. 'Are there really such things as witches – aren't they just people like us?'

The old man took a long breath. When he spoke, his voice was pitched low enough not to carry too far. 'Some of them are. There are those named as such who are probably like you, gifted with power and fumbling their way to some sort of control over it. Most of them are simply cross-eyed old folk whose neighbours don't care for them much – mutterers and wanderers and keepers of too many cats.' A smile appeared, thin as an assassin's blade, and just as quickly gone. 'And some are true witches, with the power to rend the Veil between worlds.'

'Can they summon demons, like the stories say?'

'Demons, angels – there's so little to choose between them it scarcely matters once they're here. Anything from the Hidden

Kingdom upsets the balance of the daylight world, and that balance must be maintained.' Alderan sighed. 'But mostly it's demons, yes. Order is white and cold and passionless, driven by logic. Chaos is passion unfettered, both creative and destructive energies pursued indiscriminately. Turbulence strains the Veil the most, and at those points of stress it is possible to pick a hole in the fabric.'

'What would happen if it was torn completely?'

Alderan grimaced. 'Some have had visions of that event. Most of them died screaming, like St Ioan—'

'—who saw a vision of the Last Days and plucked out his own eyes rather than see it again.'

'Exactly. The final chapter of the Book of Eador contains all that the Church dared to make public of Ioan's prophecy. There is more of it in the Apocryphae, things that give strong men night-mares.'

Gair looked around him, at the bellying sails overhead, the leaping water, bright in the sunshine. It was hard to believe that the world he could see and touch could be picked open, like peeling paint on an old barn, to expose another world beneath. Surely he should be able to sense it, somehow? He'd read about the Hidden Kingdom; as a boy he'd been enthralled by stories of spirits and demons and creatures of the fey, but they had been exactly that, stories. He had never truly believed that the Hidden Kingdom was really there, beside him, as close as his skin.

'How come I don't know any of this? How can you know this other world exists if you can't see it, or touch it, or . . .?' He spread his hands helplessly. He could not organise his thoughts into coherent questions. There were simply too many, too much to take in.

'As far as the people who raised you were concerned, it doesn't exist.' With rather a sad smile, Alderan added, 'People don't like to think too hard about the world in which they live, you know. They don't care for change, and as long as each day continues pretty much like the one before, they're happy. If you told them that heaven was not above and hell was not below, but they were actually the same place and it exists alongside our world, a shadow's depth away, they'd say you were touched by St Margret and send you to the sisters at the asylum-house.'

Gair felt his knees go weak; he needed to sit down. Everything in his life that he had always taken on trust had been tipped up and sent tumbling away from him, like apples from an overturned cart. Part of him wanted to chase after them, to catch them and pile them all up into some kind of order. The other part waited for them to stop bouncing. He needed more time to make sense of it all, for nothing was the same any more, nothing at all.

'What about the storm?' he asked at last. 'Does Captain Dail know about it?'

'He as good as said so last night, when he helped me put you to bed. It's unusual for storms to come out of the northeast at this time of the year – they normally come from the south, off the deserts. Someone was playing games with the weather.'

'Who?'

Alderan looked thoughtful. 'I've no idea. There are a few who are strong enough for a weaving of that size, and that's just of the ones I know. Storms aren't what you could call local phenomena. Their causes spread over tens, even hundreds of miles – the temperature of the water or the land, the direction of the wind, all working together or against each other over vast distances to create the conditions in which a storm can occur. Controlling all those energies and manipulating them to focus on one specific area like that takes a great deal of skill, or a strong natural aptitude for weather-Song. It took the two of us to dissipate it, remember.'

That made sense, Gair thought. The web Alderan had woven across the face of the storm had stretched further than Gair's eyes could see, though his awareness of it through his contact with the Song had reached far beyond that. If he had known more about what he was doing, he was certain he could have slid along the cords of power to the furthest reaches of the net like a bead on a string.

Intuition tickled the corner of his mind. 'What about Savin? Could he have sent the storm?'

'It's the kind of thing he'd think was amusing, that's for sure,' said Alderan. 'I don't think he was responsible, though. Savin is a liar, a gambler, and slippery as eels in oil, but I see no reason for him to try to harm us. What made you think of him?'

'I got the feeling he didn't like you very much.' Absently, Gair rubbed the brand on his palm. The scabbing and inflammation was all gone, though the scar was still red, but sometimes it burned.

Alderan grunted. 'His face makes my fist itch.'

'He said you weren't to be trusted.'

'Did he now? Well, I told you he was a liar.' Leaning back on the railing, he favoured Gair with a long look. 'Or don't you trust me?'

'You've not led me wrong so far.' *Apart from not telling me a few things.*

'And I never will, lad. You have my word on it.'

'If you and Savin don't get along, why would he be so eager to look you up in Mesarild?'

'Don't you have some sword practice you should be doing?'

'I'm just curious. He's like us, isn't he?'

Alderan gave him another of those penetrating looks. He held it just a beat past the point at which it had become uncomfortable. 'He's gifted, yes, but he's not like us. He has no respect for the Song. To him it's just a tool to be used – you saw that for yourself, didn't you? Parlour tricks. He thinks they impress people.'

'So what did you fall out over?'

'He did me a disservice some years ago,' Alderan said shortly, 'something for which I've never forgiven him. I'll die a happy man if I never have to see him – or even think about him – for the rest of my days. And that's my last word on the subject.'

'What—?'

'Don't press me on this, Gair.'

Gair held up his hands. 'I'm going.'

And with that he trotted back below decks to fetch his sword. An hour or two of practice would clear his head. If he emptied his attention of everything but the forms, what he had just learned could settle out, arrange itself into a pattern he could grasp. In time it would all become clear.

❧

When he returned, Alderan was still standing at the railing, chin on his chest, his thoughts pulled tight around him like a cloak. As he walked past, Gair wondered what on earth could have happened between him and Savin to make Alderan look so furious.

10

THE WESTERN ISLES

ෆ

From his perch above the cathead, Gair watched the islands draw nearer, evolving from an irregular line on the horizon into a series of hummocks like the humped coils of a sea serpent. After a while he could pick out the colours of the land, dark forest, green meadows, fields of tilled earth. A necklace of white foam decorated the shoreline.

As the *Kittiwake* altered course a fraction more to the north, the overlapping islands unfolded across their path, acquiring shape and definition. Tiny yellow houses clung to the slopes above long wooden jetties thrusting into the waters of a broad inlet. Greyblue mountains rose in the interior, not high enough for snow in summer but still impressively craggy, making Gair itch to explore them. On the whole, it looked as if his new home was going to be a very pleasant place indeed.

Footsteps sounded on the fo'c'sle decking and Alderan leaned on the bulwark next to him. The old man's mood had improved over recent days. He had given Gair several lessons in controlling the Song – novice exercises, he called them, simple things, not much different to what Gair had discovered for himself, such as keeping a candle lit in a draught, or making a draught to blow out a candle. Every time the Song came willingly to his call, his confidence grew.

'That's Penglas, up ahead.' Alderan pointed at the approaching islands. 'The town's called Pencruik. It means "Port of the Isles".'

'How many islands are there?'

'Twenty-three, all told, but a few of them aren't much more than sea-stacks. The ones you can see are Penglas, which is the biggest, with Penmor behind it to the left and Pensaeca to the right. The little ones next to Penmor are Penbirgha and Pensteir. There's a chain running more or less due north from Penbirgha known as the Five Sisters, which you can just about see on the horizon, but the rest are all out of sight.'

'Are they all inhabited?'

'Most of them – the ones that have a safe anchorage for fishing or are big enough to farm. Chapterhouse is on Penglas, over that hill above the town.' He pointed. 'You can just pick out the top of the tower, there above those trees.'

Gair squinted in the direction of Alderan's arm. Yes, there it was: a sliver of white against the bright sky. What would the rest of it look like?

Alderan clapped him on the shoulder. 'I think you'll like it,' he said, as if he had read Gair's thoughts. 'Dail tells me we'll be anchoring in a couple of hours, so get your things packed up. We'll be ashore by mid-afternoon.'

True to the captain's word, it was barely two hours past noon when the *Kittiwake's* anchor splashed down off Pencruik and they said their farewells. The ship drew too much water to dock at the jetty, so they were rowed ashore in the launch. Although the steep streets of the town were busy, the harbour itself was almost empty. By dusk, Alderan said, it would be full of fishing craft, and the sandboats that supplied the glass-crafters, whose work provided a good quarter of Penglas' population with a living.

The launch took them past the wooden piers, their salt-pickled timbers the colour of old bones, right up to the stone quay steps. Gair shouldered his baggage and climbed carefully up onto the quay behind Alderan, wary of the wet steps and his unsteady land-legs.

Beneath them, the oarsmen poled off for the long haul back to the *Kittiwake*.

Pencruik was a jumble of dusty cobbled streets, its tall houses rendered in pale golden plaster, with purple pantile roofs. Many had pots of herbs and bright-flowered plants on their doorsteps and windowsills, or spilling down from wall-tops. No two were the same height, nor had the same colour paint on their doors. The streets twisted about to meet at odd angles, following the rise and fall of the land, as if the town had grown there like a colony of barnacles.

In the market square, Alderan hailed a farm-wagon driver who agreed to carry them up to Chapterhouse, and they piled their belongings onto his cart. Gair made himself comfortable on some sacks in the back, whilst the old man sat up front with the wagoneer. The road zigzagged its way up into the hills above the bay. Set back from the roadway were farmhouses screened with poplars, where sun-browned children played amongst the chickens and dogs. Stone-walled vineyards, orchards of almond and olive trees and terraces of citrus fruit chequered the hillsides. To Gair, from the far north, oranges had always been rare treats; he found the abundance here staggering. When a party of fruit-pickers trooped past with laden baskets on their backs, he stared so much that a girl in dusty skirts smiled at him and tossed him one. Alderan twisted around in his seat. 'How do you like it so far?'

Gair, his mouth full of sweet, juicy orange, could only grin back. It was wonderful.

At the height of the pass the road dipped into pine forest before emerging once more into open fields in a shallow, bowl-shaped valley. A stream ran down the mountainside to feed a small lake in the valley bottom, near a prosperous-looking farm. Beyond it was Chapterhouse.

Gair knelt up for a better view over Alderan's shoulder. Chapter-house was built of white stone, speckled silver and pink, with roofs of the same purple tiles he had seen in the town. At the south end was the high tower he had glimpsed above the trees; below the tower it looked like the buildings were arranged around open courtyards or gardens. Trees rose above the gables and what appeared to be a walled orchard occupied the sunniest side. Large, arched windows were set into the walls, quite unlike the narrow slits of the Suvaeon Motherhouse, and the boundary wall looked more like it was marking the limits of the property than keeping people on one side or the other.

'It looks like somebody's country estate,' Gair said.

'It was, once. It's been extended somewhat over the years, of course – two hundred and seventy-seven students take a bit of accommodating,' Alderan explained. 'Then there're all the Masters, and the adepts who choose to stay on, never mind the servants – so nearly five hundred of us at the moment.'

'I didn't think there would be that many!'

'And how many did you think there would be?' the old man asked as the cart rumbled past the farm gates. A woman fetching in laundry from a line in the yard paused to wave to them. Alderan waved back; the wagoneer doffed his cap. 'You're not the only boy in the world born with these gifts.'

'I—' Gair floundered. 'When you said you were one of the last, I assumed there would only be a few dozen, maybe, not half a legion!'

'When I was your age, there were only a few dozen *gaeden*, and most of them were old. It was a desperate race to find students to teach before we were robbed of all our teachers. Now our Order is much less fragile, but we're still a long way short of what I would wish for. We have lost too many talents over the years, to ignorance, or prejudice, like you almost were. Or lost to imperfect control of their gifts. Every one of them is important, and should be saved if we possibly can.'

'*Gaeden*? What does that mean?'

'It's what you are, and what you will be, if you choose to join us. What I am. It means "gifted". It's an ancient word, older than

123

the Founding.' The old man smiled. 'Infinitely preferable to "witch", don't you think?'

The cart passed through the open gates into the Chapterhouse yard. An archway on the right led to stables. To the left, through another arch, were laundry lines, and Gair could see maids in white aprons with baskets of linens. Ahead, broad stone steps led up to an age-blackened oak door, studded with enormous nails. When the cart stopped, he gathered up his things and hopped down. The air smelled of baking bread, and starch, and the tang of the sea.

'Well, here we are,' said Alderan, alighting next to Gair. He looked around. 'Blast the boy, where is he? He was supposed to be waiting for us.'

Almost before Alderan had finished speaking a young man appeared in the doorway, chewing on something. When he saw them, he swallowed and trotted towards them, brushing crumbs from the front of his shirt. Over his clothes he wore a deep blue mantle that reached to his knees. The boy himself had dark curly hair, brown eyes, and an expression of elfin mischief.

'Snacking again, Darin?' Alderan asked. 'It's a wonder you're not as wide as a wagon, boy!'

'Master Saaron says I need to eat often, or I'll get sick.' Darin grinned, showing enviably even teeth. 'Sorry I wasn't here.'

'So you should be. This is Gair.'

Darin stuck out a hand. 'Pleased to meet you.'

'Likewise.'

The grip was firm and friendly. Gair estimated Darin to be about his age, maybe a little younger. From his accent and colouring, Gair guessed he was Belishan.

'I have to find out what's been happening whilst I've been away, so I shall leave you in the care of Darin here,' Alderan said. 'He'll get you fed and watered and show you where things are. You can have this evening to get yourself settled in, but I shall be expecting you to be ready by Prime tomorrow.'

124

'Ready? For what?'

'For the testing, of course.' Alderan sounded distracted, as if he was anxious to be away. 'Don't worry; it's nothing you can't manage. Darin will explain what it's all about. Now I must be off; the rest of the Council will be waiting for me. I shall see you in the morning – early, mind.'

'Don't worry,' Gair assured him, 'I'm used to keeping monastery hours, remember?'

Alderan clapped Gair on the shoulder, then strode up the steps to the door and disappeared inside.

The Belisthan eyed Gair uncertainly. 'Did you say you were from a monastery?' he asked, his voice freighted with dread.

'The Suvaeon Motherhouse, in Dremen.' Gair shouldered his bundle.

Darin's eyes flicked to the sword. 'Does that mean you're a Knight?'

'No, I never made it past novice. I was sent there in the hope that a monastic education might make me turn out normal.'

The boy is shadowkin. Such hateful words had been said – on both sides, to be scrupulously fair. Words that couldn't be taken back, that still stung. Gair slammed a lid on them. This was a fresh start, in a new place. He had to let old bones lie.

'So you're *gaeden*, like the rest of us?'

'Apparently so.'

'Then you don't go around praying all the time?'

Gair laughed. 'Oh, no – I just can't seem to shake the habit of waking up early for morning service. So, what now?'

'How about I show you your room, then give you a tour? We should have time before supper.'

Darin led the way up the steps. Inside the vestibule, bright rag rugs that would not have been out of place in a farm kitchen softened the tiled floor. Passageways led off to left and right; the wider main corridor led straight ahead for the full depth of the building. Darin pointed out lecture halls, the whitewashed cloister of the infirmary, and at the far end of the hallway, the twinned staircases leading up to the dormitories. They'd take the left-hand one Darin said; right led to the girls' rooms.

'They teach girls here too?'

'Oh, yes.' Darin grinned and rolled his eyes. 'I suppose you'll not be used to it, after the monastery and all, but don't worry. There're easily as many girls here as there are boys. You'll soon find someone.'

Finding someone was the last thing Gair wanted to think about. From the moment he had arrived at the Motherhouse he had been expected to serve the Order chastely, obediently, humbly, exactly as if he had already sworn the vows of a Suvaeon Knight. Obedience was drilled into him in the practice yards and waiting at table. For humility he'd shovelled dung in the stables, though for that he had at least had the company of the horses, whom he liked better than most people. The value of service was made plain in the fields of the tied farms, where he had earned as many blisters hoeing turnips as he had fighting with sword or lance. Chastity, in a cloistered order, had taken care of itself.

Girl after pretty girl called out good afternoon to Darin – boys and elderfolk too, but mostly girls, and some of them bid Gair welcome. They cooed over how tall he was, and swished their bright skirts and glossy hair, chattering away like so many briar-finches on a bough. He managed to talk to them without swallowing his own tongue, but Darin was as easy with them as if they were all his sisters and cousins, even the women with grey in their hair. With just a few words he had them sparkling with laughter and more than one looked back over her shoulder to smile them out of sight.

'You're popular,' Gair said as they climbed the stairs.

'It's the dimples, girls can't resist them.' Darin grinned to demonstrate. 'But I have to be good now. Renna threatened to put my eyes out with a poker if she caught me looking at another girl.'

'She's your sweetheart?'

'We've been walking out since last summer. She's one of the housemaids.' Then Darin stopped, lips pursed thoughtfully.

Gair followed his gaze across the hall. A long-legged Syfrian girl descended the other staircase, a book open in one hand as the other trailed down the polished banister. Thick, corn-gold braids hung down well past her waist.

'Oh, I'd like to get tangled up in that,' Darin murmured. He watched her until the turning to the library took her out of sight, then with a shake of his head, flashed a smile back at Gair. 'Promise you won't tell?'

'Word of honour.'

'Good man.' Darin started taking the steps two at a time. 'You don't play chess by any chance, do you?'

'A little.'

'Would you care for a game sometime? No one on our floor will play with me any more.'

'Why's that? Do you cheat?'

Darin laughed. 'No, I just don't lose very often.'

They turned the corner into a long gallery overlooking a garden. Flowering vines clambered up the pillars as far as the third floor and a fish-pond glinted at the far end. Darin stopped at the first of the plain wooden doors on the right.

'Well, this is your room. Try not to get too excited.'

'It won't take much to improve on the Motherhouse, believe me.'

Gair lifted the latch and opened the door. The room was twice the size of his cell in the novices' dortoir. A desk and chair stood underneath one window and a bed and washstand under the other. The blue pitcher was chipped, and it didn't match the green basin, but both were clean, and the soap smelled pleasantly of herbs. He prodded the mattress experimentally. Softer than a novice's pallet, too.

'It's bigger than I was expecting,' he said, laying his belongings on the bed. 'Are all the students' rooms this size?'

'On this level, yes. They're supposed to be adepts' rooms, but we have more apprentices than adepts at the moment, so this gallery is a mixture. My room's right next door.'

The fourth wall held a tall closet, empty, but for some spare blankets and a cedar block to keep down moths. Gair closed the door and turned round to find Darin eyeing his sword.

'May I?' he asked, pointing.

'Be my guest.'

Darin drew the sword, struggling a little with the scabbard.

'Never held a sword before?'

'Nothing bigger than a carving knife. How on earth do you swing it?'

'Bring the point up further, so it's higher than your hands. It sits easier that way. You get used to the weight with practise.'

Darin did what he suggested. He swung the sword tentatively, watching the light run down the blade. 'It's pretty fearsome. Have you ever used it?'

'I've done little else the last ten years.'

'I meant *used it*, you know, in earnest – fought someone when it wasn't just for practice?'

'I've not drawn blood with it, if that's what you mean.' *I've broken a man's arm, but not shed blood.* Gair took the sword back and sheathed it.

'So you've had it since you were what, ten?'

'Eleven.'

'It looks old. Did you inherit it?'

'In a way.' His foster-father might as well be dead to him now. 'Look, why don't we go and get something to eat? My belly thinks my throat's stopped up.'

On the walk to the refectory, Darin pointed out the way to other useful places, like the practice yards, bath-house, Masters' studies and the library. Gair was looking forward to exploring that. He had loved books as a boy, read and re-read his favourites until he knew the stories by heart and hardly needed to turn the worn pages to know that Prince Corum would defeat the sea-serpent by answering its riddle, or how Jaichin Three-feathers rescued the elf-maid from the pit. Of all the things he had left behind when he rode for Dremen, he'd missed his books the most.

The refectory itself was a long, well-windowed room with rows of tables and benches, and an open serving hatch at the far end. The space was full of people, queuing with trays, sitting eating, standing talking in groups, reading alone over their plates. Many wore unbleached linen tunics with bands of green or blue around the neck and hems, or a short mantle like Darin's over ordinary clothes. Fewer still, maybe no more than nine or ten in the whole room, wore floor-length mantles; it looked to Gair as if they were being accorded a little more respect by everyone.

'What do the colours mean?' he asked as they found some space at one of the tables and sat down with their loaded trays.

'Grades and disciplines.' Darin speared a potato with his fork and gestured with it as he explained, 'Once you can do a few basic things, you're graded as a novice, and that means a tunic with a band – green for Healers, blue for the rest of us, the ordinary *gaeden*. From there you move up to apprentice, which means a coloured tunic, then adept, which gets you a mantle.' The potato vanished in a single huge bite.

'So you're an adept?' Gair started to eat. The pork stew was good, with thick cider gravy and plenty of meat.

The Belisthan tugged his mantle straight and grinned. 'Newly graded. Took me almost a year to get this far.'

'And the long mantles?'

'They're for Masters, what you get to be if you're really good. The Masters do most of the teaching, but adepts take some novice classes if there're lots of students.'

'It sounds very formal.'

'Not really. It just keeps the hierarchy straight. Apart from the grades, there're very few rules. Turn up on time, try your hardest, and no extra-curricular activity between teachers and students.'

Darin waggled his eyebrows suggestively and Gair's face warmed. There had been a few novices at the Motherhouse who lived for the weekly half-day's liberty, returning to the dortoir sleepy-eyed and grinning, their afternoon more than worth the switching it earned them. They rarely stayed long. He'd never learned their trick of turning a shy exchange of smiles into something that might give him cause to dread his next confession.

'I'll try to remember that,' he said, hiding the flush behind his cup.

'So what's your strongest talent?'

'I'm not sure. Alderan gave me some lessons on the way here, but I think we only scratched the surface.'

Certainly none of the exercises he had been set had posed much of a problem, though he remained wary of the vastness of the Song he was now able to touch. Since the storm, calling the Song felt like picking up a teacup and pouring out the ocean.

'You'll probably find out tomorrow, when you're tested. They might even grade you on the spot.'

'So what's the testing like? What will I have to do?' He used the last of his bread to mop gravy from his plate and wondered whether it would be impolite to go back for a second helping.

Darin was already finished and starting on a plate of fruit and cheese, despite having done most of the talking. He swallowed and said, 'It's very straightforward. The Masters give you tasks to perform, to find out what you can do and how strong you are. I'm best with fire. That's why I was sent here.'

'Something tells me there's a story there.'

The Belisthan looked sheepish, fiddling with an apple core on his plate. 'I set my uncle's hat alight.'

Gair choked on his wine.

'Not really on fire; it was just an illusion. You know, smoke, flames, crackling. It was very realistic.'

'How did that happen?'

'My father was always saying it was past time he was brought down a peg. One day I saw him with some other farmers, carrying on like the lord of the manor, and I suddenly thought he'd look a whole lot less self-important with his hat on fire. Next thing I knew he was running around squealing and beating out the flames.'

'And your family sent you here?'

'Oh no, not straight away – they didn't know it was me. It wasn't until I set fire to my bed that they started to suspect. I was cold!' he defended himself, seeing Gair's sceptical expression. 'I was just trying to heat the warming pan and I got carried away.'

'I take it you've learned how to control it now? I don't fancy waking up one morning to find the whole dormitory alight.'

'I'll make sure I wake you up first,' Darin promised. 'How did you find out about your gifts?'

Pushing his plate away, Gair leaned back against the wall, beaker in hand. 'Stealing marchpane,' he said. 'Small boy, high shelf.'

Darin made a beckoning gesture with his hands and Gair tipped his cup in salute. 'I didn't realise I was different until I told someone what I had done and got slippered for telling lies. After that, I kept it to myself.'

'Let me guess – you don't like marchpane any more?'

'Even the smell makes me heave.'

After supper, Darin pleaded a promise to visit with Renna and left Gair to his own devices. He made only one wrong turn on the way to the bath-house and after a leisurely soak, returned to his room. With both windows opened wide to let in the smell of the sea, he unpacked his few things and stowed them away. Afterwards he sat on the edge of the desk and looked out at the pastures, painted in all the colours of the settling sun.

So this was where he was going to be living now. It bore no comparison at all to the Motherhouse. For one thing, the scar on his hand hadn't turned a hair on anyone, and he was sure at least two or three people had seen it. Chapterhouse was also much less formal. Everyone talked and laughed as they went about the halls, and the Masters did not appear to hold themselves aloof from the students. It felt very much like a large family. They *belonged*, and they had welcomed him into their house because of what he was, not in spite of it.

Snatches of singing reached him on the wind. Vespers. Even after nine weeks away, Gair felt the pull of a familiar routine. The pattern of the day in a house of the Goddess was deeply ingrained in him; he had only to close his eyes to see the burnished Oak behind the altar, brilliant in the reflection of a thousand candles. He heard Danilar's resonant voice chanting the service, the susurrus of the response. What would the Chaplain make of this place?

Gair looked down at the Book of Eador that he'd found in the desk drawer. It was a mass-printed edition, rather than one of the sumptuously illuminated, hand-lettered volumes produced by the Church's scriptorium. The leather cover was scarred, the pages dog-eared from handling. He opened it at the ribbon marker: Beatitudes, chapter eight: *Be welcome, all ye travellers. Be welcome in the House of the Goddess wheresoever you may find it on your journeys. Be at ease in this House that your burdens may be set down and your cares lifted from your brow.*

Since he was old enough to remember the words unprompted Gair had said his prayers at night and the blessing over every meal, and there had been times when he'd been sure he'd heard the Goddess' voice speak to him. He had listened to the service and shivered with dark delight at tales of damnation, whilst he hoped with all his heart that he would find his place in heaven – although of course in those days his idea of heaven bore a strong resemblance to Uncle Merion's house at Blackcraig.

Then the Song had struck its first note inside him. Somewhere in the aftermath the services had become an agony of dread and his prayers had become desperate pleas not to be found out. He did not think She had spoken to him since – or if She had, he had been unable to hear Her. Since then, it had seemed less and less important to make the effort to speak when there was so little hope of reply.

If he were a true believer, he would be on his knees in chapel, praying for guidance and absolution from his sins, instead of sitting there on his arse . . . although if he had been a true believer, he would never have ended up here in the first place. He would have flung himself on the mercy of the Church and taken his fiery penance in the knowledge that his place in heaven was assured. He was not sure he had the courage for that kind of faith.

Without really wanting to, Gair found himself turning the pages towards the Book of Abjurations. He knew the words by heart, but he read them again anyway. Chapter twelve, verse fourteen: *Suffer ye not the life of a witch and shun ye all works of evil lest they imperil thy soul.*

Was Alderan right, and sin only existed in the minds of men? If so, was he a witch? In the eyes of the Church, the Goddess' voice on earth, most definitely. In the eyes of other people? Maybe, maybe not. He had been born with this gift; surely that made it a gift from Eador Herself. Was he a witch in Her eyes? That was something he could not answer.

11

ONE OF US

&

Chapterhouse's kitchens were accustomed to early risers. When Gair entered the refectory an hour after dawn the servants were already busy at the hatches and a good quarter of the tables were occupied. He took his breakfast of warm spicebread and tea to the same corner seat he had occupied the night before and watched the comings and goings of the others whilst he ate.

Chapterhouse's other occupants did not seem to fall into any particular type, as far as he could see. They spanned all ages, both sexes, and practically every nationality he could identify. He saw a few Leahns, long-boned and fair like him, olive-skinned Tylans, Belisthans, and a few desertmen, dark as polished mahogany. He even saw one Astolan, with that distinctive golden colouring and catlike grace. They all spoke the common tongue, but with a multiplicity of accents. The atmosphere of relaxed cheerfulness was a total contrast to the solemnity of the Motherhouse. There the novices had lived for their liberty hours, when they could go out onto the commons and run and shout and laugh themselves hoarse, grabbing as much fun as they could hold in the knowledge that it would have to last them the next seven days.

He was finishing his second cup of tea when Alderan appeared at the far doors. The old man now wore a long blue mantle over his lived-in traveller's garb, but he still managed to look rumpled.

'Good morning,' he said, arriving at Gair's table. 'Did you sleep well?'

'Very.' The strange room and different night-time sounds had kept him awake for only a little while, then he had slept like a stone.

'Are you ready?'

'I suppose so. It's difficult to say, when I don't know what I'm supposed to be getting ready for.' Gair drained his mug and set it down.

'For the testing. I assume Darin told you about it?'

'He did. He was surprised you hadn't mentioned it sooner.'

Gair was not particularly looking forward to it. He had spent so long concealing what he was that he found it difficult to be open about his gift. Calling up a glim in front of Alderan in the privacy of a ship's cabin was one thing; being asked to demonstrate his gifts to the fullest extent of his ability, in front of a crowd of Masters who were complete strangers to him? That was quite another.

He eyed the old man, waiting for a reaction to his remark, but there was none. 'What if I don't want to be tested?'

'You have to be. All students are. It allows us to assay your gift and find out what you can do, what you cannot, and what you might yet learn. Then we can give you the most appropriate training. You asked me to teach you, remember. If you refuse, we'd test you anyway – Alderan showed his teeth – 'but it's much more fun if you cooperate.'

Gair stood up. 'You know, you didn't tell me nearly as much about this place as you could have done.'

Alderan didn't seem affronted. 'I told you the truth,' he said simply.

'Just not all of it. "Deception is the handiwork of the Nameless, the Father of Lies. Be open and upstanding in all thy dealings and the Goddess shall smile upon thee.'''

135

Laughter burst out of the old man, loud and rich enough to make several people look round from their breakfast. 'Quoting scripture at me now, by the saints! Fair enough, lad,' he chuckled, holding up his hands. 'I should have prepared you for this; my apologies again. You'll do fine, though, don't worry. After what you showed me on the *Kittiwake* I have absolutely no doubt that you're up to the task.'

'Then let's get it over with.'

Alderan set a brisk pace through Chapterhouse's white stone corridors to the south practice yards. Three quadrangles were arranged around a central block that contained the armoury. Shady walks surrounded the two smallest yards, one covered entirely, the other open to the sky, whilst the third, which was as big as the other two put together, sported tiers of benches under a shingled canopy. That yard was where exhibitions and gradings took place, Darin had told him.

At the door into the changing room, Alderan stopped.

'What's going to happen?' Gair asked.

'I can't tell you; I'm your sponsor. All I can say is that there will be a number of Masters waiting for you who will ask you some questions. You must answer them truthfully, and try to do whatever is asked of you. I will also be there, but I cannot help. You must do this by yourself. Now go inside and get changed and I'll see you in the yard in a few minutes. Don't worry, lad; I have every faith in you.'

Gravely Alderan clapped his arm, then strode away down the passage.

Gair let himself into the changing room and made his way along the rows of benches to the far end, where a dark man somewhat shorter and a few years older than him was waiting. He wore a calf-length blue mantle and held an off-white bundle in his hands.

'You must be Gair,' he said, smiling. 'Put these on. They should be about your size. The housekeeper had to let down the hems for your height.'

He held out the bundle, which proved to be a loose-fitting tunic and pants of a stiff fabric that reminded Gair of sailcloth. The garments were the same unbleached colour as the novices' tunics. Gair stripped down to his smallclothes, and put them on, then folded his own things onto the bench. The generous cut was comfortable enough, but the fabric felt coarse next to his skin.

'It'll chafe a bit at first, but it softens up with wear,' the adept told him as he fingered the weave. 'You'll soon get used to it. Ready?'

The adept opened the door into the yard and led the way outside. It was still early; the whole yard was in shadow apart from the west side, where a ribbon of gold lay across the uppermost seats. The beaten earth floor was cool underfoot, but the air was dry and promised a warm day to come. Back in Dremen, where summers were short, there would already be frost tipping the grasses with silver, and geese arrowing south in great ragged skeins. Here on the Isles, summer looked set to run to St Simeon's and beyond.

The Masters were arranged in a loose semi-circle across the lowest seats at the south end. He could see Alderan, standing in the yard to one side. Apart from their long blue mantles, the Masters' clothes were as everyday as those of anyone Gair might have met on the streets of a town, with dust on their hems and scuffs on their shoes. Ranged in front of them was an odd collection of objects, including a baulk of timber, a horse trough full of water and a pile of large rocks.

'Six?' whispered the adept. 'You must be good. I only got two. Good luck!'

He bowed to the Masters and left by one of the corner arches under the stands.

Gair walked the last few paces to Alderan's side.

Four men and two women watched him. One of the women had the coppery colouring and hawk-sharp features of the south-ern deserts. Dressed in a man's shirt and breeches, she wore her sleeves rolled up to the elbows, exposing lean, sinewy forearms, and her blue-black hair was cropped short, like a boy's. When she looked up, the sloe-black eyes he was expecting were vividly, startlingly blue. The other woman, in contrast, was white-haired, plump and grandmotherly. Apart from an enormous emerald ring on one hand, she looked so homely she might as well have had flour on her cuffs.

The four men were equally different in appearance. Two were dark, and alike enough in features and build to be brothers, if not twins. Of the other two, one was fair and bearded, the other ruddily clean-shaven and inclining towards the plump. All six watched Gair with the intensity of bidders at a cattle auction. He made an effort to stand up straight and not fidget, finding that if he looked straight ahead at the empty bench between the two women, the stares were less disconcerting.

'This is Gair,' Alderan began. 'He has come to us from the Suvaeon Motherhouse in the Holy City of Dremen, to be tested in his gifts and taught the responsibilities that accompany the privilege of power. He comes to us of his free will, with the knowledge that what he is and what he will become will set him apart from others in the world, for ever. He comes to us to be *gaeden*.'

'Welcome, Gair,' the Masters intoned formally. Hoping it was the correct thing to do, Gair bowed. The grandmotherly one gave him a smile as sweet as home-made butterscotch.

Alderan stepped back a few paces, behind Gair and to the side. At once the air thrummed with tension. On the back of Gair's arms the hairs rose up as if someone had run their fingernails down his spine. Whatever it was he could feel, it was all around him, like a cage, even under his feet. A quiver of unease rippled through him that left his nerves fluttering. He was reminded of another cage, of iron this time, and had a struggle to put it out of his mind.

The thin golden-haired Master spoke first. His voice was

surprisingly deep and rasping for one so slender. 'I am Godril,' he said. 'Can you work fire?'

'I can.'

'Show me a flame.'

Gair reached inside himself to the Song. It rose up to greet him, exuberant as a puppy, filling every part of him with energy. Quickly he sought out the whispery music of flame and stretched out his hand. A small yellow flame bobbed over his palm, pulsing with his heartbeat. He steadied it then left it floating in the air in front of him. Effortlessly, Godril snuffed it out.

'This is illusion. Show me fire!'

A wisp of straw lay on the ground by Gair's feet. He held it out and lit it like a taper. Gaze never leaving Godril's face, he let it burn down to his fingers, then dropped what remained. It shrivelled to ash and disintegrated.

'Now this.' Godril pointed to the timber. It was a six-foot length of tree trunk, roughly squared off and as thick through as Gair's waist. It was freshly hewn, the sawn edges still sticky with sap. Gair concentrated. Igniting green wood was always difficult, even with a good flint and plenty of tinder, but he thought he had the trick of it now. After some cautious practice on the *Kittiwake* he'd been able to make a reliable flame; this was just a matter of scale. Carefully, he called fire to the wood. Nothing happened at first, then the timber began to smoke. He drew a little more of the Song, and a golden tongue licked the splinters left by the saw. Then another appeared. They caught, strengthened. Fed by his will, fire ran the length of the timber and leapt skywards. Bubbles of sap hissed and burst.

The tension in the air around him increased. On the tree trunk the flames dimmed to a bluish glow and almost disappeared. Gair concentrated harder. A fresh blaze sprang up and Godril stifled it again. Setting his feet, Gair reached for more of the Song.

This time his fire struggled to take hold. There was more smoke than heat; it drifted towards him, tickling his throat. Gair let the music ring louder in his mind. It skirled along every nerve, tingling, singing, delicious warmth enfolding him, but still the flames were no stronger than matchlights. He opened wider, wider still, not trying to focus now, only just in control, and the heat of it was painful. He stood under a desert sun, his skin scorching. In a few moments, he would have to surrender.

With a report like a cork drawn from the Goddess' own wine-bottle, the length of timber blew apart. Flaming fragments whirled across the yard, bouncing and smoking. Somebody swore, and the darker of the two women laughed aloud. The other frowned at the smouldering splinters and one by one extinguished them.

'You never did know when to stop, Godril.' For all the warrior-hardness of her frame, the desertwoman's voice was throaty and sensual, spiced with an accent Gair could not place. It had a smoky quality that tickled at his concentration like a feather in his shirt.

'Enough, Aysha. Now is not the time,' Godril growled. He looked back at Gair. 'I judge you can work fire.'

Next to speak was one of the brothers. Now that Gair was paying close attention, he saw threads of silver in the man's hair and beard, the darkness of his eyes contrasting with his sallow skin. His name was Barin and he commanded Gair to work water, sculpting it into shapes to order, condensing it out of the air and sucking it out of the ground. Gair sweated and fought to achieve the results demanded of him, but he did it.

Barin, with a curt nod, was satisfied. 'I judge you can work water.'

He was followed by Eavin, his brother, who spun air. Gair was obliged to create cooling breezes, blow out fire, twist air and water together into a waterspout, breathe as the Master fought to stifle him, spin a shield around himself as he was pelted with all manner of objects, both solid and illusory. He was thankful beyond words for Alderan's lessons aboard the *Kittiwake*.

Esther, the grandmotherly one, worked earth. For one so benign and comfortable in appearance, she had eyes as shrewd as a moneylender's and a streak of startling ruthlessness running through her placid strength. Deftly her plump hands shaped earthquakes and tremors, broke the rocks in front of her and melted them with fire, and Gair was alternately instructed to do the same, or stop her.

Then the four of them melded their talents, water and fire, earth and air in differing combinations, until his mind raced. Satisfying them had become more difficult. Each failure, each renewed effort brought fresh sweat to his back and chest. His temples throbbed ferociously, and only stubbornness kept him on his feet.

Finally the four Masters broke off. Gair released his hold on the Song and bent over, sucking in air to ease the tightness in his chest. When the dizziness passed and his pulse had slowed, he straightened up. Although the physical effort had been minimal, he ached in every limb and his spine was running with sweat. Soot, dirt and even blood streaked his whites.

The Masters waited, their faces impassive. The sun fell full on Gair's back now, making his shadow so short it pooled round his feet. It must be past noon, then; over four hours gone, and there were still two Masters left to test him. He mopped his face with his sleeve. At the far end, the pink-faced man smiled slightly, fingers steepled under his chin. Eyes bright with amusement, he crooked a brow, as if to ask if Gair cared to be let in on the joke.

Gair ignored him because the woman Godril had called Aysha had stood up. Her bearing made her appear taller than she was, but her frame looked oddly proportioned, longer above the waist than below. Then he realised what was wrong. She was leaning on two canes, as if her legs were too weak to support her for long. She saw him looking and stared back fiercely, daring him to pity her, refusing his compassion. Her beautiful eyes were hard as sapphires. Spreading her arms, she dropped her canes and turned her face to the sun. Her outline shimmered like heat haze, shrank, and in her place a kestrel perched on the bench.

Can you do this, Leahn? demanded her voice in his mind. With a shriek the kestrel broke for the sky.

Gair could not answer – he did not know how to project his thoughts into hers. But he could show her. He reached into the restless music of the Song for a Leahn fire-eagle. In the iron room, he had been a hawk in the mews, blinded by a hood, held down by jesses, but dreaming of the sky. Now he could fly again, and his cramped wings remembered.

Four or five wingbeats lifted him from the ground, then he circled upwards to where the kestrel hovered over the yard. The fire-eagle was a large bird, six or eight times the kestrel's size, and it did not have the smaller hawk's hovering skills, but there was a fine thermal rising off the pantile roofs of Chapterhouse that his broad wings could ride.

By the saints, it was good to stretch his wings again. He had not taken to the air since the tail-end of last winter, and he had not realised how much he missed it until he felt the wind lift him clear of the walls and the weight of the earth fell away beneath him. It was as invigorating as plunging into a cool pond on a hot summer's day. All fatigue was washed from his limbs.

Aysha's kestrel darted around him, scrutinising everything, from the shape of his talons to the ruddy-gold of his plumage. *This is a good shape. Let's see how well you handle it.*

In the blink of an eye she had transformed into a female fire-eagle and swooped towards the inland hills.

Gair glanced down at the open-mouthed Masters staring up from the yard, then dived after her.

Aysha led him a merry chase above the vineyards of Penglas. Halt she might be on the ground, but in the air she was graceful as a dancer. Banking and twisting round the columns of rising air, she shrieked aloud, just for the joy of it, and Gair followed, a mirror to her every move. After ten years, this shape fit him like his own skin.

I like this shape, Leahn, Aysha declared. *Perhaps not as swift as the*

142

kestrel, but agile and strong. *I could fly the breadth of the world on these wings.* She cocked her head. *You must learn to speak like this, so we can talk when we fly together. It will come quickly, once you know how.*

Far below them, a farmer in a straw hat walked amongst his vines. Now and then he stooped to inspect the ripening fruit, or pick off a blighted leaf. Aysha turned upwind, studying the gentle slope below. Gair climbed a little higher. The warm air that rose from the hillside held him aloft, as if he was floating in a deep bath. Maintaining position required no more from him than an occasional flick of a wing, even less effort than reaching for the soap.

Abruptly, Aysha folded her wings. She stooped like an arrow falling, straight for the farmer's hat. Gair dived after her. She was descending too fast, far too fast; surely she would—

Fire-gold wings flared, bright in the sun, then she was stroking upwards again with something pale gripped in her talons. The farmer clapped his hands to his balding pate and gaped in astonishment.

Goggling like a goosed girl! Aysha's laughter bubbled into Gair's mind. Up she soared, past him and higher still, then rolled and tumbled back down. Low over the vineyard she dropped the hat and laughed again as its owner chased after it.

Oh, that was fun! Coran calls me childish, but there's no harm done. The farmer will get his hat back . . . eventually.

Banking, she swung towards the fields of the home farm. The wind dropped to barely a breeze. Rising heat from the hillside brought Gair scents of lavender and thyme and summer-baked earth. Insects ticked and buzzed. A dog barked outside the farm gate and he smelled woodsmoke, and cooking. In its hollow, Chapterhouse sat pooled in the thick, golden light of early afternoon like a sugar-paste confection in honey.

He was reminded of Uncle Merion's house, and long summer days. He remembered the tangle of St Winifrae's Bells that grew around the windows of the upstairs bedrooms, nodding their white heads to the bees, leaded mullions winking in tawny

143

sandstone walls, and competing with the other boys to see who could slide furthest along the freshly waxed Long Gallery in their stockinged feet . . .

Most of his memories from Leah, at least the ones he allowed himself, were from that place. He had learned to swim and fish at Blackcraig, and how to sail a dinghy. He'd learned how to forget he was different. And now he could never go back. A sweet pang of homesickness twisted inside him, sharp as a splinter.

The practice yards opened beneath him. Upturned faces watched the eagles' approach.

You must fly with me again, Leahn, and show me what other shapes you know, said Aysha. *I shall teach you to be a porpoise and we shall swim to the drowned palaces of Al-Amar. Be a wolf and we will hunt the mountains by moonlight!*

Abruptly she swooped underneath him and seized his talons in hers. Startled, he flared his wings to brake, but her momentum pulled him sideways and they tumbled over and over, spiralling down towards the yard. Then as swiftly as she had caught hold of him she let go. She peeled away without another glance in his direction to land on her bench and resume her proper form. It took Gair a few moments to right himself and catch his breath, then he circled back down. The shadows were cool around him, but as he regained his normal height he caught the westering sun full in the face and had to shade his eyes to make out six astonished faces staring at him.

It started as a chuckle, deep in Alderan's belly. Then it rose, swelled and burst out in a great roar of amusement. The old man slapped his thighs and shook his head; a wide grin split his beard. *Excellent! His voice rang in Gair's head. Truly, truly excellent!*

Aysha's fathomless eyes lingered on him, blue enough to drown in. Then she said formally, 'I am Aysha. I judge you can work shapes.'

Still fighting to stifle his merriment, Alderan laid a hand on Gair's shoulder. 'Are we agreed?' he asked.

144

The Masters glanced at one another and a shiver in the Song inside him told Gair they were conferring amongst themselves.

'We are,' they said together.

As one, they stood and inclined their heads in salute. The shimmering tension expanded to enfold him, holding him as fast as if the air itself had solidified around him. At the back of his mind a doorway opened onto a vast space filled with brilliant colours. In the colours he could feel presences, waiting for his acknowledgement, but he did not know what to do. Alderan squeezed his shoulder, as if taking their cue from it, seven voices spoke directly to his mind.

Welcome, Gair, to the Order of the Veil.

One by one they made themselves known to him, so that he might recognise the patterns of their minds, then they took their leave. Aysha lingered longest, and her pattern stayed in his thoughts: ice-white, sky-blue, the grey of agates and the deep red of heart's blood. She contrasted markedly with Alderan. The old man's colours were surprisingly mellow – amber and jasper, brandy and port, with none of the sharp lines of Aysha's, but a vein of silver and black ran through them like a scar.

As Alderan left his mind, the window onto infinity closed and Gair was alone inside his head once more. Then all he could feel was the stupendous heaviness of his limbs as fatigue came crashing down on him.

'You look all-in,' said Alderan.

Gair mopped his face with his sleeve again. He needed a bath, and badly. 'At least I didn't throw up this time.'

'That's because they didn't push you too hard.'

'They weren't exactly easy on me!'

'No, but they could have been much harsher. That's why Coran was there, to make sure they didn't demand more of you than you could give.'

'Was he the red-haired one on the end, the one who didn't say anything?'

Alderan nodded. 'He was there as adjudicator. You'll no doubt get to meet him at some point. He's on the faculty.'

'What does he teach?'

'Wards and shields.' They walked back down the yard and at the door to the changing rooms Alderan paused. 'You never told me you could shape-shift.'

'You never asked.'

'Ha!' He shook his head ruefully. 'Well, I think I deserved that. You've certainly made an impression on them. I should imagine Aysha will want to work on your shape-shifting.'

'She said as much.'

'You share a rare gift. She was the only shape-shifter our Order had ever seen. Now we are blessed with two.'

'So what happens next?'

'You said you wanted to learn. We'll teach you as much as we can. After that, it's up to you.' Alderan laid a hand on Gair's shoulder. 'You'd be welcome here, as one of us. We need as many *gaeden* as we can find to maintain the Veil.'

'Can I take some time to think about it? With everything that's happened . . .' Gair paused.

'Of course. Take as long as you need.' With a smile, he turned to leave.

Gair looked over at the north stand, where the last of the Masters were filing away. Aysha leaned on her canes, her feet dragging with every step. He waited, but she did not look back.

12

PLANS

ಎ

Ansel's study was not a large room. Where bookshelves did not reach, the walls were panelled, and a large tapestry hung above the hearth opposite his heavy oak desk, which had been pushed from its usual place in front of the windows to make room for an easel, placed where it would catch the best light. Ansel himself, magisterial in his snowy-white vestments, with a psalter open on his lap, sat in a high-backed siege in the window embrasure whilst the artist fussed with the folds of the robes until they were arranged to his liking before returning to his sketch.

'Just so, my lord Preceptor, just so. Now, if you could raise your head a fraction?'

Danilar closed the door quietly behind him and folded his hands in his sleeves. He recognised the slender fellow in the painter's smock. Teuter was the finest portrait artist in Dremenir, but the Preceptor's expression made Danilar wonder how long it would be before that exquisite psalter was thrown at the man's head.

'Finally sitting for your portrait, my lord?' he asked.

Ansel rolled his eyes. 'Had to happen sooner or later,' he muttered, and shifted in the chair. The artist clicked his tongue but continued sketching, his pencil darting over the paper.

'Fetch me a cushion, will you? My arse is numb from this damned chair.'

'As I explained, my lord, a cushion will spoil the line of your robes,' Teuter fluted. 'It simply would not do to have you portrayed as some kind of invalid.'

'Ha! It wouldn't do, would it not? Since when did it *not do* to tell the truth? I'm an old man, Teuter; paint me as you see me!'

'My lord?'

Ansel gestured with the book. 'As you see me, twisted hands and all.'

Teuter pursed his lips but said nothing.

Danilar watched the sketch taking shape. A few deft lines suggested the bookshelves and window leading, then bolder strokes shaped the chair and its occupant, whose scowl was transformed into a benevolent half-smile.

After a scant five minutes, Ansel stirred. 'That's enough for today, man. I have matters to discuss with the Chaplain.'

'My lord, we have barely begun—'

But Ansel had already hoisted himself out of the chair, wincing as he kicked the swathes of velvet and satin away from his feet. 'I said enough, Teuter. Come back tomorrow.'

The painter lowered his pencil and rolled a few words around his mouth, then swallowed them unsaid. 'As you wish, my lord.' He gathered up his materials and headed for the door.

Danilar bowed him out and closed the door after him.

'Whose idea was it to commemorate our time in office with portraits, Danilar?' Ansel shrugged off his heavy outer robes and flung them carelessly over the arm of the settle. He limped to his displaced desk and sat down behind it, easing his bones into the cushions with a sigh.

'Preceptor Theudis, I think, four hundred years ago.' The Chaplain heeled round the chair opposite for himself. 'Damn silly idea, if you ask me.'

'If you'd sat for it when you were anointed, like your predecessors, you wouldn't be finding it so uncomfortable now.'

'When did I have time to sit for a portrait? Within six months of taking office I was riding out to war, and I spent the next five years in the saddle. Fine portrait that would have made, all dented plate and bloody to the eyebrows.'

'It would make a refreshing change to see a Preceptor at work,' Danilar remarked.

'Instead of all this beatific posturing, you mean? It would at that.' Ansel shook his head. 'By the saints, if that Teuter makes me look like old Theudis, all constipated with his own piety, I'll feed him his brushes through his ears.'

The Preceptor reached for the decanter and glasses on his desk and poured two generous brandies. He pushed one across the table.

'It's barely High, you know,' said Danilar.

Ansel's lips twisted. 'Don't you start sermonising,' he snapped. 'It's bad enough when Hengfors does it without you chiming in. It's too late to worry about the state of my liver now.' He took a large mouthful and swirled the brandy around his teeth, then swallowed with a sigh. 'I'm sorry, old friend. I shouldn't take it out on you.'

'Your joints troubling you?'

A grimace. 'Pain always did make me tetchy.'

'I remember.' Danilar picked up his glass, but did not drink. 'You used to roar at the healers every time they had to stitch you up.'

'And that was a few times more than the dignity of my office led them to expect, I shouldn't wonder.'

Danilar could not help but smile. In an instant more than twenty years had rolled away and he was back in the blistering heat of the desert, a sword in his hand and doubts in his heart as Ansel led the charge from the front, as he always had.

'The Gimraeli healers did good work.'

149

'Aye, they saved quite a few we thought were lost. That calls for a toast, I think.' Ansel topped up his glass and raised it in salute. 'A toast to old comrades and absent friends.'

'Now that I will drink to.'

Their glasses chimed together and Danilar sipped, letting the spirit warm his gullet.

'I miss those times.' Ansel cradled his glass on his belly. 'The company of honest men, with a common purpose, instead of all this endless politicking.'

'I don't miss the heat.'

'Or the flies.'

'Or the fear.'

'It made you feel alive, though, didn't it?' Ansel asked. 'Your pulse racing, your breath quickening. That roil in your stomach as you snicked your visor down and gathered up the reins, waiting for the signal.'

'I always kept my visor up.'

'Weren't you afraid of splinters if your spear shattered?'

'I was more afraid I'd sick up and choke on my own vomit.' Ansel laughed uproariously. 'I never knew that about you, you know. We've been friends all this time, and I never knew. How many years is it now?'

'Forty and some, since we left the novitiate.'

'A long time.' The Preceptor looked down at the glittering Oak on its chain round his neck. 'A long, long time.'

After another small sip, Danilar set down his glass. 'Somehow I don't think you sent for me in order to reminisce about the desert war.'

'To the point as always, eh? Well, it was partly to get me out of the clutches of that wretched painter, and partly because I need your advice.'

'Spiritually?'

'As a clear pair of eyes.' The Preceptor opened his desk drawer and took out a sheaf of broadsheets. On top was a tangle of message slips, covered in minute script on both sides, tightly curled from being rolled into cylinders. He tipped the slips onto his desk like so much wood shavings.

'Can you tell me why the Order spends hundreds of marks every year maintaining a network of agents who send me all this paper when it contains less news than I can find in these?' The broadsheets landed on the desk with a thud. 'What is the point of it if I can get more up-to-date and in many cases more accurate reports on the street corner for a farthing?'

Danilar frowned. 'I think Elder Cristen would be the best person to answer that, since he maintains the network,' he said.

'Cristen is a fool. The most he knows about Gimrael is that it's where the silk for his undershirts comes from. As for what his agents send, the pigeons make more sensible pronouncements than the messages they carry. Listen to this.'

Ansel rooted through the slips until he found the one he wanted. '"Minor unrest in the silk quarter of El Maqqam, quickly contained",' he read. 'And according to the broadsheet – where are we? Yes, here, four attempted arson attacks on Empire merchants' warehouses, one of which resulted in the loss of the entire stock and the deaths of a nightwatchman and two civilians who were trying to rescue him when the roof collapsed.' Ansel screwed up the message slip and flicked it towards the hearth. 'An interesting definition of "minor", don't you think?'

'Cultists?'

'No one seems to know. Oil lamps tossed through the windows, apparently. No one saw anything.'

'No one ever sees anything in El Maqqam,' Danilar grunted. 'Too afraid of looking crosswise at a Cult sympathiser.'

'And that incident isn't the half of it. There's been piracy on merchant ships, spice caravans lost in the inner desert, and that's just what's been happening where there was someone to witness it.' Ansel scooped up the remaining slips and let them shower down through his fingers. 'And barely a word of it here.'

Danilar felt a twitch of unease. 'That is . . . worrying,' he said.

'Just like the old days, isn't it?' The Preceptor grinned wolfishly. 'Twenty-four years on and we're back where we started – only my agents were actually useful then, when they risked being throttled with their own intestines if they were caught. Tell me what you make of it, Danilar. I need clear sight and plain words, from someone who spent long enough in Gimrael to know what a viper's nest it can be.'

'You hardly need me for that, Ansel. You were there too.' Despite himself, Danilar reached for his glass. A little spirit in his stomach would be comforting. 'This was how it began last time, and it ended in Samarak. Have the Church's interests been attacked?'

'I've no reports to say so, but the Cult tends not to leave witnesses, so it may take time to come to light.'

'Does the Emperor know?'

'I sent a courier this morning, although I'm sure Theodegrance's spies have already informed him.'

'Well, it's Kierim's duty to maintain the peace in Gimrael. He needs to look to his borders if he wishes to keep the Cult at bay.'

'A thousand miles of sand? No one can expect to maintain borders like that without the goodwill of the innermen, and that's where the Cult draws most of its sympathisers. There's little love between them and the people of the outer desert, even at the best of times. No, Danilar.' Ansel's mouth tightened into a line like a scar, pale and taut. 'I'm too old a warhorse not to smell battle in the air long before the trumpets ring out. It's only a matter of time before Endirion's standard flies over the legions.'

Danilar shuddered. 'I pray Goddess you're wrong. No one will thank us for fighting the desert wars over again. Last time around was enough to make me hang up my sword and turn to the cloth.'

'We may not have a choice, if the Lector declares a crisis of the faith.'

'What are we going to fight with?' Danilar asked, spreading his

152

hands. 'We are too few, Ansel. I doubt we could muster more than four full legions, even if we sent the entire novitiate to their vigils tonight.'

'Then we must direct our prayers accordingly, because I'm afraid the choice will not be ours to make.' Ansel tossed the last of his brandy into his throat and swallowed hard. Almost at once he began to cough. He covered his mouth with his fist whilst his other hand fumbled in his pockets for a handkerchief. Each cough shook his spare frame, like a gale shaking a willow.

Danilar let himself into the next room to get a glass of water from the jug on the night-table and set it down on the desk as the Preceptor hacked one last time and wiped his lips.

'Thank you,' Ansel said hoarsely. His chest heaved. 'Perhaps brandy in the middle of the day is not such a good idea after all.'

He sipped water until his breathing steadied and the unnatural colour faded from his sallow cheeks.

Danilar frowned. 'I think I should send for the physician.'

'Goddess, no,' said Ansel, waving him back into his seat. 'It's nothing to bother Hengfors with.'

'Ansel, you're not well.'

'Nonsense, I'm fine. The brandy just caught in my throat.' Folding the handkerchief back into his pocket, the Preceptor sat back. 'See? Nothing wrong at all. If you send for Hengfors he'll expect me to take one of his foul potions and they're worse than being sick. Now, we have work to do.'

He drew the pile of broadsheets towards him and swept the message slips aside with his hand. Lines of vivid scarlet streaked the yellowed paper.

Danilar stared at the blood, afraid of what it might signify.

Ansel followed his eyes and took his handkerchief out again to wipe his fingers. 'We have work to do, Danilar,' he said firmly. 'We cannot afford to be distracted now. There is far too much at stake.'

'And what good is all our careful planning if you die before it comes to fruition? I can't carry your schemes alone, Ansel. It needs you, or it all goes for nothing.'

'I know.' The Preceptor inspected his hand for any last trace of blood. 'There's time yet.'

'Enough time?'

'I think so.'

Danilar, sounding dubious, said, 'We cannot afford a mistake now. The Curia will have our hides for bookbinding if we're not careful.'

The smile that Ansel shot him was positively dangerous. 'Then we shall have to be very careful indeed, shan't we.'

⁂

Carefully blotting his signature, Ansel set the last letter on top of the pile and pushed it to the front of his desk, ready for his secretary to take in the morning. The administrative drudgery seemed to take longer and longer these days. Edicts, correspondence, initialling the ponderous minutes of the Rede and its endless subcommittees; some days it seemed as if the Order ran on paper and ink, instead of faith.

Ah, faith. Once that had been all a Knight needed, that and a strong arm. Ansel sat back in his chair with a wince and looked across his study at the tapestry. It had hung opposite his desk for more than twenty-five years, a constant reminder of his task as Preceptor. Its glorious colours were faded now, muddy with dust and age, but the story told across the three panels could still be read. At leftmost, the First Knight was anointed by the Goddess Herself; he was kneeling to receive Her blessing. In the rightmost, a much-aged Endirion stood on a hill overlooking Dremen, his diamond helm on his hip and his other hand on the hilt of his sword as he watched the construction of the Motherhouse in the valley below. In the centre panel, Endirion battled a shadowy figure on the edge of an abyss.

Most depictions of the Fall showed Endirion triumphant, his

sword ablaze as he stood shining in a beam of the Goddess' Grace and the angel slunk away or fell into a fiery pit. This tapestry showed the battle at its height. Darkness swirled around the angel like smoke, and Endirion's teeth were clenched with the effort of defending himself. Where the Knight's sword met the angel's ebon blade, black and silver sparks showered the earth.

At this moment, the duel could have swung either way, salvation and damnation so finely balanced that a mouse could starve on the difference. There was resolve in Endirion's expression, but a crease between his brows that spoke of fear. The angel's eyes were alive with dreadful, gleeful hunger and he pressed his attack fiercely, but the way he crouched suggested his weight was on his back foot, just one hammer-blow short of taking the first backward step to defeat.

Some days when Ansel looked at the tapestry, he thought Endirion would be the one defeated and the whole of history would unravel before his eyes. Other days, when the sun shone and the darkness did not crowd so thickly or so close, he knew Diamondhelm would triumph. Tonight, the battle was too close to call.

You cast a long shadow, my lord. When we meet at last, I pray you are not disappointed in my stewardship of your Order.

In the morning, he would swallow as much poppy syrup as that fool Hengfors would let him have and make the long walk from his lodging to the library behind the Rede Hall. He had an appointment with the archivists that not even Danilar knew about. It was a pity he couldn't take the Chaplain along; his brawn would be useful to lean on when the poppy syrup failed, as it invariably did. But he would take his staff, which by happy chance was functional as well as ceremonial, and he would wear his finest white vestments with the gold Oak on its chain over his heart. It would take all the force Ansel could muster, backed up with every symbol of his office, to cow the keeper of the archives. A thick fur house-robe and slippers would spoil the effect a little, but that couldn't be helped. He was damned if the Motherhouse's cold corridors would make him quake and shiver when he asked for the keys to the books that were hidden even from the Lector of Dremen himself.

13

WEAPONS

❧

Goran lifted the bottle down from the shelf and reverently blew away the dust. It was a thirty-year-old Tylan goldwine, the last of the case he had inherited from his father. He had opened the first one when he ascended to the scarlet; he had been saving the last for a special occasion. Tonight ought to be worthy of it.

Carrying his candle he climbed the steps from his cellar and locked the door behind him. With so many fine vintages sleeping out the years under his feet, he couldn't be too careful. He dropped the key back into the pocket of his house-robe and shuffled through the quiet house to his study. A large square package sat on his desk, wrapped in oilskin and tied securely with twine. He tried not to look at it whilst he made everything ready.

He had managed to resist opening it for several hours. Anticipation had put a keen edge on his appetite, but it was important that everything was just right first. He turned down the lamps until the oak-panelled walls retreated into shadow, then set the candle to its brethren ranged along his desk. Candlelight was the best for this, he'd found: good white wax candles gave the cleanest flame. The curtains were already closed and the fire well built up; his study was a cosy nest of thick wool and polished wood, with his favourite tapestry cushions on his chair and the household staff already abed so he would not be disturbed. Perfect.

From the silver tray by the hearth he took a single crystal glass and buffed it lovingly with a napkin. Then, with great care, he opened the brandy and poured himself a generous measure. The honey-coloured spirit made a delicious sound, thick and syrupy, and it glowed in the glass like the very decoction of good cheer. Humming a charming little tune, Goran settled himself in his chair and drew the package towards him.

Now. Snip the twine just so and lay the pieces aside. Unwrap the oilskin – oh, how marvellous! Dark red velvet underneath. His fat fingers twitching with excitement, he turned back the edges of the fabric to reveal his treasure.

A book – but not just any book; this was a book that Goran had spent almost a decade trying to acquire. Last year his agent had announced that he had finally located a copy in Sardauk that might be available for purchase. After ten months of delicate negotiations the bookseller in Marsalis had agreed a price that made Goran's eyes water, but he had to have it, simply had to, so he had paid the five hundred Imperials. But it was surely worth it.

Pulse quickening, he squared the book on its velvet wrapping and fortified himself with another sip of brandy. The book was hand-bound in finest ivory calfskin. It was untitled – those who knew what it was did not need to see anything so vulgar as lettering on the spine, and those who did not know did not need to know. Merely looking at it was enough to start a little sweat on Goran's brow. With great care, he opened *The Garden of Kendor*, and knew immediately that he would have paid a thousand Imperials for it and considered it cheap at the price.

Each thick vellum page was paired with a leaf of finest tissue to protect the illustration. He lifted up the first and his mouth fell open in wonder. The drawing was exquisite. Every line was fluid, anatomically exact; the artist's pen had captured all the natural grace of the nude, the quivering, vibrant energy of a life suspended in stillness. It was breathtaking, quite breathtaking. Goran reached out with his fingertip, hardly daring to touch the cheek of the lovely on the page before him. It was only a line drawing, but he fancied he could feel the downy skin, the quick beat of the blood beneath. Under his house-robe he felt the first twitch of arousal and closed his eyes, relishing it. *Yes.* He spread his knees to give himself room, then sipped a little more brandy. There was no rush. He had plenty of time to savour this feast on his table.

He let his eyes wander down over the illustration again, from the arch of the neck to the neat, flat nipples. *Slowly, slowly now, take your time.* His erection was growing, pushing up against his robe, and this was just the first plate! There were twenty in all, twenty perfect, glorious bodies for him to enjoy. Count the ribs down to the belly, stretched taut, the groin smoothly shaved. His heart beat faster now, he felt giddy with it. *Oh, this was truly a treasure.*

Another mouthful of brandy to warm his stomach, then he let his hand steal under his robe. He didn't want to wait any longer, couldn't wait. His fruits were tucked up tight and full already. Perspiration dewing his face, he curled his fingers round his aching member and began to stroke.

Someone pounded at the door. Goran shut his eyes and murmured a little prayer that whoever it was would go away. Then his eyes flew open again and his busy hand fell still. Who could it be at this time of night, out here at his country estate? The pounding came again, and damn it if his housekeeper wasn't rolled up in her eiderdown in her bedroom at the rear of the house. He would have to answer the door himself. Damn, damn, *damn.*

Carefully he laid the tissue back down over the drawing and closed the book. Mopping his face with the napkin, he unlocked his study door and waddled out into the vestibule. The thick outer door shook in its frame as the caller knocked again, more insistently than ever.

'Yes? Who is it?' Goran snapped.

'We need to talk, Elder,' said a voice he dreaded to hear again. His tumescence wilted. Hastily adjusting his robe, Goran slid back the bolts and swung the door open. Frosty air swirled round his legs. A slight, fox-faced fellow in travel-worn clothes leaned against the wall. He had a rent in his jacket as long as his hand.

'I believe I told you not to come here, Pieter.'

The man pushed himself away from the wall and straightened up. He looked tired, and his wandering gaze seemed even slacker and more unfocused than usual. 'I have information. May I come in?'

Goran stepped aside reluctantly. 'Why couldn't you send a note? Why just turn up here, where someone could see you?'

A vulpine smile flickered over Pieter's face. 'Your country house is more than a mile off the road and it's past Low bell, Elder,' he said, stepping over the threshold. 'If anyone saw me, then they must have been about even darker business than mine. I think our secret is safe.'

Muttering irritably, Goran led the way to his study. Pieter glanced around at the panelling and the thick tapestry hangings with a distinctly acquisitive eye, as if reckoning up the value of the furnishings. Goran was quick to flip the velvet over his book before it was added to the tally-sheet.

Then the witchfinder shrugged off his cloak and dropped into a chair by the hearth without waiting to be invited to sit. 'A fire is very welcome on such a raw night,' he remarked, stretching out his legs. Mud flaked off his boots onto the good Gimraeli hearth-rug. 'A brandy would be even more so. Don't stint with it, it's been a long ride.'

Insufferable! Goran ground his teeth as he poured a second glass. *As if it isn't bad enough that I have to use the fellow at all, the man has the gall to turn up unannounced at my private lodging in the middle of the night, and now I have to share my Tylan goldwine with him!* He handed the glass over with poor grace.

'So what news do you have? Good, I hope, to be worth disturbing me like this.'

Pieter took a mouthful of brandy and savoured it for several moments before allowing it to trickle down his throat.

The wretch thinks he can appreciate thirty-year-old spirit, does he?

'The witch still lives.'

'I paid you a great deal of money to ensure that would not be the case.'

Pieter shrugged. 'You didn't tell me he wouldn't be alone.'

The bottle chimed on the rim of the glass as Goran topped up his drink. So the boy had had help – but from whom? Impossible that anyone could have known the Preceptor would overturn both law and precedent when faced with such incontrovertible evidence of guilt. Yet he had, and someone had known it. Goran's hand steadied. There was advantage to be had from this, if he could play out his cards in the right way. He set the bottle down and pushed in the cork.

'Tell me.'

'I followed him along the Anorien road into Belistha, then down into Elethrain – had to stay well back; that witch has ears for my kind. They took ship downriver towards the Havens on a grain barge. River travel can be chancy sometimes, so I arranged for trouble to come their way.' The witchfinder drained his glass. 'I would have set a higher price if you'd told me he was armed, too.'

'You already charge far too much for your services.'

'Few people can do what you pay me for,' Pieter said. 'Scarcity affects the price, whatever the commodity.' His undercooked gaze slid sideways to the velvet-covered shape on the desk.

Goran felt a twinge of unease. Pieter always made him uncomfortable, which was why he preferred to deal with him at arm's length, through his agent. That way he didn't have to be in the same room as him and his . . . *abilities*, useful though they were. They made his flesh crawl. The thought that the repulsive fellow might have seen the object on the desk, even guessed at its value, disturbed him even more. Suppressing a shiver, he swirled his brandy around the glass.

'The man he was with. Who was he?'

'Never seen him before. Older fellow, solid-looking. A bit shabby.'

'Is that the best description you can give me? That could be half the Curia, man!'

'I didn't give him much mind. He wasn't the one I was being paid to follow.' Pieter rubbed his face wearily. 'Why do you want him so badly, anyway? He's headed downriver. With any luck the Havens waterfront will see his throat opened for you soon enough.'

'I don't pay you to ask questions, just to get the job done, which you have singularly failed to do. I don't feel the need to explain myself to you.'

'Well, see if you can feel the need to pay me another ten marks for a new horse.'

'What happened to yours?'

'Dead. I was leading him through the trees when your boy took a shot at me with a shortbow. Missed me by a prayer, hit the horse. He took down two of the lads I paid as well. All in all, it wasn't the duck-hunt you told me it would be.'

This was a development Goran could have done without. He frowned down into his glass, brain ticking busily through the possibilities. 'Do you think you could pick up his trail again?'

'It's long cold. I could try to find out where the barge stopped – the Havens is the best place to start, but the bargee's a drunk. He'll hardly remember what he had for breakfast yesterday if I ask him tomorrow, let alone three months from now.'

'But you can try.'

'Aye, I can try. For a price.'

'There always is a price, with you,' Goran grumbled.

The witchfinder spread his hands. 'I have taxes to pay, Elder. If it's charity you want, ask the Little Sisters of St Margret.'

Damn the man – damn him and all his kind. But however Goran wished it might be different, the fact remained that there were some things he simply could not do himself, so he had to hire men who could, and that took coin. No way around that. But he could wish the loathsome Pieter didn't take quite so much of it.

Kneeling by the hearth, careful to keep his back turned so that the witchfinder would not see where his hand went, Goran touched an insignificant-looking knot in the panelling. A section in the side of the chimney-breast sprang open on a concealed hinge, revealing three strongboxes on shelves built into the structure of the chimney. He lifted out the bottom one and opened it on his desk, carefully nudging *The Garden of Kendor* out of the way. Inside the strongbox were rows of leather pouches, each with a paper label tied neatly round its neck. Goran opened several and took a handful of coins from each – oakmarks, Imperial crowns, Sardauki *zaal*, Gimraeli talents – and estimated the value as he tipped them into an empty pouch. He had paid in oakmarks last time because he had not expected the hunt to cross the border, but this time he would have to be better prepared. Two hundred Imperial, give or take: that should be more than enough for the journey Pieter faced. He could not afford to take any chances, not when the high seat of Preceptor could hang on the outcome.

'This should be enough for any inconvenience.' He tossed the purse across the room.

The witchfinder caught it with one hand. When he felt the weight, his eyes narrowed, his gaze coming sharply into focus. 'Let me be sure I understand you, Elder,' he said. 'You want me to ride eight hundred miles and back again in the depth of winter just to find one witch? I could get you five for a twentieth of this without setting foot outside Dremenir. Why is this one so special?'

'Just find him.'

'Alive or dead?'

'I don't care. Just find him, damn it, or I'll send you to the questioners in his stead!'

Pieter pushed himself to his feet. 'I'll send word when I'm near.' He set down his brandy glass and shouldered his cloak. 'A pleasure to be of service to you, Elder, as always. Allow me to see myself out.'

With a sardonic little bow, he left and closed the door behind him. A moment later Goran heard the front door close as well, and feet on the gravel path outside, walking away. He shuddered. Goddess, what a repellent creature the witchfinder was, if a necessary one. He closed his strongbox and returned it to its hiding place, closing the panel with a click. Then he poured himself some more brandy. It took several sips to dispel the chill. What he needed was a distraction, something to take his mind off the unpleasantness of the last hour and let his subconscious work through this new information to see how it could best be used.

Eyeing the clock on the mantel, he rubbed his ample belly contemplatively. It was not too late; he could still enjoy a stroll in the *Garden* before he retired. He settled himself in his chair, but Pieter's news had so soured his mood that not even the exquisite agonies of Kendor's torture-garden could rouse him again.

❧

Scrambling backwards on his rump Gair fled the clammy embrace of his bed-sheets. His throat was raw from shouting and his heart hammered against his breastbone. No matter how he panted, he couldn't draw a breath. The air in his room was too thick with heat. When he swung his legs over the side and sat on the edge of the bed, even the floor clung to his feet.

Another nightmare of the questioners. Gair shuddered. What had brought them back out of the shadows now? He rubbed his hands over his face, then raked them back through his sweaty hair. Why couldn't he leave them behind?

Who is your demon? What is your familiar? Speak, boy, and be saved! Saints, it was hot in his room, and airless. He pushed himself to his feet and flung the windows as wide as they'd go. Cool night air stole in, scented by the sea. *Better*. Leaning on the windowsill, Gair made himself take deep breaths. *Much better*.

The water in the pitcher on the washstand was tepid, but better than nothing. He poured some into his palm and rinsed the staleness from his mouth, then splashed more over his face and neck. Rivulets ran over his body, but did little to cool him.

It had only been a dream, but the pain had felt very real. He touched his belly where the bruises had been. They were long gone now; from collarbones to crotch his skin was unmarked, ridged only by the muscles underneath. No scabs, no dried blood, no raw red welts. His flesh remembered the lash vividly, but nothing showed on the surface. Surely he was safe now.

He hadn't felt the witchfinder crawl over his mind since the raid on the *Trader Rose*. Perhaps the seeker had lost his trail there on the river, or simply given up. Maybe he had been luckier with the bow than he'd thought. Whatever, he had to believe he was safe on the Isles, or he'd never be free of the questioners.

A blackbird chattered outside. Wings whirred; a dark shape darted over the silvery fields and disappeared into a hedgerow. Dawn barely smudged the eastern horizon. He should try to get some more sleep, if he could in that disordered bed. He glanced at it. No. The thought of pulling that damp sheet back over him made him shudder.

In his closet were several clean sets of whites. He pulled on a pair of the loose canvas trousers. The adept who'd been with him at his testing had been right, they had softened with wear as he had worn them most mornings over the past two weeks. Shouldering his sword belt, he let himself out into the corridor.

The rest of Chapterhouse slumbered; even the cooks were still abed, though it wouldn't be long before the kitchen fires were lit and the bread set to bake. But for the time being Gair had the place to himself. He padded through the corridors, turned left past the changing-rooms and made his way out into the smallest practice yard. Simiel was fading into the dawn sky, but there was more than enough light for his purposes, thrown back by the white walls. Up on the ridge-tiles, another blackbird flicked its wings and tail at being disturbed, then with a thin 'tsee' darted away.

Gair had developed this routine soon after his arrival at Chapterhouse: the yards were always quiet until after breakfast, so he had a couple of hours alone to get rid of the kinks of the night before and clear his head. It soothed him to work the solo forms over and over; it helped him focus, view his worries in dispassionate perspective, like seeing the landscape through the eye of the eagle. It was the only way he knew to stop dwelling on the nightmares.

Now he drew his sword and propped the scabbard against the railing. The earth floor was dew-damp under his bare feet, but it wasn't slippery. A breeze sprinkled goosebumps across his chest. That didn't matter; he would soon warm up once he began. By the time he was done, he intended to have washed off every last shred of the nightmare with clean, honest sweat.

He settled himself, wiped his hand on his whites, and began the exercise.

It took time to find his rhythm. His muscles were stiff; the first five or six forms were clumsy and his footwork poor. Gair scolded himself; he should know better. *Smoothness first*, Selenas had taught, *be smooth and the speed will follow*.

Starting the exercise more slowly, he focused on each step, each breath he took. When the birds began to chatter and then to sing, he barely noticed; when the sun peeked over the eastern wall of the yard and drew his shadow out beside him, he never felt it. All he was conscious of was the flow of his muscles as he made the sword fly. In time, the questioners were, if not forgotten, at least put back in the past, where they belonged.

With a final salute to the empty walkways that ringed the yard, Gair put up his sword. Sweat coursed over his chest and back and his whites clung to his legs. The sun sat almost a hand above the eastern wall, and glared like a demon's eye. Saints, it was still so hot! He should have brought a water jug. According to the calendar, Eventide and the turn of the year was still a full two months away. Back in Leah, the snow would have been over his knees by now, with more falling every day. The nights should have been bone-achingly, tree-shatteringly cold, not so muggy and thick that even a single sheet was too much to bear. Even after two weeks, he was no nearer becoming used to it.

Somewhat to his surprise, he missed Leah. Out there, today would have been a good day to ride up to Carterway Head, where the road dropped over the shoulder of the Great Glen and it was possible to see halfway to Leahaven, if the sky was clear. South a mile or two was the vast limestone outcrop known as the Giant's Table; he used to climb it and look out over the misty valley, feeling as if he stood on the roof of the world. There were a thousand things that he missed, from sweet heather honey to the breathless hush of the morning after the first deep snow, and they called to him. No matter how he had tried to suppress his feelings since he had left, Leah had a string tied to his heart that would never be undone.

Rolling his shoulders to ease the burn of hard work, Gair walked back to the steps where he had left his scabbard – but it had been moved, and now it was lying beside a box of oiled rags. A fresh towel hung over the railing. Someone had come into the yard, and he'd been too absorbed in the forms to notice. Flexing his grip on the longsword, he looked around.

The walkways were empty, but the armoury door stood open and a broadset man sat on a stool beside it in the morning light. Thick fingers deftly wound new whipping round the hilt of a wooden waster sword. Two of the battered practice weapons stood against the armoury wall, freshly repaired; three more lay on the packed earth by the man's feet in a litter of leather scraps, waiting their turn.

167

'Thank you for the towel,' Gair said.

'Thought you might need it. You usually remember to bring your own.' The man made the last loop and held the thong in place with his thumb, whilst he fished a clasp knife from his pocket with his free hand. 'You've good balance, but don't you get bored with the solo forms?'

'Sometimes.' Gair reached for the towel to dry his face.

The fellow on the stool swapped the towel for a bodkin from his belt and pressed the cut end down under the last few turns of leather to secure it. Then he stood up, knuckling his spine. 'Goddess, don't get old. Your back's the first thing to go,' he muttered and came forward into the yard. He had close-cropped hair the colour and texture of iron filings, and a prize-fighter's face. Dark brown, almost black eyes flanked a much-broken nose, and his left cheekbone was crumpled under an old scar. When he smiled, the scar lifted his upper lip into a villainous sneer.

'Haral. Weapons-master,' he said. 'Who taught you the sword?'

'Selenas of Dun Ygorn.'

'Up at the Motherhouse, yes? I see.'

The waster blurred in his hand and swept in towards Gair's ribs. Instinctively he raised his blade to block it, but the stocky Syfrian had already pulled his blow and the steel barely bit a splinter from the wood.

'Quick hands,' Haral said, stepping back. 'He taught you well.'

'Do you know him?'

The weapons-master stood the waster against the wall with its brothers and dusted his palms together. 'A little, from the war. Does he still have that *qatan*?'

'He does.'

'Still make you face it with just a pair of knives?'

'Sometimes it's a quarterstaff, or a broken lance. He says you never know what you might have to defend yourself with.' Gair flipped the towel back over the railing and sheathed his sword.

'Aye, that you don't.' the Syfrian grinned. 'Sword breaks, or gets

168

taken from you, you make do with the first thing that comes to hand. Saw a woman take on a *qatan* once with naught but a skillet, and didn't she make the fellow look damned foolish with it too, for a few minutes, anyways. Show me your hands.'

Gair's palms were dark from the sword's leather grip, but the scar was plainly visible. Haral didn't appear to pay it any particular mind, taking each hand in turn and rubbing a horny thumb over the calluses on palm and fingers.

'And a bowman too – but of course, you're Leahn. Probably cut your teeth on your da's old longbow, eh? Grip.'

Gair squeezed Haral's hands hard. His shoulders were burning before the Syfrian indicated he could let go. When he did, he had to flex the life back into his fingers.

'So they didn't ruin you completely. How does it feel?'

'It's not perfect, but it's good enough. Master Haral, how long were you watching me?'

'About an hour today, maybe half that every other day this week, when I had more chores to do.' He gestured towards the eastern side of the yard, where a row of mullioned windows winked over the tile-roofed walk. 'My rooms are just up there. Like Church folk, I tend to be up with the sparrows. Watching you's been a welcome distraction from book-work. With a weapon or without, I'll take on any man and give him my best, but when the armoury ledgers need balancing . . .' Haral grinned wryly. 'I don't make much of a clerk!'

He scratched his cheek, a speculative furrow creasing his brows. 'There's half an hour or so before breakfast. Care to spar with me a little?'

It was tempting, but Gair said, 'Thank you, Master Haral, but I think I'm done for the day. I have a tutorial with Master Brendan at Eighth, and I need a bath.'

'Understood – some other time, then. There's space in my classes for one more, if you've a mind for it. Twice a week. Can't

169

promise as varied an experience as you're perhaps used to, but it'll stretch you more than the solo forms.'

'That sounds good, thank you.'

'Truth told, you'd be doing me a service. Couple of my students are starting to think that there's nothing left a broken-down old war-horse like me can teach them. You'd shake them up a little.'

'If it gets me away from the Masters for a few hours, I'd sweep the stable yard,' Gair admitted. He picked up his sword and slung the baldric over his shoulder.

'Man needs to flex more than his brains from time to time,' Haral said. 'Stop by the yards day after tomorrow and you can show me what else Selenas taught you. It could be . . . enlightening.' Then he barked a laugh. 'This is one trick they won't see coming!'

14

FLIGHT

෨

Darin dropped onto the opposite bench and set a loaded breakfast tray on the table in front of him. 'You look as if you were ridden hard and put away wet,' he said cheerfully.

Gair sipped at his tea. 'About as good as I feel, then.'

'Didn't sleep well?'

'Not really. Too warm.'

'Missing the icy caress of a Leahn winter, eh?' The Belisthan spread a thick layer of butter on a slice of spicebread and took an enormous bite. 'You'll get used to it eventually. Me, I've always hated the snow. I think I was born at the wrong latitude.'

He folded the rest of the bread into his mouth and was buttering a second slice before the first was even swallowed.

Gair had a healthy appetite, but he had never seen anyone tuck into food the way Darin did. The Belisthan simply inhaled it. 'I don't know how you don't throw up, eating like that.'

'I grew up with four brothers. I had to eat quick, or go hungry.'

Darin tipped his head towards the sword propped against the wall. 'Been practising?'

'I'll get rusty if I don't.' Gair's jaw creaked as he stifled a yawn. 'Saints, I'm ready to go back to bed.'

'The Masters still working you hard?'

'You could say that. I haven't even had a free day yet. Demonstrate this, shield against that – Coran threw fish at me yesterday.' Darin almost sprayed tea across the table. 'Fish!' he exclaimed. 'Mackerel, I think. He said he wanted to see how I reacted to the unexpected.'

Coran looked soft, at first glance, but behind those twinkling eyes and rosebud mouth there was a mind of polished Yelda steel. Scorching fireballs had come as no surprise, and Gair's shield had deflected them with ease, as it had the ice-storm that came after, though a few jagged splinters had porcupined his weaving before he could bounce them away. Coran had just stood to one side, hands folded behind his back and a trace of amusement on his round-cheeked face. His smile didn't even flicker as the finny barrage began.

The mackerel had been illusory, of course, but they'd been startlingly real as they flapped across the yard and slapped off Gair's shield. He'd almost lost control of it, his jaw dropping at the sight of the gasping fish, but he'd managed to snag the edge as it started to unravel and slammed it back down into the ground.

Darin hooted with laughter as he recounted the story. 'Now that's what I call unexpected – a rain of fish out of a clear blue sky!'

'He is a deeply devious man.'

'Rather you than me! I'm not much of a shield-weaver.' Darin filched the last fig from Gair's plate.

'Hey, go get your own!'

'Quicker to steal yours – I love figs. So are we playing chess after supper?'

'Assuming I can stay awake, yes, of course. I'll try to make the game last longer than twenty-three moves this time.'

'Care to make a small wager on that?'

Gair cut the air with his hands. 'No bet!'

'Is that because you don't gamble, or because you think you might lose?'

'Both. I'll just play for the glory, thanks.'

'If it's glory you're after, I suggest you start winning a few games.'

Finally I get you to myself. Without hesitation or introduction, Aysha's voice sounded in Gair's mind, imperious as the ring of trumpets. *My study, and pick up your feet. Fifth floor, west side.* Then she was gone.

'You look like you were just goosed,' said Darin.

'Master Aysha,' Gair told him. 'Is she always that abrupt?'

'Usually, yes.' The Belisthan picked up his tea. 'I take it you've been summoned to the presence at last?'

'I thought I had a class with Master Brendan this morning, but apparently not.'

'Well, she tests all the new students eventually. I'm surprised it's taken her so long to get around to you.'

'Tests for what?' Gair asked, although he could guess what the answer would be. He drained his own mug and piled plates onto his tray.

'Hadn't you heard? She's a shape-shifter. Supposedly she's looking for someone else like her. She spends all her time flying round the islands as a seagull or some such, so I guess she's starved for company.'

'Did she test you?'

'Took one look and decided I wasn't even worth delving,' Darin laughed. 'Don't worry, there's practically no chance you've got the gift. It's incredibly rare. She's been here fifteen years and never found another one.'

Slowly Gair set his mug on the tray. If it had been up to him, he wouldn't have told anyone; he would have kept it secret, hoarded it, hugged it to himself as the one thing that could not be taken from him. Flight was his escape. He would not even have shown the other Masters, if not for her.

'Master Aysha was one of the six who tested me my first day,' he said at last.

Darin took a beat to catch on. When he did his mug banged down on the tabletop so hard he slopped tea over his hand.

'Bloody hellfire,' he breathed, eyes round as cottage loaves. 'You can—? Blood and stones! How long have you known?'

'About ten years. Darin—'

'What's it like? It must be amazing, being able to do that. Can you show me?'

'Someday, if you like. Look, I have to go.' Gair picked up his tray and started for the hatch. The Belisthan scrambled after him, trying to ask questions, finish his drink without spilling any more of it and keep up with Gair's long strides all at once. It took a none-too-subtle elbow in the ribs to make him keep his voice down so other people didn't hear. As they queued to hand in their trays Darin shifted from foot to foot like a small boy in need of a privy, gnawing his lip with the strain of keeping his questions inside.

The instant the refectory doors swung closed behind them, his indignation burst out. 'I can't believe you didn't tell me!'

'Darin, I've only known you two weeks, and the Masters have been pounding the sap out of me every day of them! When have I had time to tell you anything? Besides, it's just a talent, like being able to whistle or sing.'

'Just a talent. You can turn yourself into any other animal on the Goddess' green earth and you say it's just a talent?' Darin's laugh was incredulous. He raked his fingers through his hair, then, hands on his hips, fixed Gair with an accusatory glare. 'I can't believe you didn't tell me.'

'I'm sorry, but it's not exactly something you can just drop into the conversation two minutes after you're introduced, is it? Pleased to make your acquaintance and by the way I'm a—' Two adepts strolled up on their way to breakfast. Gair paused until they were safely inside the refectory, then continued, '—shape-shifter. But now that you know, can you keep it in your pocket? I don't particularly want to give everyone another excuse to stare at me.'

'Is that the reason you were expelled from the Motherhouse?'

'No. I don't think they ever found out about that.'

'And you're like her? You know, seagulls and things?'

'I think she favours a kestrel, actually, but yes. Darin—'

'What's your animal? Is there just one shape you can be apart from this one, or many? Is it painful?'

Gair held up his hands to stem the tide of questions. 'Slow down, slow down! I can do more than one shape, yes, but I'm best with birds – so far, anyway. No, it doesn't hurt, unless you make a mess of the change and then you feel dizzy and sick for a minute or two. If there's anything else you want to know, you'll have to ask me later. Now, *please*, can we keep this between ourselves?'

'All right, hold your furrow straight.' Darin rolled his eyes, then pressed his right palm over his heart. 'Word of honour, I'll not say anything.'

'Thank you. I appreciate it.'

'How much? Enough to write an essay for me?'

'I'll let you win at chess, how about that?'

A wide grin split the Belisthan's face. 'I already do. Just promise me you'll show me one day. Soon!'

'Done – but not in the middle of the refectory.'

'And done.' Darin pushed Gair in the direction of the stairs. 'Now go on. The Masters' quarters are the far side of Chapter-house and she'll have your tail-feathers if you're late.'

৯০

Five flights of stairs later, Gair arrived outside Aysha's apartment wondering why a woman who could not walk without the aid of sticks would choose to have her study so high up. After checking he didn't have crumbs on his shirt, he knocked on the door.

'It's open.'

He stepped inside. Whatever he'd expected, he was wrong on almost every count. Aysha's suite was airy, lavishly panelled in golden wood set at intervals with small, intricate mosaics in colours as rich as brocade. Creamy *qilim* rugs and sheepskins softened the floor. To the left was a dining table and chairs with deeply curved seats and backs padded in butter-coloured leather. To the right a pair of damask-upholstered couches flanked a pale marble fireplace in which dozens of unlit candles clustered like parishioners on the chapel steps. Arranged around them were drifts of pebbles and pieces of salt-weathered wood, polished smooth by sand and surf.

'You took your time.' Aysha was sitting at her desk by a pair of tall glazed doors, silhouetted by the bright sky outside. Her expression was impossible to read, but her voice told Gair all he needed to know.

He bowed. 'Forgive me, Master Aysha. I shall try not to be tardy in future.'

'See that you aren't.'

Planting her ebony canes firmly, she hoisted herself to her feet and turned towards the doors. Gair hurried to open them for her, letting her precede him onto the balcony.

'So tell me,' she said, 'what other shapes do you know besides the fire-eagle?'

'Birds, mostly. I seem to have a knack for them.' He closed the doors behind him. 'Master Aysha? I was expecting a lesson from Master Brendan this morning.'

'I excused you. From what I understand, you already have more than enough skill at illusion not to have to listen to that windbag twice a week.'

Gair blinked.

'What else?'

'I've tried dog, cat, deer and horse, but I couldn't hold them for long.'

'We'll work on those another time.' A brisk breeze ruffled Aysha's short-cropped hair and she turned her face into it, eyes crinkling up against the glare. 'What about a wolf?'

'I've not tried that yet.'

She faced him, fixing him with her brilliant eyes, and smiled. Her teeth were very white. 'You will.'

Spreading her arms, she let her canes clatter onto the slate tiles and Gair could sense her gathering up the Song before he saw the change begin. Then her outline shimmered, pale shirt and green breeches becoming indistinct and amorphous as smoke until, in a swirl of colour and movement she was gone and a kestrel perched on the carved balustrade. Talons grated on stone as it shook itself to settle its feathers, then it cocked its head towards him.

Well?

The Song was there as soon as he reached for it, already roused by her working, and seconds later he was perched beside her, his fire-eagle towering over her slender kestrel. Without another word she launched herself into the wind, and he had to follow promptly or else lose her amongst the gables and chimney-pots of Chapterhouse.

Aysha took to the air as naturally as if she'd been born a bird. Agile as a dancer she soared through the warm air and though Gair wore his eagle-shape as comfortably as his own skin after a decade of practice, the kestrel's narrow wings had the better of him in such close quarters and he was hard-pressed to keep up. In open skies he would have her beaten for sheer power and endurance, but her manoeuvrability there left him floundering.

Once clear of the buildings she flew due west towards the sea. A haze over the water misted the horizon, but near the shore the air was clear as fine crystal. Sunlight sparked and shimmered along the wave-crests and grey-backed gulls rode the breeze in search of food. Aysha's appearance in the middle of their flock caused consternation. Shrieking, they swooped around her in loops, clamouring at her to be on her way, but she flipped her wings and rolled easily away from them. Gair was not so fortunate, and he took a battering from their hard bills before he was able to side-slip clear and follow her up over the cliff-tops.

Aysha led him along a mazy, circuitous route that more or less followed the ragged coastline round to the north side of the island and down into a cove, little more than a nick in the flank of the island. It was barely large enough to accommodate a couple of fishing boats. The small beach was embraced by steep headlands that captured the day's warmth like a dripping-bowl under a roast.

She circled in to alight on the golden sand and shifted back to her usual form. He landed beside her, waiting for the next part of the lesson, but she simply sat down with her back against one of the haystack-sized rocks. When she saw him still standing she patted the sand beside her, to indicate that he should sit. He sat.

'You fly well,' she said. 'You're self-taught?'

'Yes.'

'Shape-shifting's a rare gift. How did you come into your talent?'

'By accident, I suppose. I was watching a fire-eagle fly over the glen and wondering how it would feel to ride the wind like that, and the next thing I knew, I was in the air.' Gair picked a piece of blackened bladderwrack from the sand and twirled it between his fingers. 'I scared myself so much I fell out of the sky and landed in a gorse-bush.'

'How old were you then?'

'Nearly eleven. It was the summer after I first started to hear the music.'

'And you had no idea what you were doing?'

'None at all. I was watching the eagle and I heard a new melody in the Song, high and wild and lonely. I reached for it, and . . .' *And the Song poured me out into a new shape like water into a glass.*

'And you flew.'

'And I flew. Not very far – but for a few seconds I knew what it was like.'

'Which was?'

'You already know. You can fly too.'

'I don't know what it felt like for you.'

Gair ducked his head, picking at the seaweed with his thumbnail. 'I felt free.'

'Did you tell anyone about it?'

'No. No one knew until I was tested, my first day here.'

'I thought Alderan looked surprised.' She smiled that dazzling smile again, combing the sand beside her with her fingers. 'The Song often comes to people like that, when there is something they want or need badly enough to make them open themselves up to it. Or something they want to escape from. Alderan tells me you are an orphan.'

'As good as,' Gair said. 'I don't know who my father was, some soldier probably. My mother gave me up to charity when I was a few days old.'

'And the family that found you took you in?'

'There were always fosterlings of one sort or another in the household . . . orphaned children from the tenant farms, cousins training to be squires, that sort of thing. One more or less made little difference.'

'We are what we make of ourselves, not what others make us,' said Aysha. 'Where we come from, how we're born – that's just biology.'

'I wish that were true.'

'You sound bitter.'

'Just realistic. I have no name, Master Aysha. Without a name I have no place, no station, except what others choose to give me.'

Blue eyes slid past him to where the surf chewed restlessly at the shore. 'Some would say that having no fixed station in life makes you the master of your own ship, with no one to answer to, no one to disappoint. There are no expectations but what you set for yourself. There's a freedom in that, don't you think?'

'Maybe.' The seaweed crumbled in Gair's fingers and he let the pieces fall, brushing the bits from his hands. 'I just wish I knew where I belonged.'

'You'll find your place,' she said. 'Give yourself some time. And if you can't find a place, make one. That's what I did when I came here fifteen years ago, and I had less to my name than you do.'

'I don't understand.'

179

'When Alderan found me I was living with the street-children in Abu Nidar, slitting pockets in the souq for my next meal. Look at me now: I'm on the inner council of a forgotten Order at the arse-end of the Empire, barely tolerated by my peers, and regarded as a freak by the students. Bird-lady, they call me. Imagine the lofty heights you could reach!'

Leaning back against the rock, she closed her eyes with a sigh. 'Forgive me. I shouldn't have said that.'

What could he say? 'Are you unhappy here?'

'No – I could be in a much worse place, believe me.' She turned her face up to the sun. 'It's such a nice afternoon. We should have brought a picnic.'

Gair stared at her. A strange lesson this was turning out to be.

'Peppered ham,' she mused. 'Honey-glazed chicken. Fresh bread, still warm from the oven. That soft goat's cheese they make here, the one that's rolled in herbs. Apricots.'

'Master Aysha?'

'Oh, and some of those maple-sugar pastries the baker in Pensaeca Port makes. They're little slices of heaven.'

'Is this part of the lesson?' His stomach growled and a flush raced up his neck, but Aysha laughed.

'Someone's sand-tiger needs feeding. We might have to pack two baskets if you're going to bring him along. So tell me what you like to eat, Leahn. What would you bring for a picnic on the beach?'

He raked a perplexed hand back through his hair. He had no idea where to start. 'Well, I like most things, I suppose. Your list sounded pretty good to me.' His lack of contribution to the banquet struck him. 'Strawberries,' he offered.

'Oh, I love strawberries. I'd never tasted them until I came here, but if I'd known what they were I think I would have left the desert a lot sooner. What else? Do you like oysters?'

'I don't know. I've never eaten them.'

'You should try them some time. Fresh from the boat, squeeze a lemon over and swallow them whole, straight out of the shell.'

Surely she didn't mean . . . ? 'Raw?'

'They taste of the sea.'

'Salty and full of sand?' he said, and she laughed.

'They're delicious, trust me. With a crisp white wine, they're incredible.'

'If it's all the same to you, Master Aysha, I'll take your word for it. I prefer my food dead when I eat it.'

Shading her eyes, she studied him. 'I didn't think you'd be squeamish.'

'Why?'

'You're a shape-shifter like me. Surely you've hunted in another form before now?'

'No.'

'Never?'

'Never. I caught a rabbit once, but I had to let it go. I just couldn't . . . you know. Kill it, eat it.' He shuddered at the memory. The fire-eagle had wanted to feast, but the rabbit's squeals had scraped at his ears and the thought of hot blood in his mouth, bitter with fear, had made his gorge rise.

'To truly understand a shape, to feel it in your soul, you must experience all its behaviours. Hunt as it hunts, live as it lives. It's exhilarating.'

'I'm not sure I could ever do that. It feels wrong.'

'That's because you're letting yourself think about it as a man.' The eagle would not even stop to consider it.' She squinted up at the height of the sun. 'Come on. The day's a-wasting and I've not seen all you can do yet.'

'I'm supposed to have a tutorial with Master Godril this afternoon,' Gair said.

'There's more to learn about the Song than he teaches. He won't miss you.'

'Are you sure?'

'I'm sure. Godril's a pompous arse. Didn't you see his expression when you flew up out of the yard? I thought he was going to have a seizure. Would have served him right, too – you'd think he'd discovered the Song, the way he goes on.' She put on a low, rasping voice that was a remarkably accurate imitation of the sandy-haired Master. ' "This is illusion! Show me fire!" As if no one but him could have the ability to do it.'

In spite of himself, Gair burst out laughing and Aysha grinned. It crinkled her eyes up at the corners, giving them an exotic tilt. They really were the most startling blue.

Walking her hands up the rock behind her, she pushed herself to her feet. Gair jumped up to offer his arm, but she barely glanced at it until she was upright and dusting off her palms. She gave him an unfathomable look. 'Manners maketh a man,' she said. 'Thank you, but I can manage.'

Then she turned and flashed into the form of a fire-eagle. A few sweeping wingbeats that kicked up sand around her and she was in the air. Gair followed close behind as they climbed up and out of the cove. Aysha circled once, then peeled off downwind, following the roll of the hills inland.

Now, Leahn, let's see just how good you are.

15

WHISTLERS
IN THE DARK

❧

Masen tied his reins around the saddle-horn in a half-hitch, enough to keep them out of the way, quick to release if he had to. He could not afford to be held up, not even for a moment. Whistlers Pass was no place to be caught after dark.

He studied the sky. The westering sun was already out of sight behind the mountains and shadows crawled from behind the rocks onto the road below. In the height of summer it was possible to ride the length of the pass between dawn and dusk. This late in the year, there was simply not enough daylight. He had set out southeastwards before first light and ridden as hard as he dared, but a third of the journey still lay ahead and he would not even have the benefit of a moon. Miriel was barely new and would not rise high enough to clear the mountains; Lumiel would not rise at all until well past the time he might need her.

Damn his luck. The Goddess must surely be laughing at him, to send him through one of the most unquiet places on earth at the dark of the moon, with the Veil as threadbare as an old sock. All he could do was put his trust in fire, and his mare's swift feet.

Masen picked up the two oil-soaked torches. He swung himself onto Brea's back, then called fire to them. They caught quickly, flames gyring in the shifting winds. Gripping a torch in each hand, he nudged the mare forward into the darkening pass. At least the road was good here. Grass and weeds had long since claimed the cobbles of the Kingsway, but the footing was firm enough for a gallop if he had to. He urged Brea from a walk to a trot and held the torches high as the last of the sunset faded from the sky like the heat from a cooling forge, leaving the heavens a glacial blue. It would be fully dark in less than an hour. Already he was unable to see much beyond the ruddy circle of light, but that could not be helped. Loss of his night vision was the price he had to pay for the security of the flames. Fire was the only thing the whistlers feared.

Keeping his own fear tightly in check, Masen pushed on, one mile, then two, then the road swung from its westward track back towards the east again, the fifth bend of the seven as it wound through the pass. Eight more miles and he would see the massive fortress of Brindling Fall rearing against the sky, blacker even than the night behind it. Two miles further to its gates, then he could start to relax. Down Roisin's Stair into Arennor, make camp somewhere near the last milecastle on the Kingsway and get some sleep. He would need it. The Pass was hard on a man's nerves.

A sudden gust of wind pushed him hard in the chest. The torch-flames snapped and showered his gloves with sparks. From somewhere behind him came a thin moan – wind between the rocks. The Brindling Mountains were sandstone, and millennia of weather had sculpted fantastic spires from them; the wind played them like a ragman's flute. Nonetheless, Masen nudged Brea into a rolling canter.

The moan faded away to nothing, then returned, rising in pitch to a shriek. *Still just the wind.* The torches were good for another couple of hours, and he would be at the Fall by then. If he could keep this pace he had little to be concerned about.

Another mile passed under the mare's hooves. The wind continued to rise and fall, changing direction in defiance of the way it should prevail, one minute tugging his cloak hard enough to choke him, the next shoving him on his way. Brea flattened her ears in distaste and ran on.

Another mile. Outside the ruddy light of the torches the darkness was absolute. Chips of ice stung Masen's face, and the chill bit through his gloves to gnaw at his fingers. Every breath smoked before the wind snatched it away.

After one more mile the dark gained a different texture as the walls of the pass steepened. It felt thicker, dense and heavy as sorrow. Anxiety tickled the pit of Masen's stomach. If the whistlers were going to show themselves, they would do it soon.

Unearthly shapes loomed out of the dark either side of the road; sandstone spires as sharp as blades fretted the wind into a whine, wound it round narwhal horns and goblin chimneys until it squealed. Masen slowed Brea to a trot. The pass was narrowest here, the Whistlers twisting the road through their crooked fingers like a ribbon. Best to be cautious, unless he had no other choice.

Keening sounded from off to his left. Another answered it from up ahead, and trailed off into a giggle. Chilly fingers of dread slipped down Masen's spine. The whistlers were abroad. More sounds from behind, audible even over Brea's hoofbeats. They had a mocking tone, the way children chanted in the schoolyard. A burst of laughter from ahead was abruptly cut off, before sounding again on the other side of the road. Brea snorted and shook her head, slowing her pace. Masen squeezed against her ribs to push her on and raised the torches as high as he could.

Stay with us.

A pale shape spiralled out of the night: pale as ash, pale as bones, too large to be a snowflake.

Why do you run?

Lower and lower it came, drifting as slowly as a falling feather, yet somehow speeding towards Masen like a stone from a sling. It whipped past over his head and he ducked instinctively.

Laughter pattered around him. *Don't be afraid.*

Then it was gone, leaving just a memory of a breeze on his

cheek and the faint, cold odour of an ages-old grave. Another pale bloom in the dark, off to his left, then two more on his right. Masen tried not to look at them, instead keeping his eyes focused on the road unrolling before him between Brea's ears, the frosty grasses gleaming in the torchlight.

Shall we sing for you? Yes, let's sing. Sing sing sing sing sing yes let's sing sing for you sing so sweet sing so sad sing to your soul sing for your soul sing you to sleep sleep dear one my dearest love sleep again to sleep once more so sad so sad so long asleep to sleep in silence silence deep so long asleep or shall we SCREAM?

Hold fast!

A dozen voices howled. The sound stabbed at Masen's ears as the pallid shades swooped around him. He crouched lower in the saddle and urged Brea faster. The mare's mane whipped at his face and the icy night wind cut tears from his eyes. He could not afford to be caught there.

Hold fast!

Brea skidded to a halt scant yards from the warmly dressed warrior who stood in the road, a heavy war-spear levelled. Masen kept his seat with some difficulty as the mare pranced and tossed her head. She whinnied in panic, but he could soothe her only with words; his hands were full with the torches. He shushed her as best he could whilst watching the warrior. The man was tall, his long hair in braids adorned with feathers. Bronze cuffs adorned well-muscled arms, and a jewelled pin fastened his thick plaid cloak. Yet the plaid had a faded look, as if washed too often, and the man's hair was colourless as spider-silk – an illusion of a man, no more real than the other whistlers, but real enough to startle poor Brea.

'Go back to your rest,' Masen called, a torch held forward. He urged the mare into a reluctant walk. 'There is no battle here.'

Hold fast! said the voice again. The spearman's lips did not move.

'And I said begone!'

With a breath of the Song Masen flicked a ball of flame from

186

the torch in the direction of the apparition. It raised its spear to knock it aside, then dissolved into smoke and snowflakes that were crushed under Brea's hooves as she stepped over the place where the shade had been. It took only a little encouragement to bring her to a trot, though her ears flicked restlessly back and forth.

More snow fell, swirling thickly out of the night to hiss in the torch-flames. From behind came a renewed chorus of tomcat yowls, punctuated with shrieks of frustration more discordant than ever.

Spite! You spite us! Scorn us mock us spit on our song! We shall sing you another song a song of spears a song of tears a song of souls long gone gone to the dust a song of stones a song of bones break the bones break the spears that broke our bones break the spears and grind the bones into the stones that sow this land that once was ours this land we bought with blood and bones.

The shades massed again, dozens of them now, drifting like clouds. He tried not to look at them directly, but there were too many to avoid. They swooped towards him with their gaunt faces and hollow eyes, their mouths stretched wide by too many sorrows, too many horrors. Here an army had died, almost an entire people, crushed between the hammer-strike of Endrion's finest and the anvil of Brindling Fall, and even now it found no rest.

Three miles to the sixth bend and the end of the Whistlers. It was too much to ask of his mount, though she would gallop until her heart burst if he gave her his spurs. The Emperor's racehorses could manage that distance flat out in the King's Circle, but Brea was no racehorse, and it was dark and she carried heavy packs. What was needed now was steadiness – a burst of speed, to put some distance behind him, then steadiness. That was something that she had in abundance.

Masen set his heels to Brea's ribs and tried to outrun the dead. When the swooping cloud of revenants was eventually veiled in the snow, Masen slowed the mare with a word. She shook a crust of snow off her face, her coat steaming, but her head was up. Masen checked his torches. They still burned, but not for much longer. He had maybe an hour's flame left in them. He hoped it would be enough. There was still another two miles or more to go.

Brea plodded on, her hooves near-silent in the deepening drifts. Masen listened for the return of the whistlers. Each time the wind sighed through the rocky pillars that hedged the road he swung his head towards the source of the sound, thrusting out his torches, but there was nothing to see but snow. It swept across the pass from north to south, silent as the shiver of an angel's wings. Cold pinched his ears with cruel fingers and his arms ached with holding the torches aloft. There was nothing to see but snow and rock and the smothering velvet night.

Treacher!

The voice sounded right behind him. Masen swung around, his heart beating a tattoo on his ribs. *Nothing.* Just more snow, glowing where it fell into the ruddy circle of the torchlight. Somewhere behind him the wind keened between the rocks and fell silent. *Nothing.* He turned back, shifting his numbed arse in the saddle.

A revenant hung in the air in front of him, close enough to touch. Long hair waved in a cloud around her head. Her skin was translucent, as if her high-cheekboned, smooth-cheeked face had been carved from moonstone. Every line of her was perfect. From smooth, milk-white shoulders to dainty feet she was lovely as the dawn.

Will you not stay? She smiled and held out her arms to him, welcoming as a woman to her lover. *Stay with me my dearest love. It is so cold without you, so cold in the night. Stay with me. We shall have nothing but time.*

Though the words were seductive, her eyes remained empty. The pale fingers that reached for him ended in the black claws of a raven and the white teeth were wolverine-sharp. Masen swung the torches together hard. A cough of flame made the revenant flinch; her smile become a snarl. He thrust the torches forward, piercing the ghost between her pale breasts. She threw back her head and howled. From the sandstone spires either side of the road, a thousand voices answered.

With a yell, Masen clapped his heels to Brea's sides. The mare reared and leapt into a gallop. Ghostly warriors rose out of the road, bows drawn, and let fly volley after volley of arrows. Had the missiles been real, his corpse would have bristled like a porcupine; instead the phantom shafts streaked through him, leaving only a chilly trail across his soul. One could not kill, but a dozen or more would leave him greatly weakened, and the bitter night would do the rest. Ducked low over Brea's neck, flames streaming back from his torches, he charged the line of revenant archers at a dead run. As arrow after arrow whipped through him, Brea grunted and stumbled once, twice. Her breathing became laboured, and foam flew from her mouth, but still she kept galloping on into the swirling snow and the hail of arrows.

Behind them the howl rose in pitch, becoming first a scream, then a shriek, thin and sharp as a filleting knife across his nerves. Then abruptly the air was silent. Though he could see no difference in the snow or the night around him, Masen could sense the pass widen, the slopes of the mountains to either side falling back, gentling, as at last he left the whistlers behind.

❧

Alternating between a trot and a walk, Masen coaxed Brea into the shadow of the fortress walls just as his torches burned out. He would have to find shelter quickly; once the snow stopped, there would be a killing cold, and the pair of them were too exhausted to make it down the Stair now. The chill of the were-arrows felt like a breastplate of ice, making it hard to breathe, difficult to maintain any sort of warmth at his core, despite his layers of clothing. Brea's head was down, her ears limp, and she stumbled as she walked. She was a bigger target for the archers; doubtless she had taken far more arrows than him.

He slid off her back to make it easier for her. 'Come along, lass,' he urged, 'just a little further, eh?'

Goddess, it was so much effort to speak. Each word had to be dragged up out of his throat as if it weighed a hundredweight. He dropped the smouldering stubs of his torches into a drift; they were no longer any use. Even his feet were too heavy, but somehow he kept lifting them out of the snow, pushing them forward in another step, then another, moving slowly under the arch of Endirion's Gate, towards the path up the looming flank of the Fall to the postern gate. Brea stumbled at his side, but she matched him step for step, yard for yard.

They would be able to enter the fortress by the postern, where the defenders had once received their supply wagons from the Greenway below. If the inner walls had not fallen in, destroyed by the storms, he should find some shelter inside, out of the snow at least, where he could build a fire, heat food. They just had to reach the entrance.

Brea whinnied and crashed to her knees. It took two attempts for her to haul herself back to her feet, and she stood shivering as snow whitened her rump. She had little strength left. Masen patted her neck. 'We've been together too long for you to think about leaving me now,' he told her, looping her reins round his hand again. 'Up, Brea, not far now.'

He wiped snow from his face and started up the slope again, only to stop when a shadow detached itself from one of the fortress' massive buttresses and stepped into the middle of the path. Masen could make out nothing of the man's appearance other than the drawn shortbow in his hands. That shape was more than distinctive.

'You should take better care of your mount, my friend.' The man spoke with the rolling accent of the Aremorian plains. 'I'll see to her needs before my own, and always have done.'

'Just as it should be.' The clansman eased the tension on his bowstring, but he kept the arrow nocked. 'We saw your torches in the pass. What brings you this way?'

'I'll be happy to tell you, clansman, as soon as I can get out of this damned blizzard.'

The clansman considered his words, then jerked his head towards the path. 'Up to the stable yard, then to your left. There is space for you at our fire.'

Not a welcome at their fire, but still better than an arrow in the gut. 'For that alone, may the Windlord favour you.'

Masen saw a flash of white teeth that might have been a smile, then the man put his fingers to his lips and blew two short, piercing whistles. A single longer whistle answered him.

'Up you go. I'll follow.'

Leading the faltering mare, Masen climbed the last dozen yards to the postern and led Brea through the black arch. Across the stable yard, yellow light spilled from a doorway and illuminated another rangy clansman standing on the threshold. He too held a shortbow in his hand, but as Masen approached, he stood to one side and held up the blanket that had been nailed up across the opening in place of a door.

Inside the low, vaulted undercroft the air was blessedly warm and smelled of woodsmoke and horses. Another clansman appeared to take Brea's reins and lead her to the far side, where five horses were hobbled. At the near end, four saddles were lying on the floor beside a fire that had been lit in what had once been a forge. Packs piled against the wall had heavy cloaks draped over them; they showed signs of hard travelling. Javelins and bows were stacked where they could be easily reached.

'Expecting trouble?' Masen asked.

The sentry returned in a gust of snow and icy air. He knocked his boots clean, then pulled the blanket tight across the door frame and secured it with a heavy stone. Like the others he was dressed in well-worn buckskins, with a quiver at his shoulder and a sheathed dagger on either hip. He had the same periwinkle-blue eyes and even features as the younger bowman, though experience had hardened the lines of his face and left threads of silver in his mane of brown hair.

'You never know what you might find in Whistler's Pass,' he said. 'Fortune favours the prepared. Now perhaps you tell us what brings you here?'

Masen eyed the two half-drawn shortbows. Either one could skewer him like a jack-rabbit at that range. He sighed. 'I'm heading for Fleet,' he said. 'The Pass is the quickest way south from the high Brindling.'

'A lonely road,' the sentry said, not relaxing his grip on his bow. 'And a cold one, at this time of year.'

Masen pulled his cloak open. The undercroft was warm; inside his thick clothes he was already sweating. 'I go where the winds blow me. What are clansmen doing so far west?'

The man who had taken Brea returned to the fire with Masen's saddle on one hip and the packs in his other hand. 'Hunting,' he said. The lightness of the voice revealed that he was in fact a she.

Masen looked more closely, and realised that her shapeless jerkin and buckskin pants concealed slender but very womanly curves.

'Your mare's in a poor way. I've fed and watered her but you'd better give her some rest if you expect her to reach Fleet.'

She leaned his packs against the others and set his saddle down, then she sat herself down and leaned back against her own saddle. Her other hand rested casually close to the dagger on her hip.

'I'm grateful, and I'm sure Brea is too. We've travelled many miles together and it grieves me to see her hurt.' Masen unclasped his cloak and folded it over his saddle. 'May I ask what it is you're hunting that brings you near on a thousand miles from Fleet?'

The sentry favoured him with a long look. Silence grew in the undercroft. Masen wondered whether he had perhaps asked the wrong question.

'You can tell him, Sor. He's *gaeden.*' The fourth clansman sat at the far side of the fire, almost lost in the shadows. Where the three others were brown of skin and hair, he was black-haired and sallow. His mouth turned down at the corners, one side from a fresh scar seaming his face from nose to chin, the other side simply of a mind to keep it company. He did not look up from the whetstone in his hands and the long-bladed dagger he was drawing across it. Steel flashed in his sloe-dark eyes as he turned the gleaming blade back and forth.

'You're sure, Kael?' Sor asked, frowning.

'Sure as I'm sitting here.' *Whisk, whisk* went the whetstone. 'I felt it as soon as he walked in. Ask him.'

Sor grunted. 'Is this true?'

Masen nodded, unbuttoning his coat.

'Duncan, is there any soup left? It's cold as the Nameless' heart out there.'

At that, Sor unstrung his bow and propped it against the wall with the others. Duncan did likewise, and set about fetching bowls and spoons as Sor took a seat by the fire.

'So,' he said when he was settled, 'you know my name. That's Duncan, my brother, Kael, Cara.' He gestured round the group as he named them.

'Masen.'

'I'm guessing from the torches, you've travelled the Pass before.'

'A few times – more times than enough, truth be told.' Masen accepted the bowl of broth and the hunk of coarse damper that Duncan handed him. 'Thank you. Those were-arrows bite deep.'

'Just as well you found us,' Cara said whilst Duncan handed round more bowls. 'They might have been the end of you if you'd been caught without shelter.'

'A wise man would avoid the Pass altogether in winter.' Sor stirred his soup.

'Well, chance makes fools of us all sometime.' The broth was thick with barley and one spoonful was enough to start thawing the chill from Masen's bones. 'I'm guessing you wouldn't be here either, had you the choice.'

'What makes you say that?' Duncan asked.

'Clan hunters this far from home, pursuing a quarry through Whistler's Pass that they're reluctant to discuss with ordinary folk?' Masen made himself more comfortable on his folded cloak. 'Clan hunters with a seeker, at that: there's a hook to hang a bloody story from if ever I heard one.'

Sor exchanged a look with his brother. 'It's bloody, all right.' He ate some more soup, mechanically, as if it were a job of work to be completed, but gave him no pleasure.

'There's a flask of good brandy in my pack over there, if you've some cups,' said Masen. 'I've a feeling we might be glad of a drop of spirit before the end of the night.'

Duncan fetched cups and flask, then returned to his supper. Masen poured everyone a generous measure and passed one to Sor, who nodded his appreciation.

'We were patrolling the Westermarch when we met a ranger, riding fast and travelling light, even for the Eldannar. They'd had an attack on their herd a day or two previously — eight mares lost, a dozen colts, half a dozen more that they'd had to put to the Goddess' mercy. They didn't know what the beast was, but it tore through the herd in the night, and it was something that killed for sport, not for food. We rode out to help, if we could, but when we caught up with the band . . .' Sor threw the last of the brandy down his throat, then set the cup on the floor. 'Don't ask me to describe what we saw in that place.'

Without a word, Masen leaned forward and refilled Sor's cup to the brim.

'They lose a few to wolves, or when the crag-cats come down to the plains in a hard winter,' said Duncan quietly. 'But nothing like this. The Eldannar said this herd was not the first to be savaged. Another was attacked, further south, and a farmer on the edge of the Southmarch said he lost twenty head of kine in one night, butchered, but none eaten.'

To Masen's right, Cara shuddered and sketched the sign of blessing over her heart.

He took a thoughtful sip of his brandy. It was not beyond the realm of possibility that there was an open Gate somewhere on the Arennorian plains, but really, the chances of that were slim. The clans lived with the Song as close as their shadows; their Speakers would have sensed a gate anywhere within twenty miles of their clan ranges and sent for a Gatekeeper. So, a rent in the Veil? That was the most likely. If it was weakening up in the high Brindling, it could easily have begun to fail here on the plains. All that was left was the question of what had come through. Merciful Mother, that could be almost anything.

Kael set down his whetstone and held his dagger up against the light to examine the edge for imperfections. Never taking his eyes from the blade, he said, 'I know what came through, *gaeden*. A hellhound.'

Sheathing the dagger, he drew another from his belt and set to with the whetstone again. Once more the brothers exchanged looks, then Duncan continued their story. 'Kael sensed the beast as soon as we were within a mile of where the attack happened. He said he could smell it, feel its wrongness with his mind. I don't understand how he does that, but he can follow a trail like this as if it was an Imperial highway. He took off after the creature as fast as he could, and he gained ground on it quickly. Perhaps it doubled back, or was lying in wait for him, but when we caught him up after doing what we could for the Eldannar we found him badly hurt, and his horse gutted like a fish. When he regained consciousness two days later, he told us what he'd seen.' His mouth twisted with distaste, and he stared down into the cup cradled between his hands.

'Maegern's Hound,' said Sor. 'Large as life and reeking like a charnel-house. He's been tracking it since he could sit a horse again. It's headed north, into the Pass.'

Masen blew out a long breath. This was worse than he could have imagined. One of the Hounds, loose now, with the Veil failing? Would the Hunt ride again? Goddess have mercy.

'I saw nothing on my journey down from the Brindling,' he said. 'Kael's right, I am *gaeden* – I am the Gatekeeper. Whilst I was in the mountains, I discovered a weakness in the Veil. If what Kael saw was true, then I'm very much afraid it has already been torn. Who knows what else might find the rent and step through?' Masen sighed. 'The situation is even more dangerous than I had realised. If you mean to continue tracking the Hound, you must be cautious.'

'I do mean to track it,' said Kael, stroking the whetstone lovingly over the blade in his hand. 'We have unfinished business, that Hound and I.'

'You'll not kill it with steel, Kael,' Masen warned him, but the clansman did not seem to be deterred.

'Nevertheless,' he said. 'I'll see it finished.' He looked up, black eyes fixing Masen through the wavering glow of the fire. 'What do you have in your pocket, *gaeden*? It pulls at me.'

'This?' Masen fished out the nail and held it up by its thread. It spun as the thread unwound, first clockwise then back again, slowing as it went. 'It's how I find the Gates to the Hidden Kingdom. I can sense them when I'm close enough, but this points the way like a compass.'

'What is it?'

'A horseshoe nail. I stumbled on it years ago, on the Belishan moors. I didn't know what it was when I found it, but the first time I passed near a Gate with it, the Hidden Kingdom tugged at it so hard it damn near tore my pocket off.'

Cara reached out a finger to touch the nail, her face rapt. 'This is from the other side? The shadow-world?' she asked, trying to take hold of it. She frowned when it slipped through her fingers like wet ice. She tried again, equally fruitlessly, then drew her hand back, rubbing her fingers together. 'It's not iron or steel, it's . . . slippery. I can't get a grip on it.'

'No flesh can. I had to tie a string round it to pick it up.' Masen held it up to eye-level, seeing his face reflected in the liquid silver surface, then dropped it back into his pocket. 'One day I'll drop it in a river somewhere and it'll be gone for good. Then I'll have to retire.'

Duncan laughed, but Kael grunted sourly and pushed himself to his feet. 'Not until all the Gates are closed, *gaeden*,' he said. 'We should have no truck with the Hidden Kingdom. There is evil there.' Shouldering his cloak, he headed for the door. 'I'll take first watch.'

Not long after, the others rolled themselves in their blankets and settled down to sleep. Masen went quietly to the far end of the undercroft to check on Brea, then fetched his own bedroll from his pack and spread it out on the floor.

He woke when Kael came back in, shaking snow from his cloak, and waited until Duncan had left to take his turn at sentry duty. Then he got up and padded to the other side of the fire where he hunkered down next to Kael.

'What do you want?' the man asked tersely, before Masen could even speak.

'Just a moment of your time, clansman. How long have you known you are a seeker?'

'What business is it of yours?' Kael pulled his blankets more tightly around him and turned his back.

'Forgive me, I'm curious. It's not a common talent.'

'Talent, you call it?' The clansman rounded on him, sitting up so abruptly Masen thought he was about to be struck. Kael's black eyes glittered like mourning jewels. 'It's a curse. Since I was ten years old I have been able to feel nothing but foulness. No joy, no love; just the blackness in men's hearts and the poison in their souls. I wish to all the gods it could be different, but it can't, so I try to put it to the best use I can. But don't ever call it a talent.'

'Forgive me. I meant no offence,' Masen said.

The clansman lay down again and pulled his blanket up to his ears. Every line of his frame was tense, as if he had to clench each muscle in his body for fear he would fly apart. Even with his eyes closed, he radiated the watchfulness of a cat about to spring. 'It's still out there, *gaeden*,' he said softly. 'Maybe twenty miles away, heading just east of north. You'd be useful in the hunt. This land is unquiet.'

'I'm afraid my way lies on another road, my friend. I have a duty to fulfil.'

'We all have a duty to rid the world of abominations such as this,' Kael said. 'No matter. I'll fetch it down alone if I have to.'

'Then may the Windlord go with you, Kael,' Masen murmured and patted the clansman's stiff shoulder. He pushed himself back to his feet, suddenly bone-weary. 'Sleep well.'

198

16

KNIGHT'S MOVE

&

Barely a heartbeat after the knock, the door to Gair's room flew inwards and crashed against the wall. Darin stood in the entrance, chess set under one arm and the other extended to catch the rebounding door. His dark eyes sparkled. 'You will not believe what happened to me today,' he announced.

Gair closed the book in his lap and took his feet down off the desk. 'Try me.'

Darin hurried in and set the chess set down, shoving a pile of books out of the way to make room. 'It was the most amazing thing,' he went on as Gair tipped the pieces out of the box and started to set up the board. 'It was my free day and I thought you might like to go fishing with me, but I couldn't find you anywhere and Renna was off to Pensteir to visit her mother, so I went down to the market in Pensaeca Port, and that's where I got this.' He thrust out his fist and opened his fingers with a flourish. There, nestled in his palm, was what appeared to be a diamond the size of his thumbnail.

Gair's eyebrows shot up. 'Good Goddess!'

'Beautiful, isn't it?' Darin's grin all but reached his ears. He tilted his hand and the gem flashed shards of brilliant colour across the wall.

'How did you afford that on your allowance?'

If anything, the grin grew wider. 'That's the best part. I didn't pay a penny for it.'

'Please tell me you didn't steal it!'

'No, no, I didn't do anything wrong. It was given to me. What do you think?'

'It's magnificent. You could buy a barony with that.'

'I was thinking maybe a duchy. Just a small one, nothing too vulgar.' Darin rolled the stone around in his palm. It spat light like a fragment of the sun and he chortled with delight.

'And someone gave you this?' Gair asked. 'I think you've missed out part of the story there.'

His friend did not appear to have heard him. He was utterly captivated by the gem. Spangles of blue and red and gold danced across his face.

'Darin? *Darin!*'

'Mmm?'

'Tell me the rest of the story.'

'Oh, sorry, I got distracted.'

'Not surprising, with ten thousand acres-worth sitting in your hand.' Gair waited for his friend to continue, but Darin was enthralled by the stone again. He rapped on the desk. 'Wake up and tell me the rest.'

'What? Oh, yes, sorry, so no, it's not ten thousand acres-worth, it's just crystal.'

'Crystal? Are you sure? It looks real enough to me.' Certainly the stone had all the flash and fire of a diamond, although Gair had only a memory of his foster-mother's earrings for a guide.

'I met a man at the assayer's office in Pensaeca. He told me.'

'You've had it assayed?'

'No, the man did. That's how he knew it was crystal.'

'You're not explaining this very well, Darin.'

'Sorry, sorry, I just can't quite believe it. It's so beautiful.' 'It's certainly turned your head around – and I thought it was

200

only girls with long braids that did that. Will you put the blessed thing away and tell me the whole story before I wring your neck like a dishrag?'

Absently Darin dug in his pocket and pulled out a small purple velvet pouch. He loosened the drawstrings, but instead of tipping the stone inside, he became caught up in admiring it once more.

Gair growled.

'All right, don't get grumpy with me. I'm just looking,'

'Darin, I hate to hear a tale half told – it drives me crazy, not knowing the end. I used to stay up all night reading because I couldn't bear to put a book down before it was finished. Now for the love of the saints––' Gair reached for the pouch.

Quick as a blink Darin snatched back his hand. 'It's mine!'

Hands held up conciliatorily, Gair sat back in his chair.

Darin dropped the stone into its little bag and yanked the strings tight, glowering. He tucked the pouch back into his pocket.

'So are you going to tell me how you came by this treasure?' Gair asked.

As quickly as he had become sullen, Darin's expression softened. 'Sorry, Gair, I didn't mean to be rude. I'm just so excited. Nothing like this ever happens to me. My oldest brother, if he fell in a river he'd climb out with a salmon in each pocket. Me, if I fell in I'd drown.'

'Can't you swim?'

'No – but that's not the point! You know very well what I mean!' Frowning, Darin seized his head in both hands. 'What was I saying? Oh, yes. I was in Pensaeca Port, walking through the market, when a man came out of the assayer's office. This little velvet bag fell out of his pocket as he put his money away.' The pouch was back in his hand and he spun it round and round by the strings looped around his finger. 'I ran after him to give it back. He told me the assayer had just said it was only crystal and I could keep it for my honesty in bringing it to him. "It'll make a pretty keepsake for your sweetheart," he said. Do you think she'd like it?'

'Renna? She's your sweetheart, not mine.'

'I was thinking I could save up and get it made into a ring for her St Winifrae's gift. Girls adore jewellery, don't they?'

'I've spent ten years in a cloistered Order, Darin – I am the last person you should be asking for advice about women.' Gair smiled. 'I know one thing, though. If you put that stone on a gold band it's going to look an awful lot like a betrothal ring.'

Darin caught the whirling pouch in his hand and looked down at it, fingering the plush fabric. 'Well, we have been walking out for a year now,' he said. Brown eyes flicked up, boyish, hopeful. 'Do you think she'd say yes?'

'Go ask her and find out.'

'Gair!' the Belisthan wailed, and Gair laughed.

'I'm sure she'd be thrilled.'

'You really think so?'

'Really.'

Tucking the gem back into his pocket, Darin finally sat down and studied the chessboard. 'Is it my move?'

'You're playing white.'

Hand hesitating over one of the pawns, he chewed at his lip. 'Actually, Gair, there's something I'd like to ask you. Will you stand for me as my second? If she says yes?'

Startlement gave way to sheer delight. Gair held out his hand. 'I'd be honoured.'

'I could ask my brothers, of course, but they're all way over there at home. You're here, and you're my friend, and, well—' Darin finally moved his pawn, then looked up to see Gair's hand, still held out towards him, unshaken. 'Oh, you will? Thank you so much! Just promise me you'll keep a hold on my coat so I don't fall over if I faint.'

'I promise.' Gair shook his hand. To be asked to stand for a man on his wedding day was an honour, and doubly so to be chosen over family. *A man's friends make the best family*, Alderan had once said. The words left an aching knot inside him that he shied away from examining too closely. He reached for a pawn and made his own opening move.

'You won't say anything to Renna, will you?' asked Darin, responding. 'I want to keep it as a surprise.'

'I'll not breathe a word.'

'I knew I could count on you to keep it a secret. I'll never forget this, Gair. You're a true friend.'

Darin's hand dropped to his trouser pocket and touched the shape of the stone, whilst the other sent his lector out into the field in a bold assault. Gair frowned over his own pieces and settled down to what looked as if it would develop into another tough game.

❧

He'd left it too late. Now the gates were shut and it was starting to rain, damn it. Smacking the flat of his hand on the stout tarred wood in frustration, Darin stepped back and cocked his hands on his hips. How was he going to get back in now? That wind had an edge to it that sliced straight through his fast-dampening clothes, making him shiver. If he had had an ounce of sense in his head, he would have brought a coat.

Well, he could either stand there getting wetter with every minute or he could walk the walls and see if there was another way in. So, left or right? Left would be best; he might find some-place where he could scale the kitchen garden wall, drop down onto the compost heap for a soft landing, and then slip back inside. His boots were already muddy; a few potato peelings couldn't make them any worse.

It was his own fault, really – he should not have stayed so long. Somehow there was always one more thing to talk about, and the conversation was so enthralling that he'd lost all track of time, never even heard the bell ring out the hour. Now it was past Second and he should have been abed hours ago. He was going to be so tired in the morning.

Blast it, the rain was getting heavier. Darin turned up his collar and jogged through the woods at the perimeter of the property. The trees provided some shelter, but they also provided fat drops that dripped from the branches straight onto his head. Now he was starting to feel cold, and he hated the cold. He definitely should have brought a coat.

Unfortunately, the kitchen wall was a few inches too tall. Darin tried to jump up, and missed three times, not even able to get his fingertips over the top. His hands slipped on the wet stone and he barked his palms on the way back down. He sucked on the bloodiest graze to try to take away the sting. Not the kitchen wall, then. Where else could he try? Of course: the leper's gate, behind the chapel, where the unfortunates had come to be shriven, out of sight of the rest of the congregation. Under Church law, a leper's gate could never be locked, except in times of direst emergency, for the blessing of Eador could not be denied to even the most pitiful and pestilential of Her flock.

Happier now, Darin set a brisk pace through the darkness round to the chapel on the east side, running his fingertips along the wall beside him to keep from straying too far into the woods. Rain was falling fast by the time he glimpsed the chapel windows, dark except for the glowing coal of the sanctuary lamp, and there was the gate, an unadorned wooden thing barely higher than his shoulders. He felt its edge for the latch. Nothing. Anxiety speeding his fingers, he tried again, feeling all around the edge from the hinge-straps to the sodden grass at the foot, but he couldn't feel a latch. How was he going to get in now?

Darin's heart began to knock against his ribs, beating a counter-point to the cold rain drumming on his head and down the back of his neck. How could he open the door? If he pounded long and hard Father Verenas might hear him, and perhaps he'd be charitable enough to leave his bed to find out the cause of it, but that would mean someone knew he was stuck outside in the rain because he couldn't bring himself to say good night to his new

204

friend. That was no good at all. There must be a latch or something, or how else could the lepers have come for their absolution?

Ha. Lepers! Honestly, why didn't he think of that before? Darin began sweeping his hands back and forth across the blackened wood, trusting touch rather than his eyes. Lepers might not have fingers, so a conventional latch would be beyond them. It'd have to be a very simple mechanism, one that could be operated without much dexterity. His hand bumped something that swung away from him; he caught it on the backswing. A mechanism that could be operated without the need for any limbs at all. In a pinch, just teeth would do.

Grinning, Darin pulled on the rope and heard the clunk of the wooden latch on the inside. Then he put his shoulder to the gate and eased it open. The hinges had been kept greased so there was barely a sound heard above the patter of the rain in the yard. He closed the gate behind him, lowering the latch back into place, then crept off to his bed with purpose fizzing like fireworks in his brain.

ை

Two days south of Fleet, the rain began. By the time Masen changed ships at Mesarild, there hadn't been a break in the clouds for a week and the Great River was a turbid brown with flood-water. Yelda came and went through a series of shimmering silver veils that swept across the sodden landscape under louring skies. Further south, the river broke its banks, inundating the fields and pastures on either side. Dripping livestock huddled in water up to their knees. Uprooted trees rolled ponderously in the current, forcing the bargee to reduce sail and slow the pace to a crawl, for fear of ramming one of them. In the villages, Masen saw more than one family being rescued from their upstairs windows by neighbours in boats.

By the time the river reached the outskirts of the Havens, whole villages stood empty. Nothing moved but flotsam on the flood.

The only animals in the fields were corpses, bloated black in death. Not even carrion-birds remained, their prodigious appetites finally sated. Foetid brown water stretched from horizon to horizon, and still the rain fell.

Masen wrapped his cloak more tightly around his shoulders and stared out over the bow. The cloak made little difference. Stout Belisthan wool could withstand most weather, but not the downpour it had endured on the journey south. He was already damp through to his smallclothes; even his boots were leaking, and if there was one thing he loathed, loathed even more than spinach greens, it was wearing wet socks.

He was in a foul mood. He'd tried to hail the Order's agent in Fleet, but with no trace of their colours anywhere within ten miles of the city, he'd taken the next trade barge south, reasoning that he could just as easily make contact with the Mesarild agent instead. After all, the capital was only three days further downriver by boat. Except in Mesarild the safe house had burned to the ground. Masen had found the housekeeper disconsolately picking over the sodden ashes. She'd gone to visit her sister, she'd told him. When she'd returned the next day, this was what she'd found. Oh the poor master, and his wife! And the lovely children — so sad, so very sad!

Well, house fires happened, didn't they? Someone left a candle lit with a window open, the curtain knocked the candle over, then smoke blackened the sky. Masen scowled at the water. How very unfortunate that it should have been that particular house, on that particular street. He'd had a decision to make then: hire a horse and go out to the nearest town with an agent, two days' ride east, or push on south to Yelda. Yelda seemed to be the logical choice; the Syfrian capital was the crossroads of the Empire, a hub for trade, and half a day west of it there was a certain quietly prosperous manor house which found a lot of work for farm-hands and domestics but otherwise attracted no attention from its neighbours. How strange, then, that Squire Matterson, his family and his entire staff and tenantry should have been struck down by breakbone fever at the harvest festival. The whole village had been in mourning, according to the mayor. The Squire was well liked in those parts, very well liked. It was such a shame.

A less suspicious man than Masen would have seen only tragic coincidence. One agent missing, a house fire, an outbreak of sickness: all so very, very sad; all about as much of a coincidence as the ground getting wet when it rained. Murder had been done there, and in Mesarild as well; he'd stake his stones on it. Probably in Fleet too, and he had an unpleasant crawling sensation at the base of his spine that said he'd find a similar story in the White Havens.

Not for the first time, Masen wished he had a stronger talent for hailing. The task of Gatekeeper was a solitary one at the best of times, and that suited him; he did not need to be at the centre of a network of agents like a spider on its web, feet outstretched to catch the slightest vibration. It had been enough to know that there were others he could call upon, should he need them, with a few days' riding at worst. That was no real hardship; his arse was surely accustomed to the saddle. Now he wished he had not put off training an apprentice. If he hadn't, he might not be having to make this journey, and the Order could have been warned weeks ago.

The northside docks were eerily quiet. Only a few barges and river-craft were moored there, and better than half of those were listing, with broken masts and splintered timbers. The stevedores on the dockside were busy shovelling a thick layer of mud from the quay, and the waterside stores and taverns were stained dark to halfway up their ground-floor windows.

The bargee pulled his kerchief down from his nose. 'Be lucky to find a ship now,' he said, easing the tiller to pass a half-submerged oak tree. 'Doubt there's a seaworthy hull left in the whole of Haven-port.'

'I'll find something,' Masen sighed. 'Damn it, I'll build a raft if I have to.'

'Plenty of lumber to be had, so long as you don't mind it green!' Cackling, the bargee adjusted his kerchief again.

Masen doubted it did much to cut the stench, a mix of stagnant pond and open grave. After two days he had more or less stopped noticing it, but he suspected it would take a week of hot baths and burning every stitch he wore before he would feel clean again.

A murky twilight descended as the barge tied up at a near-deserted wharf in the glovers' quarter. Masen was generous when he paid for his passage; there would be little enough profit for the bargee on this trip. Then he shouldered his pack and crossed the sodden boards to the Scarlet Feather. Lit cressets either side of the door said the tavern was open for business, despite the two-foot-high band of grime across the plaster, but the tables inside were mostly empty.

The landlord barely glanced up from an old broadsheet on the counter when he heard footsteps. 'Cellar's flooded. What you see behind me is all I have.'

'Brandy then, and a bed for the night if you have one. What happened here? A little late in the year for a storm, eh?'

The landlord grunted. 'Had nothing but storms for the last month,' he said as he poured. 'One after another, straight in off the sea. Rain, floods, hundred square miles of good pastureland turned to swamp. Southern Syfria will go hungry this winter, if the water-fever doesn't carry us all off first.'

Masen pushed a shilling across the counter, then followed it with another. 'Pour for yourself as well, goodman, whatever best pleases your throat. I was hoping to find a ship that could take me further west.'

'Be lucky if you do.' The landlord poured himself a brandy and threw it straight down his gullet. 'Most of the merchantmen let slip for deeper waters as soon as the first storm drew in. Those that didn't foundered on the surge. We're on high ground here, missed the worst of it, but I hear it travelled eighteen miles upriver.'

Masen sipped his drink. The brandy was no goldwine, but it was passable, and potent enough to start warming him from the inside despite his sodden clothes. 'I saw flooding as far north as Yelda,' he said, flicking another pair of shillings onto the counter. 'Syfria's been hit hard.'

'Aye, that she has, but she'll rise again, just like she always does. Can't build a city with its feet in the water just to cry when they get wet.'

The measures the landlord poured this time around were more than healthy. He saluted Masen with his glass and drained it in two swallows. 'Room won't be much. I've given my best to those who've lost their homes. It's up in the attic, but it's dry.'

'That's more than enough for my needs, thank you.'

'I'll see about finding you something hot to eat.' The landlord flicked his glass-cloth over his shoulder and disappeared into the back room.

Masen frowned unseeing at the broadsheet. No ships. Not what he needed to hear. No agents upriver, and now no ships. The roads out of the Havens would be impassable too, either under water, or so mud-choked not even the redoubtable Brea would have been able to wade her way through. Just as well that he'd left her at a livery stable in Fleet, though Goddess only knew when he would be able to fetch her.

No, a ship or a boat of some kind was the only way he could carry his news further west. This part of Syfria was low-lying, barely a span or two above the high-water mark; what the landlord called high ground was merely twenty, twenty-five feet above the sea. The city itself was built on a network of canals that connected the many mouths of the Great River and a goodly portion of its population made their living ferrying passengers from one side to the other. Surely he would find someone still plying their trade who could take him down to the docks in the morning? Then he'd have to hope there would be a fisherman or coastal trader who could take him west. Masen hefted his fast-emptying purse. He prayed there would be enough gold left, or he might have to start building that raft after all.

17
LESSONS

&

'Now this is quite a weapon.' Haral held Gair's longsword across his open palms so that the other students gathered around could see it.

There were about twenty of them, almost all several years older than Gair. Their whites were worn with hard use, and they leaned on their wasters with a kind of relaxed alertness that said the practice weapons could be snatched back into the air in a heartbeat.

'Thirty inches of good Yelda steel, double edge, two-handed grip in the Leahn style. Fine craftsmanship. Well used, but well tended too; a credit to its keeper. Now, some of you will be thinking that it's not much to look at, yes? Because it hasn't got gilding and jewels crusted all over it? On a battlefield, jewels are just extra weight, and a battlefield is what this sword was made for.'

Taking hold of the hilt, Haral hefted the sword expertly. 'Balance is good, a shade on the heavy side, but that's what gives it stopping power. This will halt a charging horse in its tracks, take the head off a lance and shear into plate armour. That is its function. This blade, gentlemen, is not for duelling, or parting silk handkerchiefs in the air to impress the ladies, Sorchal din Urse, don't think I don't know what you get up to in the Red Dragon of an evening.'

Some of the students chuckled and a swarthy splinter of a man standing behind the weapons-master acknowledged the laughter with a florid bow.

'No, this blade is not for any of those things. It has one function and one alone, and that is to chop an enemy into dogmeat as efficiently as possible.' Haral turned to Gair and offered him the hilt. 'Show us what you've learned from the Knights.'

Sword in hand, Gair moved a few paces to his right, away from the group of watching students. Haral fetched a similar weapon from the armoury and joined him as Gair set his feet comfortably apart, letting himself relax until his muscles seemed to flow and a sense of calm settled on his mind. Automatically he brought the longsword to the salute, then returned it to the advance guard. Selenas would have been proud of him.

Haral returned the salute, took up his stance and then suddenly lunged. Gair swept the blade round and away and returned the compliment, forcing the weapons-master to block him. Steel rang on steel as, alternately attacking and parrying, they began to circle.

Gair realised almost immediately that Haral was as good a swordsman as Selenas, and possibly a better tactician, trying to force him round to face the sun, a ploy which the Master of Swords would have declared beneath the honour of a Knight. Gair let him push a little further, then as Haral lunged he sidestepped and brought the longsword crashing down in a two-handed blow that should have broken the weapons-master's grip. Haral winced but held on, wheeling to scrape his sword out from under Gair's. Sparks showered onto the dry earth.

The stocky Syfrian grinned. 'Well done! I see you know the classical forms. Now let's see how well you can string them together.'

With that he launched another assault, swinging his heavy longsword with the power of a smith and the deft control of a duellist. Gair could have been back in the yard at the Mother-house. Though Haral was as different in appearance to Selenas as a

212

side of beef was to a strip of boiled leather, they had the same absolute confidence, the same perfect awareness of body and blade.

Gair could parry, but he had few chances to counter-attack and when he did Haral apparently read his mind. He held his own, but that was all.

Gritting his teeth, Gair pressed his attack harder and managed to gain a yard or two, but he could not hold it. The older man's experience was beginning to tell. A last attempt slid harmlessly aside, then Haral put up his sword and stepped back. Breathing hard, Gair did likewise.

'Not bad, not bad at all. Could almost be one of my own students.'

That gathered a few smiles from the rest of the class and one disdainful look from a tall, too-handsome youth with the dark colouring of a Tylan. Gair wondered if the Tylan was one of the ones grown lazy with the lack of a good match.

'Gair was trained at the Suvaeon Motherhouse, in the Holy City of Dremen,' Haral said, addressing the group again. 'Taught differently to you, but no less thoroughly. You may learn something from each other. Now pair off and show me how much you remember from last week. Gair, work with Arlin there.'

So Arlin was the Tylan. Gair extended his hand. 'Pleased to meet you,' he said, but Arlin simply picked up his waster and walked away, swishing it in circles to either side as he found a clear space amongst the pairs of students. Gair sheathed his longsword and propped it on the armoury steps, out of the way. There hadn't been any call to be rude, but perhaps that was just Arlin's way. Nonetheless he took his time selecting a waster of his own from the rack outside the armoury, sighting along each bruised and splintered wooden sword in turn until he found one that was still reasonably straight.

Out of the corner of his eye he saw Arlin standing with his weight casually on one hip, but he slashed the air with his weapon, left and right like the tail of a balked cat. Gair did not let himself be hurried. After exercising with a real blade the waster seemed oddly light despite being weighted; he swung it a few times to get the heft of it. Arlin sighed theatrically at being made to wait. *Let him.* Gair rolled his neck and shoulders and sighted down the weapon again. *Two can play.*

'When you're ready,' the Tylan murmured as Gair walked out to join him.

'I'm ready if you are.'

He saluted the way he'd been taught and set his feet. Arlin didn't return the gesture, nor did he appear to be interested in sparring, until he launched himself forward, weapon arcing down. Wood met wood with a sharp crack. The impact jolted Gair's wrists, though he moved quickly enough to parry and escape the worst of it. Fresh splinters appeared on the waster in his hands.

'You said you were ready. If you're the best the Church can turn out, I fear for the Suvaeon's future.'

Gair bit down on a retort. Letting his emotions rule him was a sure way to lose. Adjusting his grip, he waited. The second attack was not long in coming, but he was better prepared. The practice swords clashed once, twice, then paused a beat before Arlin rained a flurry of blows in Gair's direction. For a few crowded seconds he could do nothing but defend. His opponent was good, very good; light on his feet, and quick as a whip. But would Arlin be as quick with four pounds of steel in his hand instead of a piece of wood? As they circled warily, trading occasional blows as each sought out a weakness in the other, Gair had a suspicion that he would.

'I thought you were going to show us some swordcraft, church-ling, not dance steps.' Arlin's tone was mocking.

'Sorry, I mistook you for a girl.' As soon as the words were out of his mouth Gair wished he'd stuck to his resolve and said nothing.

Arlin's eyes widened, then his face turned as flat as dressed granite. He took two careful steps to his right then swung in fast and hard. Gair blocked the blow high then had to block again wrong-footed as the deflection became a whistling roundhouse slash that would have opened him to the breastbone with a real blade. Undeterred, Arlin pressed in close. Parrying again and again, Gair got his weight back over his front foot. That made it easier to soak up the force of the Tylan's attack; after a few seconds he could press an attack of his own.

Arlin gave ground reluctantly, then they broke apart to circle again.

Gair was sweating freely. Without taking his eyes off his opponent for a second, he shifted the waster from one hand to the other so he could wipe his palms on his whites. Arlin took the opportunity to attack. Gair swung his weapon high to block. The impact of the blow jarred, but he turned his wrists neatly, twisting the practice sword away and stepping forward into the space. His own attack was repulsed with a series of rapid counter-blows, the wasters rapping together so fast they blurred.

For the better part of an hour, neither of them could hold the upper hand in their duel for more than a few seconds. Gair had a height advantage and a longer reach, but Arlin had speed and suppleness to spare, and damn him, but he wasn't tiring – unlike Gair, who could feel fatigue in the burn in his muscles, the growing heaviness of his limbs. He would have to make an end to this quickly.

'Had enough yet, Church boy?' Arlin asked, earning himself a warning scowl from Haral, who prowled the perimeter of their contest with a quarterstaff.

Gair gritted his teeth. 'Don't think so. How about you?' He lunged in again, feinting towards Arlin's left side. The Tylan had a tendency to lead to his left and leave his flank slightly exposed, but he was so quick with a riposte that Gair had rarely managed to penetrate his guard on that side. Even then he'd only succeeded by putting the full weight of his upper body behind the weapon. That

215

tactic couldn't work for long. Now it was time to see if he could accomplish it with guile as well.

Though Arlin's defence remained as quick as ever, his weapon swished harmlessly through empty air as Gair ducked and stamped forward, the blunt wood jabbing squarely into his opponent's midriff.

Arlin's expression flickered briefly to dismay and he hissed a curse.

'Well done.' Haral thumped the earth with the heel of his staff to acknowledge the contact. 'A point to you, Gair.'

Arlin gave no sign that he had heard. He swiped his sleeve over his glistening face and then wiped his palms, all the while fixing Gair with a gaze as unblinking as a snake's. He settled back into position, ignoring the formal salute, and almost immediately struck hard.

Wrong-footed again, Gair defended until he could get his feet under him and mount some kind of coherent counter-attack. Arlin still showed no sign of fatigue, whereas his own shoulders were on fire with exertion. He fell back on Selenas' teachings, using the classical defences, until the furious energy of Arlin's attack faltered. Then Gair lunged to exploit the opening. He was rewarded with a clout on the side of his head that sent him sprawling.

For a second or two Gair's skull rang like the Sacristy bell at All Hallows. When he touched his temple his fingers came away bloody. Distantly he was aware of Haral's rumbling bass congratulating Arlin on recovering the point and cautioning him to be careful of a fellow student's eyes, but all he could see was scarlet on his fingers. His limbs had no strength; only the sturdy waster jammed into the earth kept him from falling over.

A hand touched his shoulder.

'Are you all right, Gair?' Haral asked.

He nodded, and immediately wished he hadn't when his stomach threatened to part company with his breakfast. When it steadied again he levered himself back to his feet. Blood trickled down his neck. Bunching up his tunic he dabbed at his stinging face.

Haral's horny hands grasped his head and turned it into the light so he could examine it.

Over the weapons-master's shoulder, Arlin smirked.

'You'll not need stitching, but I think you should see a Healer,' Haral said, releasing him. 'You'll have a fair headache come morning.'

Another headache. Wonderful.

'One more point,' Gair said.

'What?'

'I want to fight one more point, Master Haral.'

The Syfrian frowned. 'There is no place here for revenge, Gair.'

'One point, to settle the match. That's all.'

'And then you'll go to the infirmary?'

'My word on it.'

'If you're sure about this, I'll let it go to one more point. But no more, you hear?' he said, levelling a finger at Gair.

'Yes, Master Haral.'

Grunting, Haral retrieved his staff. 'Final point, gentlemen,' he declared. 'Then it will be time to stop.'

Arlin looked surprised, his lips already shaping a protest. Taking station opposite, Gair tugged his bloody tunic off over his head and threw it aside. It stuck to him, dragged at his skin; he could move more freely without it. As he set himself at the guard, he saw movement in his peripheral vision. The other students had stopped exercising and formed a loose ring around the two of them to watch. Sorchal, wrists rested casually on the waster across the back of his neck, caught Gair's eye and tipped his head in salute.

Arlin had noticed the spectators too. He shrugged at them, as if it was all the same to him whether Gair wanted to take another beating, and took up position.

The first few strikes Gair turned aside without any attempt at a counter. He wanted to know how tired Arlin was, but it was difficult to guess. His head felt so bloated and strange that time itself dragged. Blood running from his hairline tickled the corner of his eye; he had to wipe it on his shoulder to keep his vision clear.

Arlin feinted quickly, closing in like a hawk on a sparrow. Wasters cracked together, scraped round and broke free. Gair recovered quickly enough to step in with an attack. Arlin parried, but gave ground. Gair pressed home his advantage, using his longer reach to probe Arlin's defences. Again the Tylan led left but feinted right; Gair struck hard, forcing a clumsy parry. Whilst Arlin was off-balance, he struck again and again, driving him onto his back foot, then into taking a half-step backwards. Wood crashed on wood, punctuated with the scuffle of feet and grunts of effort. A flicker of uncertainty crossed Arlin's face. His counters became less sure as crashing blows numbed his wrists and forced him to give more and more ground.

A fierce exultation grew inside Gair. He hardly had to think about his thrusts and slashes now; they were as automatic as if the battered wooden sword in his hands was an extension of his arms. The blood at the corner of his eye became no more than a minor annoyance, one he could ignore. His whole consciousness was focused on compelling Arlin to make a mistake. Gair feinted left and right, and Arlin brought his weapon round to parry, but he was too high. Gair swung in, two-handed, and the weighted wood thumped against the Tylan's side.

Arlin's breath whooshed out of him and he folded round the weapon like a sack of meal. He hit his knees but managed to catch himself with one arm; his other hand clutched his ribs as his breath came in hoarse whoops.

For just a few seconds, Gair felt only exultation. The match was his. Then the reality hit him. Flinging his weapon aside, he dropped to his knees next to Arlin, but the Tylan snarled a curse and shoved him away, then sobbed again, hugging the pain in his chest.

'Let me see, lad, let me see.' Haral was there, carefully lifting Arlin's tunic to lay a hand on his ribs. Arlin cried and swore again.

Letting the tunic fall, Haral rocked back on his heels.

'I think there're a couple of ribs broken, so we'd best let Saaron take a look at you,' he said. 'Gair, go with him.'

'No!' Arlin shrugged away Haral's proffered arm and struggled to his feet, glaring.

'Nonsense, boy,' said the weapons-master. 'You're grey as gruel! Saaron will never forgive me if you faint in the corridor and fetch yourself a broken head.' He held up a hand as Arlin began to protest. 'Don't argue. Just go to the infirmary with Gair. You've done enough damage to each other for one day.'

Shoulders hunched around the pain, Arlin made his way to the steps up from the yard.

Gair followed a couple of paces behind. As they turned into the infirmary cloister, he ventured an apology. 'I'm sorry, Arlin. I wasn't aiming to hurt you.'

Well, maybe a little bit. Mainly he'd wanted to win.

Ahead Arlin stumped on, giving no indication that he had heard.

Gair sighed. At least he'd tried. He dabbed cautiously at his face with his tunic. The bleeding had lessened, but it still hurt. He could only imagine how it looked.

At the infirmary Arlin tugged the bell-rope, then fumbled the door open, leaving Gair, following behind, to fend it off with his arm as it swung back in his face.

He closed it quietly behind him. The waiting room was empty. Across the room the surgery door stood ajar, but Gair saw no one inside. 'Saaron can't be far away,' he said. 'I'll fetch him.'

Arlin glowered and eased himself down onto a bench, one hand held to his injured ribs.

Gair stepped into the surgery. Yellow blinds covered the large skylights and came halfway down the windows. The tiled walls were damp, as was the large surgery table, as if someone had recently scrubbed the place down, but of Saaron there was no sign. He was about to leave to try the Healer's study next door when he heard footsteps. The door opposite was pulled open by a slender young woman in a green Healer's mantle.

'I thought I heard the bell,' she said. 'I was in the dispensary. Can I help you?'

'I'm looking for Saaron.'

'I'm afraid he's not here. There's spotted fever in Pencruik; he's gone down to help.' She put down the clay jar she carried and raised the blinds, letting sunlight fill the surgery. 'What happened to your face?'

'I got hit with a practice sword.'

'You're one of Master Haral's students?'

Gair nodded. The girl looped the blind cords around their hook and came towards him. Close to, he saw that she was Astolan. Her red hair was tied in a thick braid over her shoulder, but little curly wisps had come free to form a halo around a fine-boned, golden-skinned face. Large, tawny eyes slanted up at the corners, like a cat's. She took hold of his chin and tilted his face towards the light.

'It looks superficial,' she said. 'Hop up on that stool and I'll clean it for you.'

'I think you should see Arlin first,' Gair said. 'Master Haral thinks he might have broken ribs.'

The Astolan girl's brows arched. 'Was he the one who hit you, by any chance?'

'Yes.'

She rolled her eyes.

Arlin cursed and yelped his way onto the surgery table, where the Healer deftly sliced open his tunic with a scalpel. An angry welt across his ribs was already staining purple-black, and his breathing sounded shallow and tight.

'Ouch,' she said and laid her hand over the welt.

Gair sensed her call the Song, although the tone of it was unlike anything he had ever felt before. The hairs on his arms stood up, as if they'd been stroked with a feather. She closed her eyes and moved her palm back and forth across Arlin's ribs, almost as if she were listening to his injury. Without thinking, he strained to hear what she heard, and at once the Song leapt up inside him.

She looked back over her shoulder. 'Do you mind?'

'Sorry.' Hurriedly he checked the Song, and she turned back to her work.

Her concentration now was absolute, her face utterly still and her awareness elsewhere. After some minutes she straightened up, the Song quieting within her. 'Well, Master Haral was right. One rib fractured cleanly, one that's just cracked. What did he hit you with, a tree?' She gave Arlin a smile. The Tylan turned his head away without speaking and her smile faded. Her glance flickered across to Gair. 'I'll start it healing, but I'm afraid I can't discharge you until Saaron has examined you. He should be back first thing tomorrow.'

Again Arlin said nothing. The Healer laid her hands over his ribs and called the Song once more.

Gair wanted to watch what she was doing, but he made himself resist the pull of her power, looking out of the window instead, at a couple of novices who were weeding the herb garden whilst a green-mantled adept moved along the rows snipping seed-heads into a linen bag. Behind him, the Song's rhythmic pulse became slow and somnolent. When it stopped, he turned round.

Arlin's head was lolling.

'Is he asleep?' Gair asked.

The Healer nodded. 'It often happens like that. It's a side-effect of the healing process.' She gestured to the stool. 'Why don't you sit down so I can clean that graze?'

With the briskness of long practice she fetched a basin of water, some swabs and a bottle from the shelves that lined the wall. She poured a splash of the bottle's contents into the basin and swirled it around with her fingers. With a swab soaked in the solution, she bathed away the crust of blood from Gair's temple and cheekbone.

'Now then,' she said as she worked, 'are you going to tell me what happened, or do I have to drag it out of you?'

'What do you mean?' Gair asked, although he suspected he knew. The solution stung his abraded skin, making him grimace.

'I mean, he's got two fractured ribs and you've had your face laid open. That's a little more than horseplay.'

'Arlin doesn't appear to like me very much.'

'That much is obvious.'

'Master Haral paired us off to practise together, and when I won the first point he didn't take it well. Things started to deteriorate after that.'

'He hit you, so you hit him, yes. I understand.'

'I didn't mean to hurt him.'

The Healer's tawny gaze flicked over his shoulders and arms, then she raised one eyebrow a fraction, encompassing in that tiny gesture her professional assessment of just how hard he could strike if he chose.

Shame squirmed inside him. 'I let my temper get the better of me,' he admitted.

'Were you provoked?'

'A little.'

'Then I think it's honours even.' She discarded the soiled swab and used a fresh one to pat the wound dry.

Gair yelped at a sudden sharp pain.

'There must be a splinter in it. Let me see.'

The Healer fetched tweezers from a drawer and bent close, holding the skin taut with the fingers of her free hand. Gair tried not to flinch, but the wound was tender and the tweezers were cold. Carefully she drew out two slivers of wood, depositing them on a swab. Then she cleansed and dried the area again.

'That should help it heal,' she told him. From the dispensary she fetched a twist of paper and handed it to him. 'Here. I think you might need this.'

'What is it?'

'A powder for the headache you're going to have later.'

He touched the tender swelling. 'Is it bad?'

'You'll be a picture tomorrow.' She smiled. 'Mix the powder in a cup of water and drink it straight down. It doesn't taste very good, I'm afraid.'

'Few medicines do, in my experience.'

'Then this one will be no disappointment. I'm Tanith, by the way.'

'I'm Gair.'

'From the Holy City, yes. Your reputation precedes you. May I?' She took his left hand and turned it over. Cool fingers examined the brand; the merest thread of the Song tickled him and was gone. 'I wish they wouldn't do this. So much damage, and for what?'

'I think the Church feels my sin is severe enough to be marked prominently.'

'It's barbaric. You're lucky it's healed as well as it has.'

'Alderan did the best he could with the supplies he had.'

'Saaron and I keep his scrip well stocked. It's just a pity he didn't have room in it for a Healer too, or you'd have been spared most of this scarring.'

Gair shrugged. 'If wishes were crowns we could all be rich,' he said. 'Thank you for the powder, and for treating this.' He gestured to his face.

'You're welcome. Next time, I suggest you duck.'

18

NOW WE HUNT

ભ

Gair took a detour to the bath-house to clean up before he went back to his room. The looking-glass in the changing room showed him a large bruise forming by his right eye, with a raw red welt in the middle where the skin had been flayed away. He felt around the edges of the swelling cautiously. He feared Tanith was right; by morning his face would be purple from cheekbone to hairline.

He washed and changed back into his everyday clothes, then climbed the stairs to his room with his bloody whites bundled under his arm. When he arrived he found Darin perched cross-legged on his desk next to a stack of neatly folded laundry.

Darin opened his mouth to speak and Gair held up his hand. 'Don't ask,' he said. 'I don't want to talk about it, I just want to take this powder and make the pain go away.' He dropped his whites on the chest at the foot of the bed. He emptied the powder into a beaker, added some water from the jug on the night table then took a mouthful.

It was so bitter he almost spat it straight out again. 'Goddess in glory!'

'Hold your breath,' Darin advised. 'You don't taste it that way.'

'I was holding my breath.' Gair grimaced into the cup. The powder was even more bitter than athalin, if that was possible. He bolted the stuff down and chased it with another beaker of water to try to rinse the grittiness away. That did not help much either.

Darin solemnly offered him a tin box. 'Fudge?'

'Thank you. That stuff was *awful*.'

Chewing the sweetmeat, he flopped onto his bed with his back against the wall. 'So. To what do I owe this honour?'

'I was hoping you'd help me with my history assignment for Master Donata.'

'What's the subject?'

'The Battle of River Run. I thought you might know more about it, since you were trained by the Knights.'

'You mean since I had Church history drummed into me for a decade.' Gair kneaded his eyes, then hitched himself more upright and tried to concentrate. 'What do you need?'

'Well, it was one of the last great battles of the Founding. Gwlach brought his entire war-band to face the Knights, out-numbering them more than four to one, yet the Knights won. How did they do it? It shouldn't have been possible.'

Darin was correct; it should have been a rout. Twelve legions of Church Knights against some fifty thousand Nimrothi warriors were impossible odds, even allowing for the Knights' armour, their discipline and the sheer crushing weight of a heavy cavalry charge. The Nimrothi were horsemen born, they should have scythed round the Suvaeon flanks and hamstrung them as cleanly as a wolf-pack bringing down an elk.

Instead the Knights had ground out a victory over fifteen days of the bloodiest fighting ever recorded in the Founding or any other war in the history of the Empire. It had cost Gwlach and many of his chieftains their lives, and broken the clans so utterly that the northern borders of Arennor and Belistha had been secure for a thousand years.

'According to most of the Church historians, it was strength of faith. They carried the bones of St Agostin the Defiant in a casket at the head of the army; maybe that helped.'

'But how did they win? That's what I don't understand.'

'I don't understand it either, I'm afraid.'

'Damn it,' Darin muttered, his brow furrowing under his mop of curls, 'I was counting on you for a good mark.'

'All right. You tell me the exact assignment whilst I put these away, and we'll see what we can figure out.' Gair pushed himself onto his feet and picked up the pile of clean clothes.

A beam lit up Darin's face and he began to ferret through his pockets. 'Thanks, Gair. I've got it written down somewhere. How come you're so neat, anyway? I never saw the point of putting clothes away. They're just going to get crumpled when you wear them, so why worry about hanging anything up?'

'You never had the threat of a birching to encourage you to pick up after yourself. Habits like that are hard to break.'

Without looking up Gair opened his closet and began separating his shirts from the rest of the pile balanced on his arm.

'It's here somewhere – a-ha!' Darin flourished a creased scrap of paper he'd found amongst the pocket-litter now strewn across Gair's desk. Smoothing it with his hands, he read it through. 'She wants an analysis of the background to the battle and its effect on the economic and political stability of the northern provinces over the next hundred years. It's worth twenty marks.'

Gair hardly heard a word. All his attention was focused on the middle shelf of his closet and the neatly folded blue fabric, set just so in the centre.

'What's the matter? Did the laundry starch your smallclothes or something?' Darin poked his head round the edge of the closet door. 'Blood and stones!'

Slowly, Gair set down his other clothes on the shelf. Gut tightening, he lifted up the garment and shook out the folds. Blue wool pooled on the floor at his feet. Once on, he guessed the mantle would reach his ankles.

Darin whistled reverently. 'Try it on,' he urged. 'I bet it fits.'

Gair held it against himself. The length was perfect, just skimming his boot heels. He pulled it on and a square of paper sycamored down to the floor. It had a stiff, expensive feel. The brief note was signed with a single initial in a bold, cursive hand. He held it out for Darin to see.

'A for . . . ? It's not Alderan, he doesn't loop the descender like that,' Darin said.

Gair looked again at the initial. The author favoured a broad-nibbed pen and very black ink, but there was no doubt in his mind that it was a woman's hand.

'Aysha,' he said.

He tucked the note in his pocket and adjusted the hang of the mantle. As far as he could tell, it couldn't have been better cut if he'd gone down to the tailor's shop in person.

Darin simply stared, eyes filled with hopeless envy. 'I think it suits you.'

'Really?'

'Really.'

Aysha had brought this? Gair smoothed the fabric over his chest, wishing he could smooth away the butterflies underneath. So she felt he was ready to be a Master, felt it strongly enough to make the difficult journey up into the dormitories. Certainly his control of his gifts had leapt ahead since those few lessons Alderan had given him on the *Kittiwake*. He was capable of doing so much more now, quite apart from the shape-shifting, though he didn't have the casual skill of the other Masters, or the confidence that came from a lifetime of practice. But to be a Master himself? Surely it was too soon for that. He had been on the Isles barely more than a month, for Goddess' sake.

Gair slipped the mantle off and folded it carefully, then put it on the top shelf, right at the back, behind his winter cloak, where it could keep company with the pouch of silver.

Darin was aghast. 'What are you doing? Why are you putting it away?'

'I haven't earned this yet.'

'But you've been tested!'

'I wasn't raised to Master, though – at least, not so far as I know.' Gair rubbed his forehead. He hoped Tanith's powder started to work soon. The headache had settled in like an un-welcome tenant. 'Actually, I don't know what I am. They still haven't told me.'

'Isn't that what this means?' Darin frowned, puzzled. 'There's usually a presentation from the whole Council, but that's just a formality. You're ready when someone says you're ready, and she's saying you're ready.'

Gair thought about the few words he'd kept his fingers over when he'd shown Darin the note now nestled against his hip and had to breathe deeply to quell a flutter in his belly.

'Somehow I don't think the rest of the Council sanctioned this.'

'You could always ask her – I mean, she was part of the testing, wasn't she? And she's on the Council. Ask her.'

He supposed he could thank her for the gift, but he could not help but wonder why she had chosen to deliver it this way. Why slip it into his closet for him to find? Why not just hand it to him?

'I'm supposed to have a lesson with her tomorrow. I'll see if she mentions it.'

Darin laughed. 'In other words, you're too frit to ask. Not that I blame you, mind; she scares me spitless.'

'She's not that scary,' Gair said absently, leaning back against the closet door. Bewildering, maybe. Opinionated, fiercely inde-pendent, bold. The last time they had flown together she had exulted in her mastery of the air, the Song a huge, soaring swoop in her as she danced around him. She had laughed for the sheer joy of it, the rich sound bubbling into his thoughts, then seized his talons in hers and sent the two of them tumbling through the pellucid mountain air. He remembered her tipping her face up to the sun like a cat on a wall with the wind pressing her loose shirt to her frame—

No. She was supposed to be his teacher. He had no right to be thinking of her in that way. It was entirely inappropriate . . . but now that he'd thought about her, her image would not go away.

Especially those eyes.

'Hello-o,' Darin sang.

Gair blinked.

'You were a mile away. That knock on the head stirred your brains, I reckon.'

'Sorry.' Goddess help him, he had to get a *grip*.

'I still say you should ask her.'

'Mmm. I'll think about it.'

A bell sounded outside, followed by banging doors and hurrying feet.

'Supper!' The Belisthan lunged for the door. 'We'd better be quick, or there'll be none left.'

Gair waved him away. 'You go ahead. I'll catch you up in a bit.'

'Sure?'

He nodded and Darin was off like a terrier after rats. The Belisthan might be led by his stomach, but Gair was too tired and sore to run. He touched his bruised face and winced. Even thinking hard might not be such a good idea.

Slowly he took out the note and read it again. *We make such a pretty pair*, she had written. Only half a dozen words, but taken together they had at least the same number of interpretations. If she'd given him an Arkadian puzzle-box it would have been easier to figure out. He slid the note back into his pocket and walked down to the refectory for a supper he felt too full to eat.

The Master of Novices had always taken a stern line on personal hygiene with the boys and young men in his care. Baths had been frequent, with plenty of soap, but there the similarity with Chapterhouse ended. The Motherhouse baths were housed in a lamplit, dripping cavern beneath the vaulted footings of the dortoir, and contained a large communal pool barely hip-deep on a man and a smaller plunge pool. The former was filled by a sulphurous hot spring, the latter by a stone culvert that fed directly from the River Awen, occasional frogs and all. There was no privacy there for a boy standing uneasily on the borders of man-hood. Gair had quickly grown tall enough to leave the taunts and flicked towels of the other novices behind, but for the younger, skinnier lads, bath time had been a parade of misery until their bodies filled out and furred up.

In contrast, the baths at Chapterhouse occupied a long tiled room well lit by high windows. A double row of sunken baths was fed by a network of verdigrised copper pipes that spread out from a hole in the far wall like tentacles from the monstrous copper boilers in the next room. Each tub was built large enough for four, though there were rarely that many bathers at once. Wooden shelves of towels and washcloths stood at the head of each one, and waist-high partitions divided each bath from its neighbours to provide at least some scope for modesty.

Gair sluiced off the last of the soapsuds and leaned back against the tiles. The hot water was soothing, but nearly an hour of soaking hadn't managed to overcome the aches in his muscles. However he might complain about the other Masters, Aysha worked him no less hard. In the fortnight since she had first summoned him, she had called him another eight or nine times, usually early in the morning, when she could be sure the other Masters hadn't even finished breaking their fast, and he had lost count of the miles they had flown and run across the Isles in shapes other than their own. Today was supposed to be his free day, his first since his arrival, and she'd summoned him whilst he

230

shaved, bursting into his thoughts so suddenly that the razor nearly carved him a second smile.

His bruised face had elicited only a raised eyebrow and a wry enquiry as to whether the other fellow looked as pretty, before they had taken flight for the uplands. Aysha had shown him how to shape a whitejack deer, then laughed when his first efforts made some real deer bound off into the silvery birch trees, tails high in alarm. He had countered with a heavy-antlered red stag from Leah, and bellowed so loudly that it was her turn to take fright. A squirrel-shape had streaked into the nearest tree, from which he had been pelted with spruce cones. Her aim had turned out to be as deadly as her wit and he had a stinging right ear to prove it.

Although the time he spent with Aysha was counted as a tutorial, it could hardly have felt less like a lesson. There was no structure and little formality; what they did depended on how her mood moved her, and sometimes that meant showing him something new. Yet he didn't mind: after hours of rigorous mental discipline in the lecture halls with the other Masters, it was a relief to get out into the air and just be. He'd always preferred outdoors to in, and besides, Aysha was good company. She respected his silences without having to be asked; she seemed to know or sense somehow when he wanted quiet, but when he didn't she challenged and questioned him, threw up her hands at his stubbornness, then made him laugh with her acutely observed mimicry of the rest of the faculty. Her particular target was Godril. She made it her hobby to deflate his ego whenever the opportunity presented, though no one was immune. Recollecting some of her more wicked observations when facing the sandy-haired Master across a lecture hall meant biting the inside of his cheek hard to keep himself from grinning.

Brilliant colours brushed against his thoughts.

You owe me a favour, Leahn, Aysha said in his mind.

Gair looked round the bath-house, but in the middle of the day it was empty of anyone who might send for the infirmarians if they saw him talking to the air.

'Why?'

Eavin was looking for you.

'What for? It's supposed to be my free day.'

As soon as he said it he winced, afraid she might think he was complaining about her demands on his time.

He has novice classes today, and sent one of the students to fetch you. I didn't think you'd be too interested in showing a gaggle of children how to spin a waterspout, so I diverted him.

'Master Eavin won't be pleased.'

Her laugh made him shiver as if he'd felt her breath on his ear. *He's a grown man, he'll get over it. Besides, it's your free day. Come on up.*

'Ah, Master Aysha, I'm in the bath.'

Tempting, but we'll save the fish shapes for another day. Don't be too long.

'Yes, Master Aysha.'

I don't think you need to call me that any more, you know. Just Aysha will do.

'If you're sure? I mean, you are one of my teachers—'

She was smiling now, though he did not know how he knew that – but he could feel it, like sun on his face. For some reason, he flushed.

I'm sure. Now run with me. My feet itch.

Then she was gone, as abruptly as she had appeared. Gair raked his fingers through his wet hair. He could have said no, he supposed, said he was tired or that he had something else to do, but somehow that never occurred to him at the time. Aysha's presence was so vivid, so compelling, it pushed everything else right out of his mind. With a groan he heaved himself onto the edge of the tub and reached for a towel. What the hell, the water was getting cold anyway.

Aysha's balcony was still in shade, but out past Chapterhouse's walls the sun shone and the wind tossed the tops of the trees with a restless hand. Mare's-tail clouds streaked the pale bright sky as if painted on with a brush.

'Wind's changed,' Aysha said. 'Backing round to the north. I think we might have seen the last of summer for this year.'

'I was wondering when winter would get here,' said Gair. 'It feels strange for the weather to still be so mild so late in the year. In Leah we'd be tobogganing by now.'

'Tobogganing? What's that?'

'A toboggan is a sledge – a wooden platform on runners,' he explained, seeing her expression remain blank. He sketched one in the air with a finger. 'You sit on it at the top of a snowy hill, push off with your feet and ride the sledge all the way down to the bottom.'

'And then?'

'You drag it back to the top of the hill and do it over again. It's fun.'

'Sounds cold and wet to me.' She shuddered.

'Does it ever snow here?'

'There's plenty over the mountains, but not lower down, saints be praised. I don't like the cold.' A tingling along his nerves told him she had reached for the Song. 'Come on. North winds always give me the fidgets. Let's go chase some rabbits.'

In seconds Aysha's kestrel shape was darting away down the valley from Chapterhouse and over the orchards of the home farm. Gair followed as a fire-eagle. It really was a glorious day. Autumn as he recognised it had finally arrived and it painted Penglas as vividly as a chapel window. Fiery reds and yellows lit up the lowland forests, and the fields were chequered with pale gold stubble and the brown of ploughed earth. Higher, where the landscape began to fold itself into mountains, the flaming broadleaf woods gave way to steely spruce and evergreens and the air had a tang of frost. Winter was undoubtedly on its way, but the sun on his back said it still had some miles to go.

On the north side of the island, the land was steeper and less forgiving. Neatly terraced fields girdled the slopes with stout fieldstone walls, and sandy-coloured sheep browsed the scrubby grass. Unlike the ones Gair was accustomed to, all thick fleece and slot-eyed skittishness, these were more like goats, with beards and heavy spiral horns, even on the ewes. They suited the rockier terrain, which in its turn suited the fire-eagle. Where expanses of sun-warmed rock gave way to the sudden drops of knife-cut valleys, the chillier breath of the north sculpted the air into a cathedral of glass through which an eagle-shape slid as easily as a prayer.

It was not the only bird Gair could shape. Thanks to Aysha there were nearly a dozen different birds he now knew well, from owls to finches, but in this form he felt most comfortable. It was familiar, well worn-in, like an old pair of boots, and unless instructed otherwise, this was what he always came back to when there was flying to be done.

He watched Aysha up ahead of him. Although she had not mentioned it directly, he knew she'd been alluding to the mantle when she'd said he needn't call her 'Master' any more. It remained at the back of his closet, where it had been since the day he had found it. He hadn't even allowed himself to try it on again, though he had opened his closet doors and almost reached for it once or twice. He knew he ought to thank her for the gift; he'd tried a dozen times to work out ways he could introduce it into the conversation, but no matter how he arranged the words in his head, the speech sounded forced, even when practised in the privacy of his room. And then there was the note — saints, that had even more layers of possible meaning . . .

Abruptly, Aysha peeled off into the valley below. At some time past the earth there had slipped; the ground was strewn with pale bones of fallen trees, all down the scar and piled in a heap at the bottom where the col met the river valley. She swooped down to perch on a rock above a beck. Almost immediately her kestrel transformed into a timber wolf. She sat on her haunches and watched his approach with large amber eyes.

Do you know what to listen for? she asked as he resumed his human form beside her.

'I think so, yes.'

Gair took a moment to catch his breath. This was a new shape; he would need to concentrate. Although he was no longer so afraid that the Song would get away from him and become something destructive, the first few moments after any shape-change were dizzying. Aysha had the knack of flowing from one form to another with barely a break in her stride. He could only dream that he would one day have that much control.

He sifted through the Song. The melody he sought was as elusive as the wolf itself. Wolf-song spoke of crisp snow, and hot breath on a bitter, starlit night. As he let it pour into him, he changed. Limbs shortened and senses sharpened. Muscles shifted into strange new configurations that felt alien at first then became intimately familiar as the shape took hold. Even his thoughts, in that part of him which was wholly wolf, were transformed. Everything he had ever read or learned about wolves, their behaviours and complex societal structures, suddenly made sense. It was all there inside him, written in his bones, as much a part of him as the thick brindled fur.

The she-wolf inspected him critically, pacing around him in a circle.

Good, she said. *But your tail should be a little fuller and your ruff needs to be heavier and your chest deeper, unless you want to be mistaken for a youngling.*

Standing up, Gair concentrated. His shape felt better afterwards, like clothes made to his measurements rather than hand-me-downs to grow into. He shook himself, enjoying the way his pelt

235

moved over him. This felt good, right, somehow, similar to the way he felt as a fire-eagle, only now he had the power not to fly but to run, to leap, to chase, fleet as the breeze, and leaving as little trace of his passing.

Excellent! Aysha's she-wolf stood beside him, alert and grinning.

Now we hunt.

19

CATCH ME
IF YOU CAN

෯

In the spring, when the flower-boxes were in bloom and jewelled every window and roof-garden with brilliant colour, eight days in the Havens was a feast for the eye and the nose. In the aftermath of a storm, when water-sickness stalked the canal-sides and the dead-boats poled their cargo through the foetid night, it was eight days in hell.

Masen lowered the wooden cover over the inn's well and dusted off his hands. Water-Song was not his strongest gift; whilst it was easy enough to give the Scarlet Feather a supply of clean water, it was beyond him to ensure it for a greater part of the city. The water-table was contaminated, and that meant he had to clear the well morning and evening. Before long, he would have to do so three times a day. There were too many unburned dead upriver, too many choked sewers spilling back onto the streets, for his work to be anything other than a delaying action.

'If only it would stop bloody raining,' he muttered. Rainwater could be collected for drinking if the wells failed, but it also prevented the river from returning to its pre-flood level and stopped the roads drying out so food could be transported into the city and travellers could get out.

'Patience, my friend,' said the landlord, tamping tobacco into his pipe-bowl. 'Patience. North winds always bring rain at this time of year.'

'Aye, well, my patience is about exhausted, Darshan. I've a long way still to go and I can't afford to be cooling my heels here.'

'Until the Goddess wills it different, you're stuck here with us. Might as well get used to it.' Darshan shook out his taper and puffed contentedly.

Masen grunted. 'Don't take me amiss, I'm happy to help as much as I can, but I need to be moving. It's imperative I deliver my message as fast as I can.'

'Can't you . . . you know?' Darshan twirled his fingers. The stocky Syfrian had accepted Masen's revelation with more equanimity than most, simply observing that when a nail needed driving, any hammer would suffice.

'No, I'm too far away. Some are better than others at speaking over great distances. Unfortunately, I'm one of the others.'

The innkeeper inspected the glowing pipe-bowl as smoke trickled between his teeth. 'You're not in livery, so you aren't on the Emperor's business. What could be so pressing that doesn't have Theodegrance's seal on it?'

Every day, the same question, or one like it. Darshan, perhaps uniquely amongst barkeeps, was unable to distinguish when to talk and when to polish his glassware in silence. Masen had no wish to be rude, but his temper shortened as his chances of finding a ship before Eventide grew progressively longer.

'My business is my business,' he said, and headed for the kitchen door. 'I'm going down to the docks.'

Ignoring Darshan's call after him, he strode along the wharf to the junction with the Greenwater. The boards squelched under his boots from all the rain, but he didn't have to walk far before he found a skiff idling near the pier, a sodden orange pennon hanging limply in the stern indicating it was for hire. A sharp whistle brought the waterman out of his doze and he poled his craft over to the nearest ladder.

'Deepside docks, please.'

Masen tossed the waterman a coin and climbed down into the skiff. Without a word the man pocketed the fare, struck the little jack-staff holding his pennon and pushed off from the canal-side, poling steadily through the rain-pocked water.

It pained Masen to watch the city drifting past. He had visited the Havens many times over the years, and he had fond recollections of it, from whooping like a child to see the midnight fireworks for All Hallows to dancing until his feet bled on Fools' Night, loving and being loved on linen sheets and silk – and once, memorably, on a priceless antique *qilim* with a flame-haired carpet merchant whilst her guests twittered and drank fine wines in the next room. All his memories of the city, from the grand salons of the Kingswater to the canalside taverns, were of laughter. He had never had memories that stung him to tears.

Despite Darshan's brave words that Syfria would rise again, this part of it at least looked beaten. Every building was sodden to the knees, the thick white stucco already scabrous and crumbling. Many of the warehouses and stores had been torn open, either by looters or hungry people desperate for food. Those that hadn't been ransacked had ruined merchandise piled outside, and dispirited owners leaning on brooms surveying the damage. Masen saw furs, leathers and fine furniture worth thousands simply abandoned on the dockside, too blackened and water-fouled to be of worth even to scavengers.

A few more boats were on the water today. That might have been a sign that Syfria's keen commercial instincts were as yet undamaged, if the craft hadn't been weighed down with hastily tied bundles and dead-eyed children. People were leaving, even though there was nowhere for them to go. The Havens was on its knees.

Storms were common in southern Syfria in the autumn. Why

had this one hit them so hard, lasted so long? He looked at the sky: still the same dull clouds pressing down, the same clammy, waterlogged air, so that he felt as if he was breathing soup. And still the rain fell, warm as tears, streaming down his face, clouds weeping for the destruction the flood had wrought.

The waterman turned his craft deftly to avoid the gilded skeleton of what had once been a pleasure-barge, then swung right onto the Kingswater. Mooring posts tilted drunkenly, their bright paint discoloured and their stylish charges now mostly in flinders. Shattered timbers projected from the murky water like bones from a stock-pot. Even the cormorants that stalked the waterways the way pigeons ruled other cities had vanished. Masen closed his eyes. He could not bear to look any more.

He opened himself to the Song and skimmed through the city's colours looking for a familiar pattern. There were several dozen untapped talents amongst what remained of the populace, but not the shining kaleidoscope he sought. He'd made some discreet enquiries of other innkeepers, and a few of the merchants in the jewellers' quarter, but he'd met with blank stares and shrugs for the most part. No one seemed to know the whereabouts of a silversmith called Orsene, not even the owners of the shops on either side of his. They had found his door kicked in and his workshop ransacked, and the apartment upstairs showed signs of a hasty departure. No one could say when he had last been seen.

At the head of the deepwater docks Masen thanked the boatman and hauled himself up the ladder onto the wharf. Not a single ocean-going hull remained intact. Workmen were moving about on one or two of the least-damaged craft, but their hammering and sawing had a desultory air to it, as if they saw no real point in trying to make repairs. They did not even look up when Masen walked past and onto the longest pier. He had to scramble over smashed timbers and felled masts; tangles of rigging threatened to trip his feet. Broken hulls bumped and groaned on the current but Masen kept walking, out towards the stone pillar at the end of the pier where the western harbour light had once stood. The handsome domed light was smashed, its artfully curled and gabled metalwork now fit only for scrap, but he climbed the rain-slicked steps to the very top and set his back to the stone, staring out to sea.

This was the furthest west he'd managed to reach, and it was still nowhere near far enough. But every day at Tenth he came out here, resolute in his intent to find a ship, anything that could carry him further on his way, though every day he saw nothing on the horizon but more rainclouds. Closing his eyes, he reached for the Song.

It came to him as eagerly as ever, a fresh, bubbling, vital thing, untainted even by so much death around him. Embracing it, he sent his awareness skimming over the sullen grey waves and their awful flotsam, out as far as he could reach. Three miles, four, and nothing. With a little more effort he could reach six miles, past the horizon and well into the deep-water channels favoured by the larger merchantmen, but nothing was stirring on the sea. Teeth gritted, he pushed further, straining his meagre talent for another half a mile, another furlong, whatever precious advantage he could gain. *Nothing, nothing, nothing.*

Where had all the ships gone? The Havens was the busiest port on the southern coast. There should have been silk-boats and spice-traders from the desert, pearl-fishers from the Maling Islands – the Pearlmarket off St Caterin's was second in importance only to Abu Nidar. Surely the storms hadn't sunk them all? Some must have escaped, found another port—

Where were all the ships?

He had to reach further out. He drew more of the Song and used it to push his senses beyond seven miles, though his temples throbbed ferociously and his pulse beat in his ears, his face. Jaws clenched, lips drawn back with the strain, he flung out one more silent, despairing shout . . .

Then he had to let go.

Panting, despite the stench in the air, he laid his head back against the wet stone and let the rain wash over his face to cool him. It was no good. He had almost burst his heart, and for what? Just more nothing. He beat his balled fists against the stone.

Goddess, he was so tired! He slept passably, ate as well as he could with what provisions the Feather had, though those supplies would soon be exhausted, yet he felt weary to the bone. He was ground down by the stench and the dreary days and the miasma of hopelessness that had settled over what had once been a vibrant, gaudy city.

Who hails?

The voice came clear and golden as a shaft of sunlight.

Masen's eyes flew open. Someone had heard him! Somehow, somewhere, someone had heard. Reaching out, he sought the speaker's colours.

Who hails? she called again, her accent lyrical and alien.

My name is Masen. He could not detect the presence of his interlocutor, but sent the image of his own colours out in the hope that she, with her greater talent, might be able to catch them.

You are far away, Masen. Your sigil is unknown to me. I know – please, I need your help.

My ship is four leagues south-southwest of the pearl islands. What aid can I render you?

Four leagues off the Maling Islands? Masen gaped. She was some two hundred and thirty miles away, and yet she spoke as clearly as if she were leaning into his ear! If anyone could save him now, a sea-elf could. If she was willing.

My lady, the Veil is weakening. I must bring this news to the Guardians. I entreat you, can you give me passage west?

The sea-elf was silent.

My lady?

When her voice returned, it was brusque, impassive. *There is pestilence in your city. We cannot approach.*

Lady, please, reconsider! The Veil concerns us all. If it is rent apart, your seas will die. Everything will die.

I say again, Masen of the white city, we cannot approach. We will not approach. May the wind speed you on your way.

Lady! Shipsinger! Please, help me!

The lady did not answer. Masen strained his ears and his senses for another word, but there was nothing to hear but the sigh of the sea, the hiss of the rain and a booming silence in his own skull.

Lady, please!

Another voice came back, sharp as a dagger. *The lady has spoken. Do not press her.*

I do not seek to press her, Shipmaster. I only beg her for her aid. I fear for the Veil, and the ending of an age.

The Shipmaster paused, but the sense of his presence did not fade. It was cool, considering.

You are of the Guardians?

Yes, Shipmaster. I am Gatekeeper to the Order.

You would not speak lightly of such threats, no?

Never. I am sworn to the protection of the Veil.

Another pause.

Two days. Watch for us on the flood-tide, and be ready.

❧

Two wolves burst from the birchwoods and raced each other across an alpine meadow. Tails waving, tongues lolling, they charged through the long grass, snapping at each other like two cubs allowed out of the den for the first time. Back and forth they ran, criss-crossing each other's path, jinking and turning with the sun warm on their backs and yellow birch leaves drifting through the air. Rabbits drummed alarms and scattered into the grass; partridges exploded from beneath the wolves' feet and whirred across the pale sky. They had no reason to suspect that the two predators charging towards them were anything but real.

Damn it, she'd gone to ground again and Gair had lost track of her. He looked round, but saw no sign of Aysha. Wind rippled the grasses, which were thick enough to hide a whole pack of wolves, but he saw nothing moving through them. His ears told him of a stream nearby, and rockfinches calling, but that was all. Lifting his muzzle he sifed the air for the musk of a she-wolf, but found nothing. So she had to be downwind. Slowing to a trot he turned towards the lower slope just as a brindle shape burst from beneath a juniper bush.

Caught you!

Her chest met his shoulder hard and bowled him over. Instinctively he twisted to grab her, but somehow she already had his ruff in her jaws and they rolled down the slope in a tangle of limbs. Claws scrabbled for purchase, bodies writhed and strained to be the one uppermost when the tumbling ended. When he finally got his feet under him and shook her off, she dropped her chin onto her paws for as long as it took him to begin to relax. In a flash she was away again, yipping with excitement.

Gair launched himself in pursuit. He had needed this. After so many days in the lecture halls and practice yards, it felt good to play. Aysha's enthusiasm was infectious and they ran tireless rounds of tag, leaping out at each other from whatever cover the terrain provided, jumping over bushes or down from rocks, pouncing and wrestling and revelling in the agility of their borrowed shapes.

Downslope, the meadow opened out as they neared the headwaters of the river. The wind was more boisterous there, colder, edged with the promise of winter to come. He was hardly aware of it through his thick fur as they tumbled over and over through the grass. All he felt was the exhilaration of the hunt: hot breath, strong muscles bunching to leap, quick jaws ready to seize and subdue. She was more at home in this form than he; it took his full weight across her back to finally bring her down.

Aysha kicked out, digging her claws into the turf. Gair couldn't hold her, and before he caught a breath she'd flipped him onto his back and pinned him, her wolf-face grinning down at him.

I win!

Laughing amber eyes became blue as she released the Song, her body stretching into its usual form. Gair followed suit. He was only a second or two behind her, but it gave Aysha more than enough time to plant a kiss full on his startled mouth and be off again with her tail waving high over her back.

Catch me if you can!

☙

Gair surveyed the chess board in front of him. It would take more than luck to survive this game. A distressingly large number of his pieces stood on Darin's side of the table. He had managed to make up some ground in the last few games, earning a couple of wins and several draws, although the Belisthan was still ahead on total victories. His bold, dashing style occasionally proved to be his undoing against Gair's patient opposition, but tonight he had the game trussed up like an Eventide goose. All that was missing was chestnuts.

'I think I'm going to have to concede,' Gair said.

'No you're not.'

'What do you mean? You've got me completely boxed in. If I move a single piece you'll just pounce on my queen and then it's checkmate in two.'

'Trust me, my friend: there is a way out of this dog's breakfast you've made of your game that would allow you to leave this room with your head held high and your honour intact. You're just going to have to work for it.'

Darin rocked his stool onto its back legs, grinning fit to split his face like a honey-melon. 'You've still got a way out.'

'The only way out of this is a hands-to-heaven miracle.'

'Smugness is not becoming, you know.'

Gair folded his arms on the table and propped his chin on them, frowning at the board. The knight on the right only had one move available to him that wouldn't leave him immediately vulnerable, and that was backwards into wide-open territory, four squares from Darin's nearest piece. He only had three pawns left and he was using them to protect his queen. No matter how he stared at the little carved figures, he couldn't see a way to earn even a draw. He simply hadn't seen it coming.

'I can't see it.'

'You're not looking hard enough.'

Growling in frustration, Gair surveyed the board again, one piece at a time. Darin continued to swing back and forth on his stool, tossing the little velvet pouch from hand to hand.

'This isn't like you, Gair. What's thrown you off your game?'

Yet he should have seen it; there had been more than enough clues. How could he have been so blind? Had he been asleep? Saints have mercy, what the hell was he supposed to do?

'Gair?'

It had begun innocently enough. They had passed the afternoon in a whirl of stalking and being stalked, no different to a dozen other such days. Then he had returned to his human form to find his two arms full of woman, and she'd taken full advantage of the momentary disorientation that followed a change. Holy Mother, his *teacher*.

Catch me if you can!

Reaching out, Gair fingered the least-essential of his three pawns. He hadn't caught her, of course, no matter how hard he'd tried, and she had taken great delight in taunting him about it. He still didn't know how to speak with his mind, so he couldn't answer back, and each over-shot leap or missed lunge with his jaws had simply made her laugh as she danced out of his way.

To cap it all, she had pushed him into a stream – blindsided him, bowled him over into a foot and a half of water straight down from the snowline, and hadn't even had the decency to wait within range of the spray when he shook himself.

But that kiss had lingered long after he had run his coat dry. For a brief interval, not much more than a heartbeat, her mouth had clung to his, as sweet as a promise of redemption. He had said a few days ago that she wasn't scary, but dear Goddess, she was scaring him now – or at least the way she made him feel was as close to fear as made no difference. Sweating palms, dry mouth, heart thumping so hard on his ribs it was almost painful – all she had to do was turn those eyes on him.

If he had to tell someone, he supposed it would be Darin. They had become firm friends over his time on the Isles; surely he could trust him. After all, the sunny-faced Belisthan hadn't breathed a word about his shape-shifting since learning of it. His teacher! What in the name of all the saints was he going to do?

Gair rolled the pawn round on its base with his fingertip, still trying to find the right move. Darin twirled the little velvet pouch around his finger on its string, humming tunelessly.

'Bad move?'

'Let's say I wouldn't, if I was in your position, and that's all the help I'm going to give you.'

Gair still couldn't see the move the Belisthan insisted was there. Goddess, his concentration was in tatters. And he couldn't see any way for anything to happen between them, not that had any chance of working out. She was on the Council, and he'd not even been graded as novice yet, regardless of the mantle at the back of his closet.

'I'm beaten, Darin. You know I am. Why don't you just let me concede, then I can slink away and lick my wounds?'

'No chance,' the Belisthan chortled. 'Your stunning gameplay got you here; now you're going to play yourself out of it.'

20

WHAT LIES IN DUST

The answer had to be somewhere here. With so many books, so much stored knowledge in this room, one of them had to contain what he sought. But all Ansel had found so far were secrets. Secrets and lies.

He scowled as he closed the volume in front of him and pushed it towards the back of the table to join the dozen others discarded over the last hour. He did not have time to read every book there; all he could do was skim a few pages and try to gauge from that whether it might be the one he needed. That was the only way to winnow the stacks of crackling parchment and mouldering leather bindings that weighed down the shelves around him, but the fear that he might overlook the one volume he needed gnawed at him constantly.

A diffident cough behind him said the librarian tasked to assist him had returned. Ansel smoothed his expression as the reedy young man in the brown robe placed another pile of books at his elbow.

'The last books from that shelf, my lord,' he said.

'Thank you— Alquist, wasn't it?'

'Yes, my lord.' A smile flickered nervously across his acne-scarred face, then took fright and fled. 'Um, my lord? Will that be all?'

'No, my son, I have work for you yet.'

The next book was a monstrous thing with warped wooden covers held closed by straps, which had taken two librarians to wrestle onto the table. It was unlikely to be what he sought, yet he could not afford to dismiss any of them on the basis of size alone. Opening it elicited a grunt of effort, though the stiff pages were in rather better condition than the binding had given Ansel reason to expect; the ink, on the other hand, was faded to near illegibility. He brought his lamp closer. Dear Goddess, it would take him a week to decipher the first page of pinched script.

'Only it's past Evensong now and the archives are supposed to be closed. The keeper—'

'Tell me, Alquist,' Ansel sat back in his chair and quite deliberately let the golden Oak on his breast catch the light, 'who is Preceptor of our Order? Me, or the keeper of the archives?'

'You, my lord, of course. But the keeper—'

'The keeper,' said Ansel crisply, 'will keep. Thank you, Alquist. I shall ring for you when I have need of you.'

The librarian folded his hands in his sleeves and bowed, but not before Ansel had seen the twist of misery that distorted his expression.

'Of course, my lord,' he said and retreated to the main library.

Ansel watched him go, lips pursed. No doubt the keeper of the archives would have some strong words for the boy, but that could not be helped. He made a mental note to see to it that the lad was not punished for being unable to overrule the Suvaeon's highest officer, then a further note that the keeper himself might need pricking with a very large pin. The man had a vastly inflated idea of his own importance – just whom did he think he was protecting? The living, breathing Church, or Preceptors long since gone to dust?

Harrumphing, he turned his attention back to the book before him and struggled through a few lines. Ah. Transcripts of the Leahn witch trials, early Second Empire. If he had the time, it would have made interesting reading, but alas, indulging his personal curiosity was a luxury he could not afford.

He heaved the cover closed again, releasing a bloom of dust into the air that made him cough. The spasm did not last long, but it left a tightness in his chest like steel bands around his lungs. He would have to see Hengfors soon, damn it, who would no doubt try to forbid him from leaving his rooms. He could not allow that – not yet, anyway. Once he had found what he needed, well, Hengfors could do his worst then – but not before.

The next few volumes on the table were quickly dealt with. Delirious rubbish, for the most part; he barely had to read a paragraph of each one before recognising that it could join the ever-growing stack on his right. The last but one book was a herbal, no doubt added to the Index because of the homely recipes for charms that interspersed its painstaking tracts on the medicinal properties of Syftian marsh plants. When it too was closed and set aside, and there was just one book remaining, Ansel reached for the brass handbell next to his lamp and rang it. Alquist could empty one more shelf before he let the lad slip away to his rest.

The final book was unadorned, unremarkable. Quite small, not much taller than the length of his hand, its binding was flaking and the flyleaf was badly foxed. Not an auspicious start. It was hand-written; the script was neat – not a scribe's hand, but certainly that of a man well accustomed to a pen. Ansel turned the fragile pages carefully, letting his eye skim over the densely worded text until a particular name arrested him. He went back to the beginning of the paragraph and read it through.

At first light, we received word of the siege. The messenger was near-incoherent with exhaustion; four days riding, with barely four hours rest! It would have been the death of many a man, but these plains rangers are hardy as their horses, it seems.

The siege continues. All roads into the valley are held by the enemy, and they are well dug in, if I can use such terms to describe their en-campment, though the tactics of assault on a fixed position are alien to

250

them. They make no attempt to undermine the walls or bring them down with siege-engines. Instead they are content to wait for starvation to hand them the keys to the gates. The city itself is well supplied, so Caer Ducain is far from falling yet.

Caer Ducain. The beginning of the end of the Founding Wars. The date at the top of the page confirmed it. *At last.* Unless he was very much mistaken, he had in his hands Preceptor Malthus' journal, and his search was almost over.

Footsteps approached from the library behind him and he let the book close.

'Thank you, Alquist, you can start on the next shelf now,' he said, adding, 'Our task would be much simpler if someone had thought to catalogue this archive, or even just dust it from time to time.'

A brown robe appeared in his line of sight. From the rope girdle dangled a bunch of keys that in the right hands would have made a creditable substitute for a morningstar. Unfortunately, the keeper of the archives did not have such hands.

'Master keeper,' Ansel said expansively, sitting back in his chair, 'how kind of you to stop by.'

The keeper inclined his head a fraction. 'Lord Preceptor.'

Even the man's voice was bloodless. From pallid pate to narrow sandalled feet, the keeper resembled something found at the bottom of a rendering kettle after pouring off all the tallow. Pale skin covered long, fleshless bones that sketched out the approximate shape of a man under the robe. His deeply shadowed sockets held eyes as dark and unblinking as those of a snake.

'Have you found what you require, my lord?'

'The search continues, alas. This section of the archives seems to be somewhat disorganised.'

The keeper's pale lips twitched. 'We have many books, my lord. More than three hundred thousand volumes. Recataloguing such a collection . . . takes time.'

'Indeed. How many are there in this room, in your opinion?'

Turning his head, the keeper surveyed the ranks of wooden shelves that stood like infantry battalions awaiting inspection, ranging out into the darkness past the golden circle of lamplight that surrounded the sole reading table. His expression did not change. 'I could not say.'

'If they were catalogued, I'm sure you could have told me the precise number, down to the last loose folio.'

'Quite so, my lord.' Dark orbs returned from their contemplation of the unseen far wall and focused on the book between Ansel's hands. 'Something of interest, Preceptor?'

Ansel added the book to the stack. 'No, just another herbal, I'm afraid. Syftian marsh plants and the remedies obtainable therefrom. Did you know, Vorgis, that you can prepare no fewer than seven different tinctures from the spotted frogbit?'

'Is that so? How fascinating.'

'Indeed. Ah well, onwards we march. Those journals must be here somewhere.'

'Journals, my lord?'

'Yes, journals,' Ansel said. 'Some of my predecessors were ardent diarists, and reading their journals would give a very personal perspective on the Order's history. So much more human than Brother Chronicler's dry script, don't you think?'

'Perhaps so – although I prefer history to confine itself to facts, rather than opinion.'

'If I were looking for history, my dear keeper, I would be out in the main library, where there are windows and an approximation of fresh air. What I am searching for here are the men behind the history, because it was these men who made the Order what it was, and what it has become.'

The keeper's eyes glittered. 'And you think you will find those journals here, my lord?'

'They're certainly not out there.' Ansel jerked his head towards the door behind him. 'According to your most thorough catalogue, that is. Unless they were mis-shelved.'

'Mis-shelved?' Vorgis' near-invisible eyebrows rose. 'I can assure you, there are no mis-shelved books in the Suvaeon archive. Not one.'

'You can be sure of that, keeper? Out of three hundred thousand volumes?'

'Absolutely sure. This is a *library*, my lord, not a common lending-house.' One pale hand touched the keys as if to be reassured that they were still there. 'And now the archives are closed. I shall see to it that these books are returned to their proper place.'

'Oh, I'm not quite done yet, Vorgis. I think I need another half an hour, if you don't mind.'

'I'm afraid that's quite impossible. The archives are closed.'

'I need another half an hour.'

The keeper's lips pursed. 'My lord Preceptor, when you came to me three weeks ago and . . . demanded access to the archives, I felt you were pursuing a fool's errand. Surely after all this time, if you have not found anything, it means that there is nothing here to find?'

'That's certainly possible.'

'Quite so.' Vorgis folded his hands together again at his waist. 'Shall I escort you to the door?'

'No, thank you, Vorgis. I'm not done.'

'I will be locking the archive very shortly. You are welcome to stay until the morning, but I do not think that would be advisable given your . . . condition.'

The man was quite intolerable. 'Threats, Vorgis? From you? I am surprised.'

'I made no threat, my lord.'

'Good, because if you had, I might have been forced to knock you onto your bony arse!'

The keeper blinked. 'My lord?'

Leaning on his staff, Ansel heaved himself to his feet, ignoring the fiery needles that stabbed his joints. He dug in the pocket of his

253

house robe and produced a shiny brass key, which he held up between finger and thumb.

'The archives close when I say, master keeper, and not before. You would do well to remember that.'

'But there is only one key—' Vorgis' hand twitched towards his girdle, then pointed accusingly at Ansel. 'You had it copied!'

'As is my right and prerogative as the principal of the Suvaeon Order.'

'How?' The key never left the room.'

Ansel showed his teeth. It was most satisfying to see Vorgis nonplussed. 'Candles,' he said. 'Good white candles, that give such a fine light for reading. The spilth will hold an excellent impression of a key.'

Vorgis blinked again. 'I am the keeper of the archives!'

'And you should remember who appointed you so!' Ansel roared, then had to bring his voice back to a gentler pitch when the steel bands tightened across his chest. 'I have work to do here, master keeper, and you can help me or hinder me. The choice is yours.'

'My lord, I must protest. These books are extremely precious—'

'Then you should take better care of them! The dust in here could choke a coal-pit mule.'

'—extremely precious and I cannot allow these archives to be opened at will!'

'*You*?' Ansel leaned forward on the table. '*You* cannot allow it, Vorgis? I am Preceptor.' He thumped the iron heel of the staff onto the flagstones underfoot and it rang like the Sacristy bell. 'If I wish to open the archives, I will open them. If I want to read every last book and scroll and tattered endpaper in the entire Index, then *I will read them*. Do I make myself clear?'

He had not intended to shout, but it had had the desired effect. For the first time, Ansel saw the keeper of the archives lost for words. Vorgis' eyes were fixed on the golden Oak, hypnotised by the way it swung gently back and forth on its chain.

'Vorgis! Do I make myself clear?'

Ansel's voice snapped the keeper out of his reverie. He blinked again and smoothed one pale hand over his scalp. 'Abundantly so, Preceptor.' The ghost of what might once have been a smile tightened the corners of his mouth then was gone. 'Good evening to you.'

With a stiff bow, the keeper stalked out. At once, Ansel reached for the handbell again. Damn the dust in this room! His chest was now dreadfully tight and a tickle at the back of his throat signalled an imminent bout of coughing. He didn't dare let it begin without a glass of water to hand or it might never end. He should have kept a tighter rein on his temper, not let himself be goaded into shouting. Damn Vorgis, and damn all the secrets the Order kept, even from itself.

'Alquist? Alquist!' The skinny librarian reappeared at his elbow.

'Oh, there you are, my lad. Would you fetch some water? There's too much dust—'

The tickle intensified. Ansel fumbled for his handkerchief as the cough began to hack its way out of his lungs. Pain sawed through him with each heave of his chest and he wheezed like leaky bellows as he tried to catch his breath.

Alquist stared, horrified.

Ansel waved him away and slumped back into his chair as cough after cough sent coloured lights wheeling across his sight.

By the time Alquist crept back into the room with a pitcher and cup, the worst was over and the spotted handkerchief was once more tucked out of sight. Ansel accepted a cup of water gratefully and sat sipping at it until his rasping breaths eased.

The young librarian hovered by the table. 'Are you unwell, my lord?' he asked.

'No, lad,' said Ansel, mustering a smile, 'just too old and tired for all the dust in here.'

The boy fingered the cover of the witch-trial transcripts and wiped his hand on his robe. 'It doesn't seem right to me,' he muttered. 'Why aren't they better taken care of?'

'No one cares about these books, Alquist. They're here because we're too ashamed to make them public, and too afraid to destroy them.'

Alquist's face froze. 'Destroy them?' he repeated. 'They're *books*! Books shouldn't be destroyed.'

Ansel gave him a creaky laugh. 'Be grateful you weren't alive to see the Inquisition at its height. The Church burned books by the thousand.'

'But that's not right!'

'Ah, my son, you have the soul of a true librarian. To you, all knowledge is precious, even the profane. I've a mind to promote you to keeper of the archives if I live long enough.'

'But Master Vorgis is keeper of the archives.'

'The keeper of secrets, perhaps,' Ansel snorted.

'My lord?'

'Just an old man's ramblings, lad. Don't pay them any mind.' Setting down his cup, Ansel picked up Malthus' journal again. A bead of scarlet winked at him from the cover and he dabbed it away with his fingertip. There was enough blood on those pages already, he suspected, albeit the kind that did not leave a stain for everyone to see. He rubbed his fingertip with his thumb, watching the smear of scarlet become a smudge, then nothing at all. After Samarak, there had been so much blood and filth blackening his fingernails that it had taken a week to scrub it away. It had been a lot longer than a week before he had felt that they were clean.

'Do you know your history, my son? Can you tell me who was Preceptor of our Order at the end of the Founding Wars?'

'Preceptor Malthus,' said Alquist promptly. 'He led our army to victory at Riannen Cut.'

'Indeed he did, well done.' *Well done for parroting what they taught you in the novitiate, at any rate.* 'Alquist, the night is wearing on and you must be tired. I have just one more task for you, if you would be so kind. Do you see this book? Are there any others like this, in the same hand?'

'I'm not certain, my lord. I think there might be, on the next shelf.'

'Can you bring them to me, please? Then you can go to bed.'

'I'll be as quick as I can, my lord.'

'Oh, there's no rush. Take your time. I've plenty to read here.'

21

NORTH WINDS

ତଙ

Autumn stormed down from the north in huff and bluster. Gales battered Penglas, rattling Chapterhouse's window casements and shrieking round the chimneys. Gair hadn't flown in three days and already felt confined by the walls. The wind drove Aysha as mad as a caged bear.

He looked down at the teacup in his hands. Fine Isles porcelain, delicate, translucent stuff the colour of sea-foam, far more fragile than the stout pottery mugs he was accustomed to in the refectory. More was the pity; if it had been one of them its mate wouldn't now be in shards on the hearth where Aysha had flung it a few moments earlier.

She sprawled on the couch opposite, feet up, boot-heels digging carelessly into the ivory damask as she chewed at a hangnail. This wasn't the first time the weather had kept them indoors. They had passed those other times in conversation or debate, but now the north winds scraped across her nerves like a rasp. It was proving hard on her crockery.

'Would you like some more tea?' he ventured.

She scowled at him. 'No.'

Her moods always worsened with the weather. She grew irritable, restive as a horse stabled too long, and Gair knew no way to soothe her. At the Motherhouse there had been a covered yard with a deep peat floor where the horses could be exercised when going outside was impractical, and all but the most surly animal had responded well to a thorough brushing and a sweet warm mash afterwards. Somehow he didn't think a basin of bran was going to help here.

Kneeling at the hearth, he refilled his cup from the teapot keeping warm by the fire and sat back down on his couch. The first sip told him the tea was stewed, but in order to reach the little cupboard above Aysha's desk where the honey-crock was kept, he would have to pass her seat, and she had blistered his ears once already for making too much bloody noise on the wooden floor with his damned boots. He resigned himself to a tongue-curlingly bitter drink and not for the first time wondered why he didn't just leave her to her sulks.

He knew why, of course, though it had taken that day on the mountain to make him finally acknowledge it. There was a reason for that little leap inside whenever her regard lit on him, an explanation for why he found such grace in her smallest gesture, and could scarcely concentrate on what she was saying for watching her hands as they talked.

What he should do was walk away – make his excuses and decline each time she called to him outside his scheduled tutorials. She was on the Council of Masters, he was a student, and Chapterhouse had rules. There was nothing he could do to change that; he should just accept it. But Holy Mother forgive him, he could not bring himself to say no to her. So he stayed and tried to pretend that nothing had changed, but since that kiss had brought everything so sharply into focus, nothing between them could ever be the same again.

'Damn it, I'll have no nails left,' Aysha muttered. She folded her arms across her chest and shoved her hands into her armpits to keep them away from her teeth.

The movement pulled her shirt tight across her breasts,

emphasising the curves, and Gair had to drag his eyes down before she noticed his stare, then had to haul them further down past her snug moleskin breeches to the rug. That was the only safe place to let his eyes rest.

Remember she's your teacher! he told himself firmly. That was all very well, but she hadn't acted very much like his teacher when she'd kissed him, had she? Without thinking, he took a deep gulp of tea and nearly choked, it was so bitter. *It was only once, and it was over a week ago.* Not that you're counting the days or anything. *It was nothing.* So much nothing that you can't stop thinking about it, eh?

No good came of arguing with himself about it. No matter how many times he tried, there was never anything new to hear. Aysha was under his skin as firmly as a spinewort barb, and just like the thorn, the only thing to do with that was endure the itch until it grew itself out. He renewed this resolve daily, but every time she fixed him with those stormy eyes he felt it crumble like a sand-castle undercut by the tide.

'You should go,' she said at last.

'If that's what you want.'

She looked away. 'I'm not fit company for civilised folk, Leahn. Stay here and I'm liable to take it out on you instead of the china.'

'I could use the shield-weaving practice. I've missed at least three tutorials now.'

Blue eyes flashed and for a second he thought he'd said the wrong thing. Then her lips curled up at the corners just the barest fraction and she shook her head at herself. She pressed her fists to her head and growled in frustration. 'Gah, how do you put up with me like this? I feel ready to climb out of my own skin.' Tipping her head back, she rubbed her hands over her face and sighed. 'Go on, go. I'll be all right if I can just get some sleep. A hot bath should help, and if it doesn't I've got a bottle of brandy.'

'Are you sure?' He set down his cup on the hearth and stood up.

Outside the wind shrieked past the windows and the draught stirred the curtains.

Aysha shifted restlessly on the couch.

'There's nothing I can do?'

'I'd ask you to wash my back, but there's an evens chance that I'll try to drown you in the tub instead. I'm sure you can find something more interesting to do than keep company a crabbed old witch like me.' She flicked a look towards the door. 'Go on. I'll be fine.'

Out in the corridor, with the door safely closed behind him, he had to lean against the wall and close his eyes. *Aysha in her bath.* Had she been serious? Mother have mercy, he thought she had. Images unfolded in his mind, and he was powerless to stop them. Candlelight. Water pearling on her tawny skin. Saints, a foamy sponge in his hand as he soaped her back in slow circles. He let his head fall backwards onto the stone. And all he had to do was go back into her apartment and say he'd take his chances with the drowning. Dear Goddess. She was his *teacher*.

If he'd thought he would have been granted absolution, he would have gone straight to the confessional and surrendered his impure thoughts to the impartial ear of the lector, taken his penance and been happy to do so. Yet he knew that it wouldn't stop them. In his heart, in the depths of the night, he didn't want to stop them, though they made his blood pound in his veins. So why didn't he go back? Why was he pushing himself away from the wall and heading for the stairs, trying to convince himself that it was the right thing to do?

He was halfway down the third flight of stairs and no closer to an answer when a familiar voice called his name. Turning round, he saw Alderan stepping out into the corridor, closing his study door behind him.

'I was wondering where you were,' the old man said. 'I don't see you around the place much these days. Are you well?'

'I am, thank you. You?'

The wind flung rain at the windows opposite, rattling on the glass like gravel.

'Oh, tolerable,' Alderan said. 'I'd be better if it wasn't so wretchedly damp. It plays hob with my knees.' He gestured at the corridor ahead that led out of the Masters' wing and, folding his hands behind him, said, 'Walk with me a while. It's been a long time since we talked. Have you had your supper yet?'

Gair fell in beside him, wondering where the conversation was heading. He had a feeling that he knew, and against all rationality it raised his hackles.

'Not yet,' he said. 'I wasn't hungry.'

You are, just not for food, his conscience reminded him with a guilty pang.

Alderan's brow furrowed in concern. 'Are you all right?' he asked. 'You look like you've got colic.'

Was it so obvious? 'I'm fine.'

'Have a glass of warm milk and honey to settle your stomach.'

They turned right onto the main corridor, then left towards the refectory. Knots of students passed them, and the occasional Master. Alderan acknowledged them all with a nod or a word, then asked pleasantly, 'Lessons with Aysha going well, I take it?'

'There's a lot to learn.'

'Enough to explain why you've been missing tutorials with the rest of the faculty?' Alderan pushed open the refectory door and stopped on the threshold. His expression was grave, gaze steady. 'I'm afraid I expected rather better of you than that, Gair. I thought you would be a much more . . . disciplined student.'

'We cover a lot of ground. Sometimes the time gets away from us.'

'I'm sure it does.'

'What was it you wanted to talk about, Alderan?'

'You, in a nutshell.'

Gair blinked. This wasn't what he had been expecting at all.

'You have a prodigious talent, you know. One of the best I've ever seen. If you choose not to develop it, well, that's your right and your decision, but if you'll forgive me I think it would be a terrible waste.'

'And you think I'm wasting it learning more about my shape-shifting.'

'I'm worried that you might be focusing your energies too keenly on one aspect of your gift to the detriment of the rest of it. And I don't want you to lose yourself.'

'Meaning?'

'Aysha warned you, I assume? About going too deeply into the shape-shift, staying too long? She told me about it once, not long after she arrived here. Fair made my blood run cold, thinking about becoming too much the animal whose shape you are borrowing and losing the way back. You can still hear the Song, you just don't have the capability to make use of it. That would frighten me, were I you.'

'She made the risks clear to me,' Gair said carefully.

In fact Aysha had been quite dismissive of them, maintaining that it was necessary to throw oneself fully into the shape in order to truly comprehend and *be* the animal. Gair had always been more cautious; he'd never let the urge to hunt overwhelm him.

Alderan pursed his lips. 'It would be a great shame if we were to lose you, Gair. You could be a tremendous asset to the Order, you know. Godril thinks very highly of you, and he's notoriously hard to impress.'

Gair faced him, hands on his belt. 'What exactly are you trying to say here, Alderan? If you think I'm spending too much time with Aysha, then please just say so. I'm not a child; you don't have to tiptoe round the subject in case it scares me.'

A small smile creased the old man's beard. 'That wasn't at all what I meant, lad,' he said kindly, and squeezed Gair's shoulder, letting go with a pat. 'Just have a care for your timekeeping, that's all. We still have some things to show you which might be useful to you one day. Good night.'

With that, the old man ambled off into the refectory. Gair watched him go, feeling as if he'd been having an argument all by himself. Maybe the north wind was getting to him as well.

❧

The wind had been against the *Morning Star* for most of the journey. She had spent a week fighting a gale that veered from westerly to nor'easterly, tacking some eight hundred miles for a total advance of not much more than a hundred. Every furlong had been fought out against opposing seas, and the sea-elf ship had paid a heavy price for it. Her sleek shoulders were pared of paint down to the wood, and one of her sails had already burst from throat to foot.

The Shipmaster rested his hands on the hilts of his belt knives and bared his teeth at Masen. 'Lucky for you we were already bound this way, Gatekeeper,' he called, 'or I'd never forgive you!'

Masen spread his hands in apology, then swore and had to lunge for the railing as the next pitch of the bows almost knocked him from his feet.

The sea-elf rode the roll of the deck with the poise of a dancer, his long legs flexing to absorb the motion.

'I'm grateful to you, K'shaa, more than I can ever say.'

'It may take more than your gratitude to appease the lady, however.' K'shaa gestured towards the stern where the Shipsinger stood, her hands braced on the tiller and her long hair flying around her face. 'I fear she has not yet forgiven me for overruling her decision not to take you aboard.'

'I understand. How is she faring?' Masen asked.

'She is tired. Though she does not admit it to me, I can hear it in her voice.'

Masen could hear nothing but the moan of the wind and the crash of waves into the bows, but he could feel a tug at the Song from a powerful weaving. He wiped spray from his face.

'I could help her,' he said. 'I cannot sing the ship the way she does, but I could share the burden of working the Song.'

K'shaa shook his head, pale braids swinging. 'It is her task, Gatekeeper. She will not surrender it, certainly not to you.'

'I only want to help. It is the least I can do to pay for my passage.'

'Then I wish you luck persuading her so. She is a proud one, my sister.' Then he smiled, slanted eyes sparking. 'But you may ask her, with my blessing!'

Hand over hand along the railing, Masen made his way aft, careful to keep out of the way of the other sea-elves as they moved about their tasks. Once he gained the edge of the stern-deck, he reached for the Shipsinger's colours.

Her Song tingled along his nerves.

My lady!

She frowned but did not answer. Her sea-green robe flapped in the wind.

Lady, I can be of assistance.

Mouth clamped in a tight line, she shook her hair out of her face. Clenched teeth and narrowed eyes gave her marble-pale face a feline cast. Still she said nothing.

You have not slept in two nights, lady. Let me help you, and together we can speed the Star on her way.

The Shipsinger fixed her eyes on the grey-green ocean ahead. The stiffness of her spine showed no sign of bending. Well, luck favoured the bold.

Masen hung onto the railing until he got a feel for how the ship rode the waves as it breasted each swell and dipped into the following trough. Then he leapt across the sloping deck and clamped his hands onto the tiller either side of the Shipsinger's, her slender body inside the circle of his arms.

Cat-green eyes fixed him over her shoulder. *You presume too much, Masen of the white city!*

265

Then let me answer for my presumption with the sweat of my back, for I would gladly sweat for one as lovely as you.

Delicate brows shot up. So the lady was not immune to flattery when reason failed.

The temptation to kiss her perfect mouth was almost enough to overcome his fear of the knives on her brother's belt. Instead he inclined his head courteously. 'At your service, my lady,' he said and let the Song flood into him.

At once he could feel the quiver of life in the wood in his hands and under his boots, the skirling song of wind and water thrumming through the very fabric of the ship. The Shipsinger stared at him a moment longer, then her expression softened a fraction and she turned her face into the wind. He felt the caress of her mind, cool and elegant and alien, then she drew on the Song through him and together they set their wills to driving the *Star* through the hostile waters. Now he had to hope that she would arrive in time.

᳇

Back in the dormitory, Gair saw a light under Darin's door and wondered if the Belisthan would have time for a game of chess. Luck had been running his way of late and he was enjoying a run of six victories in a row, though each had been hard fought. Something so purely cerebral might be just the thing he needed to distract himself from the rather more visceral subject that had been occupying him lately. Maybe he could even dredge up the courage to ask for some advice.

When Gair knocked on the door, there was no answer. He knocked again, then opened the door just far enough to lean in and say Darin's name.

The Belisthan was slumped across his desk, perilously close to the guttering stub of a candle.

Gair hurried to move the candle out of the way, then lifted Darin's shoulders and leaned him back in his chair. He had overturned his inkwell and there was a spreading black stain over his tunic and what looked like it had once been an essay. Next to it, the stone for Renna's betrothal ring sparkled on top of its velvet pouch like a raindrop on a rose.

'Darin, wake up.' Gair shook him gently. 'Come on, you've got to wake up now.'

Darin's eyes fluttered half-open. They were glazed and his breathing was irregular.

'Come on, Darin. You're covered in ink, look.'

The boy's head lolled again. Gair wondered if he was drunk; he certainly had an intoxicated look about him. But his breath did not smell of wine, and thinking back, Gair could never recall him drinking very much. Suddenly he remembered something Darin had said when they first met.

'Darin! Wake up! When did you last eat?'

The Belisthan tried to say something, but whatever it was came out as a moan. Gair swore. Propping him up as best he could, he searched quickly round the room for some food, but there was nothing. A trawl through his pockets and then Darin's was similarly fruitless.

Gair swore again, louder this time. He would have to get him to the infirmary. He carried Darin's slight frame out into the corridor and kicked at the first door he came to. 'Open up, Clovas! I need your help!'

The door was opened by a skinny twelve-year-old in nightshirt and adept's mantle. He blinked uncertainly when he saw Gair with an unconscious Darin over his shoulder. Further down the corridor, other doors opened, and voices demanded to know what the racket was about.

'Run down to the infirmary and tell the first Healer you find that Darin is sick and that I'm bringing him down.'

The apprentice stood there, his mouth open.

'Clovas, this is serious.' Gair grabbed the boy's arm and hauled him bodily from his room. *Run!*

With a startled yelp, Clovas hared off down the passage. Gair followed as quickly as he could, ignoring the stares and questions from the other students. In no time at all the whole corridor was awake and milling about.

Gair's swearing reached new levels of fluency. 'Out of the way, damn it!' He beat at them with his free arm, but they were confused, and slow to respond. 'Come on, move yourselves!'

In frustration he reached for the Song and detonated illusory fireballs the length of the passageway to clear his path. Startled students fell back with shouts of fright, apart from a couple of adepts who demanded to know what he thought he was doing. 'I haven't the time to stand about arguing – *let me by!*'

He shouldered his way between them, ignoring the complaints as they trailed after him. He hurried down the stairs and as he moved out across the cloister the wind moaned between the pillars and threw wet leaves in his face. Not far now: past the entrance to the practice yards, left into the cross-passageway and bless him, there was Clovas, bobbing in the wake of Saaron's scarecrow figure.

The grizzled Healer beckoned Gair into the surgery. 'Bring him in, bring him in.' Saaron gestured at the surgery table. 'Lie him down there.'

The Healer produced a scalpel from a drawer and slit open Darin's ruined tunic and shirt, then pressed his ear to the boy's chest to listen to his breathing. He sought a pulse at neck and wrist with deft fingers and clicked his tongue. 'Slow, dreadfully slow. Prop him up in a sitting position, will you?'

Gair held Darin's shoulders against his chest with one arm and used the other hand to support his chin.

Saaron disappeared into the dispensary and returned a few moments later, stirring something in a beaker. 'Let's get some of this into him.'

With the spoon, he dribbled a little of the liquid into Darin's slack mouth.

Gair thought he smelled honey. 'What is it?'

'Honey and warm water,' Saaron told him. 'Darin has something called sugar-sickness. If he doesn't eat regularly, or goes without food for too long, he can lapse into a coma, like this, and if it's not treated quickly enough he could die. I've seen it happen, especially with children. They don't understand what's happening, and they can't describe it, so their symptoms go undiagnosed.' Another spoonful went into Darin's mouth; the youth spluttered and swallowed weakly. 'How long since you found him?'

'Only a few minutes. He was slumped over his desk. I thought he'd just fallen asleep over his work, but I couldn't wake him up. I looked for food in his room, but I couldn't find anything.'

'Quick thinking. You're Gair, aren't you? Tanith has told me about you.' Saaron lifted Darin's eyelids and peered underneath. 'How's the head?'

'Fine now, thank you. Is he going to be all right?'

'I should think so, yes. And that's due in no small part to the promptness of your actions, I might add.' Saaron put down the beaker and scratched his head. His iron-coloured hair stuck up in all directions, as if he was unacquainted with the concept of a comb. 'Darin's supposed to have a box of sweets, fudge or something, in his pocket all the time, so that if he starts to feel unwell he can eat something. He's probably lost it – he's such a scatterbrain I'm amazed he doesn't forget who he is sometimes. Can you help me carry him through there, do you think?'

The Healer waved a hand in the direction of the door that led to the ward.

Together they carried Darin into the whitewashed room. Long rows of beds lined the walls, with curtains that could be pulled out to provide privacy. Saaron led the way to one of the few individual rooms at the far end, for those patients who needed absolute quiet. A bed was already made up, with the covers turned back, and in a matter of moments Darin was stripped and tucked up warmly.

'I'll have one of the adepts sit with him until he wakes up,'

Saaron said. 'We shall have to keep a close eye on him. He's not been this bad in a very long time. I'll let you know how he is tomorrow.'

Gair walked back to his room with Clovas hovering at his heels. The hubbub had died down, and most of the students were back in their rooms, but a few were leaning against the walls watching as the two affronted adepts put their case to Master Barin. Their chorus reached new heights when they saw Gair approach.

Barin beckoned him over, and Gair saw Clovas into his room before going to the Master.

'Did you throw fireballs at these two, Gair?' Barin asked in his deep, mellow voice.

'I did.' It was the truth; he wasn't going to argue about it. 'Darin was unconscious and I was trying to get to the infirmary. These two were in my way and wouldn't move.'

Barin's lips twitched. 'I see. Thank you, gentlemen,' he said to the adepts. 'You can go back to your rooms. I think I can take care of this now.'

They made to protest, but a raised hand silenced them. Drawing their mantles around them sniffily, they stalked back down the corridor.

Barin sighed. 'Do you have a habit of making enemies?' he asked. 'First Arlin, now those two.'

Gair was startled for the second time that evening. 'How do you know about Arlin?'

'Do you think we Masters don't talk to one another?' All Chapterhouse knows Arlin tried to break your head and you cracked his ribs. I believe there're wagers on which of you kills the other first.' Barin sighed again. 'Gair, you can do things without thinking that adepts like Maarna there couldn't manage with a week's notice and a red-hot poker in his drawers. Now I know you don't go out of your way to flaunt your talents, but you should be aware that there are some people who resent you for them.'

270

'Like Arlin?'

'A case in point,' Barin agreed. 'He is a very fair talent himself, and a fine swordsman – the finest we had, until you put a kink in his tail with your Suvaeon training. Not only that, you're strong in your gift as well. I'm sure I don't have to spell it out for you.'

Gair knew very well what the dark-haired Master meant. The last time he'd gone to the practice yards before breakfast, he'd returned to his water-jug to find someone had salted it. The time before it had been laced with pickling vinegar. He had no evidence, but he was fairly sure Arlin was responsible, even though they never exchanged so much as a word in Haral's classes.

'Unfortunately, Arlin is one of those people who cannot forgive another man's good fortune,' the Master went on. 'Unless he can best you at something, he will never be content. I would suggest you let him get the better of you at swordcraft once in a while, but you're Leahn, and I doubt your pride would let you.'

They had reached Darin's door, where they stopped. Barin laid a hand on Gair's arm. 'Watch yourself, Gair,' he cautioned. 'There are people who will be envious of your talents, people who will resent you, through no fault of your own. These people can do you mischief, and they will, because they are accustomed to being the centre of attention and you are diverting it away from them, simply because of what you are. Remember that.'

'I will,' Gair promised.

'Good. Now I can expect to see you for my tutorial tomorrow, yes?'

'Of course, Master Barin. You have my word on it.'

'And a Leahn's word is writ in iron, so I shall hold you to it. I'm sure my brother will be pleased too. He tells me his pupils are weary of scouring Chapterhouse for you, only to find Aysha has spirited you away.'

Gair winced. 'I suppose everyone knows now,' he said gloomily.

'Those of us who were there on the day can work out what it

means when a novice reports that Master Aysha says you're studying with her. The other students have no doubt put the clues together as well. It's hard to keep secrets in a place like this, you know. Students gossip worse than old women on washday.'

Gair could have wished it was different. She might not care who knew about her abilities – indeed, she positively brandished them in the face of the rest of Chapterhouse – but he did not feel comfortable with that. After hiding it for so long, it was too personal to share with the world. Still, the dice were cast now, he would just have to get used to it.

Barin stepped back and began walking down the corridor. 'Remember, half-Prime tomorrow, and not a second later!'

22

RUMOURS

❧

It was no good. He would have to start again from the beginning. Lowering his sword, Gair walked back up the yard. He'd paid for his punctuality the day before with a gruelling tutorial under Barin's critical eye, and it had been difficult enough to focus on the Song with rain drumming on the windows of the lecture hall and the winds moaning in the chimney like revenants without worrying about Darin as well. Now a full day had passed with no news from the infirmary, chewing further holes in his concentration. He'd almost taken off his own toes on that last pass.

He mopped the sweat from his face and chest with a towel and drank a cup of water. This early it was still dark, but he'd strung glims along the edge of the walkway roof and their blue-white light was as bright as noon, though it gave no warmth. If he stood still for too long the blustery wind would steal the heat he'd built up in his muscles over the last hour or so, in which case he might as well give up and go back to bed.

He settled his feet in first position, then brought the sword slowly, carefully, to the salute. He would return to the most basic forms, the ones he knew the way he knew how to breathe, and try to regain his focus from there. Otherwise Haral would send him straight to the novice class tomorrow.

First position. Deep breath. Hold it a beat . . . and begin.

No sound but the wind and the scuffle of his feet on the cold earth, the thin hiss of air over blade. Gair kept his breathing slow and regular, and gradually the rhythm came to him. *Smooth, fluid transfer of his weight from foot to foot; balance and counter-balance flowing together.* The faster he moved, the more his thoughts slowed towards that point of perfect glacial clarity where he did not need to think at all. His muscles already knew what to do.

When he reached the end of the yard, he began again from the beginning, stepping through each figure, block-parry-thrust, to the rhythm in his head. Selenas used to clap it out for them, pacing back and forth along the rows of sweating novices. Though the wiry Master of Swords was far away, Gair could still hear the precise beat for each exercise. It ticked along like a heartbeat and his feet followed, dancing him through the forms.

Better. Much better. He might not disgrace himself in Haral's next class after all. The weapons-master had assigned him a new sparring partner last week, an ox-like Syrian who looked slow and plodding until he got a weapon in his hands. Gair had found himself duelling a whirlwind with the solidity and strength of a castle wall. He had nearly come unstuck more than once during the session, until he'd got the measure of his opponent. Even so, by the end of the class it had been a real effort to uncurl his fingers from the waster's grip. He intended to mount a much more accomplished defence next time.

The sun was almost up when he felt someone watching him. His heart sank. He was in no mood to tolerate Arlin and his cronies today. The adulteration of his water-jug had only stopped when someone tried to drop in a raw ladybonnet pepper and discovered the hard way that Gair could weave a trigger-ward that snapped like a gin-trap. He'd felt the ward collapse behind him, but he'd continued with his forms so he hadn't seen who had broken it. Next day one of Arlin's friends, Benris, had been sporting two splinted fingers. There matters had remained, in an

274

ill-tempered draw, but Gair knew without a doubt that the game was by no means over.

He would not let them ruin the concentration he had worked so hard to regain. If they were determined to have their fun, they could damn well wait until he was done. Fighting to retain his focus, he slashed and turned his way towards the end of the form. Ten more steps. Eight. Three. Turn, and *finish*.

The blade flashed blue-white as it caught the glim-light and came to a halt levelled at Sorchal's throat.

The swarthy Elethrainian perched on the walkway railing threw up his hands in mock alarm. 'Quarter, sir knight! I yield!'

Breathing hard, Gair put up his sword. 'Forgive me. I was expecting someone else.'

Black brows rose. 'Who's up at this time of the morning?'

'You are,' Gair said mildly.

Sorchal's eyes sparkled. 'Only because I haven't been to bed yet.'

'A good night at the Red Dragon?'

'You could say that.' The Elethrainian hopped down from the rail and extended a hand. 'I don't believe we've been properly introduced. Sorchal din Urse, hedonist and ne'er-do-well.'

Gair wiped his sweaty hands on his whites and returned the clasp. 'Gair. Excommunicate Leahn bastard.'

Sorchal's grin was made roguish by a chipped front tooth, and combined with his emerald eyes and dark good looks, Gair began to understand some of the stories he'd heard.

'I like you already. Ride your own road, only dull people play by the rules.' He glanced at the eastern wall, where a bright thread of sunrise gleamed above the tiles. 'Do you always practise this early?'

'Most days. I like the quiet.'

'And it keeps you out of Arlin's way,' Sorchal said. 'I suppose I ought to thank you, Leahn. It's past time someone put that

275

arrogant heathercock on his arse. I just wish I had the skill to have done it myself.'

'I've seen you in Haral's class. You're good.'

The Elethrainian demurred, pulling a face. 'The longsword's not really my weapon. I'm better suited to the rapier. Easier to snip the ribbon from a girl's hair.' He made a deft flick with an imaginary sword. 'If I tried it with that cleaver of yours, I'd probably part her head from her shoulders, and then where would I get my kisses?'

'Her grieving mother, perhaps?'

'A vile calumny!' Sorchal declared. 'It was a wedding, not a funeral, and the lady in question was the mother of the bride, not of the deceased.' His affronted expression became another dazzling grin. 'Although your version does add a certain spice to my reputation as a scapegrace of the first water, you have to admit.'

Gair picked up his towel and slung it over his shoulder. It was time to stop if he was going to have a bath and something to eat before his tutorial with Coran.

'From what I've heard, it's a wonder you haven't been run through by an outraged husband already.'

'The trick, my friend, is not to be caught. Besides, I'm surprised you don't have your own flock of turtledoves, all this exercising with your shirt off. Married or maiden, women love to watch a man sweat.' Sorchal winked, then laughed when Gair ducked his head to hide a flush.

'Forgive me, I shouldn't tease,' he said, trying hard to look contrite. 'Now I've kept you long enough, and my bed is calling me. If you happen by the Dragon one evening, I'd be honoured to stand you a glass of whatever best pleases your throat just for the expression you put on Arlin's face.'

With that he swung his coat over his shoulders and ambled off across the yard, whistling. When he reached the door, he paused.

'By the way,' he called, 'I have five Imperials on you to win. Don't let me down!'

Gair bent down to pick up his belongings. Sorchal's conquests were the stuff of legend in the dormitory – he made Darin seem positively chaste – but he was so affable he was difficult to dislike. Even his towering arrogance was leavened with enough humour that it was charismatic instead of offensive.

After bathing and changing his clothes, Gair walked back to his room to drop off his sword. Opening the door, he found Tanith at his desk, flipping through one of the books he'd borrowed from the library.

'*Prince Corum and the Forty Knights*,' she said, holding it up. 'One of my favourites too. Just don't believe what the author says about Astolans. I don't think he had ever met one.'

'The ears?'

'Completely unpointed, as you can see.' She closed the book and returned it to the pile. 'I thought you might like to know that your friend Darin is awake and thriving. Saaron says that thanks to you, he should make a full recovery.'

'That's excellent news!' Gair's tiredness fell away. 'Can I see him?'

'Of course. I'll walk you down there. Is he always so energetic? We're having a hard time keeping him in bed.'

Outside in the dormitory court the wind still roared. Dead leaves whirled around their feet and the flagstones and rooftops gleamed like pewter under a louring sky.

'Forgive me if I'm being rude,' Tanith asked as they walked, 'but have you been graded yet? You're the only person around here apart from the staff and the children who doesn't have a mantle or a tunic.'

Gair thought of the carefully folded blue wool at the back of his closet. 'No one's said anything yet,' he told her, which was truthful enough. 'I suppose they haven't made their minds up.'

'But you've been here how long – three months? I've never known the Council take so long.'

'Maybe they just don't know what to do with me.'

She looked at him curiously. 'I remember when you were caught up in my healing – from what I saw then you seemed very strong, stronger than anyone I've come across in my time here except some of the Masters. What are you studying?'

'Everything, I think. I have weapons-practice twice a week with Master Haral, Master Coran for wards, Barin, Eavin, Esther and Godril for the four elements, and anyone else who feels like it for whatever they want me to try whenever I'm not doing anything else.'

Tanith's eyebrows arched in surprise. 'You're strong in all four elements?'

'I seem to be. There's nothing I've tried yet that I haven't been able to grasp eventually.'

The Astolan Healer stared at him and then breathed a word in her own language that had the rhythm of something most unlady-like. She held out her hands towards his face. 'May I?'

He shied back. 'Depends on what you're going to do.'

'It won't hurt.'

'That's what Master Brendan said when he wanted to find out why I found illusions so easy. He left me with a headache so bad I was seeing double.'

She laughed. 'Don't worry, I only want to look at you.'

Her hands came to rest on either side of his face and she closed her eyes. Her mind stroked over the surface of his thoughts like a feather, not unpleasant but a little ticklish.

'What are you doing?'

'Shush. I need to concentrate.'

Warmth and light flushed into him so abruptly it made him flinch. The delving washed through him from crown to toes and back again, making his nerves tingle and his skin sensitive. He became conscious of prickly wool trousers, chill stone striking up through his boots, his hair on the back of his neck, all the thousand and one everyday sensations that his mind usually screened out.

Tanith opened her eyes and as she took her hands away, the sensations faded. Her eyes had a curious, appraising quality that made him think of a jeweller assaying a gem.

'Without further testing I couldn't say what your full potential would be,' she said slowly. 'A full assay would take two Healers and probably half a dozen Masters, given what I've seen so far, and it would be far more exhaustive than your initial testing. It's not often done, you see, only in special cases.'

'And?'

'Well, I'd say you're probably a special case. I'll ask Saaron to put it to the Council next week, and then we'll see. At least you'll know your grade, one way or the other.'

At the infirmary Gair swung the door open for her and followed her through the waiting room to the ward. There were few patients, so most of the beds were empty. Tanith paused at the desk to exchange a few words with the Healer on duty, then pointed along the ward.

'There he is, right at the end,' she said.

Darin certainly looked better. His colour was good, although he had such dark shadows under his eyes that it looked like he should be sporting a broken nose. He was sipping a glass of cordial when he heard their footsteps and looked up.

'Gair!' he exclaimed, putting the glass on his side-table. A huge grin split his face. 'How've you been?'

'Tired, mostly.' Gair found himself a stool and sat down. 'What about you? Quite a few people are asking after you.'

'Oh, I'm fine. Another day, then Saaron says I can leave.'

'That's good to hear. You scared me half to death when I found you lying there unconscious.'

'I hardly remember anything about it,' Darin told him, pulling a face. 'One minute I'm making a regular dog's breakfast out of my essay for Donata, the next I'm flat on my back being spoon-fed honey by a gorgeous redhead.'

'Not a bad exchange.' Gair smiled.

'It's almost a shame to be spoken for. That Tanith is incredibly beautiful.'

Gair glanced along the ward, but the Astolan had gone. 'Master Donata told me to say she hoped you would be feeling better soon and you've got an extension until the end of next week on that essay.'

Darin's grin widened. 'More than enough time for you to write it for me, then. Promise you'll help me?' he pleaded. 'I always get better marks when you do.'

'Maybe you need to spend more time studying and less mooning over Renna.'

'I do not moon!'

Laughing, Gair tilted the stool onto two feet so he could lean more comfortably against the wall. 'If I get the time, I'll go over your assignment with you and help you work out the kinks, I promise, but the Masters keep me pretty busy. Do this, show me that, do it again, practice, practice, practice – it's all I can do to get them to give me time to sleep at nights. They still haven't made up their minds about grading me, either.'

'Haven't they?'

Gair shook his head. 'Even Tanith remarked on it. Is it rare?' For them to take so long to decide, I mean?'

'I've no idea,' Darin said. 'I've only been here two years, and everyone I know was graded almost immediately. Maybe the Council is having to make up a new category for you. You're easily the strongest of us, especially with the—' He gave a meaningful tilt of his head and lowered his voice. '—you know.'

'It's just a talent, Darin.'

'Yes, yes, so you say. Has Aysha ever said anything about the mantle?'

'No. It's like it never happened.'

'You still have it?'

'In my closet.'

'Maybe you should wear it in the refectory one day,' Darin suggested lightly. 'Might spice things up a bit. Did you know that half of Chapterhouse thinks you're her lover?'

The stool crashed down onto all four feet. '*What?*'

'You're always disappearing to her study for hours at a time. If you don't talk about that other talent, what else are people going to think?'

Gair's face began to burn. 'Darin, she's one of my teachers!'

'So? It wouldn't be the first time the rules have been broken.'

'I can't believe you'd even give the idea house-room. It's absurd.'

'There's a saying where I come from that rumours have the wings of eagles and truth can only walk. Give it enough time and everyone here will know the names of your children before you've even creased her sheets.'

'Darin, I'm not her lover, I swear.'

Even as he said it, his conscience reminded him of one or two occasions when he had been precisely that, tireless and tender, in the seclusion of his own head. The memory of those dreams flushed him scarlet. 'You're obsessed with sex,' he said weakly.

'I can't help it. Renna won't let me go below the waist and it's killing me.'

'As I recall, Renna has more than enough above the waist to keep your hands full.'

'She's got plenty of apples, but I want the whole orchard. I know, I know, the sacred act of union entails a commitment that is not to be undertaken lightly, but chastely, soberly and fiddle-de-dee.' The quotation from the marriage ceremony was delivered in Darin's idea of a priestly drone. 'That's all very well but my stones are turning blue.'

'I don't think I need to know that!'

'You've got to tell me what's happening between you and

Aysha, though. You owe me that much. It's really just shape-shifting? Nothing else?'

'Nothing but fresh air and healthy exercise, I promise. And lots of tea and arguing when the weather's bad. She hates the cold.'

'Uh-huh.'

'Don't look at me like that, I'm telling you the truth. We fly a lot, or go up into the hills as wolves, that sort of thing. She's taught me some new shapes, and how to improve a few I hadn't quite got the trick of, but that's all.'

'You know, you never did show me that.'

'You won't take my word for it?'

'I believe you, Gair; I'd just like to see it for myself, if you don't mind.'

'Here?'

'Now's as good a time as any.'

Gair closed his eyes and reached into himself for the Song. It filled him in an instant. He let the music enfold him, then dipped into it and found the shape of a fire-eagle. The flat surface of the stool made perching difficult and his talons gouged runnels in the varnish, so after a few moments he changed back.

Darin's eyes were so wide they looked ready to fall out of his head. He swore, colourfully and at some length. 'I have never, ever, *ever* seen anything like that before! It's incredible. How long have you been able to do that?'

'Since I was eleven years old.'

Flopping back against his pillows, Darin shoved his fingers through his hair. 'I don't know what to say.'

'That's a first for you.'

'Thank you.' The Belishan gave him a sickly smile.

'You're welcome.'

Tanith reappeared on silent slippered feet, carrying a cup which she set down on the nightstand. 'I'm sorry, but I think Darin has perhaps had enough for one day, and he has some medicine to take. Shall I walk you to the door?'

Darin grumbled, but was mollified when Gair promised to visit again the following day, after supper. He left the Belisthan drinking his medicine and pulling faces at the taste and walked with Tanith to the infirmary entrance. As soon as he stepped over the threshold, Aysha was there in his head, clamouring for his attention and demanding to know where he was. He winced; she was shouting.

'Is there something wrong?' Tanith asked.

'Master Aysha.' He gestured at his head. 'She wants to know where I've been.'

'The infirmary's shielded,' Tanith told him. 'It has to be; the chatter of hundreds of minds working with the Song at once interferes with our concentration. It's very distracting, like trying to hear what one person is saying in a crowd. The duty physician is excluded so that messages can be passed back and forth, but I suppose she didn't know you were here.' She tipped her head to one side. 'You could shut her out and only answer if it's convenient for you.'

'I don't know how,' he admitted. 'I can't communicate like that.'

'Really?' Tanith gave him another appraising look. 'You are a strange one. You have come such a long way with your gifts, but you haven't stumbled across the ability to speak with your mind.'

'There're quite a few things I haven't stumbled across. The Masters are always commenting on how I find the difficult things easy, but haven't yet picked up the simple ones.'

'It happens sometimes, even among my people. We don't quite know why. It might be something similar to the way some babies learn to speak and walk before others.'

'My foster-mother used to say I was a slow starter.'

Tanith smiled. 'There you are, then. It'll come to you in time. Now you had best be going. I can feel her impatience from here.'

'Actually, I'm due a tutorial with Master Coran this morning.'

'Oh!' Confusion eddied across Tanith's face, then became a

blush. 'Well, it's past Prime, so you'd better hurry. If there's one thing that irks Coran, it's lateness. Good day to you.'

With her cheeks as dusky as one of his foster-mother's roses, she hurried back into the infirmary.

As he walked towards the lecture halls, Gair was uncomfortably certain that she had heard the rumours too. He tugged the cord from his hair, finger-combed it into an approximation of neatness and tied it back again. Mother have mercy on him, he'd thought his shape-shifting was enough to set tongues wagging. Now he had another reason to ensure he stuck to his schedule of tutorials in future, or he'd be keeping Chapterhouse in gossip to the end of his days.

23

FAITH

☙

Wrapped in a thick robe, Danilar stood at the window of his lodging and sipped his tea. Morning was his favourite time, and winter mornings especially, with the sky thin and blue as Western Isles crystal and the world holding its breath for the first bird. Into such a hush, he was sure, the Goddess must have spoken the Word that sparked life into Her creation. The new day was always filled with such promise.

Across the quadrangle, a light burned in the Preceptor's window. Dawn on a winter's day, and the old man was already up. Or perhaps he had been awake all night. Ansel kept erratic hours these days, drowsing in the afternoons, shuffling through the empty corridors late at night. Hengfors opined that old people often needed less sleep than younger men because they were less active, but he could not stifle the rumours that the Preceptor's wits were failing.

Tea finished, Danilar donned some warm buskins for the walk down to the Knights' Chapel. Hoarfrost crisped the few remaining leaves on the shrubs in the quadrangle, and the cold flags of the sanctuary promised another, harder frost to come. Genuflecting deeply before the altar, left palm out in the sign of the Oak, he breathed thanks that the rumours were not true.

In the vestry, he dressed a tray with a plain linen napkin and set out the small silver cup, box and plate for the sacrament, replicas of the larger golden pyx that gleamed on the high altar. He decanted some blessed wine into the cup and laid another napkin over the tray, then carried it out through the side door into the corridor that led towards the Preceptor's lodging.

As Danilar balanced the tray on one hand to let himself into Ansel's study, Hengfors stepped out, his scrip over his shoulder.

The heron-faced physician greeted him. 'He's taking the sacrament alone?' Pale eyes stared down his nose at the tray.

'The chapel is cold. He finds it hard to kneel for long, now. How is he?'

'His joints are paining him more and more,' Hengfors said, head dipping on its long neck. 'I have never seen him look so frail. I will do what I can, of course, but his life is in the hands of the Goddess now.'

'They are gentle hands, I am sure. If it is time for Her to call Her son home, She will call him softly.'

'And you will know that best, Danilar, as Her voice on earth.' Hengfors chuckled. 'Good day to you.'

'Good day, Hengfors.'

Danilar nudged the door open with his hip, then pushed it closed behind him with his heel. Finding an uncluttered part of the desk on which to set the tray was difficult. He frowned. The Preceptor had always been a tidy administrator; it was unlike him to leave it like this, with drifts of paper, books lying open, a half-eaten meal abandoned on top of a stack of ledgers.

'I'm too old to waste my time putting things away,' said Ansel. He sat in a chair by the hearth, propped up on pillows and with a blanket over his knees. A single candle burned on the mantelpiece, illuminating a book open in his lap but shrouding the rest of the inglenook in shadow. His twisted hands twitched over the pages like spiders.

'Have you brought the sacrament?'

'I have, my lord Preceptor.'

'Well, over here, man, over here!' The voice was quavery, but the temper was as steely as ever.

Danilar suppressed a smile. He placed the tray carefully on Ansel's lap, lifted the top napkin and draped it across the thin chest.

Bright eyes glared at him from the pinched, sallow face. 'Don't treat me like an invalid, boy! I'm not drooling yet.'

'Quite. Are you going to be quiet for the blessing, or am I going to have to gag you?'

'You wouldn't dare!'

'Wouldn't I?' Calmly Danilar lifted the lid on the silver box and removed a wafer. He held it out and sketched the sign of the Oak in the air with it. 'You have the good temper of a bear with a broken head, but we all love you very much and I will see to the safety of your immortal soul if I have to tie you down to do it. This is the bounty of the Goddess that She gave us that we Her children would not starve. Open wide.'

He placed the wafer on Ansel's tongue. The Preceptor pulled a face at the taste of the herbs and salt, but swallowed it. Danilar lifted the cup and made the sign of the Oak again, then offered the wine.

'This is the bounty of the Goddess that She gave us that we Her children would not thirst.'

Ansel drank with much more relish. He had always had a taste for Tylan red. Eyes closed, he leaned forward slightly so that Danilar could draw the Oak on his forehead.

'This is the bounty of the Goddess that She gave us that we Her children should not falter. Be at peace in the certainty of Her love. Amen.'

'Amen.'

Danilar covered the tray with the napkin again and set it on the desk. Then he sat down in the chair across the hearth from Ansel with his feet stretched out to soak up the fire's warmth. 'Has there been any news?' he asked.

287

'None. I thought we might have heard by now. Do you still think we have done the right thing?'

'I am certain of it.'

'I cannot help but feel I have left too much to chance,' Ansel said with a sigh. 'Well, it's too late now. Too late for everything, except faith.'

'And hope.'

'And hope as well, but it's a precious thin branch on which to hang everything. Precious thin.' He shook his head. 'There are so many things that I always wanted to see, Danilar, that now I know I never will.'

'Such as?'

'Oh, just fancies, those trivial things that lodge in a man's heart in the course of his life.' His expression grew faraway, faded eyes seeing landscapes Danilar could only imagine. 'Midsummer's Eve in the Northern Isles, when the sun does not set but hangs in the midnight sky like a lantern. The view from the highest peak in the Archen Mountains. The throne room of the Caliph's palace in Abu Nidar – did you know the walls are supposed to be a hundred feet high and covered entirely in gold leaf? They say he has a drinking cup hollowed from a single diamond, and a wife for every day of the year.'

'The Caliph of Abu Nidar is a barbarian infidel.' Danilar folded his hands in the sleeves of his robe.

'True,' Ansel conceded, 'but a fabulously wealthy one. Is it just me, Danilar, or do you think infidels have a rather better time of it than we do?'

'I understand the Caliph has to employ bodyguards and a food-taster, and spends his days pondering which of his cousins and nephews will try to murder him next.'

'I think I could live with that, if I were as rich as him.'

'That's a perilously heretical thought, Ansel.'

The Preceptor grunted sourly. 'Old age does that to a man.

Once your time starts running out, you start thinking about all the things you should have done with it.'

'Are you doubting your vocation? So late in the day?'

'Don't be ridiculous. I'm hardly going to recant at the gates of Heaven, am I? If I had my time over again, I think the Goddess would still speak to me in my heart and call me to Her service. Sometimes I wonder what I would have done if She had not, but it's just a game. I am content.'

'I am glad to hear it,' Danilar said, and smiled. 'All will be well, Ansel.'

'I hope so,' the Preceptor sighed. 'It's too late to change anything now. We have cast the dice. Only the Goddess knows which faces they will show when they come to rest.' He looked down at the book on his lap, smoothing the pages over and over. 'There is a letter, on my desk. Can you arrange to have it delivered?'

'Of course.'

'It has a long way to go. Perhaps I should have sent it sooner, not left it so late, but I didn't know . . .' He closed the book with a snap, arthritic fingers gripping the worn binding tightly. 'I am blind, Danilar. I am fumbling in the dark, with no clue as to what I might be treading on, what I might stir up, and I am very afraid that I will not be here to see the outcome. It is torment, not knowing. I just wish there was some way that I could find out what will be!'

'You know that is not possible, Ansel,' Danilar said gently.

'I know. Visions and oracles are the province of the Caliph of Abu Nidar and his like. Still, it would be good to know.'

Sinking back against his pillows, Ansel closed his eyes and his lips moved soundlessly, as if he prayed for strength and guidance.

Danilar watched him, thinking how frail he had come to look in recent weeks. Winter weather was unkind to him, stiffening his joints until every movement stabbed him with red-hot needles. Only heat brought any relief. The Preceptor should have spent his last years in a kinder climate. The Suvaeon maintained a retreat in

Gimrael, in the Glass Hills above El Maqqam, where the savage heat of the plains was tempered by cooling breezes. It was peaceful there, and more comfortable than a house of the Goddess should decently be. That would surely soothe Ansel's old bones, but Danilar feared the journey alone would kill him now. It was far too late; too late for everything, now, except faith and hope.

Danilar crossed to the desk, where a letter he had not noticed before was propped against the inkwell. He slipped it under the napkin on the tray and reached for the door handle.

Ansel's head turned on the pillow. In the shadows cast by the candle Danilar could see nothing of his expression but the glitter of his eyes.

'I envy you the strength of your vocation, Danilar,' he said, his voice so soft that it was barely louder than the whispering flames in the grate. 'Mine has worn thin over the years. Lately when I listen for the voice of the Goddess in my heart, I can scarcely hear it for the beating of my own mortality.'

'Maybe She is closer than you think.'

'Aye, maybe She is.' Ansel's silhouette changed fractionally. It might have been a smile. 'Good day, Danilar.'

Back in the vestry, the Chaplain took off his surplice, shook it out and hung it up in the closet ready for next service. Then he carefully rinsed and dried the silverware and stowed it away in the velvet-lined pyx-chest. Only when all the chores were done did he sit down and look at the letter sitting on the tray. The name and address on the front was written in Ansel's spidery hand. Something small but solid, quite heavy, nestled inside the folds of parchment. Once he would have wondered what it was; perhaps even asked. Now he knew better.

Tucking the letter into a pocket of his robe, Danilar let himself out and locked the vestry door behind him. Later he would go down into the city, after evening service. A man lived by the Water-gate who could be trusted to carry out tasks discreetly; Danilar had used him before and knew he could be relied upon to keep his silence. He would want to be paid well for this one, though, to go so far at this time of year, when the return journey would take him into the teeth of winter. Still, there remained gold enough. All that was in short measure was time.

☙☙

He should not have come. Whatever he was being paid, it was not enough for stinking canals, and sin as thick in the air as the heat that made it so hard to sleep, heat that was unseasonable even for southern Syfria. He'd had to spend a month in it, eating their strangely spiced food and trawling the dives and doss-houses of Haven-port looking for a man he was beginning to think did not exist. He should not have come.

Pieter adjusted his mask again. The sequinned thing sat too close against his face, and the forked ribbon that was the serpent's tongue kept catching in his mouth when he talked. But he'd needed it; an uncovered face in the Havens on Fools' Night was conspicuous.

One more tavern to try. A couple of cups of cheap brandy and some artfully worded questions had led him here; he hoped it would be a fruitful visit. There were only two pigeons left in the cage he had brought from Dremen.

He peered round the corner again. The place looked quiet enough. Footsteps sounded behind him, and a stifled giggle. A man's voice, too deep to make out, was followed by a woman's purr of pleasure. Pieter glanced back over his shoulder. A burly fellow with docker's tattoos and a raven's mask had his hands all over a slim girl in a gauzy costume that barely reached her knees. As he watched she spread her legs and slid the docker's hand up between her thighs. The raven fondled her, then backed her up against the wall, fumbling at the front of his trousers.

Pieter blinked. *Had she no shame?* The girl's mask looked expensive, and she had the pale, soft flesh of gentle birth. Yet there she was, with her buttocks clutched in tattooed hands, rutting in an alley in full view of the raucous revellers staggering down the main street. The docker grunted, his thrusting hips picking up speed, and the girl clung to his shoulders with her head thrown back and her moth mask swinging from her fingers in time with their coupling. *Shameless!*

This city, on this night, was no place for a man of faith. Pieter dragged his eyes away from the brazen display in the alley and crossed the street to the tavern. Too many people, drinking and fornicating as if their actions were ephemeral and could be discarded on the morrow with the masks, when their old lives crept back into their rooms with the morning sun.

He glanced through the tavern window. Yes, there was the man he sought, alone in a corner nursing a pint mug, with his dog curled round his feet under the table. 'Forgive me intruding, friend, but are you the master of the *Trader Rose*?'

Pieter pushed through the door and crossed to the counter, where he bought a bottle of brandy. Then he carried the bottle and two cups to the bargee's table.

Skeff peered up at him. 'Aye, that I am.'

'Mind if I sit with you for a spell?' Pieter set the bottle and cups down in the middle of the table and pulled up a stool.

Skeff eyed the bottle speculatively. 'Sure,' he said.

'You run to Mesarild, don't you? Ever pick up passengers?'

'Mebbe. When there's coin to be had, only a fool turns it down.'

Pieter poured two measures from the bottle and pushed one cup across the table. 'I'm looking for a friend of mine, came down this way from Mesarild in the summer. I'm worried something's happened to him. Do you think you might have seen him?'

'Might have, might not. People need a ride from here to there, I don't ask no questions, so long as they pays me.' He drained his mug in two noisy slurps, then wrapped his hands around the cup of spirit, but did not drink. His one bleary eye sharpened. 'You say you're a friend o' his?'

'I'm afraid he might have met some trouble. The river's been bad for bandits this past year, so I hear.'

'Aye, terrible bad.' Finally Skeff raised the brandy to his lips and took a slug.

It might not have been anything like as good as the Elder's goldwine, but the bargee smacked his lips and beamed all over his saggy face.

Pieter's own cup remained untouched. 'Anything you might be able to tell me would be helpful,' he prompted.

'Did take some passengers, this past St Tamastide. What's he like, your friend?'

'Tall lad, Leahn. Travelling with his uncle.' Pieter topped up Skeff's drink and tried not to smile as the bargee's eye fixed on the golden liquid rising up the cup. 'He wears a sword across his back.'

'Aye, I saw him. Nice lad. Had manners.' Skeff raised the brimming cup. 'Good to have him aboard. Bandits was terrible bad that trip, terrible bad. He helped see them off when they came for the *Rose*.'

'Lucky he was there, then. You brought him down to the Havens?'

'Before the storms. Dunno where he was headed after. Never said, and I don't ask no questions.'

So the trail ended there. A month of waiting and searching in this appalling city, all for nothing.

'There's nothing more you can remember?'

Skeff drained his cup and set it down, turning it round and round between his hands. Pieter filled it again, just in case it helped.

'Not from that trip. O' course, I seen his uncle afore, few times, mebbe twice a year. Sometimes on his own, sometimes not. Said he had a house on the Isles.'

Pieter's spirits rose. 'The Western Isles?'

'Aye, think so. Said the climate suited him. Might know where your friend went. There're ships to Pencruik now, since the storms stopped.'

Good news at last. Standing, Pieter slid the half-empty bottle across the table to Skeff. 'Thanks for your help, friend,' he said. 'Keep this, with my compliments.'

Then he hurried back out into the sultry night. The Western Isles weren't that far, and he'd been careful with the gold Goran had given him. There was more than enough left to pay for passage. Finally, he had something to report.

24

A CHANGE IN
THE WEATHER

❧

Ten days short of Eventide, winter finally arrived on Penglas. A hard frost silvered the landscape overnight and left a shawl of white over the inland mountains that reminded Gair sharply of the Laraig Anor. He had a free day, his first since he'd given his word to Master Barin, but he was spending it alone. Aysha hadn't called him. He wasn't sure if she would ever call him again.

In the last few days the wind had backed to south of west and brought some welcome sunshine. The instant the weather changed she stepped into his thoughts, colours vibrant, compelling. *Come fly with me.* But he had given his word, and that he could not break. Morning and evening she railed at him, demanding, imprecating, occasionally lapsing into some lyrical desert epithet that made his ears burn even without translation. Though ignoring her twisted a guilty knife inside him, he stuck to his timetable and attended all his tutorials.

This morning, the fifth-floor apartment on the west side of Chapterhouse was silent.

Snow-crust crunched under Gair's paws, sparkling like sugar in the low sun. The perfect day to be a wolf. In the creased and folded uplands of Penglas were deep drifts to bound through, and shaggy-coated deer to chase. He had thought a run in the snow would help him think, but he might as well be chasing his tail. All he could think about was her.

Not for the first time he wished he had the knack of speaking with his mind. He'd searched for Aysha's colours in the shimmering cloud that was Chapterhouse, trying to puzzle it through from first principles, but either she'd shielded herself or she was not there. He'd tried and failed to write a note. Climbing the stairs and knocking at her door would be simple, yet he'd shied from that idea like a yearling colt.

Maybe he should have chosen a different shape. The last time he had run as a wolf, he had been with Aysha. He could still taste her mouth, feel the pressure of her lips. If only he'd seen it coming. If he'd guessed what she was going to do he could have reacted, responded somehow. Instead he'd just lain there in the grass like a gaffed salmon and let her get away.

He leapt a frozen beck and ran on. But what would he have done, pushed her away? Kissed her back? Maybe seized her by the scruff and made her his, right there on the mountainside, in the way of the pack?

Goddess help him, what was he thinking? She was on the Council of Masters, in a position of authority over him. If their roles had been reversed and he'd been the one stealing kisses, she should have slapped his face and he would have considered it no less than he deserved. That was the way he'd been raised. From the moment he was old enough to understand that boys and girls were different he'd been taught to offer his arm, to bow, to be gentlemanly, and the Knights had put a good gloss polish on that. Aysha exploded through the Suvaeon chivalric code like a firework through a windowpane.

The warning tingle came too late. Powerful paws struck him hard between the shoulders and sent him rolling into a drift. He bounced back to his feet and shook himself, spraying snow crystals into the air. The other wolf pounced again, growling deep in her chest. Teeth sought his throat. He staggered under her weight, then heaved her off to one side. Her paws scrabbled for purchase in the powdery snow, but the jaws buried in his ruff did not let go. Gair tried to wrench himself free, falling onto his side. The she-wolf kicked back with her hindquarters and sent them rolling down the slope. Biting, clawing, snow in their ears and stinging their nostrils, they fetched up hard against the roots of a fallen tree, with the full weight of the she-wolf driving her paws into Gair's ribs.

Amber eyes glared down the long muzzle at him. Lips curled back from sharp white teeth as the growl increased in pitch and volume. Then she snapped. Hot breath washed his face before her jaws clicked closed a hair's-breadth from the end of his nose.

You need to learn your place, youngling.

Gair released the Song. His body stretched back into human form, but it did not help his situation overmuch. Though he was tall, the she-wolf was almost as long from muzzle to plumy tail, and she had all her weight behind her as she bore down on his ribcage. His throat stung where her teeth had grazed his skin.

'Master Aysha.'

Where the hell have you been?

'I gave my word to Master Barin that I'd attend all my tutorials. Today's the first free day I've had since then.' His breath steamed on the chilly air. Though he spoke softly, his voice still seemed loud enough to shatter the mountain morning.

The she-wolf glared a moment longer, then settled back on her haunches. *A man of honour. A rare beast, these days.*

Gair sat up. Snow had got down the back of his jerkin to make an uncomfortable damp patch in his shirt. He felt his neck and his fingers came away with the tiniest smear of scarlet. He would have to be careful shaving for the next day or two, or else start to cultivate a beard if he was to prevent people knowing he had come within a whisker of having his throat torn out.

The she-wolf licked her chops and lay down with her head on her paws. *Sorry about that.*

'I'll live.'

At least you're still practising. She lifted her head again, ears pricked. *There're a few whitejack in the next valley. Hunt with me?*

'Master Aysha, this conversation would be much easier if you taught me mindspeech.'

Call me Aysha. Out here, I am not your master. Hunt with me and I'll teach you.

'Teach me and I'll hunt with you.'

The she-wolf cocked her head to one side. *A bargain?*

'A bargain.'

Then it is done. She stood and lifted her muzzle to scent the air, smoky breath wreathing her face. With a yip she bounded for the trees. *Catch me if you can!*

&

Aysha pressed her hands to her temples and propped her elbows on her knees. 'Goddess in glory,' she groaned, 'you don't know your own strength.'

'Sorry.'

'You're supposed to introduce yourself first, like knocking on a door, not come roaring in like a charging *lyran*.'

'I'm sorry!'

'All right.' She straightened up and made a beckoning gesture. 'Come on, try again – but gently!'

They sat beneath a rocky overhang near the head of the valley, where the snow had not yet reached. A thick carpet of pine needles made a comfortable place to sit for the lesson. Gair took a deep breath and let it out slowly. Now, her colours. He found them straight away, a brilliant constellation in the vast, dark place in which the Masters had greeted him after his testing. Reaching out, he brushed against her pattern and waited for her to acknowledge him. It was rather like knocking on a door, though what he knocked with was nothing so solid as knuckles, and the door was as intangible as a dream.

Aysha greeted him graciously, then invited him to step inside. She had created a hollow within the folded patterns of her colours, a lobby in her thoughts. Apart from the gently swirling hues, he saw nothing, but the sense of her presence was very strong.

Much better, she said.

It's easier than I thought.

You would have worked it out for yourself eventually, I think.

Gair wasn't so sure; inviting another into the very heart of his gift, the way she had invited him, felt too much like baring his chest to a blade and trusting the hand that held it not to drive it home. It went against every instinct he had.

Exploring cautiously, he realised what he could perceive was only the tiniest fraction of her. There was more, he was sure of it. Though the five physical senses did not strictly apply in this place, wherever it was, something analogous to sight told him there were layers of colour behind this surface, intricately shaded with emotion and memory.

He reached out, and she slapped the back of his hand.

No peeking.

Sorry. He drew back. *Can you show me how to do that? Close parts of me off so no one can get in unless I invite them?*

Like me, you mean?

Gair started guiltily and she laughed.

Now it's my turn to apologise. I know I pounce on you.

I don't mind. But sometimes you do shout a bit.

Her colours swirled with amusement.

Gair was fascinated, seeing and feeling laughter instead of hearing it.

I'll show you some other time. You're not ready for it yet – you need a lot more practice.

She drew back further and he guessed this was an invitation to leave. He departed as gracefully as he could manage.

'I only know your colours, so far,' he said when contact was broken. Not strictly true; he could recognise a few of the other Masters, but he doubted they would welcome him in for a chat. Except maybe Alderan.

'Then you'll just have to practise on me until you're safe to be let loose on the population at large without giving us all a migraine.'

※

A chill wind gusted across Aysha's balcony. Pellets of frozen snow rattled on the slate tiles and stung hands and faces as she and Gair completed the shape-shift back to human form.

Ducking against the squall, one arm raised to shield her face, Aysha limped to the doors. The instant she opened them, jade-green brocade curtains enveloped her like a conjuror's cloak round a caged dove.

'Wait—!' Gair hurried after her.

Too late.

'*Khajali*!'

Brocade ripped and the brass curtain rod clattered to the floor.

Gair pushed past the remaining curtain and found Aysha slumped next to her overturned desk chair, smothered in yards of fabric. He dropped to his knees beside her and lifted the heavy brocade off her head. 'Saints, are you all right? Are you hurt?'

Murderous blue eyes glared at him. Her free arm shoved him away. 'Of course I'm all right! Haven't you ever seen a cripple fall over before? Give me some room, damn it.'

Bent curtain hooks pattered onto the rug as she tugged at the fabric wound round her body until she'd freed her arms. Ignoring his proffered hand, she snatched up her fallen canes and levered herself onto her knees, then tried to stand. Her left ankle buckled and with a cry of rage and pain, she sprawled back at Gair's feet. '*Khajal me no suri jarat!*' Flat-eyed as a bathed cat, she clenched her jaws so tight every breath whistled through her teeth.

300

Gair slid an arm round her shoulders and the other under her knees and picked her up, curtain and all.

'Leave me be.'

'Aysha, you can't stand.'

'I said leave me be – are you deaf or just dense?' A balled fist thumped his shoulder. 'Put me down.'

The next blow grazed his jaw. He jerked his head back. 'Stop that.'

'Put me *down*!'

'Will you hold still? I'm only trying to help.'

'I don't need anyone's help. I'm fine!'

Kneeling, he set her on the couch by the hearth. Aysha glared at him, then hauled back his fist.

Gair grabbed her wrist before the punch landed. 'That's enough.'

'*Ayya qi makhani!*' Her other hand landed a stinging slap across his ear.

'I said that's *enough*!' He wrestled her hands into the small of her back. Aysha twisted her shoulders left and right, trying to free herself, and he tightened his grip.

Storm-clouded eyes flashed. '*Bhakkan! Me no suri jarat!* Let me go!'

'Not until you promise not to hit me.'

'Bastard! You're hurting me!'

'Your word, Aysha!'

White teeth chewed up curses and spat them in his face. She didn't repeat a single phrase as her passionate mouth sculpted a torrent of invective that filled his ears like song.

Gair couldn't help but stare. It didn't matter what she said as long as he could watch her say it. Aysha furious was the most beautiful thing he had ever seen.

She glared back, panting. Every breath pushed her breasts against his chest. 'What are you staring at? Let me go.'

'I want your word.' He wanted to kiss her.

'Fine. You have it. Now let. Me. Go.'

He released her wrists. Aysha rubbed at the fingermarks blooming on her cinnamon skin. 'You hurt me.'

'You were trying to hit me.'

'You deserved it.'

'For picking you up off the floor?'

One dark brow arched. 'Spare me the knightly courtesies, please. I'm not some helpless *ammanai* milksop who takes to her bed if she so much as pricks her finger with a tapestry needle!'

'You would rather I just left you there?'

'I'm a cripple, you slugwit.' Scorn stung like a cold razor. 'Sometimes I fall over. I am quite capable of picking myself up again – Goddess knows, I've had enough practice. I do not need to wait around for some man with more hair on his arse than brains in his head to come and do it for me!'

Gair threw up his hands. Impossible woman. Beautiful, impossible woman, and he wanted to kiss her so much it hurt. 'Are you done, or do you want to insult me some more?'

A gust of wind threw hailstones in through the open balcony doors and he flung them closed with the Song.

Aysha seized his shirt collar in both hands. 'I'm not done,' she said, and kissed him.

The Song flew out of Gair's grasp. Soft lips, stronger than he'd expected. They teased his mouth open, letting him taste her. Goddess in heaven. He took hold of her shoulders and pushed her away. 'We can't.'

She stared at him, cheeks flushed. 'You don't want me.'

'It's not that. Master Aysha—'

'I told you, Leahn. Just Aysha.'

'You're on the Council of Masters. I'm only a student. There're rules—'

'Stupid rules!' she flared. 'Rules for children, to save them from themselves. Neither of us is a child.' She let go of his shirt, smoothing out the creases, and her hands carried on smoothing, right into his open jerkin. Gair swallowed, mouth suddenly dry as fingertips traced his collarbones, mapped out the planes of his chest.

'It wouldn't be right.' She was his *teacher*.

'That doesn't make it wrong.' Down further, outlining the ridges where his abdominal muscles contracted under her touch.

Holy Mother. He reached for her hands to stop her when she got to his belt, but they slipped out of his grasp like fish.

'Kiss me.'

No more than a breath on his face. Gair shut his eyes tightly. 'I can't.'

'Why?'

'Because I'm afraid that if I start kissing you I won't be able to stop.' He opened his eyes again. 'You scare me, Aysha. The way you make me feel scares me. I don't know what to do around you. I—' Whatever he'd been about to say piled up in his throat and died. She was so close. Too close.

He lunged for her mouth, found it, and somehow it fitted to his. Her lips parted under his tongue. Kiss after kiss, urgent, hungry. Fingers tangled in his hair, her body supple in his arms. *Yes.*

'I want you.' Her words were crushed between kisses. 'I've wanted you since the moment I saw you fly.'

She tugged his shirt from his belt. Gair shucked off his jerkin, snatched his shirt over his head and gathered her up again. Her touch skittered over him like flames, making him shiver even as he burned.

Aysha's scent permeated every breath he took: linen and winter and sweet soft skin. The deeper he drew it into his lungs, the more he wanted her.

White teeth nipped at his lip. She hitched forward on the couch, straddling his hips. Goddess, yes! He pulled her closer and she folded her legs around him. The couch creaked under their combined weight, feet skidding on the hardwood floor. Aysha's shirt had rucked in the small of her back; Gair slipped his fingers underneath.

She gasped, 'Cold hands!'

'Sorry, I—'

'No, don't stop. I want to feel your hands on me.'

She fumbled the buttons open, let her shirt fall down her arms. Gair's hands shook. Swordsman's calluses snagged on her filmy chemise, but he peeled the silk off over her head.

Tawny breasts spilled onto his chest. 'Touch me.' Another kiss, another nip that jolted straight to the base of his spine. 'Touch me, please . . .'

She was warm, firm, sleek as a cat. She arched under his caress, pushing into his hands, pressing her hips against him. The couch feet squealed again.

Goddess, he wanted her so much, ached with it. He lifted Aysha up and laid her on the thick *qilim*.

'Make a light.' She heeled off her boots, wriggled out of the rest of her clothes. 'I want to see you.'

A thought flung a fistful of tiny glims into the air, then he had no more thoughts at all, only sensation: Aysha's mouth under his, her hands undressing him, cool fingers on his overheated flesh, guiding him into her . . . No time to waste; no time to wait. She moved with him, body rising to meet his, over and over. Her arms locked tight around him.

'*Khalan bey*,' she whispered. '*Khalan bey!*'

❧

Tanith poured another cup of peppermint tea from the pot on the hearth and settled back into her chair. Oh, her feet hurt. She had been in the infirmary since breakfast, supervising the adepts making a batch of flagwort ointment. Normally she rather enjoyed concocting the various medicaments to restock the dispensary, but flagwort ointment, she freely admitted, she loathed. The iron-hard roots had to be simmered in vinegar until they softened, then pounded into a paste, then the paste – which stank even worse than the boiling vinegar – had to be beaten into a neutral emollient base.

By the time the bowls were ranged neatly on the shelves in the cooling room the afternoon was well advanced and the wretched stuff still had to be decanted into jars, labelled and put away. She kicked off her slippers to rub her aching feet. The novices could do the labelling tomorrow for a little extra credit, she decided. It would be useful for them to learn that there was more to Healing than just the Song.

It was a pity she would not be there to see the rest of her students take their mantles. She had been dreadfully nervous with her first few classes, but it was so rewarding to see them grasp new techniques under her guidance, and to watch their confidence growing along with their skills. When she had first come to Chapterhouse she had never imagined that she would one day be teaching, but Saaron had had no hesitation in recommending her to the rest of the Council. She would find it a real wrench, leaving the students behind when the time came to return to Astolar.

She opened her book at the ribbon-marker, but the light was fading towards dusk. Reaching for the Song to make a glim she sensed the resonance of another weaving close at hand. It wasn't any of the other Masters, but the pattern seemed familiar: emerald and amber, with moonstone-white and obsidian and a deep wine-red, threaded through with glittering gold and strands of lustrous pearl. Whoever it was had not learned to guard their colours; they swirled tumultuously, scintillant with powerful emotion. Then she heard the faint, unmistakable sounds coming from the floor above and snatched her awareness away.

Oh. So that was how the land lay. Quickly she spun a glim over her shoulder and focused on her book, trying to ignore the heat in her cheeks. It was no business of hers what others chose to do in their private time, even if they themselves did not care who heard them. No business of hers at all. Now, Barthalus' *Essays on Government*, chapter four. She really ought to finish it tonight. Barthalus' prose was dry as dust, but his book remained the definitive work in its field. With luck it might help her navigate the shoals of the White Court – but only if she could manage to read more than the first three sentences before becoming distracted by the passionate rhythm from the apartment above.

What was she *doing*, listening to them like that? Face aflame with mortification she darkened the illusion spread across her ceiling until all the constellations of Astolar sparkled over her. Evening filled her room with a soft breeze and the sweet song of nightingales, but it was not enough. She knew who wore those colours now. She shut her eyes, her book sliding from her lap to the floor, teacup forgotten in her hand. Spirits hold her and keep her, she knew who he was.

It was difficult to avoid overhearing the students gossip, in spite of her best efforts. Their prurience had shocked her almost as much as discovering just how well informed they could be. Now she knew for certain that at least one of the rumours was true.

❧

The tattoo on the nape of Aysha's neck was about the size of a gold Imperial, a stylised crescent moon with an arc of stars between the horns. Gair propped his head on his hand and studied it. He had only seen a tattooed woman once before: the Painted Lady at the fair, who wore the lives of the saints in her skin like the Book of Eador made flesh. There had been scarcely an inch of her not illuminated, but he could not recall what she looked like. The tattoo Aysha wore measured no more than an inch across, and he could not drag his eyes away.

She was sleeping now, cradled in the curve of his body. Her breathing was slow and regular, one hand curled like a half-open flower beside her face. Careful not to wake her, he drew the ruined curtain that served them as a blanket up to her shoulders.

'You're staring,' she murmured, eyes still closed.

'I can't help it. You're beautiful.' Leaning down, he put his lips to the crescent moon. 'I didn't know you had a tattoo.'

'It's my slave-mark. That's the sigil of the trader who first sold me.'

Gair jerked his head back. 'And you *kept* it?'

She shrugged. 'I liked the design.'

'I was going to say I liked it.'

Aysha turned over, curiosity quirking her brows. 'And now you don't?'

'No.'

'Because it marks me as someone's possession? I've never known any different, Leahn. My mother was property, so I was property too.'

'It's repellent.'

'It's just ink,' she said gently.

'I mean what it signifies. I don't like the idea of you belonging to someone.'

'Someone other than you, you mean?' Amusement sparkled in her eyes. 'Are you jealous?'

'People are not objects to be owned.'

'You are, you're jealous!'

He pulled her close and kissed her. 'Maybe a little.'

'Why, sir knight, I'm flattered.' Another kiss, longer this time. Aysha pushed her fingers into his hair as it fell around her face. 'You should keep your hair long. It suits you.'

'Do you think so?' He raked it back, but it flopped forward again like a Barrowshire's forelock. 'I was too afraid to go near the barber at the Motherhouse in case he tonsured me when I wasn't looking.'

She tucked a few strands behind his ear.

'I like it. Bring your comb and razor sometime and I'll trim it for you, if you want.'

'You can do that?'

'That's how I made my living in the souq – I apprenticed myself to a barber. I was cutting hair before you were shaving more than once a week. Speaking of which' – she stroked a fingernail along his stubbled jaw – 'I could give you a good shave too.'

Gair rubbed the tingle from his chin. 'Is there something wrong with the way I'm doing it?'

'Not at all, but the desert way gives the closest finish. It's the berassa oil. If I could find a shop here that sold it, I could give you the best shave you've ever had.'

He smiled. 'Modest as well as beautiful.'

Aysha rolled her eyes. 'I should warn you, Leahn, I outgrew *The Summer Knight and the Snow Queen* when I was nine. If you start composing sonnets it will go badly for you.'

'That book's not a very accurate depiction of the life of a Knight, you know.'

'Just as well. I'm not a very accurate depiction of a lady,' she said, and drew him down.

Gair lost himself in her mouth. He should have been exhausted from their coupling, but her hands gliding over him erased any fatigue. In no time he was hard again, more than ready for her. She arched her back, pushing her breasts towards his mouth. He closed his lips around first one berry-dark nipple, then the other.

'Stay with me,' she whispered when he lifted his head. 'Stay the night.'

Above them, the mantel clock chimed a soft Second.

'It's getting late.' Goddess knew he didn't want to leave.

'Late is only early seen from the other side.' She hooked a heel behind his knee and pulled his thigh between hers. Kisses nuzzled his neck, his throat. 'I'll make sure you're on time for your tutorials.'

'Won't people ask questions? I mean, a student in the Masters' wing first thing in the morning?'

She tilted her hips up and took him inside.

He groaned.

'Let them ask,' she said. 'It's none of their damned business.'

25

ALL THINGS END

და

We begin our march tomorrow, at first light. It will be hard, near on five hundred miles and three weeks in which to do it, but if the siege is to be lifted before the city starves, we have no other choice. Gwlach's sorceresses cannot be allowed to continue like this.

I am astonished by their ferocity. I had no conception that women could be induced to perform such acts of brutality. I know that the female of any species can be provoked to defend her offspring, her mate, but these women are under no provocation at all. They simply raise their hands at their chief's command and blood rains down.

Ansel laid his head back and closed his eyes. In the light of a single candle, Malthus' small, precise script was difficult to read. Daylight was better, but the days were so short now in the heel of the year and he had so little time in between the duties of his office to read through the three volumes that Alquist had found. So candlelight it had to be, and late in the evening when his secretary had gone to bed and it was unlikely anyone would come to disturb him and learn that he had smuggled them out of the archive. No doubt Vorgis would discover their absence eventually, but the keeper seemed to be more concerned that nothing in the archive was disturbed than in maintaining an accurate register of what was there and what was not. He hoped it would be enough time.

This evening, I asked the First Knight to join me for supper. It occurred to me that I knew very little of the man beneath the white surcoat. I know the Knight, whom the men call Fellbane, who rides at my right hand and whose sword I have relied on these past ten years, but I know nothing of the man. I do not know if he was wed or had a family, another life before he received his calling. I do not know if he plays chess, or can fashion things from wood or metal with his hands. In a few short days I must ask him to die and all I know of him is that his shield is first in the air above my head when arrows darken the sky. If I do not know him, the words of the eulogy will be ashes in my throat.

❧

The *Morning Star*'s motion was easier now that she had rounded the Horn of Bregorin and gained the wide waters of the Western Sea. The long, slow swells of the ocean had rocked Masen as gently as a babe in his cradle and he had slept the night through for the first time in weeks.

He looked up at the beams overhead, spangled with reflections from the dancing seas outside, and wished he didn't have to move. He wanted to stay in those few seconds after waking, where all was warmth and contentment and the horrors he had seen were only a memory from another lifetime. But he couldn't ignore the urgency of his mission, no matter how much he wanted to. All things had to end eventually.

Masen turned onto his side. K'shelia sat on the edge of the bunk, naked as a peeled switch, stroking a comb through her silvery hair. He watched the ripple of muscle in her back and arm, remembering. Reaching out, he ran his fingertip down the furrow of her spine.

She shot a smile over her shoulder. *We are almost within hailing distance.*

Thank you. He sat up, rubbing sleep from his eyes.

K'shelia flicked her hair over her other shoulder to comb that side. Jade eyes lingered on him, tracing the shape of the muscles layering his torso and the many scars that seamed them. Her own skin was as flawless as a pearl. *You sleep soundly,*

The bosom of the waves makes a fine pillow, my lady.

A flicker of uncertainty darkened her gaze and she lowered her comb. *You jest at my expense, yes? I am unfamiliar with your humour.*

I did not jest. Kneeling behind her he put his arms around her waist and pressed a kiss to her shoulder. *I meant it most sincerely, in every sense of the words.*

Slowly he slid his hands up to her breasts. They were small enough that his square palms smothered them.

K'shelia laid her head back, long pale hands covering his as he caressed her. Her touch was cool, and delicate as snowflakes. *It has been . . . interesting. I will think fondly of you, Masen.*

And I will miss you too, Shipsinger. Whenever I find myself on open water. The golden buds of her nipples had firmed to points. He plucked at them gently, making her breath catch.

Is there time?

There is always time for love.

Then just once more, for remembrance?

Masen kissed her slender neck. She smelled of the sea, of salt and wind. Even her skin tasted clean. He let his right hand drift over her belly down to the junction of her thighs. She opened them a little and he dipped his fingers into the silky folds of her sex. The ivory comb clattered to the floor.

Later, when he came up on deck and she stood at the tiller next to him, her eyes were composed and remote again. There was not even a flush in her cheek to betray what they had shared. That saddened him a little; he had always striven to leave his bedmates glowing with lust or laughter, or both, if he could manage it. But he had never taken a sea-elf to his blankets before, and their souls were as deep as the oceans they roamed. She might not show anything now, but he would always have the memory of what he had seen and heard in her arms.

Show me the sigil of your friend and I will attempt to reach him.

Thank you, my lady. Masen showed her the pattern of colours he sought.

How far away are we?

Two days, if this wind holds.

It has taken longer than I'd hoped.

Even I cannot Sing the Star into the teeth of the wind, Masen. She has done her best.

I know. I am grateful beyond words. For everything you have done for me. Did he imagine it, or was there a trace of a smile? There and gone, fleeting as the sparkle on the crown of a wave? He could not be sure, but there was no mistaking the brush of her colours against his thoughts, as intimate as a caress. No disguising the glow there.

Let me know when you have established contact and I will give you the message to send. We have no more time to lose.

∾

'You have very nice hair for a boy,' said Aysha, combing it through.

'Thank you.' Gair adjusted the towel around his shoulders. 'You have very short hair for a girl.'

'I cut it short when I lived in the souq. It made things easier if I looked like a boy. I got to like it.'

'You cannot expect me to believe that you ever passed for a boy.' Reaching round behind him, he ran his hand over the seat of her breeches.

She rapped his crown with the comb. 'Behave. When I was young I was as flat as a freshly pressed shirt. The curves came later.' The razor hissed over the comb. 'Anyway, I haven't the patience to look after long hair. All that primping in front of a mirror – I'd rather have my fingernails pulled.'

Cut hair sifted down to the bathroom floor around Gair's stool as she combed and trimmed and combed some more. He watched her in the mirror on the wall. Her hands moved quickly, deftly, the blade flashing in her fingers.

He'd never had his hair cut by a woman before, not even as a child. Even considering the woman was the same one on his pillow when he opened his eyes that morning, and each of the two mornings before – and saints, he was still waiting to wake from that dream – it was a remarkably intimate experience. Her fingers moving through his hair, over his scalp, left his spine tingling. The sensation so absorbed him that several seconds had passed before he realised she had looked up and was watching him watching her. Her lips barely twitched, but the crinkle at the corner of her eyes betrayed her amusement.

'So.' He cleared his throat. 'Why was it better to be a boy in the souq?'

'It was safer,' she said. 'Young girls with no parents were sought after, even crippled ones.'

'I'm almost afraid to ask.'

'Goddess, you're such an innocent. For the pleasure-houses, of course.'

'Oh, of course.' Gair's ears burned. He should have realised, despite his cloistered education. He had been too young to take much of an interest at the time, but he'd seen them in Leahaven, certain poised, elegant women who kept their complexions pale with parasols and who could collect the attention of every male over the age of twelve and a dark stare from every female just by walking down the street.

'I was friends with one or two of them,' Aysha went on, combing out another section of hair. 'They told me it wasn't such a bad life in the better houses. They had fine clothes, their rooms were decorated in silks, and there were toughs on the door in case any of the patrons cut up rough. They even got a share of their price. Not all the houses were so civilised.'

'I can imagine.'

'Believe me, you can't. Some of the things people were

prepared to pay to see or do, or have done to them . . .' She shuddered. 'Anyway, I decided I'd give myself where I chose and took up a trade to earn my way. Once I'd learned to drop my voice an octave and walk without swinging my hips it was easy enough to pretend.'

'Weren't there boys in the pleasure-houses too?' he asked carefully. 'Some men incline that way.'

'There were, but indentured prentice-boys were left alone. Not that I didn't have one or two handsome offers,' she added, flashing him a wicked glance. 'Although Jalal had a habit of standing at the back of the shop stropping his largest razor when certain individuals came to call, and for some reason they never wanted to stay long.'

'Do you miss him?'

'Jalal? Yes, I think I do. He had gold teeth and a glass eye that he would pop out and polish on his shirt if he didn't like the look of you. He let half a dozen of us street children sleep in the back of his shop. In return we took care of him, swept the floor and cooked his meals, that sort of thing.' Her voice had the warmth of real affection and her eyes were briefly a thousand miles away.

Watching her, Gair felt an odd little twist of pain in his chest. 'I know so little about you,' he said.

'Oh, I think you know pretty much everything now,' she replied lightly, with just enough emphasis on the 'know' to make him curse his fair complexion again.

Saints, that took some getting used to. She was so matter-of-fact about what they did in private, and so open and earthy when they did it, that she left him breathless.

She took a step back to scrutinise his hair fanned out over the towel and make sure the cut was even. Then she smiled at his reflection. 'There. Much neater.' Aysha folded up the towel and flicked it across his back and chest to clear it of cut hair, then dropped it on the floor. 'Wait here a moment. I've got something to finish it off.'

With that she limped out into the bedroom. Gair fetched his shirt from the hook on the back of the door and pulled it on.

Aysha's private bathroom resembled a grotto, tiled in undersea shades around the walls, sandy-gold underfoot. It did not take much imagination to picture her in the deep tub. Her bath-oil scenting the air was enough to quicken his pulse.

When she returned she carried a blue velvet pouch which she held out to him.

'What's this?'

'Your name-day gift.' She laughed at his expression. 'Don't tell me you forgot what day it was.'

'We weren't encouraged to remember anything but saints' days in the Motherhouse. I'd completely lost track. How did you know?'

I asked Alderan.'

He upended the pouch into his hand. It contained a silver object the shape of an oversized finger ring, engraved with borders of Leahn knotwork. Round the middle ran an inscription in Gimraeli, all jagged peaks and hooked descenders with ripples between like a child's drawing of waves.

'It's called a *zirin*. It's for your hair.'

She showed him how to work the concealed catch and the sprung grip inside. Then she gathered his hair into a horsetail and clipped the *zirin* in place.

'There,' she said, smoothing his hair through her hand. 'Better than that ragged piece of cord, eh?'

'I don't know what to say. Thank you.' Gair fingered the cool metal as he studied his image in the mirror. The *zirin* was heavy on the back of his neck, but it looked secure. Handsome too, gleaming against his shirt. He didn't dare think how much it must have cost her. That sort of quiet elegance usually came at a price.

'What's the inscription?'

'Oh, just a quotation from a poem about the desert.'

'Al-Jofar?'

'Ishamar al-Dinn. Fourth century.'

'I've not heard of him.'

'He wrote the *Rose of Abal-khor* verse cycle and was banished from the Gimraeli court for it, on pain of death.'

'Were the poems that bad?'

'Actually, al-Dinn wrote some of the most beautiful verse I've ever read. He's a favourite of mine.'

'So why was he banished?'

'The *Rose of Abal-khor* was the name given to the prince's third wife, and the poems are profoundly erotic.'

Gair clapped his hand over the *zirin* and stared at her.

'Please tell me the inscription isn't a quotation from that!'

'Relax,' she laughed. 'It's nothing you couldn't repeat at the dinner table, I assure you.' Lifting herself on her toes, she wrapped her arms around his neck and offered her lips for a kiss.

'Joyous remembrance, Leahn,' she said, touching his face. 'Now get out of here before I give in to temptation and muss up your haircut.'

'I like the sound of that.' He kissed her playfully, nibbling his way down her neck.

With a girlish giggle, she twisted out of his arms. 'Stop that. You haven't got time.'

'Later?'

'Maybe.'

'Will you tell me what it says?'

'Maybe that too. Now go, or you'll be late for chess with Darin again.'

&

Alderan cupped his hands and scooped warm water over his face and neck to rinse away the last of the soap, then checked his reflection in the looking-glass above the washstand. Better. His beard now ended in a neat line below his jaw and he'd shaped it over his cheeks so that it was symmetrical. Much better. He turned his head left and right to check for stray whiskers – ah.

Picking up his razor, he leaned towards the mirror with his head angled. Carefully he set the edge against his skin.

Guardian.

Damn it! He dropped the razor into the basin and stared at the thread of scarlet trickling down into his beard.

Yes?

Forgive me for intruding. The accent was as lilting as birdsong and the colours presented to him were sea-foam and sunshine over aquamarine blue. Not a pattern he recognised.

I am K'shelia, Shipsinger to the Morning Star. I have a message for you from the Gatekeeper.

Masen? What was he doing on a sea-elf ship? Unease prickling down his spine, Alderan straightened up, the cut on his cheek forgotten. *I am listening, my lady.*

Assemble the Council. The Veil is failing.

Saints and angels. This is the whole of the message?

Yes, Guardian. The Morning Star will reach Pencruik in two days, if the winds are willing. We shall make the best haste we can.

I understand. Thank you, Shipsinger. Our Order is in your debt.

Do you have a message to convey to the Gatekeeper?

Tell him I will do as he asks. We will convene as soon as he arrives. I pray Goddess we will not be too late.

Very well. Until we meet, Guardian, I bid you farewell.

And the lady was gone. Alderan leaned on the washstand and let his head fall forward. Well, all things ended in time. Men did not choose the when. He could have wished that it were not quite so soon, though, that he had had a better chance to prepare. He would just have to make the best of it with the tools he had. Unheeded, blood dripped from his neck into the water, spiralling into threads, disappearing from view.

The third book was incomplete.

Ansel let it drop into his lap and kneaded his eyes. According to the date at the top of the page, the journal ended abruptly on the eve of the battle at River Run. Malthus was known to have survived, though wounded, so why did it stop? The first two volumes had been crammed with his musings and observations; what had occurred to make him set down his pen? Had the book been misplaced in the furious advance, put away by his steward and somehow overlooked? Would he have started again with a new notebook, and did that mean there was another volume still waiting to be found in the archive, sleeping amongst the Apocryphae?

Ansel muttered a curse that he had not used since the battlefield, then followed it with a prayer for forgiveness for the coarseness of his language, although he was sure She would understand his frustration. How cruel fate could be, to bring him so far along the path then abandon him so close to his goal. How bitter the taste of disappointment on his tongue.

He flicked back a page or two and re-read the final entries. Malthus' descriptions of the march from Mesarild had been perforce brief, but even those few hasty words scratched into the book at the end of each day had been potent as spells. Ansel had felt the desperation, been harrowed by the sight of men and horses falling through sheer exhaustion and having to be left where they fell because the legions could not stop. Men marching until their feet bled through their boots, marching well into the night, then seeing the first league of the next day behind them before the sun even crested the horizon. And then to expect them to fight when they reached their destination!

But they had fought. Somehow, with wooden limbs and weapons that weighed them down as if forged from lead, the legions had fought. They had secured first one road into the valley, then another, and they had lifted the siege. The city's defenders had committed everything they had to a final sally from the gates and the two-pronged attack had caught Gwlach with his back to the river and his warriors in disarray.

How sweet the taste of our first victory! Like water from a spring on the mountainside, so fresh and invigorating, it washes the tiredness from our limbs and dulls the sting of our hurts, which have been many. Tomorrow we will grieve for them and say prayers for their souls, but tonight we will celebrate, for we have done good, if bloody, work this day. Who knows how many lives we have saved? Could that number be reckoned, we might consider we have bought them cheaply indeed. Without Fellbane, I fear we would have seen a very different end.

Then the next day's entry:

Gwlach has withdrawn to the north of the valley and regrouped. He knows we cannot press our victory just yet. Men and beasts must rest, be fed, for us as well as him. I have sent out scouts to watch him and they report that he has sent riders north, west and east. Intelligence from Caer Ducain's garrison commander suggests this is where he has placed his reserves, numbering at least ten thousand more men. This tips the odds in his favour, in weight of numbers at least. We cannot know how many more sorceresses he can call upon. If we are to strike against him we must strike hard and strike soon, before his reserves can be ranged against us.

On the eve of River Run, when the tide of battle irrevocably turned in the Order's favour, the day's entry was short. Two paragraphs, no more:

I spoke with Fellbane again today. He is a simple man, by which I mean uncomplicated. He sees his task very clearly: it is the right thing to do. To do otherwise would be to do wrong. Oh, for such clarity of purpose! I must perforce look beyond the morrow. The need is great, the end is just, of that I have no doubt. It is the means that tears at me like wolves in my soul.

He accepts the task with which I have charged him with such equanimity, his strength of faith puts mine to shame. I am humbled by him. I pray to the Goddess Herself that one day his shade may find the grace to forgive me for what I have asked him to do in Her name.

And that was that. Malthus had written no more. Despair reverberated through every word; the very book trembled with it. Ansel heard the long-dead Preceptor's voice in his mind, felt his anguish, and wanted to cry out to him to finish his account, to finally set down the truth of what happened on that day. Even if no eyes but his ever read it, someone would have seen it and acknowledged it for what it was instead of hiding it away in shame like an out-of-wedlock child.

He let the book close and smoothed his hands over it. Secrets and lies underpinned the fabric of his beloved Order like the stones and mortar beneath the Motherhouse. It was past time they were brought into the light. The Suvaeon should wear their scars proudly, as badges of honour, however disfiguring they might be. They showed that it was not the battles he had won that shaped a man's character, but the battles lost. That was what made him a man, or broke him on the wheel of bitter experience. Scars were nothing of which to be ashamed.

The fire had burned low. Ansel reached into the scuttle and tossed a block of peat into the hearth. Too late he realised he should have used the tongs; ash and sparks belched up, sending a gust of fragrant smoke into the room. He leaned back out of the way, but it was too late. His next breath brought a dreadful clutching at his chest as the cough sank its talons into his lungs again. He fought it as best he could, holding his breath whilst he prayed for the urge to pass, but it did not and the cough burst out of his mouth in a spray of blood and spittle. Spasm after spasm shook him, and scarlet drops bloomed on his white robe even as black specks swarmed into his vision.

If he could just reach the bell at the far side of the hearth! He managed one step, clutched dizzily at the mantel, fell. Relentless pain clutched his chest in its fist. Drawing breath such a struggle now. Much better to lie still, the hearthstone cool under his over-heated cheek. The frantic fluttering under his ribs would stop eventually, if he was patient. Darkness now, closing in, so soothing after so long spent struggling to read that damned book. Time to sleep . . .

Ah well. All things end.

26

DISTRACTION

Gair took the stairs to his room at a trot. He'd flown straight from Aysha's apartment to the dormitory court, despite the blustery winds, but too many people were moving along the galleries for him to be comfortable making the shape-shift back into human form, so he'd had to double back into the kitchen garden instead. From there he'd jogged through the refectory, filching an apple on the way, and battled the tide of hungry students back into the dormitory wing. One or two people paused to stare as he passed; he hoped they hadn't seen him for long enough to notice that his hair was uncombed and his chin rough.

He hadn't woken until the bell rang for Prime. His head was woolly from too little sleep; it had taken the realisation that he was going to be very late for a tutorial with Master Brendan to galvanise him out of Aysha's bed. She had stretched languidly, her body making tantalising shapes under the sheet whilst he dressed, and offered to send a note excusing him from attending as he was urgently required elsewhere. He didn't have to ask where that elsewhere would be. It had been very tempting. Her goodbye kiss had damn near broken his resolve.

He had thought the first heady days couldn't possibly last, but they had. It had been almost a month now, and if anything he was further under Aysha's spell than ever. She called to him in the evenings, her voice singing through his mind, and he went to her willingly, losing himself in her for hours at a time, most often for the night. He had taken to sitting at her desk to write his essays, just to share the same room with her, whilst she watched him from the couch like a cat. Too often the weight of her gaze was enough to distract him and then paper and ink would be pushed aside in favour of another kind of self-expression.

Somehow, he had managed to keep his word to Master Barin, though sometimes, like today, it had been a close-run thing. The apple would have to do for his breakfast if he was to have any chance of changing his shirt and still making Brendan's class on time. Back in his room he washed as fast as he could, not even bothering to warm the water in the pitcher. Shivering, he opened his closet and rooted about for a clean shirt with one hand whilst towelling himself off with the other.

He eyed the evidence of hasty ablutions. 'I didn't see you at breakfast.'

Someone rapped briskly on the door. 'Anybody home?' Darin's face appeared round the door frame. He was fully recovered now, though dark shadows still pooled round his eyes. Saaron said they would fade in time, but until they did they gave Darin a haunted appearance completely at odds with his sunny character.

Gair pulled the half-eaten apple from his mouth. 'Overslept,' he said, then stuffed the fruit back. He snatched a shirt from the closet and tugged it over his head.

'But I was here an hour ago and your bed was made up.'

A word popped into Gair's mind. He had no idea what it meant, but he had heard Aysha use it more than once and it sounded perfect for a situation like this.

Darin's eyes grew rounder. 'You sly dog,' he breathed. 'So it's true.'

'So what's true?'

'The Knight has a lady.'

'What?'

'You. You've got a girl!'

'Where did you get that idea from?'

'Gair, if you actually spent any time in the dormitory these days you'd have heard the gossip for yourself.'

Gair tucked in his shirt and refastened his belt. He didn't really have time for this, but he might as well know, if only to learn where his careful precautions had failed him. He kept his voice light. 'What gossip?'

'Unbelievable.' Darin shook his head, then started counting off on his fingers. 'Before the supper bell's stopped ringing you're gone and no one knows where. You're late for chess two times out of three, and I've given up even looking for you on free days because you're never around. Without you to help me my history grades have slipped so far down since Eventide that they're practically in the cellar. Now this morning's evidence that you're laying your head somewhere other than on your pillow and the conclusion is obvious. You, my friend, have got a girl.'

Well, the Belisthan had him there. He thought he'd been so discreet, too. Goddess, it would be so much easier if they could be open about it, but they'd so thoroughly broken one of Chapterhouse's few rules that he wasn't sure he wouldn't be asked to leave on the very next ship. Sighing, he unfastened the *zirin* and reached for his comb.

'I'm right, aren't I? So who is she?'

'Darin, I haven't really got time for this.'

'Is it somebody I know? Who? Is it Sarra, the Syfrian girl with the long braids? I saw the way you looked at her.'

'I did no such thing,' said Gair, dragging his comb through his hair. 'As I recall, it was you who swore me to secrecy about wanting to get tangled up in those braids.'

'Come on, Gair, tell me! Saints, you never tell me anything!'

'Because it's none of your business. Can't a man have a little privacy?'

'Did she give you that fancy clip for Eventide?'

He looked down at the *zirin* in his hand, turning it to read the inscription. She had told him what it said eventually, in Gimraeli. He was still no nearer a translation.

'For my naming-day.'

'So there *is* a girl, and she's got money. Someone has their boots well under the bed there. Is she in one of your classes?'

Gair tossed his comb onto the washstand and fastened his hair back. The horsetail reached down past his shoulder-blades now, despite the trim, and the silver *zirin* kept it in better check than the cord had ever done.

'Darin, Brendan will have my hide. Come on, or we'll both be late.'

Scooping up his jerkin from the bed he headed for the door. Darin darted past him and braced himself across the door frame. 'I'm not moving until you tell me.'

'You'll have a long wait, then.' Gair jabbed his fingers into his friend's midriff and side-stepped him as he doubled over.

As soon as he had caught his breath, Darin ran down the corridor after him. 'Tell me!'

'No.'

'Tell me!'

'No!'

'At least tell me how good the ride is?'

Gair stopped dead. 'I don't believe you just said that.'

'*Please?* Nothing below the waist, remember?'

'Your mind is a sewer.'

'So I've been told.' The Belisthan's grin was unabashed. 'I take it that's another no, then?'

'It's a no.'

'Spoilsport.'

326

For the first time in twenty years, snow fell over Penglas. It came softly out of the north as evening fell, drawing veils of white over the land that thickened into the night, and by morning blanketed the entire island to a depth of two or three inches.

'But it *never* snows here,' Darin complained, huddling into his cloak in the bell-tower. 'It's almost like being back at home.'

'I've missed the snow,' Gair said. 'In Leah, we'd say this wasn't much more than a hard frost.'

He focused the spyglass on the ship beating across the mouth of Penbirgha Sound. She was as sleek as a fisher-bird, with raked masts and strangely rigged triangular sails, but she wore the scars of heavy weather. Several pieces of new rigging were not yet tarred down, one sail was split and another was so creamy-pale it had to be fresh from the locker. Still, the sailors handled her neatly, bringing her about and reducing sail so that she slipped easily between the headlands.

'Looks like you were right. She's a sea-elf chaser, and coming in fast.' He closed the glass and handed it back to Darin.

'I told you it was.' The Belisthan peered towards the approaching vessel. 'Caught in that storm last week, by the look of her. Masthead pennant's little better than a rag.'

'Someone must be in a hurry. It's not been the weather for sailing lately.'

'Sea-elves are the best deep-water sailors in the world. If I was going to trust anyone to see me through a storm, it would be them. Look, they're lowering a boat.'

Gair leaned out over the balustrade. The chaser had barely slowed and already a dartlike launch was speeding across the sound towards Penglas. Apart from the oarsmen there was only one passenger aboard, though he could make out little more than a shape. As he watched, the ship's anchor plunged into the sea with a roar of chains, audible even up there on the tower, and the launch was finally obscured by the cliffs.

Darin took the glass from his eye and slid it closed, bouncing it on his other hand. 'I wonder who's coming ashore. Can you fly down there and see who it is?'

Gair reached for the Song of a gull. The melody was an untidy, jinking thing, threaded through with shimmering plaintive notes that spoke of long wings and wide skies. After the effortless power of a fire-eagle, the gull shape felt strange, but the narrower wings were tremendously manoeuvrable; gulls nested on cliff-ledges and hunted amongst the troughs of the waves, a world apart from the cathedrals of ice and stone that were the eagle's world. In a few moments he had the trick of it and barrelled downwind over the town.

At the head of the jetty a familiar speck of blue waited for the launch to come in. Gair glided closer until he could make out Alderan's face and saw him extend a friendly hand to the man with the bundle on his shoulder who climbed the steps from the water's edge. They exchanged a few words, then began to walk towards the town.

Abruptly the other man looked up and stared directly at Gair. The gaze was both curious and knowing, as if the man knew who he was without having to be introduced. Yet Gair knew he looked no different to the hundred other gulls that swooped and squabbled around the pier. How could that be possible? Had Alderan recognised him, and told his companion? Unsettled, Gair rolled away from the harbour and flew back to the bell-tower.

Darin waited on the landward side, his spyglass trained on the dip where the road from the town wound out of the woods. 'Who was it?' he asked without looking round.

'I didn't recognise him. Some friend of Alderan's, I think. He was there to meet him off the boat.'

'What did he look like?'

'Brown, mostly,' Gair said, rubbing his chilled hands together. 'Brown skin, brown cloak, brown eyes. Face like an old shoe, looks like he spends a lot of time out of doors.'

'Did you get close enough to hear what they were talking about?'

'I don't eavesdrop, Darin,' Gair chided him gently.

'Pity.' The Belisthan closed the glass with a snap. His lips were bluish from the cold, his thin fingers so pallid they looked to be all bone, stripped of flesh. The weight he'd lost when he'd been sick before Eventide had never returned; if anything, he'd lost a little more. He'd grown gaunt, and his eyes glittered darkly in their sockets, the only colour in his face now two feverish patches high on his cheeks. 'I wish I knew what they were talking about,' he muttered.

'Maybe we'll find something out later,' Gair said. 'The gossip from the town usually finds its way up to Chapterhouse inside a day or so.'

'Maybe.'

'I need to get some breakfast. I'm due with Master Eavin in half an hour.' Hauling on the rope, Gair lifted the trapdoor down to the bell chamber. 'Darin? You coming?'

'What? Oh, yes, yes.' The Belisthan took a few steps towards the trapdoor then stopped and his gaze went out towards the harbour again. Pale fingers twitched over the spyglass, turning the little brass cylinder round and round.

'Darin?'

'I'm coming, I'm coming. Don't nag.'

Gair let him precede him down the stairs. Following close behind, he could see how Darin looked out of every window they passed towards Pencruik, even when Chapterhouse's walls had risen in the way. His deeply shadowed eyes were fixed on the same point, as if they could see clear through the stone. What was bothering him? There was something, for certain; he'd even stopped complaining about a lack of access to Renna's shift. He was definitely not himself.

After supper, Gair went to Darin's room to play chess. The Belisthan did not look at all well. His skin was greyish, and the shadows around his eyes were darker, like bruises. Normally a quick-witted, bold player, now he stared at the board as if he had never seen it before in his life, and he played like it too, losing three games in a row.

Rather than start another, Gair pushed the board to one side. 'You're not yourself tonight. Are you all right?'

'Hmm?' Darin blinked at him. 'Oh, yes, I'm fine. Just tired.'

'Renna keeping you up late these days?'

'I wish.' A flash of the old Darin, then it was gone. 'I'm not sleeping well at the moment, that's all. Strange dreams.'

'What about?'

'I can't really remember. I just wake up feeling like I've had a nightmare, but I can't recall a thing about it.'

'Do you think you should speak to Saaron?'

'No, it's all right. I don't really want to talk about it.'

Gair drew the board towards him and began arranging the pieces. 'He might be able to help.'

Darin's arm swept across the table, scattering chessmen in all directions. The sleepy fuzziness was gone from his expression, replaced by a feverish energy. His dark eyes snapped. 'I don't want to talk about it,' he grated.

Gair shifted in his chair. He had never seen Darin like this before. 'Yes,' he said carefully, 'so you said. Let's set the board up for another game, shall we?' He picked up the little figures and arranged them on the board.

A few seconds later Darin's temper evaporated and he joined in, but before they had played a half a dozen moves each he was drowsing over his pieces. 'Sorry, Gair,' he mumbled, then yawned. 'I can't seem to stay awake.'

'Then go to bed. We can play another day.'

'All right.' Without another word, Darin heeled off his mud-spattered boots and lay down on his bed. Within seconds his breathing had fallen into the rhythm of a deep sleep.

Gair fetched a blanket from the closet and spread it over him before letting himself out. The Belisthan was definitely not himself, not by a country mile.

Aysha's deep bath was full, thanks to Chapterhouse's vast copper boilers and enlightened plumbing arrangements. Steam hung thickly in the air, fragrant with bergamot oil.

'For someone who looks like a village goodwife, Esther's got a mind you could crack rocks with.'

Gair massaged his temples to chase away a nascent headache. It had been a hard lesson with the matronly Master, possibly his hardest yet, drawing on the slow, deep Song of earth. He'd been the only one of the twelve students in the class who'd been able to keep up with her after the first hour, and dear Goddess, she had made him work for it.

'She scares the lights out of me,' Aysha said, wringing out a flannel in the hot water. 'I always feel she's about to turn me over her knee and paddle my behind. Close your eyes.' She spread the flannel over his face.

Gair laid his head back and let the heat soak into him. 'Oh, that's good. A private bathroom is the hallmark of a civilised society,' he sighed. 'No more secondhand soap and other people's navel lint. Bliss.'

She laughed. 'So what about my navel lint?'

'Yours I don't mind. It's other men's navel lint I have a problem with.' He dropped the cooling flannel into the water and looked up. She sat on the half-step behind him, her legs wrapped around him; his head was pillowed on her shoulder. Her tawny skin was dewy from the heat and her hair stood in soft peaks, like a cat come in from the rain.

'Do girls get navel lint?' he asked.

'I thought it was strictly a male thing, to go with the excess body hair and tendency to scratch. Hold on, I'll just find a man to check.'

'I'm crushed.'

'But you don't have excess body hair.' Aysha's hands slid down over his chest to emphasise its comparative smoothness. 'And I have never seen you scratch.' They dipped below the water. 'But in all other respects, you fit the definition.'

Gair closed his eyes, savouring her touch. It still had the power to thrill him, if anything even more so now. It didn't matter whether it was the casual intersection of two hands reaching for the teapot, or the most intimate caress; the merest brush of her skin against his left him tingling. Like this, with nothing between them but the water, it sent shivers of pleasure out through his body from the point of contact like ripples from a pebble thrown into a pond.

'Do you have to go?'

'It's a Council meeting. Sorry.'

'When?'

'About an hour.'

No sooner had his lessons finished than she had been in his mind. No sooner had he bid farewell to his classmates than he was on his way back up to the fifth floor, taking the steps two at a time when no one was watching. There was no awkwardness when she greeted him, still no feeling of boundaries redrawn into unfamiliar lines. She was just there in his arms as if she'd never left them. That had been only a little over an hour ago. A lot could happen in an hour.

'It'll only take me ten minutes to get ready,' Gair said.

Under the water, her fingers curled around him. 'I'd say you're ready now.'

The summons came too quickly. Aysha reared above him, a sheen of sweat on her skin and her colours swirling around his as she shared herself with him. The red seemed deeper tonight, dark as wine, and the heat of her was intoxicating. When someone touched her mind, he saw and felt her flinch. Her fingers dug into his shoulders.

'Damn it, not now,' she groaned. She shut her eyes and kept moving, but her pleasure was slipping away from her. She tensed again. Whoever called her did not intend to be kept waiting. With a hissed curse she slumped forward.

'I have to go,' she said against his neck.

'Was it Alderan?'

'Yes. I'm sorry.'

'Best not keep him waiting, then.'

Lifting herself up, she studied his face. 'Are you sure you don't mind?'

'If it was anyone else, I would.' He held her face between his hands and kissed her, long and slow. 'Go on. There's always later.'

'I don't know how long the meeting will be.'

'The sooner you go, the sooner it will be over.'

She eased herself off him and reached for her clothes at the foot of the bed. Gair watched her dress, enjoying with his eyes what he couldn't touch with his hands.

Aysha threw his shirt at his head. 'You're staring.'

'You're beautiful.'

'Liar.' She opened the door, shooting him a smile as she blurred into her favourite kestrel shape. Then she was gone.

Gair waited until after Vespers, but she did not return. The bed in his room felt small and cold. He had grown accustomed to having Aysha next to him when he fell asleep, and he missed the warmth of her, the scent of her on the pillow. Staying in her bed to wait for her would have been worse. Surrounded by her perfume, the echo of her presence would only have made her absence cut more keenly.

෨

The topmost chamber of the bell-tower was cold and exposed, but it suited Gair's mood. He hadn't fallen asleep for a very long time, and when he finally did, his dreams were dark and disturbing enough to wake him, gritty-eyed, well before dawn. Sword-practice had been abandoned after barely an hour; even the babble in the refectory had set his temper on edge. When a harried-looking adept announced to the room at large that tutorials had been cancelled for the day, he had been both irritated at the lack of something to occupy himself, and absurdly relieved that he wouldn't have to wrestle with the Song in his current humour.

Hunkered down in the lee of the wall Gair pulled his cloak tightly around him. Pellets of ice laced the wind and stung bare skin like horseflies. As a boy, he had gone out onto the fells with his pony on days like this, when he couldn't settle. Sometimes he'd take one of the wolfhounds for company, and they'd roam the heathery slopes of the Long Glen until he'd walked off the restlessness. At the Motherhouse there had been the top row of the bleachers in the exhibition lists, or the grassy summit of Templemount on a free day. Whenever he felt that itch in his soul he craved high places, open to the wind and sky, as if by soaking in it he could bring a little space inside himself.

Absently he reached out for Aysha's colours, skimming through the glowing patterns of Chapterhouse's other residents. A dense, vivid blue globe shrouded Alderan's study, solid as steel. The room, with the entire senior faculty inside, was still sealed up tight in a ward he knew he couldn't even begin to unpick.

Whatever message had been brought on the sea-elf ship must be dire news. It had demanded a chaser's speed, and had summoned the entire Council into a suppertime session that for all he knew had continued clean through the night. War, perhaps. Maybe Lord Kierim's efforts to maintain peace in Gimrael had finally failed, as Alderan had predicted, and the Empire was bracing for insurrection. Maybe the Church would declare another crisis of the faith and send the Knights riding out to battle.

If events had come about differently he might have been amongst them, sworn to sweat and bleed and if necessary die for the white and gold. Of course, if events had come about differently he would not be here on the far edge of the Empire, trying to find his place in a different Order, and he would never have known Aysha.

He missed her. Less than a day apart, separated by only a hundred yards and a few walls, but he missed her. It hurt more than he had ever realised it could. He told himself that she had responsibilities as a Council member, that it was her duty to attend with the others, but he could not silence the selfish little voice at the back of his head that whispered that her duties and responsibilities were what kept her from him.

Merciful Mother. He dropped his head onto his knees. What was the *matter* with him? He couldn't think of anything but her, couldn't even enjoy an unexpected day's liberty without hiding himself away in a corner and brooding on her absence. Two months ago he would have given almost anything for a few hours' respite from the Masters. Now he had it, and he couldn't think of anything better to do with it than to freeze his arse on a cold stone floor and feel sorry for himself.

Greased timbers squeaked on the floor below and Gair barely had time to clap his hands over his ears before the bell's huge mechanism began the counter-swing that would strike the hour. It seemed to go on for ever, shaking the floor underfoot, even the very air in his lungs, before the echoes shuddered away into the startled scolding of the gulls.

He took his hands from his ears and pushed himself to his feet. He couldn't stay there much longer or he'd be deaf. Stretching the stiffness from his limbs he leaned on the balustrade. From up there, the islands looked very different to the green jewels of summer. Now every one was capped with the unseasonable snow, darkened to muddy brown around the shores, as if they had trailed their skirts in a puddle. The snow bore little resemblance to what he was accustomed to in the north. The deep, clean cold of the Laraig Anor was easier to bear than these damp chills.

Most of the harbours and coves he could see were full of boats, though a few slivers of sail on the horizon said there were hardier

335

souls who'd chanced their craft in the hopes of making a catch before the weather closed in again. Off Pencruik the smacks and cobles lined up in rows, blunt-bowed, stubby-masted things amongst which the sea-elf ship rode at anchor like a Gimraeli *sulqa* in a field of donkeys.

Gair launched himself from the tower balustrade as a black-tipped gull and swooped down towards the ship. Once or twice as a boy he'd seen sea-elf rakers in Leahaven, and once a chaser beating out to sea past Drumcarrick Head, but he had never seen one close to. She was extraordinary, all sleek curves, resembling something grown rather than something made. From cathead to stern-rail every line flowed as smooth as water. Across her transom where her name would be painted was a row of golden characters unlike any he had ever seen before, but he knew she was called *Morning Star*. That much news at least had come up from town with the carters, but that was all. He didn't even know the name of her master.

Banking round the *Star's* tall masts, he passed along her port side. Two sea-elves watched him from the aft deck. Both had long white hair and sharp-boned, ageless faces. The man wore a seal-skin jerkin and carried a long knife on each hip. He was frowning. Beside him, the woman dressed in subtle shades of green inclined her head gravely as Gair passed. A gentle but firm pressure, like the wind but not like it, pushed him away out to sea.

So sea-elves had the gift as well. The woman on deck had recognised that although he might look like one he was not a gull and had acknowledged him graciously. However, she had made it equally obvious that he was not wanted near the ship. He wondered how much of that was due to a liking for privacy and how much due to the passenger they had set ashore.

The sea-elf had pushed him onto a course that would take him clear across Penglas Sound and over the outer islands, towards the Five Sisters that rose like blunt teeth from the sullen waters. The thinnest of winter sunshine silvered the wave-tops, so he followed its path towards the furthest islands. Flying in such chill air was exhilarating and the concentration required to keep him from slapping into a rising swell prevented him from brooding. Out beyond the smallest Sister he saw another sail, angling down from the north. Likely just a coble out after mackerel, but it made a good excuse to stretch his wings a little further before he turned back. He dipped his shoulder and veered north.

Gradually the ship emerged from the haze. She had a high prow, ornately carved into the head of some snarling beast, a square-rigged mast and an ensign as big as a bed-sheet flying from the stern. The flag was midnight-blue, apart from a bold white star in the centre. Something niggled at Gair, but he was curious about the carved prow and swung in closer to get a better look. In a matter of seconds he was face to face with a dragon's head, luridly painted, with glass eyes and ivory fangs.

A dragon-headed ship. A flag with a star, the brightest, whitest star of them all, the Pole Star, riding at the cross-hilts of the constellation known as the Sword of Slaine. *Nordmen*. Gair changed course. The braided and bearded warriors of the Northern Isles, with their horned helmets and double-headed axes, were rarely seen in the Empire; few chose to trade with the main-landers. Most preferred to pillage the island communities of the Eastern Ocean; Gair had never heard of them in the Great Sea before. A ruddy-bearded face appeared at the railing above a massive plaid-wrapped body, and he decided not to wait around. As he banked away he saw a splash of golden yellow that caught his eye. It was a silk shirt, open at the neck, being worn by a pale-skinned, dark-haired man who did not appear to feel the cold in the slightest.

Gair's unease became a sour taste of fear. Something was wrong. The sweet music of the Song had become a jangling dis-cord as another mind brushed against his colours. The man in the golden shirt took hold of a mast shroud to steady himself and

337

stepped up onto the bulwark, one foot on the railing, heedless of
the salt spray on his glossy boots.

Well, well, well. The voice was cool, sardonic. Familiar. *An emissary
to welcome us. Come here, little bird.* An invisible hand scooped Gair
up. *Let's play.*

27

FIVE SISTERS

༄

Savin. Gair folded his wings and darted down into the next trough. What was he doing here? Unseen greasy fingers plucked at him, forcing him to jink sideways and up once more to regain height. The hand came in again, scooping Gair up, but he managed to beat free. He looked back and realised he was well beyond the Five Sisters. They were barely visible on the horizon, just knots in the thread that was the line where sky met sea. Goddess, how far had he flown? It would be a close-run race for the islands.

Savin reached for him again, but this time did no more than tweak his tail. Gair swerved away and flew straight into a wall of solid air that batted him back the way he had come. Flapping hard, he tried to climb above it, but it was as clear as glass and implacable as a fortress wall. Savin gave him a push from below, then whisked the hand away and left him tumbling in the disordered air.

A laugh bubbled into Gair's thoughts.

Little bird, you can do better than this, I'm sure. Show me what you can do, if given sufficient motivation. The hand swatted him down towards the heaving sea. Gair plunged into the Song for the shape of the fastest bird he knew. Aysha had tried to teach him the trick of flowing from one shape to another whilst in motion, but he had never yet perfected it. Now he had one more chance to master it, or face drowning. Holding the keen, arrow-sharp melody of the raptor in his mind, he let the gull shape unravel and pushed himself towards the new Song.

A heartstopping plummet brought him within inches of the wavetops, but now he was beating his wings strongly, and his peregrine shape was able to dart clear of the pressure against his back and strike out for clear air. It was not the ideal shape to be over water, but he did not know what else to do. Heart drumming in his chest, he dived for the nearest of the Sisters.

The islands were closer now. He could make out their shapes, the necklace of white foam amongst the rocks. If he could keep drawing away, maintain the gap for a few seconds more, he might have a chance. Unseen fingers tweaked his tail again: Savin was still behind him, as close as his shadow. Somehow Gair had to find the strength to pull ahead.

The smallest of the Sisters appeared beneath him, jagged and hostile. At this time of year the sea was marginally warmer than the land, and where the two met confusion reigned in the air. A gull would have ridden it easily, but the peregrine was a creature of upland moors and Gair struggled with the conflicting currents, wings beating desperately to capture some lift. As soon as he'd gained sufficient height, he surged over the rocky channel towards the next island.

He felt Savin behind him like hot breath on the back of his neck. He could not be sure whether the pursuit was physical, or whether Savin was reaching out with his mind, and he didn't dare spare a second to look. All he could do was fly straight for Chapterhouse and hope he had enough time.

Come to me, little bird, Savin sang. *I know who you are!*

Over the second island Gair gained a little more height, but it was harder to take advantage of it. He was unaccustomed to flying this fast for this long; it was a world apart from the easy gliding and tumbling of the fire-eagle. His wings were tiring, but he could not afford to rest.

Over the channel between the two largest islands talons slammed into his back and sent him plunging towards the foaming rocks. Burning pain shot through his neck and feathers flew. He screamed aloud and, twisting free, he scrambled up into clear air above the island. Another peregrine wheeled into view ahead, shrieking a challenge. Immediately Gair felt a resonance in the Song inside him. Fear spasmed in his gut. *Savin* – and he was desperately strong.

The peregrine swooped towards him. Talons raked his back again, costing him yet more height. Gair swerved, but he was unable to recover in time. The rising slope of the island was too close and he ploughed headlong into the snow.

He panted for breath as the chill struck through his feathers, sapping his strength, making him shiver. *Move.* He had to move. Savin couldn't be far away, though he could not see him. He had to move! There, a rock. He floundered through the snow towards it, hopped up. His feathers were damp, clumped. He shook himself to settle them, and the gashes across his neck and shoulder burned. Scarlet speckled the snow around him.

Weary and shaken, Gair started to heave himself back into the air for the long flight to Chapterhouse. At once Savin slammed into him and knocked him sideways. A heavy silver paw planted in the centre of his chest, pinning him down. Behind it reared the mask of a snow leopard.

Gair's heart pounded. No matter how he kicked and flapped, he was unable to wriggle out from underneath the broad paw, and its fur was too thick for his beak to penetrate. He shrieked again as the cat's weight bore down on him.

He could do nothing as a falcon now. A little more pressure from that paw and any bird's ribcage would shatter as if made of spun sugar. Releasing the Song, Gair stretched into his human shape. Despair crouched on his chest in the shape of a snow leopard, its ebony claws pricking his skin. Fully grown, the cat could take down a musk deer at a flat gallop . . . Gair did not know the shape well enough to even attempt to meet it on its own terms. He could do nothing at all.

Walnut-sized golden eyes narrowed. The leopard shifted, silver coat bunching over heavy shoulders as another paw was placed on Gair's chest, this time just below his throat. It growled, and he gagged. Its breath stank of rotten meat.

'What do you want, Savin?' he gasped.

You.

He felt pressure on his mind far heavier than that on his breastbone, crushing his brain within his skull, squeezing tears from his eyes.

This.

Wrenching pain. Savin's presence blew through him like the first icy blast of winter, shrivelling everything it touched. Gair scrambled for the Song to throw up a shield, but Savin tore it from his grasp. The alien presence intensified. It grew stronger, heavier, filling his head, weighing him down as surely as the ocean squeezed the last breath from a drowning man.

Savin chuckled darkly, plunged his hand into Gair's memories and pulled. They came spilling out like yarn, in a tangle of brightly coloured instants: the taste of spicebread at breakfast; the breathless hush of a snowy forest; the Vespers bell over sleet hissing on a windowpane. He picked them over carelessly, snatching up what interested him and tossing aside what did not, hauling out still more as Gair's mind flooded with images, strewn haphazardly atop one another in bizarre combinations. Nothing was left untouched, and it hurt.

Gair screamed, each casual violation stinging worse than a sword-cut. Each old wound picked open welled forth new pain like pus. And still the hunt went on. His talent for shape-shifting was ruthlessly explored. Savin pushed and pummelled him through the changes, then yanked him back so quickly he could hardly recall how his own body felt. Then Savin reached deeper, to pluck out every moment Gair had ever shared with Aysha, lingering over each kiss, turning it over like some exotic curio.

You have feelings for her? A cripple?

'Please . . .' Oh Goddess, the *pain*, throbbing, pounding— *Aysha, help me!*

Then she was tossed aside in favour of every other Master Gair had ever met. Each word they had uttered was examined and discarded, each lesson winnowed for grains of whatever Savin sought. Alderan was treated to a similar scrutiny, for far longer. Snatches of conversation echoed round Gair's head.

What has he told you? Savin demanded. *What?*

Deeper he plunged, back along the threads of the years at the Motherhouse, back to Gair's childhood summers amongst the cliffs and coves of the Leahn coast, to a boy's wondering innocence at the colours of the world. Back to a first startled breath, back to sleep, back to a blessed darkness and a song sung in stillness over the rhythm of a distant pulse.

Savin returned, raging. *Where is the key? You cannot hide it from me, boy!*

Gair could not answer. His mind was paralysed by pain, deafened by his own sobbing. He was helplessly adrift in a roil of tattered memories. Savin clawed at him again and again, and fresh agonies detonated in his skull.

Where is it?

He was slipping, drifting further away—

You must know! Tell me! TELL ME!

—the darkness opening up, drawing him in—

TELL ME!

—even the pain becoming remote. It belonged to someone else now and the yammering, demanding voice faded at last into nothingness.

☙

In the end, the paralysing cold woke him, seeping into his back and limbs. His extremities had lost all sensation; his muscles were stiff and unresponsive, except where they burned in agony. Slowly, Gair opened his eyes.

Grey. Everything was grey. Featureless, colourless, as far as he could see. He tried to turn his head to increase his field of view and pain exploded through his neck. Groaning, he screwed his eyes shut and tried moving his arms instead. More pain, but it was tolerable and he could move, although something resisted him. Likewise his legs. Opening his eyes again, he lifted his right hand and brought it round in front of his face. Snow caked his sleeve and was clutched in bluish-white fingers. That accounted for the cold at least, and the greyness, he realised, was a heavy sky overhead. As the fuzziness in his head cleared, he knew he had to move before the chill overcame him completely. Gritting his teeth, he rolled over onto his belly and dragged his legs under him.

When he staggered to his feet, he was surrounded by churned, bloody snow. Movement had started at least one wound bleeding again; spatters of fresh scarlet appeared around his feet. Gair crashed to his knees. His stomach churned and abruptly heaved. Sour bile burned his throat over and over until nothing remained to throw up.

He slumped weeping into the snow as the grey sky spun and rolled above him. It took such a long time to steady, a long time for the earth to stop pitching so that he could try to stand again. Painfully he levered himself up. Blood trickled down his chest and arm and he almost fell. Blinking, he tottered around in a circle to get his bearings.

Somewhere on an island. Sea heaved sullenly off to his right and beyond that lay the humped white shape of another island. Gair was sure he should know its name, but he could not think of it. He did know that beyond that island there was another one and beyond that, home.

To cross the water to the next island he would have to fly. He was not sure if he could. Cautious exploration round the back of his neck found a mess of torn fabric and congealed blood. When his fingers brushed against the raw edge of the wound he sobbed aloud at the pain. He scooped up a handful of snow and dumped it onto the back of his neck. Cold lanced into him, stinging, burning, making him howl. Another handful and slowly numbness over-took the pain. Gasping for breath, he reached down inside for the Song.

It was not as strong as he remembered. It felt almost as ragged and bruised as he did himself. An eternity passed as he sorted through the melodies for the one he wanted. When he found it, it lay inert in his hands. He could not make it sing.

'Oh Aysha, help me,' he whispered.

He tried again. This time he felt the shape-shift begin and was halfway through it before it broke apart and he fell to his knees, retching. As soon as the nausea had diminished enough, he lurched back to his feet and tried again. He got no further, but this time he resolved not to let go. He could not afford to let go. He would not die there! Gritting his teeth against the sickness churning his stomach, he clung onto the music and willed it to carry him through.

He flew across the narrow neck of sea, one more step closer to home. Black shadows crowded into his vision and he lurched, only feet above the waves. Dizziness threatened to overwhelm him, sent him crashing into the snowy flank of the next island. Agony flooded his neck and shoulder. Scarlet seeped into his field of vision, blurring the world. He lay panting until he could summon the strength to master the pain and pull himself up the slope towards the island's crest. Before he'd reached the top, he'd fallen to his knees again.

'Aysha,' he called, 'oh Goddess, *Aysha!*'

No answer. She could not hear him. He would have to get closer, make the next change and fly, somehow. He dumped more

345

snow on the back of his neck and reached for that fragile, elusive melody once more.

చ∾

As darkness fell, Alderan climbed the stairs to the top of the bell-tower with a spare cloak over his arm. For all spring was drawing in, snow still lay thickly on the fields, pearly under the second moon. It was not a night to be out without a cloak – not a night to be abroad at all.

One by one he closed and barred the shutters, all except the west-facing pair. Spreading his hands, he called a glim so wide he couldn't wrap his arms around it and left it spinning in the centre of the chamber. White light lanced across the sleeping island, straight as an Imperial highway. He hoped it would be enough to guide the lad home. It had to be enough. It was all he could do. Then he sat down on a bench to wait.

An hour passed before he saw a flicker of movement and a kestrel streaked though the window to alight on the end of the bench. Her feathers were disarrayed and there was a wildness in her eyes.

Where is he? I've searched everywhere!

I don't know, Aysha, Alderan told her. *He's out there somewhere, but I don't know where.*

But I can HEAR him! she wailed. *Listen!*

Her colours filled his mind, and a despairing howl echoed around the inside of Alderan's head. Aysha's colours shuddered. He closed her out gently.

Have you spoken to him?

He can't hear me.

Try again, now. We must bring him home.

Alderan watched the kestrel become still and sensed her reaching out into the night, though he could not hear her. He had never seen her like this before, not in all the years he had known her, never seen her colours stretched so taut or slashed so vividly with

346

scarlet. How much longer could she bear it? Looking out of the window, he searched the darkness for something, anything that might show him Gair had found his way back.

There's no answer. Aysha's colours were frozen.

Maybe he is just not strong enough to reply, Alderan said. *Keep trying.*

The kestrel dipped her head and broke contact with his mind again. He was glad, in a way; he had felt every ounce of her pain when that hopeless shriek had stabbed at her. Something had happened out there, something awful beyond imagining. Gair was too strong to have somehow fouled a weaving and lost himself to it, Alderan knew that with a certainty, as sure as he knew himself, but doubts continued to gnaw at him as the minutes passed and still there was no sign.

He had gone looking for Gair after the Council meeting broke up, but he hadn't been able to find him in his room, the refectory or the library. Darin had not seen him since breakfast, nor had anyone else he spoke to. With concern mounting, Alderan had searched for his colours, and found no sign of them anywhere on Penglas. He had reached out to the wardens on the other inhabited islands and shown them the Leahn's pattern of emerald and amber, but one by one they reported the same thing: wherever Gair was, he was not on the Western Isles.

What's that? Aysha's presence was back inside Alderan's head in an instant. *Out towards the Five Sisters. I thought I saw something.*

Your eyes are sharper than mine, little sister. I cannot see anything.

I can – it is him, it must be! She fluttered to the window ledge, her mind straining out, then recoiled.

What is it?

Oh Goddess, he's hurt, she whispered. *He can barely hold the shape. Help him, Alderan!*

There is nothing I can do from here, you know that. That would be beyond even the strongest of us. He must make his own way back here. If he cannot, we will go out to him.

347

If he loses the shape, the fall will kill him!

He will not lose the shape, Aysha. Be strong.

She swore, her colours swirling in agitation, as Alderan stared out into the night. There it was, no more than a flicker in the silver beam from his glim. He fixed his eyes on it, willing it closer, until at last he could make out its shape.

Go, Aysha. Go back to your rooms.

But I want to be here!

No, you do not, Alderan told her. *Go. I will call you when all is well.* She protested again, but he cut her off, hating himself for it but knowing it was for the best. Reluctantly, her kestrel took to the air and darted out into the night.

Hold on, Gair.

The fire-eagle lurched through the glim-light towards the tower. Its red-gold plumage was stained almost black, its wing-beats erratic, as if all strength was gone and it was propelled by sheer will alone. It barely cleared the tree-tops outside the walls.

Alderan shrank the glim to make room. Another mind clutched at his, howling, and the battered bird scrambled over the balustrade to hit the floor in a smear of blood and feathers. Almost at once the shape shimmered as Gair lost his grip on the Song. His face was scratched and deathly pale. Bloody rents in his clothing showed raw flesh, his shirt was sodden scarlet.

Alderan knelt beside him. 'There, lad,' he said, wrapping the spare cloak around him, 'you're home now.'

Gair whimpered as the cloak brushed the wound on the back of his neck. His breathing was ragged, and blood and sweat plastered his hair to his forehead.

Alderan helped him to stand, but the young man slumped against him. 'Come on, you stubborn Leahn bastard,' he muttered, thrusting his shoulder under Gair's arm. 'Stay with me. I brought you here for a reason and I'm damned if I'm going to lose you now.'

348

Gair floated in darkness. Vast as a night sky, starless as death, it crowded around him and stretched away into unimaginable depths. He felt neither heat nor cold, saw no movement, heard no noise, not even the sound of his own breathing. There was no sensation of the passage of time, for he had nothing to measure it against, only an endless now. The void was absolute.

Then he saw a flicker in the dark, faint at first. A hazy patch appeared, silvery as the moon behind clouds. It brightened and spread, the darkness giving way grudgingly, seeming to become darker still as if the light only emphasised the blackness. When it filled his vision, he felt drawn to it. Something beyond the light pulled him closer. He was too tired to resist. So very weary. Easier to let go.

A shape passed across the light, twisted and stretched. Colours slid over it like the surface of a soap bubble. Another shape, darker this time, loomed large, then faded back to a blur in the bluish-silver light. It was familiar somehow; it tugged at his memory. Curious now, in spite of the weariness, Gair strained forward into the light and the swimming shapes.

Pain exploded through him. Colours stabbed into his eyes like shards of stained glass; his mind was wreathed in fire. He screamed, and sound tore at his ears. Voices boomed and whispered round his head, shrieked along his nerves to add to the agony. Strong hands held him down, pinned his thrashing limbs and gripped his head like a vice until he thought his skull would be crushed by those iron fingers. Waves of pain rolled through him and he howled.

A woman's face floated through the mist above him. She smiled gently and laid something cool on his face. Her lips moved; she was speaking, but her voice was sonorous and distorted, as if coming from the bottom of a pond.

Gair could not make out the words. He could not think for the pain.

She continued to smile and speak and stroke his face and slowly the pain diminished. With it went the light, and as that faded, so too did awareness, until darkness claimed him again.

28

A LETTER

☙

Danilar watched the sunrise over the rim of a mug of scalding tea in his study. The first day of what the calendar said was a new year was dawning blue and crisp as an eggshell. A good omen for the year to come, according to superstition. As Chaplain of the Suvaeon Order he could not countenance such beliefs, but he knew as well as anyone that although the Goddess moved in ways beyond the wit of man to comprehend, She was inclined to drop the occasional hint.

Today was undoubtedly one of those days. True, the cloister below his window was still waist-deep in snow, apart from the little patch he kept clear for the birds, and ice bearded every gutter and cornice, but the sun shone from a clear sky and that was enough to inspire a little hope.

Tea finished, Danilar hummed a psalm or two as he swept the path and put out water and scraps for the sparrows. A few of the bravest darted down from the ivy-covered pillars to hop about his feet, alternately watching him and their imminent breakfast with bright black eyes. They had no words with which to say grace, but he was sure that they had souls, so he made obeisance to the Goddess on their behalf with a prayer for wild creatures, then put the broom away.

As he latched the closet he heard footsteps on the far side of the cloister. He looked round to see one of the curates, padding carefully over the frosty flags towards him.

'A letter for you, Chaplain!' he called, flourishing the parchment. 'Well, for the Preceptor, actually, but the man said to give it to you.'

Could it be? Danilar took the letter from the curate. He did not recognise the hand on the front, but then he had no reason to. 'Is he waiting?'

'I sent him to the hospitaller for some hot tea. I thought it might be welcome on such a raw morning.'

'And a good thought it was,' Danilar said. 'Run and tell him I'm on my way. I'll be but a moment.'

He went back upstairs to his study to fetch a small purse from his desk. After a moment's thought, he added a few more marks from his strongbox in acknowledgement of the speedy completion of the errand. In this winter, the fellow had more than earned it.

Danilar found the messenger perched on a stool in the kitchen, nursing a large mug of tea. A flicker in the man's expression as he took the purse said he had gauged the coin in it by its weight and found himself pleasantly surprised. Then Danilar bade him finish his breakfast in his own time, and set out for the Preceptor's lodging.

Ansel's already poor health had deteriorated further over the winter. Not long after the first snows his chest had worsened, and only a few days before Eventide, Danilar had taken the sacrament to him and found him collapsed on the floor of his study, barely able to breathe. Hengfors' prognosis was grim, yet somehow Ansel had held on, as defiant to the last as St Agostin reborn.

The Preceptor was in bed when Danilar let himself in. Hengfors' assistant bent over him, a bottle in one hand, the other proffering a spoon.

'You should take the syrup, my lord,' the young man insisted. 'You won't get better without it.'

'I'm not going to get better, with or without Hengfors' concoctions,' Ansel rasped. 'Take it away.'

Danilar closed the door quietly behind him. Ansel's head turned towards him a fraction, then dipped the merest nod. The Preceptor's complexion was appallingly pale; the only way to tell him apart from the pillows piled behind his shoulders was the hectic colour in each cheek.

'My lord, I really must insist—'

'Take it away, damn it, or I'll insist you drink it yourself!' Ansel broke off, racked by coughing. He balled a stained handkerchief to his mouth.

Danilar touched the physician's elbow. 'He's a terrible patient, isn't he?' he murmured. 'Why don't you try again later, when he's in a better humour?'

The physician hesitated. 'I'm not supposed to leave him.'

Danilar applied a little more pressure to his elbow, gently ushering him aside. 'That's all right; I'll keep an eye on him. Go on,' he said, smiling, 'I'll send for you if you're needed.'

Shooting a dubious look at the bed and its glowering occupant, the physician corked his bottle. 'Well, I suppose half an hour won't hurt,' he said, then remembered his position and drew himself up to his full height, which was rather less impressive than Danilar's. 'But you must promise to call me at once if there is any deterioration.'

'I promise,' Danilar assured him, still smiling serenely.

Mollified, the physician withdrew.

'Thank the Goddess for that,' Ansel growled as the door closed. 'The vapours from that bottle were making me see double.'

'Oh, I doubt it was that bad.' Danilar drew up a chair. 'How are you feeling today, apart from prickly?'

'Same as ever. Dreadful.'

'Perhaps you should take your medicine, then.'

The old man's face wrinkled further into a scowl. 'It doesn't do any good.'

'Well, at least it can't do you any harm,' said Danilar.

Ansel grunted. 'It tastes awful. Like rotting fish.'

'Medicine is not meant to be pleasant. The quicker you get well, the quicker you can stop taking it.'

'I'm not going to get well, Danilar.'

'I know.'

'I'm beyond the reach of any of Hengfors' potions.'

'I know that, too.'

'But you're still going to insist I take the stuff?'

'It will make Hengfors feel better, even if you don't.'

'Blast it, man, why are you so reasonable? It makes it very difficult to be annoyed with you.'

'Precisely.'

What Ansel said next was short, pithy, and would have made an Imperial legionary blush, had it not been interrupted by further coughing.

Danilar held a basin for the old man to retch into and reflected that even after the Goddess had called him to Her service Ansel remained a fighting soldier at heart. When the bout was over, he put the basin back on the nightstand and covered it with a napkin. There was a little more blood, now; it could not be much longer.

Ansel slumped back on his pillows. Mucus rattled in his chest as he fought to draw breath into his lungs. His eyes were closed, the lids blue, translucent as paper. 'So, Chaplain,' he croaked, 'to what do I owe the pleasure of your company this fine morning?'

'I have a letter for you.'

Now the old man's eyes sparked. 'There is news? Read it for me.'

The letter was sealed with a disc of blue wax impressed with the shape of a swallow. Danilar eased it off with his thumb and opened the paper. The message inside ran to only a couple of lines, written in a neat, sloping hand.

'The feast of St Saren,' he said, 'unless the weather changes. Certainly no more than six weeks.'

354

He laid the paper on Ansel's blankets. The Preceptor folded it up carefully and smoothed it between his hands. 'St Saren's day,' he remarked. 'How appropriate. I just pray I'll live to see it.'

'I'm sure you will. You're stubborn enough.'

'Maybe, but you know as well as I that She'll pay scant respect to that. She'll call me when She's good and ready.' Ansel fell silent, as if his little speech had exhausted him.

Danilar walked to the window to open it a little. The room was overheated, too stuffy for a man with a chest complaint. Through the frost-patterned glass he saw a flock of robed figures in the cloister below. Faces were difficult to pick out, but the scarlet was unmistakable.

'Ansel,' he said, 'there's a whole gaggle of Elders outside and they're heading this way.'

The Preceptor chuckled. 'I was wondering how long it would take. Send them away.'

Danilar turned. 'You know what they're here for?'

'Oh, I have a fair idea. I've been expecting them any time this last month.'

'Are you going to keep me in suspense?'

'Just send them away, Danilar. I'm not in the mood for their prating.'

Danilar waited, but Ansel volunteered nothing more. *So be it, but I pray Goddess he knows what he's doing, even if I don't.* Lips pressed into a disapproving line, he went out through the ante-chamber to the apartment's outer door and opened it.

Goran was pulled up short, his hand raised to knock. 'Oh!' He blinked, heavy features more than usually florid. 'Chaplain, good morning to you.'

'Elder Goran,' Danilar said pleasantly. From the whiff of brandy, Goran was well fortified against the cold. 'Good morning. Won't you step inside?'

Goran realised his arm was still raised and lowered it, folding his hands in his sleeves as he crossed the threshold. The remainder of the delegation followed at his heels and ranged themselves in a half-circle across the doorway, rosy as robins in their ceremonial scarlet.

No doubt to make the maximum impression on a frail old man. I don't care for the way this is shaping up at all.

'Well, gentlemen,' Danilar said, 'what can I do for you?'

'We have come to see the Preceptor,' Goran began, without preamble. 'We have been concerned about the state of his health. He has been ill for some time; perhaps he ought to relinquish some of his administrative duties and concentrate on his recovery. After all, we have not seen him in the Rede Hall for more than a month.'

And so we come down to it. Danilar let a small frown crease his brow. 'So you want to reassure yourselves that he is still fit to hold the reins of power in our Order? I see. Well, I can assure you, gentlemen, that the Preceptor has been in no way inconvenienced by his recent illness in the day-to-day administration of this House.'

'Thank you, Chaplain, but we would prefer to see this for ourselves.'

'You have some doubts?'

'Yes, we have doubts!' Goran's colour heightened. 'We have seen not a hair of his head for five weeks – he could be cold in his grave, for all we know.'

'But Elder, he is most definitely not. You have read the edicts he has signed. They are all sealed and witnessed, in accordance with the law.' Danilar kept his voice even, his tone bland.

'These edicts,' Goran declared, pulling a sheaf of documents from his sleeve and brandishing them, 'could have been written by a pot-boy and signed by the Preceptor's pet monkey. What proof is there in these that his faculties are intact?'

'Ah.' Danilar folded his arms. 'Now we come to the heart of it. You are not concerned about his health at all. What you are concerned about is the state of his mind – to be blunt, whether our beloved Lord Preceptor has bats in the attic.'

Goran harrumphed, embarrassed. 'I would not have put it quite so crudely, Chaplain, but he is an old man, after all.'

'Not that old,' Danilar cut in. 'His wits are as sharp as ever, as is his temper. Ask his secretary, if you doubt me.'

'Secondhand evidence is not what we want, Chaplain,' said a new voice. A lean, fox-faced Dremenirian made his way to the front of the group. He touched Goran's elbow and the portly Elder melted back into the crowd.

'Ceinan,' Danilar said. *No surprise that you're the real leader of this deputation.* 'How kind of you to drop by to extend your good wishes.'

'Danilar,' Ceinan returned easily. 'As you can see, we are not plotting insurrection. We have come in good faith, to have our minds put at rest. That is all. We have no desire to call the Rede and move that Ansel be put aside.'

'So what exactly do you want to do?'

'Just to see him.' Ceinan spread his hands. 'Just to assure ourselves that all is well and that our Order is in safe hands.'

'I'm afraid you're going to have to take my word for it, for now. No one can be admitted to the Preceptor's presence until all risk of contagion is over.'

A flicker of irritation showed in Ceinan's pale blue eyes.

'Contagion?' Goran echoed, round-eyed.

'Why yes, Elder Goran,' Danilar said, 'black-lung fever is highly contagious.'

'Black-lung fever?' Colour drained from the Elder's face.

'Indeed. We'd hardly want that spreading through the Rede, would we? Elders dropping in droves – it would be a disaster.'

'But you come and go as you please, Danilar,' Ceinan put in.

'I have had the fever before,' he said. It astonished him how easy lying became when necessity cracked the whip. 'Many years ago, in the desert. Hengfors tells me a man cannot contract it twice.'

Goran fumbled for a handkerchief. 'You are sure the Preceptor has this?'

'The symptoms are very specific, I'm afraid. We cannot take any chances that it might spread further into the Order, or into the population at large. It can be deadly. Until such time as we are sure there is no risk of infection, the Preceptor must remain in isolation, although he is carrying out his duties as normal.'

'Why were we not told of this sooner?' one of the other Elders interjected. 'We should have been informed as soon as the Preceptor was diagnosed.'

'We saw no need to alarm you.' Danilar tucked his hands in his sleeves. 'Once the Preceptor is recovered, he will be back in the Rede Hall. In the meantime I shall convey your kind wishes to him. I'm sure he will be touched that so many of you are so concerned. Good day to you.'

Muttering, the deputation drifted towards the door. Goran mopped his face and peered back over his shoulder as if he expected to see the spectre of disease come slavering after him.

Only Ceinan lingered. 'He is still alive, isn't he, Danilar?' the Dremenirian asked. 'You know as well as I that his secretary can forge his signature, and it is an open secret where the Great Seal is kept.'

'Oh, he is alive, I can assure you, and feisty as ever. Ask Hengfors' staff, who have to nurse him.'

Ceinan smiled thinly. 'I may just do that. I know your friendship with the Preceptor goes back many years – you were novices together, were you not? How far does your loyalty go, Danilar? Would you lie to protect him, or conspire with him to prevent a fair election?'

'Who says there's going to be an election?'

Ceinan looked wounded. 'My dear Chaplain, we both know he's dying. Your little fiction about the black-lung fever was very neat, I must say. It certainly fooled them.' A jerk of his sleek brown head indicated the departed Elders.

'I wasn't trying to fool anyone, Ceinan,' Danilar told him. 'The Preceptor was not prepared to infect the whole Rede just to satisfy you that he's still right-minded and fit to tend his daily affairs. It would be foolish, to say nothing of extremely uncomfortable for anyone who contracted the disease. It's not very pleasant, believe me; it fills the lungs with reeking black mucus.'

'Hence the name, I know. I'm still not entirely convinced, Danilar. I think Ansel should come before us so that we can see for ourselves how well or unwell he is. If he is unfit to hold office, consistorial law provides our clear remedy.'

Anxiety slid another knife into Danilar's side. It was not good that Ceinan was so involved. Not good at all.

'Ceinan, I appreciate your concern,' he said. 'It is only right and proper that you should be so keen to ensure the wellbeing of the Order, but I can assure you that your concern, however well founded, is entirely misplaced. We are in very safe hands.'

'But for how much longer?'

'No one can see that far ahead. Only the Goddess knows.'

'And She's not saying, I suppose?'

'That's perilously close to blasphemy, Elder Ceinan,' Danilar warned him. 'She does not vouchsafe me Her innermost mind, but I do know how She feels about being invoked in such terms. Now I suggest that we leave Ansel to his rest. If you still want to see him, make an appointment when he is better.'

Ceinan treated him to a tight little smile and a shallow bow before gliding away.

Danilar closed the door after him with a sigh of relief. Back in Ansel's bedchamber, the old man was waiting, weak but alert.

'Well?'

'I think we may soon have a coup on our hands.'

'Nothing new. I've been expecting it. Ceinan?'

'Ceinan.'

359

'He's a subtle one, Danilar,' Ansel said. 'We must tread carefully with him.'

'I know. I had to perpetuate that story about the black-lung fever for the benefit of the others, but he made it quite plain that he wasn't taken in by it.'

'I heard. You left the door ajar.' Ansel chuckled. 'You lie well, for a Churchman.'

'Thank you, although I'm not sure that's an achievement to be proud of.'

'How many were there?'

'Nine or ten, but you can guarantee that wasn't all of them. Ceinan implied that they would have a quorum, if they called the Rede – or at least close enough to a quorum for us to be concerned.'

'His faction seems to have grown of late,' Ansel mused. 'I think perhaps we lost a friend or two when we let the Leahn go.'

'If they would have preferred to see him burn then I'm not sure I'd want to count them as friends.'

'You may be right, at that. Still, Ceinan's the one we have to watch, not his hangers-on. Does he know much?'

'I couldn't say. He implied that he knew there was something afoot, but not what.'

'As long as it stays that way, we've got as much as we could hope for. When he finds out exactly what has been going on under his nose, I want it to come as a surprise.' He tossed Danilar a little ball of paper. Traces of blue wax clung to the folds. 'Burn it.'

29

LABYRINTH

ॐ

Gair opened his eyes. He had to blink several times before the smeary shapes resolved themselves into the shadows of trees on a whitewashed wall, dancing in the breeze. Apart from the bed he lay in, the only furniture was a single narrow closet and a wash-stand, both of plain dark wood. He didn't recognise the room.

'Hello.'

A woman's voice, with a lilting accent. He turned his head towards it. Sitting on a stool next to him was a golden-skinned woman with copper hair, waves and waves of it, loose round the shoulders of her green mantle. Tired shadows bruised her tawny, tilted eyes.

'I know you.' Gair's mouth felt stuffed with wool, thick and dry.

She smiled. 'I'm Tanith, one of the Healers here at Chapter-house.'

'I remember. You look tired.' He took the beaker of water she held out to him and sipped at it. 'Am I in the infirmary?'

'Yes. Do you remember your name?'

'Gair,' he said. 'Why would he not remember his own name?'

'And your family name?'

'I don't have one.' He drained the cup and she refilled it for him.

'What colour are your eyes?'

'Grey. What's happened to me, Tanith?'

'Don't worry about that just yet. You're safe now.' She laid the back of her hand on his face. Feeling for a fever?

'Have I been sick?'

'In a way. You were attacked, and some of your memories were damaged. I wasn't sure how far the damage extended, but it seems to be confined to your most recent past. You can remember your name, for instance, but you didn't know mine.'

'Attacked? By whom?'

'Saaron will be able to tell you more. He wanted to see you when you woke up. I'll fetch him.' She stood up to leave.

Gair put out a hand to stop her and saw a freshly healed wound seaming his right forearm. 'What happened to me, Tanith? I know I was up in the bell-tower, looking at the sea-elf ship. Did I fall out?' *No. That wound is a straight slash, made with a blade, or something sharp.*

'Not exactly.' Slender fingers curled round his hand, held it between hers. 'You've suffered something called a reiving. Your memory has been ransacked, left all tangled up like a goodwife's rag-bag. I've shielded you from the worst of it, but it will take time for all your memories to come back.'

'But they will come back.'

'Oh, yes. With more healing, you'll be fine, don't worry about that.'

'And this?' Gair nodded at his arm.

'The attack was physical as well as mental, I'm afraid.' Gair lifted the sheet. Days-old bruises mottled his side, his legs, slashed with puckered, angry scar tissue. *Saints and angels, what happened to me? How much time have I lost?* Healing could repair in hours what would take the body days or weeks by itself, but still. He let the sheet drop.

'How long have I been here?'

Tanith squeezed his shoulder. 'Let me fetch Saaron.'

After she'd gone, he stared at the ceiling and tried to remember what had happened after climbing the stairs to the tower. Nothing came back to him but a vague disquiet which squatted on his mind, heavy as a storm-cloud. Memories grumbled and flickered in its depths, too brief to catch. Was that Tanith's shield?

The door opened again to admit a scarecrow-haired man in Healer's green, gaunt but grinning. 'So you've come back to us at last,' he said, plopping down on the stool beside the bed.

'Saaron?'

'One and the same. How do you feel?'

'Considering I look like a butcher's block? Tired, mostly.'

'That's the Healing. A few days' rest and some good food and you won't know you've been hurt. Even the scars will have faded in that time, unless you want to keep one or two to impress the girls? Although from what I hear, some of them don't need any impressing,' Saaron dropped a heavy wink.

'What do you mean?'

'Your little chickadee. She laid siege to the infirmary for two whole days until Alderan shooed her away.'

Chickadee? 'Two days? Is that how long I've been here?' A tiny bird of panic fluttered in Gair's chest. *Pray Goddess it won't be too late.*

'A mite longer than that, but it's not important. What matters is that you're on the mend and—'

'It *is* important – how long, Saaron? What happened to me up on the tower?'

Saaron scuffed his fingers through his hair. 'Near as we can tell, you shape-shifted and flew out over the harbour, towards the Five Sisters. K'shaa, Shipmaster of the *Morning Star*, remembers seeing you. Somewhere over the Five Sisters, you ran into Savin.'

The name chimed in Gair's head. Lightnings flared in the storm behind his eyes.

Saaron paused. 'You recognise that name.'

'Yes. What happened next?'

'He half-killed you looking for something he thought you knew.

You were able to tell us that much. How you made it back here no one knows. Alderan brought you down from the tower more dead than alive and you've been here ever since.'

'How long?'

'A few days, that's all. Gair, it doesn't matter.'

'Don't flannel me, Saaron, *how long?*' *I have to know how much time I've lost.*

Saaron's lips clamped into a disapproving line, but after a moment he relented. 'Six days.'

Gair swore. Six days was too many. Pushing back the covers, he swung his legs over the edge of the bed.

'You're not strong enough to be up, not yet.' Saaron took his arm, but Gair shoved him back.

'I have to find it,' he said. 'Damn it, Saaron, let me up.'

'Sit still a minute!' the Healer snapped. 'Find what? What are you talking about?'

'Savin is coming here,' Gair told him, struggling to his feet. 'He's looking for the key.'

'What? What key?'

'I remember it. He's coming here.' His knees buckled. He clutched at the night-table for support and the pottery beaker fell to the floor, where it broke into shards. *Too long, damn it. Far too long. Six days! I have to find it.*

But Saaron was shouting at the door, and green mantles swarmed in and surrounded him. Two burly adepts pushed him gently back onto the bed and held him down. Goddess, his neck burned. He couldn't move, couldn't throw them off. Didn't they realise what was happening?

'The shield must have weakened,' said Saaron as Tanith bent over, her hands either side of Gair's head. 'He insisted Savin was coming here, and that he had to find it, whatever it is. Something about a key.'

'Tanith, let me go.'

She frowned, and paused in calling the Song. 'He shouldn't be remembering anything yet. It's far too soon.'

'No, it's too late. Please, listen to me!'

Then Gair sank down into blackness.

❧

The maze had changed its shape. He was convinced of it. He had taken this turning before – his footprints were still clearly visible in the dusty earth – but now it led to a dead end. Impenetrable green thorn hedge grew across his path, taller than he was, joined seamlessly to the hedges on either side. Swearing in frustration, Gair turned round.

The path behind him ran arrow-straight into the distance between the hedges. He hadn't walked that far, only twenty or thirty paces. So the maze was changing behind him as well. Goddess, how long had he been here? No shadows lay on the pale, sandy soil underfoot to indicate the time of day, and when he looked up he could not see the sun, just green hedges and cloudless, summer-bleached sky. All he could do was keep walking until he found his way out.

At first he had tried to memorise the turns he had taken so that he could work his way back if one path proved false, but there was no point once he knew the maze changed behind him as well. He would never find the square where he'd started.

There had been a marble statue in the middle, a wood-nymph playing the flute, about three feet tall. Her pedestal was almost obscured by a climbing dog-rose. He wanted to find his way back to it because there had been another exit on the far side that he wanted to try. This one was leading him round in circles.

Gair turned left, then left again, and the path doubled back on itself to the right. He followed it round through five complete right-angled turns, then stopped. He should have crossed his own path by now, but he had seen no intersections, only parallel hedges eight feet tall, ahead and behind, with a dusty earthen path in between. He about-faced and went back the way he had come. The path turned to the right again, three times, then left into a small open square, about five yards across. In the centre stood a statue on a marble pedestal.

He walked up to it, not quite believing what he was seeing. It was a wood-nymph, playing a flute, but the dog-rose around her pedestal had withered. Dark green ivy scrambled through the desiccated stems to coil around the nymph's ankles. She stared down at her feet, eyes and mouth wide with horror.

Quickly, he scanned the hedges opposite for the other exit. There was only one break in the hedge, where he had entered. He hurried out and found a short path that met another at right angles. Which way to go, left or right? Footprints marked the pale dust in both directions; no help there. He chose left and followed it through two left turns, and came back to the square with the statue. The ivy had reached the nymph's knees and her hands clutched at her face. Gair jogged back to the intersection and turned right. The path led straight on as far as he could see. He shaded his eyes against the glare of the invisible sun, but saw no sign of any turning or side-path. He began walking, counting off his paces. One hundred. Two hundred. Two hundred and fifty. Green thorn hedges, eight feet high, endlessly converged ahead. Gair turned around, and there was the square behind him.

He swore. The wood-nymph's face was turned towards him and she was screaming. Her arms were pinned at her sides by the thickening coils of ivy, her waist and lower body completely obscured by dark, leathery leaves. He looked back over his shoulder; the long straight path now ended abruptly in a right turn, not twenty yards ahead. He turned and began to run.

It didn't matter which way he turned now, left or right, he did not care. He simply ran. Occasionally he stumbled and crashed into the hedges. Green thorns snagged his clothes and raked his skin, drawing blood. Cloudless, perpetual noon beat down, hammering sweat from his chest and back. He ran until his lungs burned, then kept on running. He had to find a way out of this place before the wood-nymph was strangled.

Shadowless paths stretched on and on, criss-crossing, doubling back. Turn after turn was taken or missed. The heat tightened its grip until his head pounded and his vision blurred. There had to be a way out. The labyrinth couldn't go on for ever.

His feet tangled with each other and sent him sprawling into the dust. The ground smashed the wind from him; he sucked in a breath and inhaled a lungful of dust that set him coughing. Saints, he had to get out of this place. He rolled onto his back, panting, and tried to summon the energy to stand up.

Move onto his knees first. One foot under him, push himself up. His legs wobbled like a newborn colt's, almost pitching him into the nearest hedge. He straightened up and looked around him. He stood at the entrance to an open square, about five yards across, containing only a mound of ivy in the centre. Whatever it was growing over was obscured, apart from a sliver of white at the very top. Gair stumbled towards it. The white sliver was a small arm, a woman's, slender and smooth, straining up towards the sky. A single strand of ivy wound up from her elbow, unfurling its dark leaves against her marble flesh. He was too late.

He fell back to his knees. All that running, and he was still too late. A sob shuddered its way out of him, then another, for the nymph under the ivy, for the drumming pain in his head, for his inability to find his way out.

He had failed.

Gair stared at the nymph's arm, her fingers spread in supplication. The ivy was young, the stems slender. Perhaps she could still be saved, if he could reach her. He grabbed hold of a handful of ivy and tugged. A few clinging rootlets peeled back, leaving feathery patterns on the nymph's pale form, then his hands slipped. Dark leaves showered the pale ground, but the stems did not break. Gair redoubled his efforts, jerking and tearing at the ivy until his fingers were sap-blackened and bleeding, but it was to no avail.

367

'No,' he whispered. His fists clenched. He couldn't let her suffocate. 'No!'

Cursing, he reached down inside himself for the music of fire.

Power burst forth. It spilled into his soul, boiling, rising until it filled every crevice of his being. It scoured at the guilt, raced along his veins, seared his skin. He released it, and the statue blazed.

Ivy leaves crisped in the heat, showering the earth in a parody of autumn. Stems split, sap bubbled in the cracks, and roiling, stinking smoke filled the air. Thorn hedges ignited with a rushing roar, and he lashed the flames hotter still.

Between one heartbeat and the next, the fire was gone. A carpet of cinders surrounded the statue's plinth, puffing ashes into the air under Gair's boots as crossed it. The stone was grey with soot, but not a shred of ivy remained save for a few twists of charcoal on the ground. The nymph's head was down, her arms hanging at her sides. Dishevelled hair covered her face, laced with tattered roses. He reached out to touch her and she crumbled into ash.

'NO!'

Gair fell to his knees. The marble pedestal shattered under his hands and he sprawled on his side. He was still too late to save her, and to save himself.

Smoke swirled. A thin beam of sunlight slipped through, then another and another, until there were five in all, touching the blasted earth like the fingers of the Goddess Herself. They fell warm on his face, soothing his sunburned skin. In the sky above him, a smear of green and gold and red resolved into the face of an angel, surrounded by a brilliant light that flickered with ethereal wings. The angel smiled and reached down a hand to lift him into the light.

'It's all right, Gair.'

His eyes flew open. His chest heaved, fighting to draw a breath from the air that scorched his lungs—

'It's all right,' Tanith said again, soothingly, 'there's no fire here.'

368

Gair stared around wildly. The room was dark apart from a candle on the table that silhouetted Tanith's head as she bent over him. She had her hands on his shoulders, holding him back against the pillows. The tangled sheet clung to him with sweat, and his lungs were filled with the dry tang of smoke.

'I thought you were an angel.' His throat was sore.

She smiled, stroking back his hair. 'You were dreaming.'

'I was caught in a maze,' he said. 'There was a statue . . .' The dream crumbled like old parchment, the fragments dissolving faster the harder he tried to hold on to them. He looked at his hands, expecting to see something he couldn't name.

'Saaron should have warned you there would be some strange dreams,' she said. 'Don't worry. That's all they are.'

'What time is it?' he asked.

'Late,' she said. Her arms were bare, he noticed, and her nightshift was visible under her Healer's mantle.

'What are you doing here in the middle of the night?'

'The duty Healer was worried about you, so he woke me,' she told him. 'I've been sleeping in one of the spare rooms here – the dreams were very bad when you first came back. Saaron thought it would be best if I stayed close at hand.'

'I don't remember.'

'Just as well. You endured a terrible ordeal.'

'Will I ever remember? I don't like this cloud in here.' He gestured at his head.

'The shield in your mind is to prevent you remembering too much too quickly. Try not to fight it.' She poured him a cup of water and pushed it into his hand. 'Drink this. You're dehydrated. Then tell me what you told Saaron, about Savin.'

As Gair drank he tried to recall what he had said. The exact words would not come, but he remembered the feeling of urgency, of time slipping away from him.

'Savin is coming here to look for what he couldn't find in my head, some kind of a key. I don't know when, or how I know, exactly, but when I heard his name I suddenly felt as if we were in a race, that I had to find out what he wanted before he got to it. I don't know what it means.'

'And do you still feel like that?'

He nodded. 'Not as strong as before, but yes.'

Tanith folded her arms. A frown creased her golden brows. 'I strengthened the shield,' she said softly. 'You should not be able to remember, if it was something that Savin said to you. I don't understand. You met Savin when you were travelling here from Dremen, didn't you? What has Alderan told you about him?'

'Not much. That he was a renegade of some kind. Alderan never said exactly what he'd done, but he hinted at something horrible.'

'Worse than horrible. Savin was exiled because of it, and the Council ruled that wards should be set around the inhabited islands so that he could never come back without their knowledge.' She bit her lip. 'I must tell Alderan. Try to get some sleep, if you can.'

'I'm not a child, Tanith,' he protested, then closed his mouth when he realised he sounded like one.

'I'm not tired.'

She straightened up. 'You need sleep, Gair.' Her voice was gentle and not unkind. 'Sleep and food, and in a day or two, when you're strong enough, more Healing. Then you will be well.'

'I know. But you must be patient.' She picked up the candle to take it away, then banged it back down hard enough to slop molten wax onto her fingers. She did not seem to notice. Her eyes were hard as topaz. 'Don't you realise what was done to you? Savin tore your mind apart, far worse than anything he did to your body. When you came back you were barely alive. None of us knows how you managed to hold onto the Song long enough to fly back from the Five Sisters. You were bleeding to death, barely alive, barely sane. I've spent hours inside your head stitching you back together again and I just—'

She stopped, hands clenched in the folds of her mantle, eyes
screwed shut. Her lips trembled.

Gair stared at her, startled by her outburst.

'Forgive me,' she said tightly. 'I had no right to lose my temper.
I'll see you in the morning.'

Leaving the guttering candle where it stood, she let herself out.

30

RIVEN

Tanith closed the door to her rooms and leaned back against it. Her father was right, she had lived amongst humans for too long. She had lost her detachment, left herself at the mercy of gales of emotion, just as they were, and how those gales blew!

She shut her eyes tightly. *Oh spirits keep me, what am I going to do?*

In the course of her physician's training she had studied them, those minds born with no concept of restraint, whose hands were driven to terrible deeds by passions they could not rein in. Anger that flared bright as lightning – how did humans withstand it? Did they feel that swelling storm of emotion roiling and trembling inside, despair's hard hands crushing the breath from their lungs?

Dark tides raced in the noblest human soul, depths in which only nightmares could dwell. She had glimpsed them in broken bodies, broken minds. Had she just seen the first stirrings of them in herself? Covering her face with her hands, she let her head fall back against the door. *What will the White Court make of me now?*

The first gale of tears had shocked her. The jealous pang that followed, sharp and sour as hog-apples, had left her breathless. After an upbringing of restraint, of moderation, she had been cast adrift on a surging, ungovernable sea she had no clue how to navigate. There were no charts to plot a course, no familiar stars to guide her, and she wanted to dive into those murky depths and *feel*, to rage and lust and gorge and revel in excess, not because it would make her a better physician, but, spirits keep her, because it would make her human.

She kneaded her temples. Oh, she was so tired. The Healing had been hard, perhaps the most difficult she had ever done. It had required such delicacy, yet she had had to work feverishly fast to contain the chaos the reiving had wrought before Gair's mind unravelled around her. She'd spent so many hours in the wreckage of his memories, privy to so much that he would never have shared with her, even under a physician's oath – no wonder she had weakened.

I have to go home. Once he's well, I can't stay here any longer. I thought I could resist, but I can't. It hurts too much.

Tanith stepped out of her shoes and sank her toes into the mossy floor. It was illusion, like the trees that screened the walls and the sounds of running water and birdsong, but it felt as cool and springy underfoot as the earth of the birch woods above the Mere. It was enough to restore a little calm, so she could meditate. She really was too tired, but she needed to regain her equilibrium. Her soul felt tossed about by stormy seas; she would find safe harbour for it, then she could sleep.

From the silver-inlaid chest at the foot of her bed she took a flat box and a small brass brazier and chafing dish, which she set up on the chest lid. The merest thread of the Song ignited the charcoal and whilst she waited for it to heat, she unfastened her hair from its braid and combed it out. When the coals were filmed with white ash and the air roiled over the chafing dish, she sat herself down cross-legged at the base of a birch tree and opened the box.

Inside, its multitude of tiny compartments contained other boxes, vials, silk pouches. The yarra-root she sought was wrapped in a piece of kidskin; she lifted it out, together with a clear glass vial of oil, then set the box aside. A few drops of oil went into the chafing dish first. With a knife, she shaved a fragment from the lumpy black root and as it hit the hot oil it began to smoke, releasing a fragrance as dark and rich as earth after rain. Tanith breathed it in deeply, then exhaled as slowly as she could.

Better. She could almost be back in Astolar. All around her, she let the illusion that replaced her room expand until the simple square chamber encompassed an entire valley. Gentle breezes stirred the leaves of the birch trees over her head. In the distance she heard the murmur of Belaleithne Falls on the far side of the Mere. For the first time in far too many months she felt a pang of longing for her home.

I hear you dreaming, Daughter.

Tanith opened her eyes. Coils of smoke from the yarra-root shaped themselves into the outline of the face she knew so well. It formed and reformed as the smoke rose, only the tilted eyes and narrow brows remaining constant.

'Papa,' she greeted him warmly.

Are you well?

'Just tired. It's been a difficult day.'

K'shaa tells me he has not yet sailed.

'No, not yet. I am needed here for a little while longer.'

You are needed here also, Daughter.

'Just a few more days, Papa. I have a new patient.'

He sighed. *You should have returned to us a twelvemoon ago, Tanith. I indulged you when you said you wished to become a physician, because you have a gift for it, and such gifts are not to be squandered, but you have responsibilities here in Astolar, duties that await you as a daughter of the White Court. Your continued absence is . . . most vexing.*

'I know, Papa, but I swore the Healer's oath. My first duty is to the patients in my care, and without my care, this one will die.'

You told me some of the finest Healers in their world pass through the Isles. Surely one of them can complete this task?

'I cannot leave him. Not yet. He suffered a reiving.'

The smoky outline recoiled with a hiss. *You are certain?*

'Never more certain.' Tanith kneaded her eyes. 'I have done my best. I have shielded him from the worst of the damage, but there is much more work to do if his talent is to be saved.'

A reiver loose in the world. Her father shook his head, sending the tendrils of smoke spiralling.

'This reiver is human.'

Abomination! And you expose yourself to this?

'There is no one else who can undo what he has done.'

Her father's image sighed and murmured words she could not catch, although she could imagine what they were. She had doubtless heard them before.

I am uncomfortable with the risks you take, Daughter. You have great significance to the Court, to the continued existence of our people. The merest pause, as fleeting as a breath. And you are precious to me.

She reached out to lay her palm against his insubstantial cheek and smiled.

'Don't worry, Papa. I am as careful as I can be whilst doing what has to be done.'

Does it have to be done? You cannot have forgotten what is at stake.

Tanith's head jerked up, shocked by what her father suggested. 'Is he worth the risk, is that what you are asking? Of course he is – any life is, whatever their race or station. He is a good man, Papa, as worthy as you or me or any High Seat at Court.' She stopped herself before she said too much, but her illusion quivered at the edges as her concentration slipped. Rainclouds darkened the horizon of her dream of Astolar, dimming its eternal blue skies.

But human.

'Yes, human. So many of the greatest talents are now, since our people began to withdraw from this world. If we are to be saved at all, it will be the race of men who take up arms to do it.'

Her father's image looked pained.

'I know you do not like to think of it, Papa, but our fate lies in the hands of others now. With the Veil threatened, there will be only a temporary reprieve if we withdraw from the field. War will find us, even in the Hidden Kingdom. We will not be safe.'

There are four Houses voting for exile now. Last moot, House Amerlaine cast its lot in with Denellin and the rest.

Her heart fell, though the news was hardly unexpected. 'Berec is old,' she sighed. 'He wants to see out his remaining years in tranquillity, not be riding to battle. I can understand his reasons.'

One more vote for exile and the Ten will be deadlocked. The Queen must then decide, and I know she favours peace. We are not a warlike people, my daughter.

'I know. But there are some foes even we must fight. The price of inaction is far too high.'

Ah, Tanith, her father chuckled. *When you succeed me to the High Seat, you will shake the White Court to its very foundations. I hope I live long enough to see it. When are you coming home, daughter mine? Astolar is diminished by your absence.*

'As soon as I can, Papa, I promise. But I am still needed here.'

How long?

'A few days more, I think. The physical wounds were grave enough, but it seems Leahns are not easily killed and his body is mending. It is his talent I fear for.'

He is strong, this Leahn?

'Perhaps the strongest I have ever seen. I delved him once, briefly, and I could see no limit to it.'

Does he know?

'No, although I believe he suspects there is more to his gift than he has yet embraced. Even if he did know the extent of it, it would not abet him. This is not the first time the reiver has come against him.'

Her voice trembled and even the perfume of the yarra-root could not smooth out the catch in her words. 'He almost tore him to pieces. I held him whilst he screamed until he had no more breath. I cradled his sanity in my hands and all around me his talent sparkled like the Mere under a trinity moon. That cannot be lost. His importance to the Order is incalculable and that makes him important to us all, in the final reckoning. I have to Heal him, Papa. I must.'

Her father stayed silent whilst she composed herself. Then he said gently, *There is more here than simply another patient, isn't there? You have formed an attachment to him.*

'Even if I had, another has more claim to him than I,' she said. *But you care for him.*

'I care for what might happen to this world should he die.' Vehemence heated her words. 'He could be the key to ensuring the preservation of the Veil. We live on the borders of two kingdoms, Papa, and as long as the Veil holds, we have a place. If it is rent apart, as I fear the reiver means to do, we will have nothing at all.'

I know this, he sighed, *however much it grieves me. Very well, my daughter. You must do what you must do, as must I. We each have our battles to fight now, yours with your Leahn sword and shield, mine in the council chamber. May benevolent spirits attend us both. Ghostly hands spread in benediction and he inclined his head to her. Sleep well, my daughter.*

'And you, my father. I shall come home as soon as I can, I promise.'

Good. I know Ailric is anxious to see you again.

'No doubt he is.'

Have you thought more on his proposal?

'Papa, I have no need for a husband yet, and no want for one, either.' She was too weary to face that subject again.

He would be an asset to our House, husband you well.

'He would bring us nothing but his ambition. Ailric has eyes for the High Seat and sees me as his stepladder.'

You judge him too harshly, Tanith. Please: at least consider his request for your hand. I cannot bear to think of you lonely when I am gone.

She tried not to sigh, for she hated to see hurt in his eyes, even smoky illusions of them.

'Very well, I will consider it, but please say no more to him than that. I mean to choose my own husband when the time comes.'

Her father's image shifted as if he was uncomfortable. Our blood grows thin, Tanith. It must be conserved carefully. I would not see yours spent profligately on an impure union.

'And our inheritance passes on the distaff side. No child of mine should be barred from the White Court on the basis of who sired her,' she said. Her sharpness made him flinch and she gentled her tone. 'Be at peace. When the time comes, I shall see to it that Astolan seed bears fruit on Astolan soil.'

That time should come soon, Daughter. We must think to the next generation whilst there is still a chance for a harvest.

'I know my duty,' she reassured him. 'Soon, I promise. Now I must sleep, Papa. I need rest before I can Heal him again. The shield I have placed in his mind will need renewing soon. He is remembering things that should be suppressed until he is strong enough to withstand them.'

I understand. Until I see you with my own eyes again, be well.

'And you, Papa. I miss you.'

The smoky image smiled and then became only smoke again. The yarra-root was spent, shrivelled and black. Tanith closed her eyes and took the last deep breath of its loamy scent, drawing it down into her lungs as far as she could. So much for her meditation. She still felt soul-sore and unsettled, but she did not dare risk another shaving. Too much yarra-root would leave her thick-witted in the morning and she could not afford to be less than sure of herself when she stepped into Gair's mind. There was far too much at stake now, perhaps more than even Alderan knew.

Gair knew he had dreamed again, though when he woke he had no clear recollections, only a nebulous sense of foreboding that dimmed the splash of spring sunshine across his bed, made the sparrows' chatter in the garden outside a little more strident. That apart, he felt stronger than he had the day before.

He pushed himself up into a sitting position with only a twinge or two from his wounds. Encouraged, he swung his legs over the side of the bed and eased himself onto his feet. He over-balanced immediately and had to sit down again, but a second attempt, holding the bed-post and the edge of the nightstand for support, was more successful.

The scar on his neck remained taut and tender, but the ones on his arm and thigh had faded to pale lines. Even his bruises had yellowed; they would be gone in another day. A draught from the window over the bed made him cast around for something to wear. There was no sign of his clothes, but the closet did yield a plain linen robe. He was tying the sash round his waist when he heard the door open behind him and turned around.

Tanith stood in the doorway with a covered tray in her hands. 'I didn't expect to see you on your feet,' she said, setting the tray on the nightstand.

'I nearly wasn't. It took me a moment to remember what they were for.' Gair made his way carefully back to the bed and sat down.

Tanith tilted his head away from the light to examine his neck, her touch cool, precise. 'This is healing well.'

'How bad does it look?'

'Not too bad. There will always be a scar, but not much. You'll hardly notice it once you get rid of all this.' She scuffed her fingertips through his beard.

Gair scratched his chin. 'I can't wait. It itches.'

'I'll bring you a razor later. Now have your breakfast. You need your strength.' She opened the door to let herself out.

'Tanith?' He paused. 'I'm sorry about last night. If I sounded ungrateful. I don't know how I can ever repay you.'

'Don't apologise. You've done nothing wrong.'

'Even so, I feel better for saying it. And thank you.'

The Healer smiled, her tawny eyes shining like sunlight on river stones. 'You're welcome,' she said with a dip of her head, then closed the door quietly behind her.

As good as her word, after breakfast Tanith brought Gair clean clothes, hot water and his shaving kit. Once she was satisfied that his hands were not shaking so much that he'd cut his own throat with the razor, she left him to wash in peace.

Gair took his time dressing. Although he felt much better, and better yet for something to eat, he was not quite as steady on his legs as he would have liked. The clothes Tanith had brought were sized to fit him, but not a stitch had come from his closet. The tunic and trousers were good dark green wool and the linen shirt was finer than anything he had ever had, even for a feast-day, with silver embroidery at the neck and cuffs. Even the smallclothes were new. Only the boots were his, and they had been oiled and buffed until they glowed.

He was shaving the tricky bit under his nose when he became aware of someone watching him. At first he thought Tanith or one of the other Healers had slipped into the room, but when he looked over his shoulder, he was alone. Strange. He shrugged the feeling off and continued with his shave, but the sense of presence would not go away. It nagged at him like an itch at the back of his brain all the way down his other cheek and along his jaw, growing more and more persistent.

Sparrows chattered in alarm outside, and small shadows whirred past the window. The garden fell silent. Gair looked out over the top of the mirror. A kestrel perched in the birch tree outside, fixing him with a fierce golden eye.

Kiek kiek kiek! Beak agape, it bobbed its head with each cry. *Kiek kiek kiek kiek!* In a flurry of speckled feathers, it was gone.

Gair cleaned his razor, then rinsed and dried his face. As he lifted the shirt over his head, he heard scrabbling at the window. When he turned round, there was the kestrel on the window-ledge.

380

Kiek kiek kiek!

He tucked his shirt in and reached for the latch. As soon as the window opened far enough, the kestrel swooped in to land on the bed. There its shape stretched into a cinnamon-skinned crop-haired woman in faded breeches and shirtsleeves. Her sea-blue eyes flashed anxiety and frustration in equal measure.

'Are you deaf or just ignoring me?' she demanded. 'I've been calling you for an hour!'

'I didn't know who it was.' *Saaron's chickadee?*

'Who did you think it would be, you great lump?'

Her arms wound around him and pulled him down beside her. Off-balance, he half-fell, half-sat on the bed. She took his face in her hands and kissed him hard.

'They would not let me see you,' she said. 'I thought you were dying.'

'I nearly did, from what they tell me.'

Who was she? She knew him, and knew him well – saints, that kiss! – but her name was lost somewhere in the storm clouds in his mind. Yet he knew her, he was sure of it. Knew her face, her perfume, the shape of her body against his. She peered anxiously up at him and the clouds surged, a memory pushing through them as slow and unstoppable as a ripening bud. It burst open with a silent concussion, and Gair saw a kestrel take his talons in its grasp and tumble with him through warm, clear air.

'Aysha,' he said, smiling.

The memories did not stop with her name. Wolves raced and wrestled in moonlit snows. Eagles soared. Lovers sweated to a shuddering, breathless communion. More and still more memories poured out and he was there in every one of them. Suddenly dizzy, he clung to Aysha's shoulder.

'What is it? Gair, what's wrong?'

Too many memories, too vivid: whirling shards of stained glass pierced his brain. A thousand fragments of time, disconnected and without structure, struck him with the sting of hailstones on bare skin, and burst across his consciousness like a raindrop. He shut his eyes. Oh Goddess, he was going to throw up.

'You're sweating; I'll fetch Saaron.'

She made to rise, but he clung onto her. He would fall if he let go. 'No, don't. Please.' Nausea climbed Gair's throat, filling his mouth with saliva. He swallowed it down again and again as the flood of memory continued to hurl him from moment to moment, emotion to emotion. He couldn't breathe, couldn't think, couldn't do anything but endure.

When it finally dwindled and he was able to open his eyes, Aysha was cradling him in her arms and stroking his hair. Worry clouded her face as he sat up.

'You scared me.' Abruptly she punched his shoulder. 'Don't do it again.'

'Sorry.' Gair kneaded his temples.

'What happened? Was it him?'

'No. The memories came back so suddenly. I recognised you, but I didn't remember your name. Then I remembered everything all at once.'

'What in all hells did he do to you?'

Gair let out a long breath and rubbed his hands over his face. 'Tanith called it a reiving – like a cattle raid, but inside my head. She says it will heal in time.'

'You should have let me fetch a Healer.'

'I'm all right.'

'You're not all right!' Aysha burst out. She dashed a hand across her eyes, not quite fast enough to prevent him seeing the sparkle in her lashes. 'I talked to them, Leahn. They said you were dying. They said that even if you survived, you might be damaged, you might not remember anything at all. How could you let him catch you like that? How?' She punctuated her words with more blows, flailing her fists at his shoulders. Her face twisted into a sob. 'How could you let him hurt you?'

'I'm sorry, Aysha.' Gair caught hold of her and pulled her to him. He planted kisses on her silky hair, rubbed her back. 'I'm so, so sorry. I had no idea he was out there, or that he would even recognise me in another shape. I had no idea he was so strong.'

She pressed her face into his new shirt and took deep, shaky breaths. 'When I could not find your colours, when you didn't answer when I called, I feared the worst.' Her voice was thick with unshed tears.

'I'm still here.'

'Only because you have the Nameless' own luck. I should kill you myself for the trouble you cause me.'

'I didn't mean for this to happen, Aysha.'

'I know . . . I just thought I'd lost you.' Quickly she wiped her face, blew out her cheeks and scrubbed her fingers through her hair. Then she flashed him something like her old smile.

'That shirt looks well on you, even better than I expected,' she said brightly. 'The silver brings out the colour of your eyes.'

'You had this made for me?'

'I was saving it for your St Winifrae's gift, but you needed some new clothes for when you woke up, so I had the tailor send it all down early.'

'It's the finest shirt I've ever had. Thank you.' He kissed her forehead.

She lifted her hands to his face and touched him with her Song. What she found made her pull a face as she released him. 'They've shielded you,' she said. 'That's why I couldn't find you – it masks your colours. It also cuts you off from the Song.'

He reached for it, and found only silence. It was there, he could sense it in the same way that he always had, but he could not hear it at all. The clouds were massed around it. Strange how accustomed he had become to just reaching for it and having that liquid power fill him. Without it he felt vaguely bereft.

'How badly did he hurt you?' Aysha asked.

'Nothing that won't heal,' Gair said. He pulled his shirt away from his neck. 'This was the worst.'

She touched the scar gently. 'Does it hurt?'

'Not any more.'

'What about your memories? Are they damaged?'

'I'm not sure. Tanith says she'll know more when she Heals me again.'

'Pray Goddess she Heals you quickly, then. I've missed you.' All of you.

The image she slipped into his mind flushed him to the roots of his hair, and Aysha's eyes danced. He kissed her to hide the blush, and made promises with his mouth that he couldn't wait to keep.

'Will you come and visit me later? I need to see Alderan.'

She nodded. 'Will you ask him about Savin?'

'Yes. I think he owes me the truth now. This is the second time Savin's tried to kill me, and I want to know why. I've done nothing to warrant this. Did you know him?'

'No. He was long gone by the time I came here, but I've heard the other Masters talk.' Blue eyes flicked over his face, searching. 'Have a care with him. He is not what he seems to be.'

The words echoed Savin's in the rooftop garden so strongly that for an instant Gair thought she was talking about Alderan.

'I will, but I can't promise I'll be gentle when I catch up with him.'

A smile curved her lips. 'I would expect nothing less from a Leahn.'

When he tried to stand, she seized his arm with both hands. 'I'll not let them keep you from me,' she whispered, dragging him down for a kiss. 'Not again.'

Her passion startled him, even as it reawakened old hungers. Memories of her in his arms flooded his head, drowning him in sensation. How much of it was him and how much her, pouring her need into his mind, he could not say, but it was all he could do to pull away.

'Later,' he said. His voice was husky. He felt no weakness in his limbs now; he was on fire.

'Later,' she agreed, smoothing her hands across his chest. Her touch burned right through the linen. Then she flashed into the shape of a kestrel and darted for the open window.

31

ALDERAN

ლ

Gair stepped off the stairs onto the second landing and steadied himself against the wall. The short walk to the Masters' quarters was turning out to be harder than he'd expected. He remembered the way well enough, and the corridors and stairs in themselves were not too taxing on his weakened body, but the assault on his memory had taken it out of him; he wanted to curl up in a ball with his arms over his head.

Every face he saw tickled at his memory, then suddenly filled his head with sharp colour as he recalled a lecture, a joke, a fragment of his testing. No sooner had he brushed past one recollection than another was fluttering around him, each tied to the next in a never-ending rope, like a conjurer's gaudy hand-kerchiefs.

He took a deep breath and released it slowly. At least this corridor was empty. Everything inside his head felt fragile, bright as a bruise and twice as tender; on the floors below, where the passageways were busier, even turning to acknowledge a greeting had left him floundering in broken memories. Goddess alone knew what it would be like when he faced Alderan on the other side of that panelled oak door. But he had to do it. He had to know the truth, once and for all.

Gair's knock met with a distracted acknowledgement from inside. When the door remained closed, he lifted the latch and let himself in, braced for memories to rain down on him—

—except they didn't. His first meeting with Alderan must be far enough in his past to lie outside Tanith's shield. Grateful for the relief, he closed the door behind him.

Alderan sat at a heavy lion-footed table behind a rampart of books. The fingers of his left hand marked places in one volume whilst his right traced the text of another, open in front of him. A pencil was clamped between his teeth.

'Just put it down over there,' he said, gesturing with the pencil at a side-table equally overloaded with books.

'Put what down?' Gair asked.

Alderan looked up and blinked in surprise. 'I was hoping it was my lunch, but you are just as welcome a sight.' He closed the books with their pages interleaved to keep his place and stood up. 'I would have come down to the infirmary, you know, saved you the journey. Would you care for some tea?'

'No, thank you.'

From a cupboard over the hearth Alderan took out mismatched mugs and a flower-painted teapot that had seen better days. The kettle was already steaming on its hook over the flames.

'You look better,' he said, spooning tea into the pot from a wooden canister. 'Sure you don't want some tea?'

'What I want are some answers,' Gair told him. 'I want to know why Savin tried to kill me, and I want you to tell me the truth this time.'

The old man bridled. 'I have always told you the truth.'

'Just not all of it. Every time I ask you something you give me enough of an answer to be going on with and avoid the meat of the question. I want the whole truth now, gristle and all.'

Alderan dropped the wooden scoop back in the canister and put it away. He closed the cupboard door and gestured at the hide-covered chairs flanking the hearth. 'Sit yourself down, lad.'

'I'd rather stand. Alderan, you and I need to talk.'

'And talk we shall, but please sit down. You're looming.'

'I'm what?'

'Looming. Why do you Leahns have to be so blasted tall? My joints are stiff enough without getting a crick in my neck as well.'

Teeth clamped against the tide of questions rising inside him, Gair took a seat. Alderan filled the teapot, then turned back to the desk to scribble a few words on a scrap of paper tucked into one of the books.

Gair thought it was a wonder the old man could concentrate in all that clutter. The shelves lining the walls were stacked with boxes and books, and peculiar objects of brass and glass. Scrolls piled on the window-seat like cords of wood and an archipelago of paper dotted the sun-faded rug. In the few places the clutter hadn't consumed, the dust was thick enough to write in.

When the tea was brewed to Alderan's satisfaction, he poured two mugs and dolloped a generous spoonful of honey in each. Then he handed one to Gair, having apparently forgotten that tea had been declined.

Gair set the mug down on the hearth tiles by his feet.

'Your health's improved since I saw you last,' the old man said as he settled into the other chair. 'The Healers have done good work.'

'Tanith says she's not quite done yet, but she seems confident that I'll recover.'

'You were lucky she was here. Saaron is a good Healer, one of the best, but he is a battlefield sawbones compared to her. Tanith has a deftness of touch with the mind that is really quite remarkable, even among her people. She's earned her Master's mantle twice over with you.' Alderan blew on his tea to cool it. 'Yes, another few hours and she would have been gone.'

'Gone? Where?'

'Back to her people. Didn't she tell you?'

'No, she never mentioned it.'

'On the sea-elf ship, *Morning Star*. K'shaa was due to sail the next day with Tanith on board, but she persuaded him to wait.'

'I thought she didn't finish her training until the summer, like the others.'

'Not her. We gave her her mantle last year, but she offered to stay on for another twelvemonth to help Saaron, before her obligations to the White Court called her back. That was an extremely fortuitous choice, as far as you're concerned. Without Tanith to Heal you, I very much doubt that we would have you back in one piece.' The old man sipped at the scalding brew. 'We thought for a while that we might not get you back at all.'

'Was I really that badly hurt?'

'Be under no illusions, Gair, you were dying,' he said softly. 'What Savin did to your mind, well, there's a reason why it's called a reiving. It's a violent, penetrative act for the sole purpose of obtaining something the reiver has no right to take, and it could have left you no more able to take care of yourself than a babe in arms.'

Alderan was far blunter than Tanith had been; her explanation had spared him the worst.

The old man eyed him steadily through the steam from his cup.

'Drink your tea, lad, before it gets cold.'

Gair picked up his mug. 'I don't understand what he wants from me, Alderan. I've done nothing to him – why does he want to kill me?'

'He'd only kill you if you got in his way and he couldn't make use of you. How much do you remember about him?'

'Not much, really – he came to the inn in Mesarild, then there was the storm when we were on board the *Kittiwake*, but what happened out beyond the Five Sisters?' Gair sighed. 'Next to nothing, so far. Tanith's shield seems to be doing its job.'

'You told Saaron that you thought Savin was going to come here, looking for something – whatever it was he couldn't find it in your head – and yet now you say you don't remember anything of what happened.' Alderan's eyes were sharp as glass.

'I don't remember anything definite. It's more an impression, a sense of urgency. I remember a feeling of . . . *need*. Hunger. A feeling that something he wants more than anything else in the world is only just out of his reach.'

'And that is what made you think he is going to come here? It must have been a strong impression.'

'He was right inside my head, Alderan. It doesn't get much stronger than that.'

A wolfish grin split the old man's beard. 'Fair point. I think you're wrong, though,' he added. 'Savin can't come here, and if you'll forgive me a rather long-winded story, I'll explain why. More tea?'

Gair shook his head. 'I'll forgive you the story, as long as it's complete. Don't leave anything out this time.'

'Take that tone with me again, my lad, and I'll tell you nothing at all.'

'Fine! Tell me nothing and next time he really will kill me!' Gair thrust himself out of the chair and began pacing. 'From the beginning you've told me only what you felt like about Savin. You even reassured me – more than once – that he wasn't dangerous, that he was curious about me but meant me no real harm. Then he sent a storm that nearly sank the *Kittiwake* with us on board, not to mention Dail and his crew. And now this – he appears out of nowhere and tries to turn my brains out through my ears!'

'We don't know for certain that he sent the storm.'

'Who else could it have been, Alderan? He's horribly strong.'

'Can't get much past you, can I?' Using the sleeve of his robe as a pot-holder, Alderan topped up the teapot with the kettle and swirled the tea around. 'Yes, I think it was Savin who sent the storm. He flooded half of southern Syfria with it, all because he couldn't care less what happens to anyone else once he's had his way.'

390

'What a pleasant individual.' Gair stopped pacing and leaned on the windowsill. The sudden burst of energy had drained away from him, leaving him trembly as a chick. Saints, his head boomed.

'Aye, well, you don't know the half.'

'Tell me what he wants from me, Alderan, so I can stay out of his way. I don't want to spend the rest of my life looking over my shoulder for him.'

On the hearth, the kettle pinged as it cooled. Porcelain clinked; a spoon chimed in a cup. Gair let his eyes close, wishing his headache would go.

'Savin is the son of two *gaeden*, born here on the Isles,' Alderan began. 'His mother was very young, and the pregnancy was difficult. Savin himself was born early, but seemed healthy enough, and he was prodigiously gifted – we knew that from the outset. Within a day of his birth he was calling to his mother's mind when he was hungry. We thought he might very well grow up to be the most powerful *gaeden* we had ever had. We were right.'

He sat back in his chair and sipped his tea. Gair watched from the window.

'So what went wrong?'

'As he grew, we realised that in addition to being extremely powerful, he was going to be cruel. He was killing flies from his cradle. He set them on fire, incinerated them in mid-air. As he got older, he started compelling his nurse to do whatever he wanted, from fetching toys and sweetmeats to performing tricks for his amusement. When his mother Aileann found out, she tried to punish him. He set fire to her, too.'

Horror curdled Gair's stomach.

'She was horrifically burned, and she died not long after. It would have been a mercy if it had killed her instantly.' The old man stared into his cup. His face was set, his tone colourless. 'Savin's father tried to kill him. We're not quite sure what happened, except that Teosen was compelled to turn the knife on himself. We found the poor man on the floor, on the opposite side of the room to his skin. The boy was six years old.'

Gair didn't know whether to curse or offer up a prayer. He could hardly find the words for either. 'I had no idea— That's . . . there're no words for it.'

'You've never seen true evil, have you? Bred in the bone, black-from-the-womb evil, the kind that only exists in psalms and storybooks?' Alderan's smile was sad as he lifted his tea to his lips. 'Neither had we, and we had no idea what to do with it. Looking back, we should probably have dealt with him differently, but we didn't know any better.'

'He should have been hanged for murder.'

'Probably. But there'd been enough killing and we weren't of a mind for more. So we taught him. He'd been receiving lessons almost since birth, but after the death of his parents we took them further, hoping we could channel his phenomenal abilities in other directions. We taught him everything we knew. In retrospect, that was our mistake. He soaked it up the way a suet dumpling soaks up gravy.'

'And turned all your lessons back on you.'

'Precisely. By the time he was fifteen we had exhausted our knowledge, but he was still hungry, and that's when he found a new teacher, one over whom we had no control.' Alderan refilled his cup, spooning in another generous measure of honey. 'There are books in the library which detail powers that *gaeden* long ago had, but which we have not seen here ourselves. Savin devoured these books, and he sought to unearth those lost talents for himself. When we discovered what he had achieved, and what he had brought here from the Hidden Kingdom, we had no choice but to act. We gathered up every Master, every adept, every untrained apprentice with even half an ounce of talent, and by joining together, we were able to overpower him long enough to exile him from the Isles.

'We thought that without the talismans he had been using here, he might be cut off from his demon. That was our second mistake: he already knew far too much, and he burned out the talent in almost a whole generation of young *gaeden* in the course of the weaving. We think he has spent the intervening years scouring the world for another talisman like the one he lost. *Gaeden* caught in his path have vanished – burned out, killed, driven insane, we don't know which, but we have not heard from them again.'

'And you think that's what he was trying to do to me?' Gair asked. 'Use me to find this talisman?'

'It's possible.' Alderan looked at him quizzically. 'I've been talking about demons here and you haven't batted an eye. Didn't anything from holy orders rub off on you?'

'In order to believe in the Goddess, you must also believe in the Nameless.'

'I see you've been debating philosophy with Master Jehann. I swear, that man could think his way round the inside of a corkscrew without starting a sweat.'

'Actually, it was Chaplain Danilar. One of his better sermons,' Gair said. He picked up his tea. It was almost cold, but now he was thirsty.

'And do you believe?' Alderan asked curiously, then waved the question away. 'No, that's a conversation for another day. We exiled Savin, and I think some of us thought that would be the last we would see of him. Certainly most of the people here have forgotten about him by now, or wish they could. I never have. Sometimes I have lain awake at night thinking that maybe we should have killed him whilst we had the chance, instead of just sending him away.'

'It would have saved a lot of trouble,' Gair said.

'Probably would at that. That is my failing, perhaps: I'm not ruthless enough.'

'Did he ever try to come back? Tanith said you warded the islands, but if he is as powerful as you say, why couldn't he just walk in and take what he wanted?'

'The wards we built were extraordinarily subtle. They were tuned to Savin's mind, so that if ever he came close, we would know about it. He tried a few times in the first couple of years, but he never managed to break through. He knew we were waiting for him. This is the closest he has come since then.'

'Whatever it is he thinks I have, he must want very, very badly,' Gair drained the last drops of his tea. 'I wish I knew what it was, if only so I could tell him I don't have it.'

Alderan rolled his mug back and forth between his hands, lips pursed as he watched Gair at the window. 'To tell the truth, I'm surprised you haven't figured it out for yourself by now. You're a bright lad, and you have all the clues you need.'

'Don't be cryptic, Alderan! Half my wits are still missing.'

'The battle of River Run. The siege at Caer Ducain. Riannen Cut. What do they all have in common?'

'What?' Alderan had changed direction so unexpectedly it left Gair wrongfooted.

'What do they all have in common?'

'They were decisive battles in the Founding Wars. The Knights made a three-hundred-mile forced march from Mesarild to lift the siege at Caer Ducain, then they drove the clans back north of the river. Gwlach brought up his reserves and the Knights fought them to a standstill at River Run, then routed them at Riannen Cut. Alderan, why are we talking about the Founding? It's Savin I want to know about.'

'Bear with me. How did the Knights win? Donata loves to set this question for assignments to see which of the students figures it out. I thought you would grasp it straight away. And no, I'm not talking about the mouldering remains of St Agostin the Defiant.'

'I don't know what you mean. The Knights were outnumbered, but they held on somehow — something must have turned the battle their way, but I don't know what it was.'

Alderan pounced. 'Yes, you do. You've always known — you just don't realise it. Come on, lad, *think!*'

Gair raked his hands back through his hair. Goddess, he had such a headache brewing, but he tried to reason his way through to the conclusion. Gwlach and his clans had outridden and out-fought the heavily armed but less manoeuvrable Knights repeat-edly in the early part of the campaign, inflicting savage losses on their supply trains. Then, at the front line, the Knights had come face to face with a weapon that was impervious to steel, and it was wielded by women.

It hadn't taken the Suvaeon too long to discover that women died as easily as men, but not before the sorceresses had flayed and burned and broiled them alive, and summoned obscenities from the darkest places to fling at the Church lines to wreak destruction. Yet the Church had been victorious. How? Alderan stared at him intently. *How?* What power could overcome that dark magic?

The answer drifted into his mind as softly as a flake of snow through an open window, but when it touched him it blossomed like a firework in the night sky. *Magic.* How could it have been anything else? It was the one true power in the world, and it answered to the call of anyone's gift, any intent. All it needed was the will. Oh blessed Mother, the Knights had fought fire with fire.

'The Song,' he breathed.

'Well done.' Alderan sat back in his chair. 'The very crime Mother Church tried to burn you for secured them their most notable victories in the Founding Wars. Not faith, not skill at arms or superior tactics, but guts and grit and the songs of the earth.'

'And Savin?'

'Savin is looking for a talisman like the one that Gwlach's clan Speaker used to unleash the Hunt; more specifically, what the Knights used to stitch the Veil closed again. He obviously believes it's here on the Isles.'

'Is it?'

'No. It never came here. When the Inquisition turned on the Church itself, we gave shelter to some of those gifted Knights who managed to escape, but they brought nothing with them save the clothes they stood up in and a few books. Where the rest went and what they took, we may never know. The Inquisitors were very . . . thorough.'

Gair was struggling to keep pace with the revelations as Alderan's words tumbled in his head like woodchips in a mill-race. The headache had worsened too; his eyeballs were being squeezed in their sockets.

'Do you know where it is?'

Alderan shook his head. 'Not for certain, no. I can think of one or two places where it might be, but I have nothing that points it out.'

'So why does Savin think I know?'

'Because of where I found you, in the Holy City.'

'But Alderan, I'm *nothing*! Some soldier's by-blow, an accident of nature who washed up in the Suvaeon Order for want of anywhere else to go. Even the Church wanted rid of me at the end. How could *I* possibly know the whereabouts of this relic?'

Feet clattered in the corridor outside. Someone rapped sharply on the door, then flung it open without waiting for permission. A sun-browned man in a brown cloak leaned in. He had untidy iron-grey hair and a face like an old shoe.

'You'd better come,' he said, his expression grim.

Alderan was on his feet at once. 'What's happened, Masen?'

Dark eyes flicked to Gair and back again. 'You'd best see for yourself.'

The old man strode out of the door without another word, the man in brown close behind. Gair did not hesitate; he followed them along the corridor and up the tower stairs to the roof-walks. After all, he had not been told to stay away.

A brisk breeze blew in from the sea, scouring the purple pantiles and tossing the gulls about like scraps of paper, but it only frayed the edges of the banner of smoke that rose over Pensaeca's humped green shoulder.

'We saw it at first light,' Masen said. Again his gaze flicked to

Gair, so quick that had he not been looking he would not have seen it. It wasn't a hostile look, more curious, as if deciding how much to say in front of him, and settling on caution. 'It's coming from the far side, towards Pensaeca Port. There's far too much for a house, and it's been too wet of late for a forest fire.'

That left only one possibility, and though Masen stopped short of voicing it, it hung in the air loud as a shout. Alderan grunted. His face looked carved from stone.

Gair smelled the smoke, faintly, over the tang of salt on the wind, and something stirred in the back of his mind. A ship surged out of the mists in his head, flying a huge blue banner, and with a splash of bright gold at the railing.

'Savin,' he exclaimed.

Masen swung towards him. 'What?'

'Savin – he was on a Nordman ship, off the Five Sisters. I remember now!' The snarling dragon mask loomed larger and larger with each pulse of pain behind Gair's eyes.

'Masen?' Alderan glanced at him for confirmation.

'A sandboat from Pensteir saw them at anchor off Pensaeca Port and beat round the far end of the island to put in at Pencruik instead. Six longships, the captain said, and at least one building already put to the torch. It's a fair size for a raiding party, but Savin?'

'We always assumed someone was sheltering him,' Alderan said. 'Now we know who.'

'But he would never dare come here,' Masen started.

Alderan bared his teeth. 'If anyone dared, he would. Besides, I think Gair here has the best idea of his intentions. He says Savin will come, and I'm inclined to believe him.'

'What about the wards? Savin cannot set foot on any of the inhabited islands without our knowledge.'

'He doesn't have to stir from his ship if he's got Nordmen running to do his bidding, damn him.' Fury sparked in Alderan's eyes. 'By the Goddess and all Her angels, I should have strangled him when he was born!'

Gair kneaded his temples hard, trying to counter pain with pain and think clearly, but it was no use. Waves of menace battered at the haze of Tanith's shield. In the middle of it all snarled a dragon's mask that glared at him with eyes of flame.

Frowning, Masen touched Alderan's arm and pointed at Gair. 'Should the boy be about if he's still so sick?'

More pain, worse now. Every pulse shook his bones. His skin strained so tight his blood must surely be squeezing out through his pores. He burned with it, and it was only his desperate grip on the wall that kept him from dropping to his knees. Only a tiny part of him heard Alderan barking orders, but each word stabbed his ears like a knife. The dragon roared, its scaly bulk twisting in the confines of his skull as it sought a way out.

Someone put an arm around him and helped him to sit down, leaning his back against the wall. A hand felt his brow for a fever; another lifted his chin. The brightness of the sky seared his eyes; he could hardly make out the silhouette of whoever peered into his face. A ruddy halo surrounded their head and Gair saw green against the purple pantiles; no proper shapes, only colours, churning his stomach until he thought he would spew. An acrid smell stung his nose, and then he felt nothing at all.

32

ANGEL WITH A SWORD

ଚ୭

Tanith stoppered the small bottle and tucked it away in her scrip. 'That should keep him unconscious for long enough,' she said, 'but I'll have to be quick. I'm afraid we haven't much time.'

Alderan hunkered down beside her. 'I called you as soon as Masen saw something was wrong. What is it?'

'I have a thought, though I don't know for certain . . .' She cradled Gair's lolling head between her hands and concentrated. The sweet music of the Song skirled out into him, seeking, then abruptly shattered into discord.

Tanith recoiled.

'What did you find?'

'A filthy thing.' Like plunging her hands into a cesspit. She wanted to wipe them on her skirts, but she kept hold of Gair's head. 'The worst kind of foulness. When Savin went rampaging through Gair's memories he left something behind – a tiny thing, a seed of his consciousness. It's growing.'

Alderan made a face as if he wanted to spit a bad taste from his mouth. 'Another trick of the Hidden to go with the reiving,' he muttered and swore softly. 'Can you remove it?'

'I can try. It's behind the shield I wove, so it may not have spread too far, but I won't know for certain until I look.'

'What if you can't?'

She swallowed, her mouth suddenly dry. 'If I can't, Savin will have him, mind and soul.'

Alderan's expression became grim. 'It must not come to that.'

'Then I will have to stop his heart.'

'That would violate your oaths as a Healer.'

'I may not have a choice. Would you rather I let him scream his life away? We can't let it come to that either, unless I miss my guess.'

'Astolan eyes are sharp. They see far too much.' Alderan sighed and scrubbed his face with his hands. 'Very well. Do what you must.'

Not what she could, but what she must. The thought chilled her. A Healer's oaths were to preserve life and relieve suffering, without fear or favour. To do no harm. Which would she have to break before the day was done? How much harm would she have to do to achieve the greatest good? Steeling herself, Tanith slid back into the Song.

Carefully, she edged her way through the layers of pain that were exploding in lurid colours. Even wrapped and warded in the Song as she was, she felt something of the agonies flaying the living mind around her. When she reached the grey mist that represented her shield, she hesitated. Beyond that fragile-seeming barrier would be a nightmare of half-healed, fragmented memories, childhood horrors unearthed from long-buried pits. And Savin's seed, growing like some monstrous creeper around it all. She plunged through.

Alderan motioned Masen a little further along the wall to give Tanith room to work. Only a deepening of the creases around Masen's eyes gave any clue to his anxiety, but with the familiarity of many years Alderan read it clearly.

'He'll be fine,' he said. 'Tanith can Heal him, if anyone can.'

'Savin has grown bolder,' Masen replied. 'I never dreamed we'd see his handiwork again so soon. When you told the Council to prepare for an attack, I thought you were shying at shadows.'

'I hoped that I was, but it appears I was not. At least we had some time to ready ourselves. He won't catch us unawares like he did last time.'

'There're only a few of us left who remember. Are you sure they'll be able to hold the shield?'

'They'll hold.'

Masen raised an eyebrow. 'No matter what he unleashes against them? He'll try to rend the Veil, bring through Goddess knows what.'

'I know,' Alderan sighed. 'I'm very much afraid we may see the end of an age before we're done.'

'If what the Leahn saw is true.'

'I trust him, Masen, and so far events are bearing him out. Savin's taken an interest in Gair from the start. He tried to lure the boy, then sent a storm to spite us. Now this.'

'Is the lad really that powerful?'

'He has power and to spare.'

Masen considered. 'What about Pensaeca? It's likely a ruse to draw us out.'

'Whilst Savin tries to pierce our shields through Gair's mind, yes. We wait.'

'That could cost the islanders a few lives,' Masen said, but Alderan shook his head.

'Fewer than you might think. The Nordmen raid these islands every once in a while. The people simply pack up and head inland. They know the hills and valleys like their own faces, and the Nordmen learned long ago that it gains them precious little to pursue. They take what they can carry from the coastal towns and sail north again.'

'Will they do the same with Savin snapping at their heels? How far will he press them to get a reaction from us?'

'How far will his patience last? You know as well as I that it was never among his virtues, such as he had. We can wait him out.'

'And you're willing to wager lives on that?'

'You have a knack for asking hard questions, old friend,' Alderan said, 'and wanting hard answers, too.'

'Just as you have a knack for not giving them.' Masen chuckled mirthlessly. 'Very well, I'll tell K'shaa to stand ready. He'll not want the *Star* to lie at anchor with pirates so close at hand.'

'You'd best rouse the Masters whilst you're about it. If Savin comes against us directly, we'll need every scrap of talent on the island to maintain the shield.'

'What if Gair's wrong, or worse than wrong?'

They both looked over to where Tanith knelt over the prone figure of the young Leahn. She was wreathed in green sparks, and even at that distance, her working of the Song tugged at Alderan's gift; the power she wielded was considerable.

He sighed. 'We'll wrestle that bear when it wakes and not before.' Glancing up at the sky, he frowned. Thin wind-whipped cloud veiled the blue now, and a stiffening breeze struck foam from the waves in Pensaeca Sound. 'Looks like the weather's turning,' he said. 'I think we're in for a storm.'

Ivy tendrils snaked across the dusty earth. They put out shoots as they thickened that rapidly became dark, leathery leaves veined purple like diseased organs. The tendrils moved with astonishing speed. Ahead of them, Gair broke into a run.

He slowed when he came to a corner and peered cautiously round it. Nothing. The earthen path lay empty between its green walls. He looked over his shoulder. Nothing behind either. Safety, of a sort, but he was still no nearer finding a way out. He mopped sweat from his face with his shirtsleeve and wished he had some water. His throat was full of dust.

Gentle pressure on his ankle made him look down. A purple-black shoot, no thicker than his little finger, had coiled around his boot. Tiny leaves unfurled along its length. Gair jerked his foot away and the shoot twitched spastically, then groped across the earth towards his other ankle. He backed away and collided with one of the hedges. Thorns pricked his skin through his shirt, deep enough to draw blood. He yelped, whirling around. More shoots had coiled through the hedge, and whatever they touched began to shrivel. Withered leaves pattered down through the branches, as desiccated as if they had been dead for years.

Gair backed further away. The shoot that had reached for his foot was thicker than his thumb now, and it edged purposefully towards him, dragging a little furrow in the dust. Those coiled through the hedge reared into the air like snakes. Behind them, the hedge itself was almost dead, only a few patches of green remaining amongst the curled brown leaves, and they were rapidly being smothered by leathery foliage.

He began to run again. Whippy shoots lunged for him as he passed, plucking at his clothing. Roots broke through the sun-hardened earth to trip him. He leapt clear and ducked down the first side-path that led away from the ivy. Dead end. Gair swore and doubled back to the next turning. A quick glance showed it was clear, but before he had gone a hundred yards he heard the rustle of dry leaves sifting down.

He increased his speed, though thorns raked his hands and arms when he took a turning too fast, or couldn't stop for a dead end. Soon blood flew with the beads of sweat, leaving scarlet smears on his shirt. Now dead leaves blighted every hedge, and dark strands twisted amongst the branches. With every yard more purplish leaves uncurled their hands, and swarmed through the green.

A stitch stabbing at Gair's side finally forced him to a halt and he leaned on his knees to catch his breath. His lungs felt as if they were filled with hot sand. Around him he saw no sign of ivy; perhaps he had a moment or two to rest. If only he could have found some water. His throat burned; the air itself was parched by the relentless, invisible sun. Even his sweat evaporated before it could dampen his shirt. Maybe there would be water when he finally found his way out.

Swift as striking adders, purple stems coiled around Gair's arms and ankles. They jerked him upright, then lifted him clear off the ground. Panic leapt in his chest. He scrabbled for a purchase on the leathery stalks, but they were inflexible as forged steel chains. All he tore was the skin from his fingers. Relentlessly, he was spread-eagled against the hedge behind him. Thorns bit into his back, rump and thighs; they even began to penetrate the stout leather of his boots. As more and more of them gouged his flesh, he screamed—

Enough, said a cool voice.

The ivy tightened convulsively. More thorns pressed into Gair's flesh, and fresh blood spattered the dead leaves below him.

This goes no further.

Brilliant light flooded the dusty maze. Gair screwed his eyes shut against it. His left arm burned, as if touched with iron straight from the forge, and the bond on that limb fell away. Far off, something whined in pain. Blindly, he clawed at his other arm.

Wait, said the voice.

Gair squinted through the glare and saw a robed shape with a burnished copper halo. A fiery sword swung in towards him and his right arm was freed.

An angel. An angel with a flaming sword.

Hail, Mother, full of grace, light and life of all the world . . .

The words of the devotion tripped through his head, insistent as the clicking of beads.

Blessed are the meek, for they shall find strength in you. Blessed are the merciful, for they shall find justice in you. Blessed are the lost, for they shall find salvation in you. Amen.

The angel advanced, wielding the blade as deftly as a surgeon's scalpel to sever the ropy stems like spider-silk. The fresh shoots thrusting through the hedge needed time to thicken, and in that time Gair could snap them, with a little effort. When the angel carved away the final swathe, he sprawled full-length on the littered path. Soot and blood smeared his shirt, and hundreds of tiny thorn-wounds burned as he scrambled away from the thrashing lengths of cut ivy and their stinking, oily sap.

Come, quickly, said the angel. *We must leave this place.* A hand slipped under his arm and helped him to his feet. The hedge was leafless either side of the bloody thorns. New ivy-stems reared away from the angel's sword as it swung it, ready to lop anything in its path.

'Thank you,' Gair gasped. The angel was too dazzling to look at directly.

We must go.

He stumbled after the angel as it set off down the path. Though it did not appear to move any faster than a walk, he was forced into a shambling run to keep up. It chose their way without hesitation, left, then right, then right again. Its sword blazed in one hand, whilst the other skimmed along the flanking hedge. Where it touched, new leaves appeared and turned green faces towards the sun.

Again and again the ivy lunged for them, across the earth, out of the hedges at throat-height. The angel swung its sword, and branches rained down. Fumes from the foul black sap stung Gair's throat. He lost track of how far they ran. Each turn brought only more dying hedges, or some that were completely dead, the thorn-bushes choked with ivy or torn down by the weight of the parasite. There the angel shuddered and withdrew its hand.

Gair's muscles burned. When his weary feet finally tripped him and sent him sprawling, he had no strength to get up.

The angel reached for his hand. *We do not have much time.*

'I can't. I can't go on.'

You must.

'I can't!'

405

Get up! You must, or you will be lost. The angel's fingers closed on his wrist and hauled him halfway to his knees. *I will not lose you to him! Up!*

Another tug got his knees under him. From further back along the path came the patter of falling leaves.

Quickly! Time is running out!

Gair lurched to his feet, although the effort nearly sent him down again.

Back, quickly!

The angel thrust its shoulder under his arm and they stumbled forward. Round the next corner they came face to face with ivy carpeting the earth in mottled leaves and draping in great swathes from the ravaged hedges. Roots writhed in the broken earth.

Ivy roofed the passage now. It rustled and sighed where there was no breeze to be felt, and under it shadows pooled. The stems ceased their lunging and coiled restlessly, waiting.

We must go through.

Gair lumbered back the way they had come, only to skid to a halt a few yards further on as thick ropes of ivy swarmed over the hedges towards them. The angel hissed in irritation and swung them round again. They had no choice but to go forward.

'Blessed are the lost, for they shall find salvation in you,' Gair mumbled. He could not keep his head up. Even those few words made him cough.

Hold onto that thought. The angel levelled its fiery sword. It glowed white-hot as a crack into the furnaces of heaven, and fire leapt from the blade.

A shriek augered through Gair's ears. Torn leaves rained down and the air filled with the tang of char.

Run! the angel commanded.

He staggered a step or two, then lurched forward, arms windmilling as the flat of the angel's hand connected with his rump. Ivy writhed and flailed under his boots, but this time it was more intent on cringing away from the angel's blade than in holding

406

onto him. Ducking the last few clutching stems, he stumbled out into daylight and crashed onto his knees.

We have no time, the angel said. *You must keep running!*

Drawing on his very last reserves of energy, Gair broke into a lumbering trot. Broken branches crunched under his feet. Here the hedges were more dead than alive, and the angel did not bother to touch them as it passed. Too much was lost to the ivy to be saved. With the angel supporting him, he concentrated on putting one foot in front of the other. He was desperately near his limits. Around him the ivy shuddered with its own pain.

The angel stopped abruptly, head cocked as if listening. Then it moved quickly to the right. *We are very close now. You must be strong.*

'I can't.'

You can – you are strong enough, Gair. Trust me.

Too tired to protest, Gair let himself be tugged around a corner and along a straight path where a mighty hand had swept the hedges aside. Dead boughs littered the ground. His pace slowed, but he scrambled across to where the angel directed.

There were more paths between broken hedges, more turns, then at last the angel stopped. They had reached what had once been a small square. All that remained of the hedges that had surrounded it were blasted stumps, poking up from a shroud of ivy. Branches as thick as Gair's thigh humped and coiled all around, carpeting the earth with coarse leaves that gleamed like old leather. Saggy loops roofed the square, through which only a little sunlight penetrated to illuminate the trunk squatting at the centre.

This is the heart of it. The angel pointed at the fissured black bark. *You must strike there.*

Around them, the ivy shivered. Thin shoots groped towards them but kept their distance.

'Strike with what?'

With your sword. I will protect your back, but you must be quick and sure. Strike for the heartwood, and make each blow tell.

'I don't have a sword.'

Yes, you do. Reach for it, where it has always been.

He reached over his shoulder. Raw fingers closed on the worn grip that felt shaped to fit his hand. He tugged, and the blade unsheathed without effort, winking in the dim light.

Deep inside him, something stirred. A tingling, tickling sensation stole along his nerves, into the muscles of his arm and hand, then down into the sword. Where it passed, some of his weariness washed away. Strengthened, he lifted the old sword and its blade burst into white flame.

Ivy stems lunged, and the angel's weapon darted out, there, and there. Severed creeper thrashed.

Now strike!

Gair drew back his sword. It would be good to see where he was working. An overhand blow sheared through the sagging ivy overhead, and shrieks assailed his ears as foul sap showered his shoulder and arm, but he ignored them and hacked a hole wide enough to admit a haywain. Daylight flooded in.

That was better. Stepping forward, he swung the fiery blade into the thick trunk in front of him. The shriek rose to a painful pitch, and lashing stems clutched at him, but the angel was there to cut them back. Holding the sword in a two-handed grip, like a lumberman with an axe, he struck again.

Overhead the ivy rocked and flailed. Black sap ran, thick as oil, and flashed into dust where it met the flaming blade.

Again! the angel urged. *You must reach the heartwood!*

He swung. 'Hail, Mother, full of grace—'

More wood chips, and a rising stench.

'—light and life of all the world—'

Spatter from the blade pocked the leaves around him.

Fumes from the sap made breathing difficult, and soon he was panting, which only served to draw more of the filthy air into his lungs and made him cough. Doggedly, he swung and struck, swung and struck, and chips of dark wood flew around him.

'—blessed are the meek, for they shall find strength in you—'

The shriek became a keen. The deep notch Gair had cut into the trunk widened like an obscene mouth as the crown of the ivy-tree rocked. Gritting his teeth, he drew back for another blow.

TCHUNK!

'—blessed are the merciful, for they shall find justice in you—'

TCHUNK! More chips; thick gobs of sap splattered his boots.

'—blessed are the lost, for they shall find salvation in you—'

TCHUNK! The cleft in the ivy's trunk yawned wider and wider as the weight of its branches toppled it backwards. With a splintering crash, the crown of the tree hit the earth, leaving a jagged, weeping stump. Gair reversed his grip on the sword and plunged the point into the heart of the exposed wood.

'Amen.'

Wailing filled his head. He leaned all his weight onto the cross-hilt and the steel slid deep into the heartwood. All around him branches spasmed, and bruised leaves and stinking sap filled the air. The wails trailed off into sobs, tumbling down through the registers of audibility until they were felt rather than heard, until there was silence.

33

GUARDIAN
OF THE VEIL

ʘ

Word spread through Chapterhouse like fire through dry bracken. The tenor urgency of the alarm ringing out from the bell-tower fanned the flames. Classes were abandoned, and the strongest apprentices and the adepts assembled in the yard. The weaker students and the youngest of those who were not *gaeden* were shepherded into the safety of the stout-walled chapel. Everyone else was sent to the refectory.

Alderan watched from the parapet above the foreyard. He saw none of the panic and confusion that had so hampered them the last time Chapterhouse had come under siege. Everyone knew their role and carried it out briskly, though palpable unease rippled through the population. He could taste it on the air, the metallic tang of a summer storm about to break.

Before the alarm bell's last chime faded, the defenders were in place. Blue-mantled Masters were stationed all around the walls, never more than a dozen yards apart, and one by one they reached for the Song. Even those who were too young to have been involved last time Chapterhouse came under attack knew their place in the plan and stood ready. When the defenders merged their weavings to create the shield, it would be the single most complex work of power Alderan had seen in twenty years. It did not reach as far as the one he had spun against the storm with Gair's help, but they had been only two minds. This shield would seal Chapterhouse in a tightly woven bubble that could repel an assault by siege-engines.

I hope it's enough. It's all we can do.

'I think you were right about that storm,' said Masen, squinting at the bruised sky. Clouds piled up on Pensaeca like clotted cream, and the light had taken on a flat, yellow quality that dulled colours and brightened white into starkness.

'It's starting,' Alderan said. His gaze slid along the parapet towards Tanith. Gair had bought them some time to prepare, but at what cost? He forced himself to look away. He couldn't help either of them now.

There was nothing more to do now but wait. Alderan walked along the wall, Masen following on silent feet. Twenty years ago they had stood back to back on these very walls whilst the powers of the Hidden raged around them. It was reassuring to have his old friend standing with him again. It felt right. Fitting.

'We've seen too many battles, you and I,' said Masen, as if he had read Alderan's thoughts. Alderan grunted, leaning on the wall over the main gate to look out to sea.

'We're going to have to see one more before we're done.'

'I hope it's the last. We're getting too old for this.' Masen grinned, but there was no humour in it.

'Aye, that we are.' Alderan let his head fall forward, stretching the tension from the back of his neck. 'All right, Masen. Make them ready.'

Masen reached out to the other Masters, and a moment later, a web of power shimmered into place over Chapterhouse. The size of the weaving lifted the hairs on Alderan's arms and made his scalp feel too small to contain his skull. Even without the Song, the shield was visible as an iridescence against the sky. When he embraced his power, the warp and weft broke the sunlight into

411

spangles, like crystals spun into thread. The weave was as tight as the melding of so many minds could ever hope to achieve. It had to be enough.

Alderan raised his right arm. Barin, up in the bell-tower, lifted a hand in response, then, one by one, the other Masters acknowledged him. He counted them off, all the figures tucked amongst the stacks and gables, and the brush of colours from those he could not see. He slid his awareness along the threads of the weave, checking each anchor, though he knew they were secure.

'You worry enough for all of us, Alderan.' Donata's voice dragged his attention back. She perched on a stool in the corner where the north and west walls met, her sketchbook open on her knees and her water pot balanced in the embrasure next to her. With deft strokes she drew sullen clouds mounding over a green island, whilst offshore a sleek ship leaned her shoulder into the waves.

'Does it show?'

She smiled and dabbed ochre from her palette. 'A little bit.' Alderan peered over the wall. The *Morning Star* was indeed standing out into the channel.

'How can you be calm enough to paint at a time like this?'

'How can I be calm without painting?' She held out her brush hand. 'It's the only thing that keeps my hands from shaking.'

'I suppose I should have known, after all these years. I just never thought to ask.' Alderan chuckled. 'What will you do when the light fails?'

She regarded him with a birdlike eye. 'Paint in the dark, of course.'

He patted her shoulder and moved on. All along the roof line, Masters waited: Coran, who had done this once before and surely remembered; Brendan, who had not, looking anxious. Men and women whom Alderan had known for more years than he cared to recall were now ready to fight.

Down in the yard, others watched over groups of adepts, whilst the last few children were escorted inside. Even the youngest sensed the tension. Barely old enough to speak, still they stared round-eyed from their mothers' arms, with that knowing look that small children sometimes have, when they seem old beyond comprehension.

As the minutes passed, the wind shifted to the north, oddly warm for so early in the year, then fell away to nothing. The sea grew steely. Overhead the clouds boiled, their bellies full of lightning.

'And so we come down to it,' Alderan murmured. At his side, Masen said nothing but followed his gaze across the yard to the far side where Healer's green splashed the snowy stone wall. 'Goddess look kindly on us now.'

છ

It was a blessed relief when the alarm bell fell silent. Each urgent clang had stabbed through Darin's bloated head like a spear. He had never known pain like it, and never wanted to again. He pushed himself up, lifting his head off the pillow carefully. It felt like the worst winehead in the world, except he hadn't been drinking. He'd gone to bed early because he was exhausted, still unable to sleep more than two or three hours a night without interruption, then woken before Prime wanting to die. He'd been lying on his bed with the curtains closed ever since.

Something fell off his chest as he moved and he picked it off the blanket without looking, closing his fist around it to keep it safe. Goddess, his head felt as if it had been boiled. Every hair was a red-hot needle stabbed into his scalp. His face felt raw; he could hardly bear to touch it to rub the crusts of sleep from his eyes. Maybe he should go to the infirmary. Saaron would surely have something to help with the pain. He swung his feet down to the floor. His boots were muddy and the cuffs of his trousers were badly stained. He'd have to put them out for laundering soon.

A wave of dizziness engulfed him and sweat broke across his

back. Merciful Eador, he was going to lose his breakfast. Sourness rose in his gorge and he heaved, but nothing came up. He swallowed, but could not get rid of the sting in his throat. Yes, the infirmary, before he did anything else. He couldn't think with this headache, and he needed to concentrate on what he had to do today.

Darin levered himself to his feet and made his way to the door. He left it swinging open behind him and set off along the gallery. Something for the pain, then on with his task. He had to make sure he got it right.

⁊

Nordships rounded the outer islands, square sails bellying with a wind that did not reach the walls of Chapterhouse. Alderan scowled. Weather-Song again. Well, that removed any remaining doubt about who might have sent the storm that almost ended the *Kittiwake*. He ground his teeth together, then, with a great effort, he forced himself to relax. He could not afford to be distracted by past mistakes, nor thoughts of future vengeance. Chapterhouse's safety demanded all of his concentration.

He sent his awareness further afield, over to Pensaeca, where black longships rode in the harbour and the town burned. Horned helmets swarmed through the streets, the braided and bearded Nordmen looting as they went, taking only what they could carry, the small and precious things. Anything else they left strewn in the gutters, or smashed to flinders. The market square taverns had been hit hard, judging by the gaping doors and shattered glass, and red wine ran like blood amongst the spangled cobbles.

The first raiders to emerge from the town on the southeast road met a barrage of arrows. The trees were close there, the narrow forest paths of the hinterland a maze to anyone who did not know them well. Nord after Nord whirled to clutch at the feathered shafts that sprouted from backs and legs. A grim smile tugged at the corners of Alderan's mouth. The men of the Isles might only be farmers and fishermen, but they knew how to use their bows. Even the shepherd-boys were letting fly with their slingshots, gouging eyes and ringing skulls. Pensaeca would not be easily taken.

'Can you see them?' Masen asked, intent on the longships that edged into Pencruik roads.

'Aye. They're making heavy weather of it – Pensaeca has teeth.'

Alderan dragged his attention back to the town below. Anchors splashed down now, and boats were already carrying the first wave of warriors ashore. They met no resistance. He saw a flicker of movement in the woods and orchards that lined the road out of town. Just as on Pensaeca, the Nordmen were in for a surprise if they pushed inland.

Thunder rolled across the sky and shook the air in its fist. Somewhere inside the building a baby wailed.

Gripping the stone coping with both hands, Alderan reached to his defenders. *Be ready.*

Out beyond the net of the shield, a cruising gull rolled indolently down the breeze and sideslipped out of sight. *I am always ready.*

Have a care, Aysha, Alderan called, and laughter floated back on the ether, with a brush of brilliant colour. Her crimson was bloody today, beating like a heart.

More thunder boomed out of the north. Storm clouds heaped from horizon to zenith, black on grey on sickly yellow. Light drained from the day. Thunder again, then lightning connected earth to sky like a hot wire and scorched the salt air.

Not long now. The weight of a will pressed down on Alderan's mind, a finger pushing into the soap-bubble of the world. The child's wails took on a shriller note that sawed through his ears. Even that untrained, untapped talent sensed the pressure being brought to bear on the Veil. And he, the oldest of them, supposedly the wisest, Guardian of the Veil for more than thirty years, was powerless to prevent it.

The heart of the storm seethed. Clouds gyred slowly into a vortex and the sky bulged. Alderan opened himself to the Song. Over Pensaeca the bulge pulsed, contracting and expanding rhythmically in a ghastly parody of a heartbeat. Thunder shook Chapterhouse until its windows sang in their casements. The hideous tumescence ruptured and imps boiled forth – far more than there had been last time, many hundreds more, bile-yellow and black and red as old blood, teeming across the channel on crooked, batlike wings. Thousands of them, with still more scrambling after.

'Dear Goddess,' Masen breathed, 'I never thought I'd see this again.'

'Nor me, but it's here. Courage, old friend.' Alderan reached out and clapped Masen on the shoulder.

Soon the first imps were close enough to distinguish from the swarm: squashed faces, and too-wide mouths lined with sharp teeth. In a few moments, they would reach the shield.

'Take care of Tanith, Masen,' Alderan said. 'We have work to do.'

His friend left at a trot, but Alderan did not watch him go. He dared not take his eyes off the gathering demons. Inside him the Song bubbled like a spring, fresh and clear as it had always been, waiting to take on the shape he gave it. Easy as breathing, he raised his arms and called for lightning.

The first fireball exploded in the front rank of the demons and blackened fragments showered the shield, punctuated by the squeals of the wounded as they fell heavily to earth. Greasy smoke tainted the air. Seconds later, another fireball hissed into the next rank, joined almost immediately by one from either side. Demons blew apart into offal, but the gaps in the swarm were immediately filled. The outriders hit the shield and bounced back, then flew at it again. Actinic flashes arced from Master to Master across the domed shield as claws scrabbled for purchase and wedge-shaped jaws snapped at the defenders they were unable to reach.

Alderan took a step back and reached along the weave to the other Masters. He felt strain in one or two, but he had no time to coddle them. They would stand or fall by the plans he had drawn. If they fell, others would take their places, and if the others fell, well, there were always the adepts.

Charge the shield!

The force of the weaving roared into him. Resonance upon resonance multiplied in him, expanding outwards in a heartbeat to encompass the entirety of Chapterhouse.

Now!

The shield flashed silver, and demons burned.

34

SHIELD

୧୦

Cool stone under him. Hands on the sides of his head. A scorched smell on the air. Gair opened his eyes, and they were seared by a brilliant flash.

'Holy Mother!' he yelped, screwing his eyes shut again.

'Just relax, Gair.' Tanith's voice, very close.

He dared a look.

She was bending over him, her Song lifting the hairs on the back of his arms. 'You'll be fine in a few minutes.'

The Song dwindled and she helped him sit up with his back against the wall. Above him, lightning stitched a stormy sky behind a faint pearly dome.

'What's happening?' He had to raise his voice above the chittering that filled the air.

Tanith moved round to sit against the wall next to him. Wisps of copper hair had escaped her braid and floated round her face in a halo.

'Savin tried to take hold of your mind, from the inside. When he attacked you by the Five Sisters, he left something behind in your head, a seed of his will, so that he could get back in whenever he wanted. We managed to destroy it.'

'And all this?' A flip of his hand took in the noise and smoke.

418

'Whilst I was in your mind, he attacked Chapterhouse with demons. So far the shield is holding, but there are thousands of them.'

Swearing, Gair hauled himself to his feet and looked over the wall onto a scene from a nightmare. Scaly bodies squirmed over one another, pressed up against an invisible barrier that curved over Chapterhouse like an upturned glass basin. Some were burned; their wounds bled a yellowish ichor that left smears on the barrier. Every few seconds, the shield flashed silver, blessedly opaque, to a chorus of squeals.

He spun around to see Masters, standing every few yards around the roof, maintaining the shield. Sweat sheened their faces. Hands were clenched in fists or gripping the wall coping with white-knuckled intensity. Some bared their teeth, or kept their eyes closed in concentration. The weight of their working pressed on Gair's brain.

'How long?' he asked.

Tanith peered at the sky and the pale disc of the sun behind the fringe of the storm. 'Two hours, a little more.'

'Where are they all coming from?'

'Savin's summoned them. He can't approach the islands directly, so he's sent his creatures instead.' Masen appeared at Tanith's shoulder. He laid a hand on her arm, his eyes framing a question. She nodded and gave his hand a squeeze. 'There are other worlds than this one, Leahn, if you know where to look. Savin discovered theirs a long time ago.'

Gair swore again. His head still rang from whatever Tanith had done inside his mind and he could not think clearly. The squealing of the demons was scraping across his brain like fingernails down a chalkboard. He clapped his hands to his head.

'Gair, you need to relax.' Tanith's voice again, soothing as balm. 'Sit down a minute. Try not to fight the shield.'

Curse words were all he could manage; coherent thought was impossible. The shield filled his head, pressing outwards even as

419

the weight of Chapterhouse's defensive weaving bore down from above. Then, as suddenly and silently as the bursting of a bubble, it was gone. He gasped for breath, and immediately wished he hadn't. He didn't dare imagine what he could taste on the air.

Tanith touched his arm. 'Better?'

Gair nodded. His thoughts still felt disconnected, but it was bearable.

'Is the shield still holding?' he asked.

'Yes, so far.'

'How long can they maintain it?'

'In theory, indefinitely,' said Masen, 'but people will need to eat and sleep eventually, and there aren't enough full Masters to replace everyone up here at once. Even if we rotate them in shifts, they'll tire long before Savin runs out of imps. Alderan will have to use the best of the adepts before the end.'

'I can help. I'm strong enough.'

'No, you aren't, Gair,' Tanith said firmly. 'If you were well, you'd be a huge help, but right now it's too dangerous. That shield in your head is the only thing keeping you safe.'

'Safe from what? You said we'd destroyed what Savin left behind.'

'We did, but you need time to heal – there was a huge amount of damage done to you, and I had to seal it away to give you a chance to repair it. That shield isolates you from the Song.'

If he listened, he could hear the Song inside him, swirling restlessly in response to the massive weaving all around him, but it was muted somehow, remote, more like a memory of the Song than the thing itself.

'How long, Tanith? How much time do I need?'

The way she paused for a beat before she answered told him he wouldn't like what she said. 'Weeks. Most probably months.' She took a deep breath. 'Possibly for ever.'

Before he could find the words to protest she had her hands on his arms. Her grip was surprisingly strong. 'Gair, I'm sorry, but I

420

don't know how long it will take. I don't know how quickly you can heal yourself.' Concern shadowed her eyes, concern, and a flash of pain. 'The shield will shrink over time as your mind restores order to itself, but that will happen at its own pace. I can't speed it along. It's impossible for anyone to organise all those fractured memories. All I can do is give your brain a quiet place in which it can work.'

Clammy fingers of dread plucked at him. The Song might be out of his reach for ever? He might never be able to touch it again, even though he could feel it like a flame behind glass. He might never be able to fly. No. Not that. He scanned the turbulent sky, but he couldn't see her. He couldn't bear it if he couldn't fly.

The shield flashed silver, and scrabbling multitudes of Savin's creatures returned, relentless as the tide.

'There must be something I can do besides standing here,' Gair muttered.

'The best thing you can do is find a place to rest,' said Tanith gently.

'I can't rest with this.' He gestured at the shield, and winced as it discharged into the demons. 'I can feel it, Tanith – I can't touch it, but it can touch me. I've got to find something to do. Where's Aysha?'

'She's outside somewhere. She's our eyes and ears over the island. Gair, please, listen to me. You need to rest.'

He turned to go down off the wall and had to stiffen his knees when they wobbled underneath him.

Masen's hand caught his elbow. 'You should heed the lady. She knows what she's about.'

'I can't stand idle, Masen.' He disengaged his arm. 'Thank you, Tanith, for everything you've done, but I can't stay here.'

'Gair, wait!' She caught his hand in hers and tried to pull him to a halt. 'Are you always so stubborn? Please, you're not fully healed. You need rest.'

'I've rested enough.' Lifting her hand he ghosted a kiss across

421

the back of it. 'Stay out of danger. Chapterhouse might need you later.'

She threw up her hands in exasperation as Gair strode away towards the stairs, newly healed muscles twanging in protest at the pace he set. He pushed past the discomfort; he had no time for it just now. He still had a sword he could use, if it came to down to that.

Adepts crowded the yard. Most stood silently, faces upturned to watch the roiling demons and the flashing of the shield. Some kept their heads bowed, and Gair heard more than a few prayers as he wove through them towards the main doors.

As he reached the vestibule, a hand snagged his sleeve. It belonged to Sorchal, and his other hand was on the hilt of the rapier at his hip.

'I thought they'd have you in the shield,' he said.

'I would be, if I could. Tanith says otherwise.' Gair gestured at his head. 'What about you? You're not out with the other adepts.'

The Elethrainian showed his teeth. 'I'm not much of a talent! No point standing around out there like a square wheel on a wagon. I just wish there was some way to kill these things. They're grating on my nerves.'

'Maybe there is,' Gair said. 'Why don't you get Haral to open up the armoury? Take everyone who knows one end of a weapon from the other who isn't needed elsewhere and get them equipped. We might need them to protect the Masters if the shield comes down.'

Sorchal's green eyes sparked. 'I've asked all the girls to dance with me; might as well ask Lady Death. Where are you going?'

'To do the same as you. To get ready for a fight.'

Sorchal loped off in search of the weapons-master, and Gair continued inside. The main hall stood empty, echoing to his footfalls as he hurried to the stairs and along the silent gallery to his room. Even indoors he could feel the shield as it charged and

422

discharged. It prickled over where the Song should be like yellow-balm on a skinned knee. When he came back out onto the gallery with his sword, Darin was standing uncertainly in the doorway to his room.

'Gair?' The Belisthan's dark eyes were lost in their shadowed sockets.

'Shouldn't you be down in the yard with the others?'

'There's something I've got to do first.' Darin's left hand plucked at the front of his shirt. His right was balled into a fist. His gaze flicked down the gallery then back again, but was unable to settle, hunting for something to rest on.

Gair looked closely at him. 'Are you all right?' he asked. 'You're very pale.'

'I'm just scared.' A sickly smile. 'I can hear them screaming. They're all screaming.'

'There's no one else here.' Gair frowned. 'Who's screaming, Darin?'

His slight shoulders lifted, then slumped again, as if he hadn't the strength to keep them squared. 'Everyone,' he said, then turned and walked away.

'Darin, wait!' Gair called after him. 'Darin!'

The Belisthan walked on towards the far end of the gallery, away from the stairs. As he rounded the corner Gair debated running after him, even jogged a few yards along the passage, but when he leaned out over the balustrade he could not see anyone. Darin must have gone into another room. Gair called his name again, but there was only an echo for an answer.

❧

Back on the parapet, two of the Masters had been replaced. Tanith knelt over a blue-robed figure in the lee of the wall by the kitchens, but she was too far away for him to see who it was. Above the gates, Alderan still watched over the shield. Gair climbed the stairs to stand next to him. Scant feet away was a roil of sharp teeth and flat black eyes.

'Relentless, aren't they?' Alderan said. He eyed the sword. 'Pray Goddess things don't get so bad we need to go hand to hand with them.'

'Tanith's shield cuts me off from the Song. At least with my sword I don't feel quite so useless.'

The old man laid a hand on his shoulder. 'If it weren't for you we wouldn't have known he was coming, so you're far from useless. You paid a high price to give us a few days' warning, and believe me, for that I'm grateful.'

Overhead the shield flashed and more shrieking demons fell away. Through the bluish haze Gair could see more longships closing on Pencruik. Fire-arrows leapt into the anchored sandboats and fishing vessels, adding to the smoke that billowed across the sound from Pensaeca. An early dusk was falling as the storm clouds finally smothered the sun. Then Savin's imps resumed their scrabbling and cut off his view.

'What exactly is this talisman he thinks we have, Alderan? You never got a chance to tell me.'

'The Nimrothi call them starseed. The stones are prized by the clan Speakers, because they enable them to draw more deeply on the Song than they could unaided. That's how they tore the Veil in the first place, and how Corlainn sealed it up afterwards.'

Gair frowned. 'Corlainn the heretic?'

'Corlainn Fellbane should have been raised up a saint, not burned at the stake.'

'He condemned himself, Alderan; by his own admission he used dark arts to summon demons. Wait—' Gair corrected himself as his brain made the connections. 'That's how they held Riannen Cut when Gwlach brought up his reserves, isn't it? That's how they turned the battle – he used the starseed!'

Alderan inclined his head in salute. 'And Corlainn paid for it with his life, to protect the Order's reputation. He was a hero,

Gair, the kind folk should write stories about: a plain-spoken, good-hearted soldier who was not afraid to stand shoulder to shoulder with his men and bleed for them. He should never have been asked to make that sacrifice, but he did it because he believed in something greater than himself.'

'And the Church repaid him by ensuring he was recorded in the histories as a treacher and apostate.' The shield sizzled and stank. 'Another sin to call them to account for. What about the starseed?'

'After he'd taken it from Gwlach's clan Speaker, he used it to stitch up the rent she had made in the Veil, sealing the Wild Hunt away again. After his arrest, he surrendered it to the Suvaeon. History is silent as to its final resting place.'

'Is it here?' Gair asked.

Alderan shook his head.

'But Savin thinks it might be? That's why he's coming against us?'

'That, and there's other knowledge here – books, people, all things he could find a use for as he searches for that starseed. We cannot let him back into Chapterhouse.'

'What would he do with it if he found it? Rend the Veil?'

'Oh, he can do that already.' The old man jerked a hand towards the rent in the clouds that was still spewing demons. They were thick as blowflies round rotten meat. 'It's already wearing thin, according to Masen. With the starseed, Savin could destroy it completely, and from that, there is no coming back.'

Another flash overhead.

With mounting horror, Gair realised where Alderan's story would end. 'Holy Mother, you're talking about the Last Days!'

'"And Eador did cast down the Angel into the Abyss, there to remain for all eternity. She commanded that the Angel's name be not spoken, that He should dwell in nameless darkness, forever in opposition to Her will. Should ever the Angel escape the Abyss, there will be much weeping, for a darkness shall cover the land and in it shall be the ending of all things."'

Even curse words failed Gair now. *The ending of all things.* The Book of the Last Days was the final book in the gospels, St Ioan's apocalyptic visions of a battle between heaven and hell. He had been raised to fear such things, and now Alderan had told him that he might live to see those events unfold within his lifetime.

His mind reeled. 'I can't believe—— Why would he want to destroy the Veil? Why?'

The old man smiled sadly. 'You'd have to ask him that, because I simply could not say. Much of the Book of Eador is based on legends, scraps of legends, really, from a time further back than even the clan Speakers can recall, but there is truth in it too. The hell of the Book is one aspect of the Hidden Kingdom, one of the many worlds that exist beyond the Veil. If the Veil were to disappear, there would be nothing to prevent those worlds inter-secting with our own, and the creatures that inhabit them have no love for men — least of all those creatures that mankind once banished there.'

'Doesn't Savin know this?' Gair demanded. 'Doesn't he realise what he's doing?'

'I'm sure he does. I'm also quite sure he doesn't care. Savin would take the world apart stone by stone to find the tick, then not be bothered to put it back together again when his curiosity was sated. Maybe he thinks the Nameless will be so grateful to be free that He will reward him in some way. I don't know. I only want to stop him.'

For a moment, Gair saw Alderan's true feelings about Savin: loathing, fear, and deep, deep regret, and over it all, an ocean of sorrow. Then the old man's expression closed up, drew all the pain inside and hid it away.

'Let me help,' he said. 'Please, Alderan, you could use me.'

'I can't, lad. If Tanith removes that shield before you're healed, you'll almost certainly be lost. I won't take that chance. I think there is work for you to do yet, but it's not here and not now.'

'What do you mean? I don't understand!'

The shield above them flared again, but this time the light was weaker, webbed with blue and purple. The Song inside Gair resonated in response to something, but he did not know what.

'Alderan, what just happened?'

Alderan didn't answer. His eyes were searching the fabric of the shield as he drew on the Song.

The weight of the weaving above Gair became oppressive. His nerves crawled as if he had fire-ants in his skin. 'Something's wrong,' he whispered, straining to feel what it might be. He yearned to touch the Song, but it was locked up tight behind the silk-fine, steel-hard wall of Tanith's shield.

Alderan's hand pressed in the middle of his back. 'Get down off the parapet, Gair. I have a feeling we may yet need your sword.'

Deep inside Chapterhouse, someone screamed.

35

ARROWS IN THE AIR

୨୦

The Rede-bell rang, silver-bright, and sent the Citadel's doves clattering around the Sacristy spires.

Pausing in his dictation, Ansel peered at his secretary over the sheaf of notes in his hand. 'I thought we were still in recess,' he said as a stray dove whirred past the windows.

'The Rede is not scheduled to reconvene until after St Saren's.' The young clerk frowned over his daybook, long fingers flicking through the pages. 'I have nothing in my book, my lord. Someone must have called an extraordinary session.'

Any Elder could do so, with the support of two seconds, if he could convince the clerk of the court he had sufficient reason. Ansel had done it himself, years ago, when the Curia had dithered about sending the legions to Gimrael. He tossed his notes down onto the desk.

'Run down to the hall, will you, and see who rang the bell? Those letters will keep.'

'Very good, my lord.'

When the clerk had gathered up his writing case and closed the door behind him, Ansel stared unseeing at the administrative detritus that cluttered his desk. So the first arrows had been loosed. The timing was perfect: spring recess almost over, and many of the Elders still at their parishes. Much easier to find a quorum then, with so many of the Curia out of the city and out of reach.

With a roar of rage, he swept his arm across the desk. Pens and correspondence scattered onto the faded rug. *Damn them! Damn them to the Nameless' dark!*

The door opened to admit a husky, sandy-haired youth in novice's grey. Blue eyes watched the papers sifting down to rest, then his fingers flickered through the shapes of words.

I take it you heard the bell.

'I heard it,' Ansel growled. He hoisted himself from his chair and winced. Leaning on his desk for support, he tested his weight on his aching knees.

Goran?

'Aye, or his puppet-master. Goran's cunning as a ragman's dog, but I'd bet my stones he's not the one orchestrating this.' Ansel took a tentative step towards the door to his bedchamber and fiery needles stabbed through his joints.

So who rang the bell?

'I've sent Euan to find out.' Another step, and more pain. He let go of the edge of the desk, but had to grab on to it again when his knees threatened to buckle. 'I've been waiting for this, Selsen. I could see them manoeuvring. Like jackals,' he spat. 'Wait until their prey is weakened, then attack in numbers to bring it down.'

And then they feast.

'Ha! They can try.'

What the boy signed next brought a tight grin to Ansel's face, despite the pain.

'We are in the House of Eador, you know. Only I'm allowed to swear with impunity.'

I'll say five Hail Mothers and a Domine Me before I go to bed.

'All twenty-eight verses?'

Of course. Selsen folded his hands in his sleeves and offered his

Preceptor a face that shone with honest piety. *And in Greic, to show proper respect.*

A full Domine Me in the elegant, formal tongue of Greic that only scholars could read would take the lad an hour and a half. 'Show-off. Fetch my robes from the closet, would you? I'm going down to the hall.'

Are you sure? They'll make it harder for you to walk.

'They'll also make it harder for me to be ignored.'

Selsen's sandy head dipped to hide a smile as he glided towards the closet. *Mother always said you had a strange sense of humour.*

'And you have her sharp tongue, I see. Take care it doesn't cut you. Is there any poppy syrup left in the bottle on the nightstand?'

Doors opened and closed; fabric rustled. The novice emerged from the bedchamber with his arms full of pearly silks and swathes of velvet that he draped over Ansel's chair.

The bottle's empty but for a few drops. Fortunately, I have learned where Hengfors keeps the keys to the dispensary. He produced a small bottle from a concealed pocket of his robe and held it out.

Ansel popped the cork with his thumb. 'My boy, you are a great comfort in my hour of need,' he said. Tipping back his head he took a generous swig of the cloying syrup.

Be careful with that – too much and you'll sleep through the Rede.

'I know what I'm doing.'

It shows.

Ansel slapped the cork into the bottle and threw it back. 'You have some latitude with me, but I suggest you don't abuse it.'

Selsen gave the merest half-bow, blue eyes not in the least contrite. *Yes, my lord.*

Even in thieftalk the boy managed insolence. A glower washed off him like rain off a roof-tile. Just like his mother.

Ansel shrugged out of his woollen house-robe and reached for the clothes Selsen had brought out. The high-collared silk shirt slithered over his back, chill as ice. Despite himself, he could not suppress a shiver.

Afraid, old man? You survived Samarak, you'll survive this. When there're arrows in the air you raise your shield and you hold, damn it!

He jerked the shirt closed and began to fasten it. The tiny pearl buttons were wilful; each time he chased one down and brought it close to its buttonhole, it popped from between his fingers. Wretched things. A pox on the tailor who'd stitched them! He fumbled for another button.

Selsen's square hands intervened. *Here, let me help.*

Damn his age, that he couldn't even fasten his own clothes now, but had to let someone dress him. An idiot child could be taught to manage his buttons and laces – gah! Ansel ground his teeth as the novice deftly fastened his shirt front and cuffs. He held out his arms for the shirt to be tucked in and the heavily brocaded robes lifted onto his shoulders.

I feel like I'm armouring you for battle, the boy signed. *First your arming-jacket, then your breastplate* – he smoothed the brocade, with its glittering thread-of-gold curlicues – *then your surcoat.* He picked up the heavy velvet outer robe, satin lining whispering as he shook out its folds.

'Goddess knows it weighs as much as war-plate.' Scowling, Ansel thrust his arms into the sleeves. 'And it's about as hot, too.' Already the shirt was clinging stickily to him, and he couldn't get to it through the layers to pluck it from his skin. 'Well? Am I presentable?'

Polished vambraces and greaves would look stunning, but I think you'd fall over.

'Cheeky whelp. Just give me my staff, before I paddle your backside like you deserve.'

I still don't think all that regalia is wise.

'Maybe not, but you were right, you know. We are going into battle, so by the Goddess we'll go caparisoned in silk, with all our banners flying.'

The Rede-bell rang again, and the corners of Ansel's mouth turned down. Only a quarter of an hour left, and then things

431

would end, one way or the other. Time to go. He pushed himself away from his desk and straightened up. The poppy syrup's numbing hands were already at work, stroking and soothing his crumbling joints. It would wear off eventually, and there would be a price exacted of him for walking so far, but he'd pay that bill when it came due.

A glitter of sun on gilding caught his eye. His scabbarded sword hung from a peg on the end of the bookshelves by the window, its coiled belt dusty and cracked with disuse. A pity he couldn't have found an excuse to have that on his hip when he walked into the Rede Hall. Leaning on that mighty two-handed hilt made even treacherous whoresons sit straight in his presence.

Selsen followed his gaze. *It would make them remember who governs this Order, at any rate.*

'Then I'll save that for the last,' Ansel grunted. 'When there's nothing left but to do or die.'

For now they get the steel hand in the velvet glove. Selsen plucked the Preceptor's formal robes to hang straight, and brushed a speck of lint from the sleeve. Then he grinned wolfishly, and looked so much like his mother that Ansel's heart ached.

'Ready?' he said, hoping the gruffness in his voice would be taken for determination. 'Let's meet them on the field.'

&

Danilar looped the bell-rope around its hooks as the echoes of the last stroke shivered into silence. So much for Goran's attempts at secrecy. Now the whole Motherhouse would know – including, the Chaplain hoped as devoutly as he hoped for his own redemption, the Preceptor. Please Goddess, Ansel had heard. Please Goddess, he could reach the hall in time.

Quietly letting himself out of the small door at the foot of the bell-tower, he cocked an ear for sounds of commotion, but the long vestibule remained empty. Nothing stirred in the sunlight slanting through the high windows but the banners hung from the vault and the doors between the pair of mailed guards remained closed. If anyone inside the Rede Hall had heard the bell, it hadn't stirred them from their plots.

Danilar's fists clenched. Whatever flaws Ansel might have, however the Curia might disagree with his stewardship of the Order, there was a procedure to be followed to resolve differences. The rule of law must be obeyed, or what remained but chaos? Anxiety and righteous anger quickening his steps, he strode back to his lodging to change into his formal robe. As Chaplain he had no vote to cast in the consistory court, but he was entitled to be there when they sat, and there was too much at stake for him not to be.

Elder Festan cocked his fists on his hips and scowled at the sentry in front of the iron-strapped doors.

'What do you mean, you can't open them?' he demanded.

'The Rede is already in session, Elder,' the sentry said woodenly, staring straight ahead over Festan's shoulder. 'The doors can only be opened from inside.'

'But how can they be in session with half the Curia cooling its heels out here, and the Preceptor besides? I order you to open those doors!'

'I'm sorry, Elder. I can't do that.'

'Why you—,'

'Leave him be, Festan,' said Ansel. 'Shouting at the poor fellow might make you feel better, but it won't change matters. If they've got a quorum they can start the Rede without us, and they can stay in there as long as they want. You know that. Now peace, and let me think.'

Twenty-four scarlet robes clustered around him in the vestibule. Ansel had found them milling in the corridors on his way down to the hall, unsure why they'd been summoned. They had fallen in behind him, a tail to a blazing white Preceptorial comet, only to find it knocked from its orbit by the closed doors of the Rede Hall. Twenty-four. It couldn't possibly be enough.

If only Festan was right and he could order the doors opened. If he could face them, he was sure he could prevail. But if the Rede was called and a quorum sat, they acted with the full authority of the Curia, and their deliberations could only be interrupted at their behest. There weren't even any handles on the doors on this side.

Rhythmic squeaks from further down the corridor dragged everyone's head round. Elder Tercel, too frail to walk now, was being pushed in his wheeled chair by his brother Elder Morten, almost as stooped and silvered as his charge. Others hurried to help, tripping over each other's words in their haste to explain. Two more. How many were still to come?

There must be something we can do, Selsen signed.

'Don't drop your colours, we're not done yet.' Ansel peered over the shoulders of the crowd, hearing more footsteps. Danilar strode into the vestibule with the ends of his stole whipped out behind him, a piece of paper crumpled in his fist.

'Thank the Goddess you heard, Ansel. I was afraid the bell might be too late.'

'It was you who rang, not them?' Festan asked, and Danilar nodded.

'Pure chance I looked out of the window when I did, and saw a dozen Elders crossing the court, all robed for the Rede. I came straight here, but the doors were already closed.'

Festan scowled. 'I can scarcely believe it. Treachery in our own house!' Shaking back his full sleeves, he stalked up to the doors and pounded on them with his meaty fists. 'Open up! Open in the name of the Preceptor!'

Dust sifted down as the doors shook in their frames. Several other Elders added their voices to his, chirping their concern like sparrows at a cat in the garden.

Danilar held out the paper to Ansel. 'Here. I met your secretary

434

on the way and he thought this might be useful. It's the absentee list for the first scheduled session next week.'

Ansel smoothed the crumpled sheet between his hands and scanned the names, counting. Eighteen absent, so eighty-one attendees. Fifty-four hierarchs for a quorum. A faint hope began to warm his breast. Could it be possible? He ran his eye round the room again to check his count and the hope dimmed. Twenty-six wasn't enough to challenge them.

Silently, he offered the paper to Selsen, who read it and handed it back, grim-faced.

Behind him, Festan continued to pound the doors and demand admittance.

'Saints and angels, Festan, let it be,' Ansel sighed. 'There's nothing we can do for now but wait and see where the arrows fall.'

He leaned on his staff as the tide of righteous anger that had carried him this far began to ebb. So it would end on a bureaucratic technicality. How ironic.

'Arrows?' barked a voice. 'Has war finally broken out in Gimrael?'

Ansel looked round to see scarlet robes melt out of the Lord Provost's path as he strode into the room in hunting leathers, slapping his gauntlets across his thigh in time with the rap of his boot-heels. With him was another Elder garbed for the hunt, his quiver still across his shoulder.

'Not yet, Bredon,' Ansel said. Eadwyn made twenty-seven. Deadlock.

'So what's going on? I was in Eadwyn's deer-park with a clean shot when he heard the bell. Someone owes me a buck.'

Insurrection, Selsen signed, and the Provost's brows quirked upwards.

'Thieftalk? I thought only spies and slitpockets used that, not Suvaeon novices.'

I grew up in Haven-port, my lord. A man cannot help where he comes from. May I borrow your dagger?

Bredon frowned, but produced a skinning knife from his boot top and proffered it hilt first.

Selsen took it and walked to the hall doors, bowing his way past the smouldering Festan.

The sentries stirred uneasily, glancing from the Lord Provost to Ansel and back.

'At ease,' Ansel said. 'Selsen?'

Trust me. Carefully the novice slid the knife-blade between the two doors below the latch and worked it upwards until it clicked against something. He set his shoulder and heaved, and the left-hand door swung inwards an inch or so under its own weight.

'Impressive,' said Bredon, taking his knife back. 'Growing up on the waterfront has given you all sorts of skills. Who are you, young man? I could find a place for you as a marshal.'

My name is Selsen, my lord. I'm visiting from the Daughterhouse at Caer Amon.

'So where is this going, Selsen?' Ansel interrupted.

For answer, Selsen pointed at the Lord Provost and smiled.

Bredon's dark eyes registered confusion at first, and then his lips twitched as he worked it out. Hand over heart, he bowed. 'I accept your nomination under the fourth amendment, my lord Preceptor.'

Of course. Who would have thought a novice from a backwater Daughterhouse could be so finely versed in consistorial law? He looked to Tercel, who steepled his bony fingers under his chin and nodded.

'Selsen, my boy, you never cease to amaze me,' said Ansel, a grin threatening to break his composure. 'Let's see this done.'

Beautifully balanced as they were, the Rede Hall doors swung open with a hearty shove from Selsen and scattered the two sentries inside. Surprised Elders swivelled round in their seats, and on the Preceptor's dais Goran choked on his speech.

Ansel stood in the doorway and stared at the assembled Elders. A few stiffened defiantly under his eye, but a few more cringed. *And well you might, duplicitous curs!* His belly roiled with rage. *What were you promised to support that fat slug's ambitions?*

Bredon and Danilar took station either side of him, and behind him he heard the remainder of the Elders taking their seats. When the shuffling and rustling finally faded away, he let his gaze rest on Goran, standing in front of the Preceptor's chair with its carved Oak backrest, and dared the man to look away first.

'This,' he announced, 'is an illegal Rede.'

'We convened a quorum of available Elders, as mandated by consistorial law,' Goran declared. 'We are quite within our rights to vote——'

'Shut up, Goran.'

'——to vote on issues concerning——'

'I said be *quiet*!' Ansel struck the floor with his staff. 'One more word out of you before I'm done and I'll have the Lord Provost arrest you.'

Goran drew himself to his full height, colour rising in his cheeks. 'On what charge?'

'Why don't we start with contempt for the process of law, and work up from there?' Ansel roared. 'Marshals!'

Behind him, the four sentries stamped to attention.

'How dare you!' Goran blustered. 'You have no authority to do such a thing!'

'Don't I?' Ansel glared at him. His voice quivered with rage. 'I am Preceptor of this Order.'

'Not any more.'

Silence held the hall breathless in its grip.

Ansel's knuckles whitened on his staff. 'I beg your pardon?'

'You were put aside by majority vote as unfit to hold office. I am Preceptor now.' Triumph sparkling in his piggy eyes, Goran gestured to the clerk at the desk below him. 'The vote has already been recorded in the ledger.'

Fury boiled up Ansel's throat, sour as the urge to do violence.

'Unfit, am I? Let me tell you who is unfit for holy office, Goran! Who keeps their own staff of questioners, even though they were outlawed with the Inquisition?'

Goran blinked, and the assembled Curia sucked in their breath.

'Did you think I didn't know that you use those questioners to inflict pain on young men for your own personal gratification?' Bredon laid a hand on Ansel's arm. 'Is this true?'

'It's true, I just couldn't prove it,' Ansel hissed back. 'None of the poor wretches he abused is still here to testify against him.'

'Dead?'

'All bar one.'

Puce-faced, fists trembling at his sides, Goran burst out: 'Lies! I won't stand here to be slandered by you, Ansel. Your tenure is over. Marshals, I demand you remove this man from the chamber.'

'Can you produce this witness?' Bredon whispered under restless mutters from the watching Elders.

'I sent him away from Dremen for his own safety.'

'That's good enough for me.' The Lord Provost raised his voice. 'Hold fast, men.'

'What are you doing? Arrest that man!' Goran levelled his finger at Ansel. 'You're finished, do you hear me? You've been clinging onto office on the strength of your war record for far too long – you should have stood down years ago.'

'At least I have a war record to be proud of,' Ansel retorted. 'Where were you when the fires burned, Goran? Where were you when the legions rode out against twice their number at Samarak, when the arrows were so thick in the sky they made midnight of noonday? Tucked up snug on your father's estates like a hen on her nest, weren't you?'

A raspy cough broke out with the words, but Ansel could not stop now. His blood was up the way it hadn't been since the desert wars, when his life had depended on steel and stones and a strong

438

horse under him. He dashed moisture from his lips on the back of his hand.

'I was there.' A hand plucked at his sleeve but he shook it off. 'In the blood and the muck and the stench and the flies. I was there because I swore an oath to defend the faith with my body and my soul, though it might cost me my life. You all swore that same oath when you received your spurs. Is this what we are become?'

'The Order has changed since the desert wars, Ansel,' Goran fired back. 'Our numbers have dwindled, the faith is diminished. Swords and rosaries are not enough any more. If we are to reverse this decline we need a new hand at the helm, a new voice to rally the faithful.'

'And you think that voice is yours? You think you have the stones to sit in that chair?'

Ansel thrust out his hand to point at the Preceptor's seat and saw crimson smeared across it, speckling his brocaded sleeve. Another cough flayed his lungs and he staggered, saved from falling by Selsen's shoulder under his arm.

'Yes, I do. Look at you,' Goran scoffed. 'You're dying, old man. Go out to pasture where you belong.'

Ansel straightened up with an effort. The coppery taste of blood filled his mouth and he spat onto the marble tiles to clear it.

'I am where I belong,' he said, biting off each word. 'For the Oak and the Goddess, to my last breath. What do you stand for, Goran, that makes you so much better suited to lead than me?'

'It's over, Ansel! We have voted for a new Preceptor, accept it!'

'Um, the vote is void, Elder Goran,' the clerk squeaked.

'What?'

'It's void.' Brother Chronicler clutched his papers to his chest, a shield against the stares levelled at him. 'There was no quorum.'

'There were fifty-four names against the motion, man!'

'Yes, but there are eighty-two Elders present,' the clerk rushed out, shrinking down inside his black robe under the weight of scrutiny. Next to him, Tercel and Morten nodded.

'Count again,' Goran ordered.

'The count is correct. Elder Tercel confirmed it for me. Under the fourth amendment to the Curial Code as established at the Grand Rede, in times of emergency the Lord Provost assumes the rights and responsibilities of a full Elder of the Suvaeon Order.' Brother Chronicler's voice dropped to a whisper that rang loud as a shout in the sudden stillness of the hall. 'Twenty-eight to fifty-four means you have no quorum.'

A heartbeat's silence, then the Rede Hall exploded into uproar.

36

BREACH

~

Alderan embraced the Song and merged his mind into the weaving. Gair was correct; something was very wrong. The taut fabric enfolding him was pulled askew, creating a point of weakness. One of the Masters anchoring it was failing. Dear Goddess. Quickly he searched along the web of minds and counted the patterns one by one. To his right Masen's colours appeared and the strain eased a little, but even with his old friend in the weave, the shield continued to weaken.

Not enough, Masen said. *What's happening?*

I wish I knew. Everyone's here, but I can feel the weave being torn.

Where's the Leahn?

I sent him down off the wall. He could feel it happening, Masen, even shielded. I've never known a talent like his.

Except one.

Except for one.

In front of him the demons chattered furiously, redoubling their efforts to claw through the shield. Purplish smears suffused the weave now, and each discharge was palpably weaker. Scaly forms piled on top of one another, as if sheer weight of numbers would prevail. Or as if they knew something that the defenders did not.

Masen, there's going to be a breach, right here! Get every Master you can find to reinforce the weaving!

Feet clattered on the parapet stairs and new colours appeared along the shield. Strength washed into him, fresh water into a stagnant pool, and Alderan drew deeply on the Song and flung it out into the weave.

What the hell is happening inside? he demanded of anyone who could hear.

Donata's voice floated back, as calm as ever. *One of the adepts is coming, I'll ask. Did you hear it too?*

I heard it.

The weaving lurched and pain stabbed Alderan's brain. Colours along the shield flickered then flared as their owners threw themselves back into it. Another stab. The demonic chittering increased in pitch and the creatures poured towards a point on his left. A surge of power charged the shield, but instead of the incandescent flash he expected, a line appeared down the curve of the weave as if drawn by the hand of the Goddess herself. Then it opened up.

Breach! Alderan yelled. The Song came eagerly to his call and spilled into the weave. Masen, Barin and a dozen others did the same, but it was not enough to stop the spiny limbs clutching at the edges of the breach, allowing misshapen bodies to spill through. Almost at once a silvery veil appeared above the adepts in the yard below as someone had the presence of mind to erect a shield over them. Alderan thanked the saints for whoever it was who'd kept their wits about them, then recoiled in horror when the demons turned on the unprotected Masters instead.

A pattern of colours winked out over by the stables. Alderan felt the wrench, but the weaving held. How much of the Song could he spare to defend himself? Behind him he heard the distinctive sound of steel on leather. Gair touched his arm briefly, then the Leahn was off, longsword swinging into the approaching swarm. Elsewhere on the parapet lightning arced across the stones and the air filled with the stench of char.

We must close this, Alderan! Masen cried. *We can deal with the ones under the shield, as long as no more get in.*

It'll take more power than we've got.

There's no one left, my friend, unless you want to start using the children.

Alderan swore foully. *Damn you, Savin, you bastard!*

Already the adepts' shield had begun to bulge and discolour. They didn't have much time. From across the yard an unfamiliar voice barked orders and Alderan spared a handful of seconds to glance round. A young man with a rapier was directing parties of apprentices to wherever the imps were thickest, and they set to with whatever could be wielded as a weapon: spears, quarter-staves, even rakes and hoes from the kitchen garden. Those who had swords were paired with those who hadn't; in twos and threes they set about the demons with the dedication of veterans.

Alderan offered up a prayer. Some of those voices yelling defiance were alarmingly treble.

Still more demons pushed through the breach, and another set of colours winked out. Pain flickered back and forth across the weaving like scarlet lightning.

Someone's holding it open! Masen sounded strained.

Who?

Donata!

That's impossible!

There's something not right about her colours, Alderan. She's not entirely in the weaving.

Alderan made himself look along the roof-walk towards Donata's station. Through the smoke he saw a figure standing at the wall, head tipped back. It couldn't be her weaving, surely. His mind refused to accept treachery from her. He skimmed a thought out along the shield towards the breach. A gateway, being held open to admit the demons, and Donata's colours were threaded through it. Impossible. He probed the weave; the colours shimmered and settled, but Masen was right, they were odd somehow.

Then he saw a dark shape on the pale stone. Watercolours spilled around it, bright as broken butterflies. He moved in closer.

Donata's face was ashen, and her scalp and temples were criss-crossed with scratches. Dark hair was tangled in her hooked, bloody fingers. In her place stood Darin. His body twitched with the forces that raced through it, and his sunny features had slumped into a horrified mask. Alderan heard the Song in him, wild and skirling and utterly mad.

Now he could see what Masen had sensed. The colours were Donata's, but apart from the illusion of her presence, Donata was gone, and only a fragment of Darin remained, just enough to focus the shield weaving until such time as Savin chose to tear a hole in it. Somehow he had managed to suborn the Belisthan's mind and use it to pierce the shield from within.

He is nothing but a tool to you – not a person, not one of the Goddess' creatures, as worthy of life as any other, but a tool. A means to an end. Alderan trembled with a rage he had thought he would never feel again.

It's not Donata, he told Masen. *Her colours, yes, but it's not her underneath them.*

We must close that gateway.

I know. I'll call the adepts.

◈

Gair saw Tanith at the end of the walkway by the stables. She knelt with a fallen Master's head in her lap, struggling to work a Healing on him while maintaining a small defensive shield around them both. He hefted his longsword and chopped his way through. Scales and talons pattered down onto the walk, Chapterhouse's snowy stone stained now with yellow and black. The Astolan flashed him a grateful look, then let her shield go and bent over the fallen Master, Brendan, Gair saw, grey-faced and horribly wounded in the abdomen. Wielding his sword, he kept the demons at bay whilst she worked to staunch the bleeding.

'Thank you.' She was breathless.

'Is he going to be all right?'

A rust-coloured imp darted along the walk and he cleaved its head in two then kicked the body off the parapet.

'I've done all I can up here. He's stable for the moment.'

Gair looked back at her. Her hands and gown were bloody and there was a streak of soot on her brow.

'We can't hold for long against this, Tanith. For every five I kill there're another ten coming through. You've got to let me help Alderan close the breach.'

'It would put you in harm's way, and that's a violation of my oath.'

'There's no choice.' Another yammering creature met the edge of his blade. 'Take down the shield.'

She chewed her lip. 'I don't know what you're going to find behind it. You might not even be able to reach the Song.'

'Do it, *please*. You know how strong I am – they *need* me.'

Golden hands reached up, seized his head, and her presence swept through him like an avenging angel, then the shield was gone and Gair's brain filled with nightmares.

Darkness and pain washed over him. He dropped the sword, crashed to his knees as fragments of memories, things buried and long forgotten, were dragged back out into the light, the sweetest of memories torn and commingled with childhood horrors. Nausea clawed up from his guts and he vomited.

When the violent cramping receded, Gair reached for the Song, which thrummed underneath the dissonance in his thoughts. It was so close – but every time he tried to grasp it, he missed. Gritting his teeth, he willed it to come to him.

Astonishing music filled him, clean as mountain air. The nightmares were pushed back and masked by the joyful power he now held. Above him, he saw the weave anchored on the sobbing minds either side of him. Without quite knowing how he did it, he touched the intricate fabric and slid into it.

445

Colours streamed around him. Some he recognised, some he did not. Some flickered through garish parodies of their usual shades as incredible pressures were brought to bear upon them; others were so dimmed they were close to being extinguished. The Song rose up and flowed out along his awareness, and anchor by anchor, he stretched out his arms and gathered them up.

Who is that? demanded an unfamiliar voice.

It's Gair, Masen. Alderan. Are you all right, lad?

Not really, but I can hold it long enough for you to close the breach. Someone's weaving a Gateway. I'll need all the strength you can give me.

I've a better idea, Masen interrupted. *Drop the shield altogether and re-weave it without Donata's colours. If we force it closed, we might not have anyone to question afterwards.*

Alderan paused for only a second. *Agreed. Stay with me as long as you can, Gair.*

What had happened to Donata? No time to ask. The Song poured through Gair in a river, though he couldn't help but dread the cacophony he knew awaited him when he eventually let it go. But that was then, not now, and in the now he rode it as a ship rides on the wings of the wind.

Ready? asked Masen.

I'm ready.

The shield winked out. Demons surged forward – and with the chime of a tapped wine glass, the transparent dome snapped back into being, catching Savin's creatures as it closed and slicing them into pieces. Fragments tumbled down, showering the defenders with filth. Outside, the horde yowled in frustration.

Charge the shield! Alderan's voice rang out. Now!

For an instant, every shred of Gair's being flashed white-hot. The flow of the Song did not diminish one iota, but he had less control now. The other Masters were holding him; he was merely a conduit. That was all he could be, at the moment. It took every-thing he had to resist being swept away.

446

A sharp pain in his arm, then another, and he opened his eyes to see a triangular mouth lined with sharp teeth about to take a bite out of his face. Steel flashed and the imp fell away, its talons leaving bloody rents in his sleeve.

Tanith had his sword in her hands and an expression of fierce concentration. *Too close for a fireball, sorry.*

The demons closed in again. As if drawn by his gift, dozens of them fluttered and scrambled along the walkway. Tanith could shield or fight, but not do both, and Gair didn't have enough control over the Song to help her. Like the angel he had seen once before, she raised the sword and blue flame wreathed the blade. Demon blood crisped and flaked off. Then the swarm was upon them.

Dimly, Gair felt exhausted Masters disengage from the shield. Lightning stalked across the yard. Fat raindrops burst on the stone around him with the sound of tiny thunderclaps, but where they struck his skin he barely felt them. Tanith had done her best, but already blood was streaming down her arm, and soon she wouldn't be able to lift the sword.

The shriek of a raptor pierced his skull, and red-gold feathers swept across his field of vision. The fire-eagle laid about with beak and talons, scattering pieces of imps everywhere. She was bright as the sun before him, magnificent and deadly. Yellow ichor spattered the stone walk, and yet each imp she tore apart was replaced. Some were in flight, dodging her powerful wings to dart in to scratch and bite. There was more red than gold in her plumage now, and panic rose inside Gair. He couldn't help her like this. Desperately he called upon the Song for more than he had ever dared to hold.

Wild-water music scoured through his consciousness and he held on by only his fingertips. It seared like flame, shimmered like the breath of winter. Every fibre of his body was bloated with it. This was that day on the road against Goran's Knights, magnified a thousandfold. But now he knew what to do.

Blue-white lightning arced from demon to demon and shattered skulls as if they were eggshells. Rain fell in silver sheets from the tormented sky, plastered his clothes to his skin and flashed into steam where it met the lightning.

But still more demons swarmed around Aysha, and golden feathers flew as black claws tore. Again and again she lunged with her beak, ripping, gouging, but too many imps clung to her and she staggered in flight with the weight of them on her back. There was a spray of blood, and her wings lost the wind. She screamed, just once, and brilliant colours brushed across his thoughts—

—and were gone.

Gair answered with a scream of his own, wordless, furious, despairing. The shield over Chapterhouse shuddered with his pain and flew into shards.

He didn't see where she fell. He couldn't see anything at all but vengeance, and as the storm broke he reached out for every last twist of wrongness he could feel. With the Song raging inside him demons were crushed by invisible hands and broken like twigs. Malformed bodies littered the walkways around Chapterhouse and strewed the fields outside.

Some scrambled for the safety of the luridly lit clouds, where the Gateway into their own world wavered on the brink of closing. None of them reached it in time.

In the harbour black ships crowded on sail and forged through the burning wreckage of the sandboats for the open sea. Gair reached for them too, but it was too far, and he was near the limits of his endurance. The most he could do was set fire to the stern flags and let the flames harry them north.

Too much. Finally, he slumped against the wall, spent. His hands were clenched so tightly on the stone coping that he couldn't feel his fingertips, though the fingers themselves screamed with cramp. Helping hands turned him around, but he had only one purpose now, and he stumbled away from them.

Gair found Aysha propped against the stairs from the parapet. Tanith was there; she had spread her Healer's mantle out like a blanket, so that he would not see. *Too late.* There was too much blood on the stone for him to be anything other than too late.

He knelt beside Aysha. Already her cinnamon skin was grey with her ghost. She breathed fast and shallow, eyes blue-black as bruises. Any tears were lost in the rain on her face.

'I'm here, *cariamh*,' he said. With a thought he spun a small shield to keep the rain off. He maintained his hold on the Song, to keep the nightmares at bay. 'What were you doing, charging in like that? You could have got yourself killed.'

'Had to do something, Leahn,' she whispered. 'The adepts were overrun.'

'And there I was thinking you came to save me.' Gair struggled to force breath past the crushing pain in his chest.

'Wouldn't waste my strength. You can take care of yourself.' She tried to laugh, but it came out as a sob. 'Goddess, that hurts!' Her hand seized his sleeve. Fingers knotted in the fabric, white as bones.

'Just rest a minute. Tanith's here to look after you.'

'There's nothing she can do for me now, you know that.'

'Nonsense, you'll be fine.' The inanities kept coming; he couldn't seem to stop them.

She shook her head, telling him no. 'Always loved you, Leahn. Never thought I'd be the first to go.'

'You're not going anywhere – I won't let you.' He dared a glance at Tanith. The helpless look she returned nearly broke him. 'Just rest, *cariamh*.'

'Is Chapterhouse safe?'

'I think so.'

'Good.' Another spasm of pain made her sob. 'Gair? Will you hold me? I'm cold.'

Thunder shook the sky. The storm swept over Chapterhouse in waves, but under the shield there was stillness. Carefully Gair slid

449

his arm around Aysha's shoulders and cradled her head against his neck.

'Better,' she sighed.

He pressed his lips to her forehead, glad she couldn't see his face. In a few seconds her breaths were shallower, her head drooping. Gently he lifted her chin and kissed her mouth, so that the last thing she felt would be something other than pain.

37

THE FORGE

'Gair?'

He opened his eyes. Masen's face swam into focus.

'It's over, Gair.'

'I know,' he rasped, 'I just need to rest for a while.'

Masen gave him a look that said he understood, then strode away. Though the storm had eased to a grumble, it was still raining. Water streamed over the walls, sluicing away the blood and char, washing Chapterhouse clean. Green mantles were busy in the yard where too many small bodies lay broken.

Gair wanted to close his eyes again, but Tanith had spoken and he had to focus on her face. Tears and shadows haunted her gaze. She was apologising, kneeling in a puddle, her dress stained with blood and muck. Her hands implored him to understand that it had happened too fast and she had reached Aysha too late.

'You did what you could, Tanith,' he told her gently. 'Go and help the others.'

A tear spilled over her lashes and cut a trail through the grime on her face. 'If I'd been quicker I could have saved her. There were just too many of them and they were—'

'I know.' He didn't want to hear it said.

'Please forgive me.'

'There's nothing to forgive.' He managed a smile for her, Goddess knew how, with the knowledge of what lay under the green mantle. Aysha's head rested on his neck like the weight of the world. 'Go on. Have Saaron take a look at your arm, then help the others.'

'What about the shield?'

Inside his head there was only quiet, and a sense of something held back. He could not detect what it was. He touched the Song, but grief threaded it with a lament. 'I seem to have put it back.' She looked shocked. 'That's impossible!'

Gair felt her gather the Song as she reached out to him, but he leaned away. 'Go to Saaron, Tanith. Please. You're bleeding. This will keep for a while.'

She let her hand fall and got slowly to her feet. Dripping corkscrews of red hair framed her face. The stricken look in her eyes was more than he could bear. It was a relief when she turned away.

When she'd gone, Gair closed the shield around him and locked out sound. The storm became a murmur. People passed silently, floating through the silvery veils of rain. Safe inside, he cradled Aysha against him and closed her beautiful eyes.

❧

It took the better part of four days to make everything ready. The infirmary overflowed, and the chapel vaults were turned into a mortuary for the bodies. Men came up from Pencruik with axes and saws to cut timber for the burning. Some brought their wives to help in the infirmary, older women for the most part, for whom the washing and wrapping of the dead held no fears.

On the rise that overlooked the harbour the sheep-cropped turf was turned back in a huge circle and wagons rumbled back and forth, feeding the growing pyres. Even from up on the fifth-floor balcony Gair could smell the new wood. Overlaying the scent of pitch pine and sap was the sharp-sweet spiced oil that would mask the smell of burning flesh.

It would be a fine day. Winter still had the islands in its grip, but that grip was less sure in the sunshine, and the pastures sparkled as if sown with diamonds. Soon new grass would push through the yellowed thatch of the old; the buds on the trees had already begun to swell. Such an irony, then, that Chapterhouse should be giving up its dead when all around it new life emerged.

Gair looked down at the glass in his hand. A glorious example of Isles glasscraft, the base and stem were deepest purple that shaded through amethyst to silver at the rim. Less than an inch of brandy remained in the goblet, but it overflowed with memories: walking through the market in Pensaeca Port to buy her Eventide gift, with Aysha riding on his shoulder as a goshawk and hooting with amusement only he could hear when the merchant boxing his purchase enquired diffidently if that magnificent bird might be for sale. Mulling wine as winter winds moaned in the chimney. Mending the glass she'd smashed in a fit of temper when they'd fought over something foolish, then marvelling how she could always pick out that one from the set, even though they all looked the same. She'd said she could feel his weaving of the Song. It had become her favourite. It was the one in his hand now.

He drained the glass, the heavy spirit trickling down to heat his stomach. That was the last of it; the decanter was empty, for all the good it had done. He wished he could have swallowed the recollections with that final mouthful, but they were still there, and they peopled the void inside him with ghosts.

When Gair turned to come back inside he saw Alderan at the door, one hand on the latch. He hadn't wanted to be disturbed, but it had had to happen eventually – and today, if no other day. At least he'd had a chance to wash and shave. He set the glass down on the desk.

Alderan's expression did not flicker as he took in Gair's

appearance, and noted the fine blue wool that hung from shoulders to heels.

'It looks well on you, lad,' he said at last.

'I thought she might appreciate it.'

'I'm sure she would.'

Gair straightened the edges of the fabric over his chest, though they didn't need it. The cut was perfect.

'Did you know?'

'I did. You hadn't earned it when she gave it to you, though we could all see your potential. You have a remarkable gift. Now it's yours by right.'

Gair dipped his head, just once. He wasn't wearing the mantle for himself.

'Did you find out anything?'

'A little. Donata's mind was taken over and her gift subsumed. That was what Savin used to hold the Gateway open. An illusion of her colours was left in the weaving to disguise what he was up to, to buy himself some time.' Alderan sighed and looked suddenly weary. 'There's too much we don't know how to do, too much knowledge lost to us. I'd hoped to be better prepared before we had to face him again.'

'And Darin?'

'Darin was his cat's-paw. Savin could never come at us directly because of the wards, so he sent an agent. It was sheer blind bad luck that Darin was the one he gave the token to.'

'Token?'

'He was holding it in his fist when we found him. A crystal, cut and polished to resemble a gemstone. It probably had a glamour woven around it to ensure Darin kept it close by. Savin tied strings to him through it. I'm sure you can work out the rest.'

Guilt wrenched at Gair's heart. 'Darin was going to have the stone set into a ring for Renna. A betrothal ring. He asked me to stand as his second.'

'Gair, I am so sorry. I know he was your friend.'

454

And I was too wrapped up in myself to see what was happening. The knight's move, the one that comes at you sideways, from the angle you least expect. He looked away. It was some time before he trusted himself to speak.

'At least he never woke up.'

'No, that's one thing we can be thankful for, I suppose. Once Savin took control, I think Darin only knew what was happening for a very short time. When the shield was taken down, his body was alive, but the spark that made it a person was gone. His heart stopped the following day.'

Gair flinched. He would miss the Belisthan's ready laughter, his mischievous sense of fun. Darin had been the first friend he'd made at Chapterhouse; it had been like having a brother. He was surprised how much it hurt, surprised he could still feel that much hurt after what he had seen. He'd thought he was numb to it.

'You were right, Alderan,' he said abruptly. 'About Savin. He sees everything as a tool towards his ends, even other people. They're just pieces on a chessboard, to be sacrificed when expedient.'

'That's one thing I wish I could have been wrong about.' The old man grimaced. 'It would have spared us all an ocean of pain.'

'How many did we lose?'

'In all, twenty-four. Nine adepts, including Darin. Eleven apprentices. Brendan, Tivor, Donata.'

'And Aysha.'

'And Aysha.'

He hadn't said her name out loud since it happened. For an instant she was there in the room, watching him from the couch; the scent of her skin was in his nostrils and her colours danced through his mind. He shut his eyes tightly. Still he saw the other images: dark blood, torn flesh – the other thing all those bottles of brandy had not been enough to drown. Gair opened his eyes and found his hands clenched into fists at his sides.

'I'll see him burn for this. By the Goddess, I'll set the torch myself.' It came out as a growl.

Alderan said nothing, but watched him with sorrow in his eyes.

'He killed *children*.' Gair's chest tightened, his voice choked by the weight of everything he had suppressed. 'Little boys and girls no higher than this, who could barely light a candle with their talent. He brought demons and he let them kill children.' *And her. Holy Mother, please, take care of her for me. Take care of them all.* 'He killed my friends, twenty-four people who had never harmed him, never raised a hand against him. I won't let him get away with that. I can't. I will see him broken.'

Strong hands gripped his arms. Alderan's voice was low and fierce. 'Gair, I know you're hurting. You want to see Savin punished, and so do I. I understand, believe me. He took someone from me too, and I mean to call him to account for that, as well as for what was done here. But not today, lad. Not today.' He tightened his grip briefly, enough to force Gair to look at him. 'All things in their season, Gair. There will be a reckoning, I have no doubt of it, but today we've got other things to do.'

Alderan was right.

'I can't begin to tell you how sorry I am,' the old man said.

Gair couldn't speak yet; Alderan embraced him firmly and he hugged back as hard. There was some comfort in that simple gesture, and he clung to it.

'I miss her.'

'I miss her too.'

It was lame, inadequate, too small. Those three words could not do her justice, nor could they begin to express the yawning sense of loss. Tears threatened, and his face twisted up as he fought to keep them at bay.

'I miss her too. We did not always see eye to eye, Aysha and I, but I respected her enormously. You were good for her, I think.'

'I thought you didn't approve.'

'We don't have many rules at Chapterhouse and that was one of them, it's true. But such things rarely wait for approval from mere mortals. You had the Goddess' blessing, the pair of you, and there is no higher power.'

Steadier now, Gair straightened up and took a deep breath. 'Thank you.' Another deep breath. He ran his hand over his hair and checked the silver *zirin* at his nape was still secure. He wiped his eyes, just in case, and forced the memories back behind the walls he had constructed.

'Ready?' the old man asked.

'As I'll ever be.'

Alderan's mouth twitched into a small smile, fond but also sad.

'Let's go and say our farewells, eh?'

Chapterhouse held its breath as they walked through it. There should have been clattering feet, banging doors, the hive-like hum of busyness that usually filled the place, but their feet made the only sound. Stairwells, cloisters, even the main yard stood empty and still. Out through the gates they went, and climbed the rise with its view of the home farm and the road down to Pencruik. Pensaeca Sound shimmered like pewter, whipped into whitecaps by the wind. Overhead, high, thin cloud veiled a pale sky.

The entire population of Chapterhouse was arranged in a loose circle around the three pyres. Staff wore their everyday clothes, Masters and adepts their mantles, which were snapping in the boisterous breeze. Every face was solemn; even the smallest children, peering shyly round their parents' legs, knew something important was happening and kept silent. Gair and Alderan made their way to the head of the circle, where a brazier flamed.

Verenas, the chaplain, waited for them, snowy vestments billowing and the Book of Eador in his hands.

Each pyre was as tall as a man and gleamed with oil. On top, the linen-wrapped bodies were anonymous as cords of wood. Which was hers? Gair had no way to tell. The shrouds gave no clue even which were men and which women, though the smaller forms of the children were distressingly easy to pick out.

As Verenas recited the service for the dead, Gair hardly listened.

He chanted the responses with the rest of the mourners, knelt to receive the benediction, but his thoughts were elsewhere. In his mind he rode the sky above, felt the crisp air thrum through his feathers as he soared, and another eagle echoed his every move.

When the last amen faded, Alderan held a torch to the brazier. It took a moment to catch as the restless flames snapped back and forth. Then the old man turned and offered the torch to Gair.

He fixed Aysha's colours in his mind, vibrant as a stained-glass chapel window with the sun behind it. Close to the pyres, the air was heady with spiced oil; that much sappy young wood needed help to ignite, so they'd had to use a lot. It filled his lungs and made it so hard to breathe.

Go with the Goddess, carianh.

Then he put the torch to the pyre. In moments the flames roared into the air and heat struck his face like a blow.

Carianh. Beloved. He wished he'd said it more often. He should have told her every time the word sounded in his heart – when she'd read Gimraeli poetry to him by firelight, when they had lain together in silence with her fingers twined in his. Every single time.

Sparks fountained up, spiralling around the column of flame. Gair spread his arms and drew on the Song. The melody came from somewhere beyond the white heat of a furnace, keen as the edge of a blade. It was the sound of heaven's own smithy, in which the stars were forged. Flecks of silver appeared in the inferno before him, then spread to the pyres on either side. Gradually argent replaced the orange and gold, then the silver turned steely, became blue.

Now the heat drove him back, a pace at a time, but he continued to call the Song. He would make the flame as pure as he could, to let Chapterhouse's dead be carried heavenwards on it without the taint of smoke and ash. It was all he could do for them now, for her.

Finally, he allowed his tears to fall.

458

Tanith watched from a distance, wrapped in her cloak. She hadn't seen the Leahn since that day. He hadn't opened his door to her, or anyone else, and she'd been reluctant to intrude on his grief, however much Healing she was sure he needed. He seemed whole enough, dressed in clean clothes, his hair neatly combed, but it was the eyes that betrayed him, grey as flints and remote as the northern sea. His control of the Song was as sure as ever, though she still had no idea how he'd managed to shield himself from the damage Savin had done to his mind. She had seen that for herself, and the memory was enough to make her shudder. One day, she feared, Gair would fly apart under the strain.

If only she could have reached Aysha in time, she could have saved her, and spared him this pain. But time could not be spooled backwards like a bobbin of yarn, and what was done was done. She rubbed the fresh scar that ran down her forearm. She would always wear it, no matter how many times it was Healed. That was her reminder of her failure. She should have tried harder. She would have stood in front of the demons and let them devour her instead, if it could have prevented the wound Gair had taken to his heart.

Tanith closed her eyes to stop the prickle turning into tears.

'A strange ritual,' said K'shaa at her shoulder. 'We give our dead to the sea, not to fire.'

She opened her eyes again and quoted the sea-elf burial ceremony in a voice that only trembled a tiny bit.

'"We are born of water, and to water we return. Let our sea-brother be taken by the water and carried home to the Mother until the tide brings him back to us once more."'

K'shaa inclined his head, long braids stirring in the breeze. 'Well spoken. Tell me, do you always do this?' A crook of his fingers took in the blue flames that coruscated skywards.

'No. I've never seen this before. I think it is something new.'

'I have seen many new things of late,' the sea-elf said. His voice lilted with regret and not a little disapproval. 'Much is changing,' Tanith folded her arms deeper inside her cloak, suddenly chilled.

'Do your people read the future, K'shaa?' she asked. 'Do you see signs and portents in the heavens, hear rumours on the wind?'

He cocked his head and regarded her with tilted eyes. 'I hear storms coming,' he said. 'I smell the lightning in the womb of the clouds and read the waves. Those are the only portents I know.'

She watched Gair, bathed in the light of the pyres. His eyes were closed now, and tears shone silver as they coursed down his face. *So much pain in there – how does he bear it?*

'I hear the storms too,' she replied. 'I fear the one coming may be the end of us all.'

EPILOGUE

❧

One. White light ran down the sword-blade as Gair swung on his heel. *Two.* Steel on steel, spitting sparks into the dirt. *Step into the space, roll wrists. Three. Shift weight, balance, reverse the thrust.* Sorchal danced away with inches to spare. *Turn again. Two-handed grip to meet Arlin's lunge.* Cross-guards locked, the two blades framed the Tylan's face. Momentum powered Gair's arms up, sending Arlin's sword skittering away. *Turn.* The sword hammered down overarm and broke Sorchal's grip. Gair took two quick steps to face Arlin again. *Charging in. Sloppy.* He met the Tylan with his shoulder, pinned his arm and twisted the sword out of his hand. It thudded into the dust. *And done.*

Arlin scowled and shoved him away. Gair grabbed his wrist, whipped the Tylan over his shoulder and sent him crashing onto the ground on his back.

'Nicely done,' said Sorchal, wiping his arm across his sweaty brow.

Gair shook his head. 'Still too slow.' There was too long between each blow and counter-blow, too much time in which everything could change. A heartbeat was an eternity between two swords. He had to be faster. 'One more time?'

Sorchal sighed. 'One more time.'

Panting, Arlin rolled onto his elbow and sat up. His sweat-damp whites were caked in dust. Gair offered a hand to help him up. The Tylan glowered at it, lip curled.

'Why do you do this?' He spat dust from his mouth, the spittle just missing Gair's bare feet. 'Ask me here every day?'

'You're the best sword at Chapterhouse,' Gair said, arm still outstretched. Finally Arlin took it and Gair pulled him to his feet. He retrieved his sword, wiping the dusty blade on the leg of his whites.

'You know I don't like you, Leahn.'

'You don't have to like me. Just fight me. Ready?'

Arlin snarled. 'Always.'

❧

'Goddess, I'm getting too old to be matching blades with bucks like him.' Haral mopped his face with the towel slung round his neck and dropped onto the bench next to Alderan.

Alderan grunted, but did not look round from watching the yard below. Three swordsmen clashed, whirled, broke and clashed again. Sunlight sparked off their blades as steel rang on steel in the still spring air.

'How long today?' he asked.

'Three, three and a half hours. About the same as yesterday.' And the day before, and the one before that, every day since the funeral. A worm of worry gnawed its way a little deeper into Alderan's heart.

'He makes it look like dancing.'

'He does at that. Not the best I've ever seen, but, sweet saints, he's close. More than a match for anyone here.'

'He needs rest. Time to grieve.'

'Maybe this is how he chooses to deal with it.'

'Maybe. *I wish he'd weep, or howl, or drink himself insensible. Do something human, anything but this relentless focus.*'

Haral's hand clapped his shoulder. 'We all find our own way

through loss, Alderan,' he said gruffly. 'You had your way, I had mine, when it was my turn. Gair has his.'

He stood, and Alderan looked up at the stocky Syfrian.

'You know what he's doing, don't you?' *Turning himself into a weapon, honing himself like steel on a stone. A weapon with only one purpose.*

'Aye, I know.'

'It's dangerous.'

'He's young, Alderan, young and hurt.'

'I don't like it.'

'He'll survive.' Haral shaded his eyes, watching the Leahn move between his opponents, and murmured, 'Though I pity whoever gets kissed by that sword.'

'He's not healed yet. Savin will kill him without batting an eye.'

'You don't know that for sure. You told me what Gair did with the shield, how he took it all on by himself. He can stand toe to toe with that bastard, don't you worry.'

But I am worried, more than I've been for him since the reiving.

As Haral walked away, Alderan turned back to the duel in the yard below and worried a little bit more.

❧

The carter handed Tanith down onto the cobbled wharf, then blushed like a sunset under his scruffy felt hat when she kissed him on each cheek. He chirruped up his mules and clattered back into Pencruik, waving over his shoulder. She waved back until he was out of sight.

And so it was over. Her last contact with Chapterhouse vanished into the bustle of the dockside and she could put off her departure no longer. She'd waited as long as she could, but the *Morning Star* had to be away on the tide, and so did she. Stevedores bustled past her, hefting bales and rolling barrels to the stores tender moored further along the dock, their feet slapping on the cobbles. Only a few water-casks remained; one more trip and the *Star* would be fully provisioned and ready to go. Even as she watched, a launch pushed off from the sea-elf ship out in the bay and began rowing in, oars rising and falling like the legs of some water-beetle.

In spite of the blue skies, the breeze off the harbour was chilly. Drawing her coat more closely round her, she turned towards the sea-ladder to wait for the launch. Next to it stood Gair. Arms folded, Master's mantle stirring round his boots, he watched her approach, his face as closed as it had been since that terrible day. Then he laid his hand over his heart and bowed deeply enough for his hair to fall forward over his shoulder.

'My lady Elindorien.'

'My secret is out, it seems.'

He straightened up. 'Alderan told me. I had no idea you were a Daughter of the White Court.'

'That title doesn't mean anything outside of Astolar, you know. Here on the Isles I'm just a Healer. That's all I've ever wanted to be. Please don't bow to me.'

'Not even when you are Queen?'

'Especially not then, not unless the whole Court is watching.' *I can't bear to see you bowing to me.* 'Promise me you won't bow.'

His mouth turned up a little at the corners, but there was no smile in his eyes. 'I promise.'

'I didn't want to leave without saying goodbye, but I couldn't find you.' There had been no trace of his colours, not in the library or the refectory, the practice yards, his study. Well guarded or absent, it had made no nevermind; no one had known where to find him, not even Sorchal.

'I was up and out early today. Sorry.' Grey eyes flicked away, off over the purple rooftops of Pencruik to the blue-white mountains beyond. They came back to her face, then slipped away again, down to her necklace. He reached out a finger to the delicate glass flowers.

464

'That's pretty.'

'A farewell gift from my students. There're earrings to match, see? She held her hair away from her ear to show him.

'They are going to miss you.'

'I'll miss them, too. I've really enjoyed teaching here.' She stopped herself. What was she saying? Nothing – stupid, empty words, noise to fill up the space between them, not what needed to be said. Not what she wanted to hear. She touched Gair's arm.

'Will you be all right?'

'Probably.'

'The shield?'

'It's holding.' He took her hands in his. 'Don't worry about me, Tanith. I'll be fine. You've got more important matters to think about now, being High Seat of your House. The White Court.'

Feet clattered on the sea-ladder and K'shaa stuck his head over the edge of the dock. Sea-coloured eyes glanced from one to the other; his expression remained neutral.

'We leave on the tide, my lady.'

'Thank you, K'shaa. I won't be long.' For a wonder, her voice was steady, but her heart was dancing a reel. She turned back to Gair and he kissed her hands.

'Good luck and Goddess speed you.' He made to turn away, but she seized his arm. Spirits, he was tense as a horse about to shy.

'Wait. Please.' On an impulse she hugged him. 'I'll miss you.'

A second or two passed before he returned the embrace. She was pressed close, close enough to smell his scent of leather and steel, a fresh shirt and the musk of warm skin beneath. *Spirits keep me, I can't bear this.*

'Thank you, Tanith. For everything. I know you helped her when—' He broke off, swallowed hard. 'When she needed you.'

'I wish I could have done more. I am so, so sorry.'

He let her go, looking away again, eyes too clouded to read. 'You did everything you could. Take care,' he said, and brushed her cheek with a kiss.

465

Turning her face into it, her lips caught the corner of his mouth. Not much, but enough. It had to be enough. 'Remember these.' She touched his colours with her own, rosy and golden as the dawn, beaded with jade.

'I will.'

A scrape of foot on ladder-rung reminded her K'shaa was still waiting. It was time to go. She took a step towards the sea-ladder, then turned back.

'What will you do now? Where will you go?'

'I'll find him, and then I'll make him pay for what he did here.'

'Don't put yourself in harm's way, Gair.'

A half-smile quirked his lips. 'Too late.'

Then he strode away along the dock. She felt him reach for the Song and his shape blurred into a fire-eagle, stroking up into the air. It flared its wings, swooped past her, close enough to stir her hair around her face, then it was gone, vanishing into the bright sky, far out of her reach.

She had to let him go. He was not for her, and never had been. Only time and distance would persuade her stubborn heart otherwise. Tanith turned around and jogged elbows with a man walking past.

'Oh! Forgive me, sir,' she said, stepping backwards out of his path.

Swinmmy blue eyes met hers and sharpened. Then he smiled and the sharpness was gone. 'My fault. I'm still skewed from the boat.' He hitched his bundle up on his shoulder. 'Can you recommend a good inn here in town?'

'The Red Dragon is popular.' She pointed. 'Up that street and across the square; you can't miss it.'

The man smiled his thanks and set off up the street.

Tanith swung herself onto the sea-ladder and climbed down to where K'shaa waited in the *Star*'s launch.

'Time to go home, K'shaa,' she said. The sea-elf handed her into the boat, and nodded to his coxswain, who whistled the port-side oarsmen to pole off from the quay. She watched the distant chaser riding the swells at the limit of her anchor-chain, a racehorse tugging at her reins. It was past time to go.

The End

The story continues in *Trinity Moon*,
Book Two of the Wild Hunt

ACKNOWLEDGEMENTS

On the long road to publication, it has been my privilege to connect with fellow writers all over the world and share their stories. Several of them, like Debbie Bennett, have become very good friends. My heartfelt thanks go out to two in particular, Greta van der Rol and N. Gemini Sasson, whose boundless patience and enthusiasm helped me make it to the finish line.

Of course, this book wouldn't be here at all without my agent, Ian Drury, and my wise and wonderful publisher Jo Fletcher and the team at Gollancz. It's been an amazing ride so far; let's hope it continues for a very long time.

But most of all I must thank my husband Rob, who when I had lost all faith in myself, believed in me enough for both of us.

THE CULTURE OF ANCIENT INDIA

DISCARD

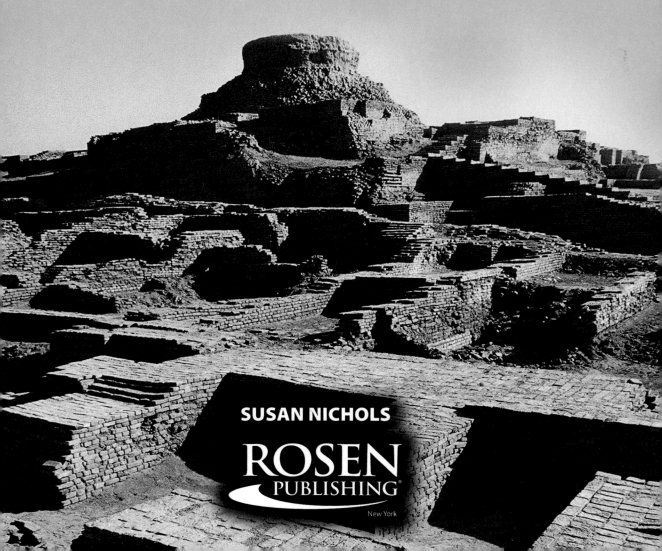

SUSAN NICHOLS

ROSEN
PUBLISHING®

New York

Published in 2017 by The Rosen Publishing Group, Inc.
29 East 21st Street, New York, NY 10010

Copyright © 2017 by The Rosen Publishing Group, Inc.

First Edition

Library of Congress CataloginginPublication Data

Names: Nichols, Susan, 1975-
Title: The culture of ancient India / Susan Nichols.
Description: First edition. | New York : Rosen Publishing, 2017. | Series: Spotlight on the rise and fall of ancient civilizations | Includes bibliographical references and index.
Identifiers: LCCN 2016000817| ISBN 9781477789209 (library bound) | ISBN 9781477789186 (paperback) | ISBN 9781477789193 (6-pack)
Subjects: LCSH: India--Civilization--To 1200--Juvenile literature. | India--History--To 324 B.C.--Juvenile literature. | India--History--324 B.C.-1000 A.D.--Juvenile literature.
Classification: LCC DS425 .N53 2017 | DDC 934--dc23
LC record available at http://lccn.loc.gov/2016000817

Manufactured in the United States of America

ANCIENT VS. MODERN INDIA

India has fascinated Western people for centuries. Some Western writers—Hermann Hesse, Rudyard Kipling, E. M. Forster, Frances Hodgson Burnett, and Ruth Prawar Jhabvala—use India for their settings and explore its history and culture as themes.

Although the urge to explore Indian culture is genuine, many works have confused ancient and modern India. Modern India has only had distinct borders since 1947, while ancient India covered far more territory, including what is now Pakistan, Bangladesh, Sri Lanka, and parts of Afghanistan and Iran.

However, modern India is founded on ancient India's rich history, during which two of the world's most important religions were established: Hinduism and Buddhism. The people who lived in the various regions of ancient India also developed their own languages, many of which are still in use by Indians today. These include Hindi, Sanskrit, Tamil, Urdu, Malayalam, and many others. In fact, there are more than 780 languages spoken in India today.

Modern India is composed of many religions and ethnic groups, each with a distinct culture and language. These cultures trace back to ancient civilizations.

INDUS VALLEY CIVILIZATION

Civilization is a way in which humans organize themselves into societies or communities. Before people were civilized, they were nomads. They traveled in groups, and they hunted for their food. When most of the animals in an area had been killed, the nomads traveled to a new area.

What made people decide to give up their nomadic life and stay in one location? The answer is that they stayed where they would be guaranteed a steady supply of food.

India's first major civilization was the Indus Valley civilization, in which people settled in the valleys close to the Indus River around 7000 BCE. Like most early civilizations, the Indus Valley people made sure they had access to water for farming and growing food.

The 2,000 mile (3,219 kilometer)-long Indus River, one of the longest in the world, empties into the Arabian Sea. It gave people more than just food—it also gave India its name.

This illustration of the ancient Indus Valley shows how people built their towns and cities close to the mighty Indus River.

FOUR LAYERS OF MOHENJODARO

Most people in the Indus Valley lived on farms, but around 7000 BCE, two great cities emerged: Mohenjodaro and Harappa.

Even though Mohenjodaro means "mound of the dead," approximately thirty-five thousand people lived there during four periods of ancient history. Archaeologists know this because they found four layers to the city as they excavated it, or dug it up. Mohenjodaro's center featured a large building, which may have been used to store grains.

Most houses were organized around the city's center and made of mud bricks. Most were two stories high but had an open courtyard in their centers. The roofs of the houses were wide and flat and used for cooking in the open air.

Mohenjodaro had an efficient sewer system that allowed dirty water to be removed from houses and shops. The citizens dug almost seven hundred wells, which allowed freshwater to be pulled from the ground for daily cleaning and cooking.

Mohenjodaro, one of the largest cities in the ancient Indus Valley civilization, is one of the oldest cities in world history. Parts of the city remain today.

HARAPPA, JEWEL OF THE INDUS VALLEY PEOPLE

Harappa has come to represent the Indus Valley civilization so much that many historians refer to it as the Harappan civilization. It was discovered in the early 1920s by British archaeologists.

Like Mohenjodaro, Harappan homes were lined up neatly in a grid pattern around a large central building. They were constructed of mud bricks. These thick walls provided good insulation, keeping the homes warm during the colder months and cool during the warm months.

Keeping their homes clean was an important aspect of the Indus Valley culture. Good hygiene helps control the spread of diseases. Most houses had baths and indoor toilets, which made these homes very comfortable for their inhabitants.

Life in the city was very sophisticated. It was a bustling, busy place, home to thousands of people. There were shops and businesses belonging to blacksmiths, carpenters, and other skilled workers. Some craftsmen included bead makers, who sculpted and glazed beads—called faïence—from stones.

Indus Valley cities were designed to be clean and hygienic. The covered sewer drain seen here shows how advanced the plumbing system was in Harappa.

ECONOMY OF THE INDUS VALLEY

Archaeologists have excavated many clues about the economy of the Indus Valley people—pottery, faïence beads, seals, jewelry—and concluded that they were manufacturers who created products from stone, glass, and some metals, such as copper.

They were also a trading people. They had a vibrant economy, in which they traded goods with other cultures, connecting with them through the use of boats.

They traveled far and wide across the ancient world to trade their products. In fact, archaeologists had known for years that the ancient Sumerians and Egyptians had had a wealthy trading partner. Eventually, they realized that coins found there could be traced back to Harappa and Mohenjodaro.

They also built their cities to last, showing that they valued good engineering and architecture. The Indus Valley cities depended on the Indus River for fertile soil and as a connection or route to other settlements, but they also knew the dangers of flooding and built citadels that protected their cities from the raging waters.

This children's toy, found in the Indus Valley city of Mohenjodaro, was shaped from terra-cotta; it portrays a goat with wheels.

THE RELIGION AND CULTURE OF THE INDUS VALLEY

One of the mysteries of the Indus Valley people is their religion. There is no evidence of temples or other sacred sites in the ruins unearthed by archaeologists. Did they have a belief in a deity or system of deities? This is difficult to know.

However, it is certain that their culture was rich and vibrant. They had stringed musical instruments to produce music. Also, the Indus Valley artisans left behind many statues depicting realistic human figures. One famous sculpture is called the Dancing Girl of Mohenjo-Daro.

The Indus Valley people created a written language that has come to be known as Indus Script. It is the oldest form of writing that has been discovered in India. Unfortunately, historians are still unable to decipher the language's system of symbols and markings.

The Indus Valley civilization's decline is also a mystery. The culture seems to have been ended by a massive flood around 1300 BCE.

Art flourished in the ancient Indus Valley. The Dancing Girl sculpture, found in Mohenjodaro, tells us that art was an important part of life in ancient India.

THE RISE OF THE MAURYA DYNASTY

The Indus Valley civilization faded, most likely due to a major flood that destroyed its cities. It is also possible that their trade-based economy failed. The civilization did not disappear all at once, but gradually declined as cities were abandoned and production of goods stopped. Other civilizations continued to grow and develop in the region of the Indus River and in other parts of the subcontinent, but nothing so great as the Indus Valley civilization.

By 321 BCE, however, there were signs of a new empire emerging. Its leader, the great Chandragupta Maurya, who demonstrated great prowess and strength, had humble beginnings. An orphan, he was raised by Kautilya, a wealthy politician. Some sources say he was actually sold to the politician as an apprentice or servant. However Chandragupta met Kautilya, the relationship improved his life. Kautilya taught him the art of war and military strategy. Eventually, Chandragupta raised an army, defeated the current leadership, and seized power.

This painting portrays the first Maurya emperor, Chandragupta, (*right*) and one of his advisors, Chankaya.

THE DEATH OF CHANDRAGUPTA

Chandragupta Maurya overcame attempts to remove him from power by having a band of spies throughout the region. The Greek army, led by Alexander the Great, had sought to control the Indian subcontinent for years, and now, even after Alexander's death, they attempted to attack India again. However, Chandragupta defended his land. His empire, now known as the Maurya dynasty, unified greater India under one leader for the first time.

Toward the end of his life, Chandragupta became a follower of the religion known as Jainism. He also became saddened by the starvation in his empire, and he handed over the reigns of the empire to his son. In 297 BC, he traveled to a cave in Shravanabelogola, where he spent five weeks meditating and fasting. According to legends, that is where he died.

His son, Bindusara Maurya, worked busily to expand his father's empire. He became the father of the next king—the great Ashoka.

According to many accounts, Chandragupta Maurya died after several weeks of fasting in the Bhadrabahu Cave, in Karnataka, India.

A CHANGE OF HEART FOR ASHOKA

Ashoka was a vicious ruler. Legends were told about his brutality. One story claimed that he had killed his brothers in order to succeed his father. He had people put to death on a whim.

During his reign, Ashoka ordered his army to invade the city of Kalinga, which resulted in the deaths of more than one hundred thousand people. Soon, another legend emerged about Ashoka: according to the story, the terrible suffering Ashoka had inflicted on the citizens of Kalinga devastated him. Not only had so many died, but their city had been nearly destroyed. For the first time, Ashoka regretted the violence he had caused.

As a result, he had a tremendous change of heart—one that would have an impact on the entire Indian subcontinent. He converted to a new religion known as Buddhism, which had emerged around 500 BCE but had not been adopted widely.

The Dhauli Girl Shanti Stupa, a peace pagoda in Orissa, India, depicts the emperor Ashoka being moved to follow the teachings of the Buddha.

THE EDICTS OF ASHOKA

Now, thanks to Ashoka, many people in the Mauryan Empire became Buddhists because it was the religion of their king. Perhaps they had begun to see what a positive impact it had on him. Previously a cruel leader, Ashoka was now a man of peace.

Ashoka changed many aspects of life in the Mauryan Empire. He put new laws into place. These laws, or edicts, were carved into stone and displayed on rocks and pillars throughout the land. Known as the Rock Edicts and the Pillar Edicts, they spread the new message of Ashoka's reign: peace and nonviolence.

One such edict explained the concept of dharma:

There is no gift comparable to the gift of dharma … And this is: good behavior toward slaves and servants, obedience to mother and father, generosity toward friends, acquaintances, and relatives … and abstention from killing living beings.

This is one of several pillars that bears the Edicts of Ashoka; it was originally located in Haryana but was brought to the city of Delhi.

BUDDHISM

Approximately five hundred million people practice Buddhism today, although most live in China and Southeast Asia. Why did Buddhism appeal to Ashoka? What transformed a murderous king into a benevolent leader?

Buddhism specifies what actions humans must take to improve their lives. Buddhists believe that because humans often fail to improve, they will continue to be reborn into new forms after death. This cycle of birth and rebirth will continue until it is broken by achieving nirvana.

Perhaps Ashoka realized that his actions were causing more suffering, and he hoped that teaching Buddhist ideas would help others begin their journeys on the Noble Eightfold Path, which includes three parts:

Wisdom, which can be attained by having right view and right intention;

Ethical conduct, which can be attained by practicing right speech, right action, and right livelihood; and

Concentration, which can be attained by striving for right effort, right mindfulness, and right concentration.

This depiction of the Buddha was painted on a cave wall in Maharashtra, India.

ACHIEVEMENTS OF THE MAURYA

The Maurya Empire grew steadily and soon covered a vast amount of territory, protected by a mighty military. The Mauryan emperors controlled and funded one of the world's largest armies at that time: six hundred thousand infantry, thirty thousand cavalry, and nine thousand war elephants!

The empire was also united by a strong central government. Chandragupta had established a capital at the city of Pataliputra. The empire was divided into four sections, each with its own head of government, known as the kumara. The kumara had a council of ministers who aided him in decision making. The kumara of each province reported to the emperor. The emperor had his own council of advisors, known as the Mantriparishad.

The empire's strength was also due to its wealth. The Mauryans were skilled producers and traders, and they utilized the Silk Road. Over 6,000 miles (9,656 km) long, this network of roads connected Asia to Africa, the Middle East, and the West.

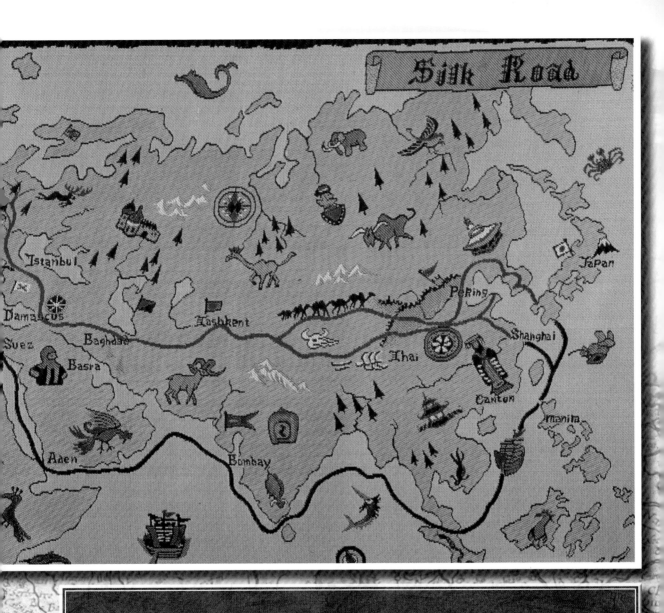

The Silk Road was actually not one road, but a series of ancient highways that connected Asia to Europe. It was a system that linked people and cultures.

MAURYAN LITERATURE AND ART

One of the most widely spoken languages in the Indian subcontinent was Sanskrit. At first, Sanskrit was a spoken language only. But then a script called Brahmi—originally created to serve another language, Prakrit—was applied to it. This gave Sanskrit a written form. Kautilya, who had raised Chandragupta and who had been appointed his chief advisor, wrote a book in Sanskrit, the *Arthashastra*, which was a guide about seizing and maintaining political power.

Ashoka's edicts were mostly carved in Sanskrit on pillars throughout the empire, although some were carved in Greek and some in other Indian languages as part of the mission to convert people to Buddhism. Missionaries traveled the Silk Road to spread the message of Buddhism. The idea was that Ashoka's edicts would be spread.

Many of his pillars were also remarkable for their artwork. The symbol of modern India is the lion, which appears atop many of Ashoka's most famous pillars.

During his reign, Ashoka was represented as a lion, which is the state symbol of modern India. The triple lion tops one of his great pillars.

THE GUPTA DYNASTY EMERGES

A shoka died in 232 BCE, and one of his successors was murdered in 185 BCE. The strong central government that he, his father, and his grandfather had cemented began to crumble.

The large provinces of the empire began to take on more control over their territories, and they developed into their own small kingdoms. Therefore, over the next several centuries, each established its own dynasty—a line of leaders or kings, language, and culture.

Around 320 CE, a strong and powerful dynasty emerged. Chandragupta, a local king, already ruled over a collection of smaller states when he decided to marry a princess from the ruling family of another region. Uniting their two families made Chandragupta the powerful ruler of a very large portion of the Ganges region. It became clear that Chandragupta wanted to unite India, which had been fragmented for centuries. However, it would be his son, Samudragupta, who would actually build this empire and make unification a reality.

A gold coin, dated from the fourth century CE, depicts King Samudragupta, a great leader of the Gupta dynasty.

CONQUESTS OF SAMUDRAGUPTA

Samudragupta ascended to the throne in 335 CE and put his plan into motion almost immediately. It is possible that he wanted to recreate an empire like that of the Mauryans. At least one of Ashoka's great pillars is said to have been seized and reinscribed with Samudragupta's name to make it appear that he had issued these edicts.

Samudragupta was a talented and fierce military leader. He began conquering other independent states and adding them to the growing Gupta Empire.

An empire is expensive to maintain, however, and so he forced the kings of some states to pay him fees on a regular basis to allow them to stay in power. This is called tribute. The system allowed some kings to stay on their thrones rather than be swallowed by the Guptas.

Samudragupta's son was named Chandragupta II after his grandfather. His vision for the empire was the most ambitious of all.

One of the Gupta dynasty's most influential leaders was Chandragupta II, who conquered many new territories as he united India.

REIGN OF CHANDRAGUPTA II

Chandragupta II became emperor in approximately 380 CE. He strengthened and expanded his army and actively seized lands belonging to other rulers. One of his most important conquests was the defeat of the Shakas, who ruled over a vast amount of land in the west. The Guptas eventually controlled all land north of the Himalayas, the whole Indus Valley, and most of the eastern kingdoms.

Chandragupta II was a great patron of the arts. In fact, under his rule, India experienced a golden age of art, literature, and music. Much of the art and culture associated with modern India is rooted in the Gupta era.

Chandragupta II also welcomed new ideas and theories. Even though he was a Hindu, he tolerated other religions, such as Buddhism, which thrived during his reign. In fact, a university devoted to Buddhist theology was built during the Gupta era. Jainism was also practiced freely and thrived during this time period.

Hinduism is a religion in which adherents worship several deities. This carved wood image portrays the god Krishna, an avatar of the major god Vishnu, playing a flute.

RELIGION UNDER THE GUPTAS

Just as Ashoka Maurya championed Buddhism, the Guptas championed Hinduism, which is the most common religion in India and Nepal. It is practiced by almost one billion people worldwide. Hinduism has no common set of scripture, although many Hindus place great importance on ancient texts known as the Vedas. There is not one clear founder of the Hindu faith, which is one of the world's oldest religions.

Hinduism shares very close ties with other faiths, such as Jainism and Buddhism. Many Hindus believe that life is a cycle of birth, death, and rebirth, known as samsara. One's rebirth depends on karma, or the consequences of one's actions in a previous life.

The three major gods of Hinduism form the Trimurti, or trinity of deities. They are Brahma, the creator, Vishnu, the preserver, and Shiva, the destroyer. Vishnu has many incarnations or avatars, because according to scripture, he was born nine times.

The three major gods of Hinduism—Shiva, Vishnu, and Brahma, known as the trinity—are depicted here, paying homage to Mahadevi, a female deity.

37

A LITERARY GOLDEN AGE

Chandragupta II was a great patron of the arts. India's classical period of arts and culture was ushered in during his rule.

Chandragupta II supported the career of a man named Kalidasa, who has been called the William Shakespeare of India. He wrote in classical Sanskrit, the official language of the Gupta Empire.

During this time, other literary works were produced, including the *Panchtantra*, a collection of lovely stories, and the *Kamasutra*, a guidebook for love and romance. Other, older works were rewritten, such as the *Mahabharata*, a war story about the Bharata dynasty. Another Sanskrit retelling is that of the *Ramayana*, the tale of Rama, a popular Hindu deity who is one of the incarnations of Vishnu.

Many Gupta-era fables made their way across the empire and were later incorporated into *One Thousand and One Nights*, also commonly known in English as the *Arabian Nights*. These include the tales "Aladdin" and "Ali Baba and the Forty Thieves."

The Ramayana is a beloved epic poem considered one of the great works of Indian literature. This is an illustration of one of its tales. The Ramayana was composed in Sanskrit and dates back as far as 1500 BCE.

SCIENTIFIC AND ARTISTIC ACHIEVEMENTS

Under the Guptas, science and the arts flourished. Chandragupta II sponsored the Navaratnas, or the Nine Jewels—scholars who advised him on artistic, mathematical, and scientific developments and produced work in those fields. Scholars from across the empire were welcomed to India to conduct experiments and advance mathematics.

Gupta-era mathematicians developed the modern number system, which was later adopted by Islamic scholars and eventually made its way to Europe. They also created the idea of the decimal system, based on the number 10, as well as the concept of zero to represent a lack of quantity.

Buddhist artists and architects built stupas, tall shrines to commemorate holy people, which eventually became known as pagodas after becoming popular in China.

A famous medical text, the *Sushruta Samhita*, explained ayurvedic medicine and surgical practices. Astronomers proposed the idea that the Earth actually revolved around the sun, and other scientists observed that the Earth was actually round.

Dhanvantari, an avatar of Vishnu, is the Hindu god of medicine. Many medical advances were made during the Gupta Empire.

archaeologists Scientists who study artifacts and fossils to learn about past human life.

avatars Incarnations, or the human or animal forms of gods.

cavalry Soldiers who ride horses in an army.

citadels Fortresses or castles.

civilization A stage during which humans organize themselves into societies or communities.

deity A god or goddess.

dharma In Hinduism and Buddhism, dharma refers to a person's duty.

dynasty Rulers of a country who are all part of the same family and who inherit in succession.

edicts Laws or orders.

faïence Glazed beads crafted by the Harappans.

fasting A spiritual ritual that involves denying oneself food and sometimes even water for a sustained period of time.

hygiene Practices that lead to good health and sanitation.

infantry Foot soldiers.

kumara A regional head of government who reported to the Mauryan emperor.

nirvana A state of enlightenment that Buddhists hope to reach in their lifetimes.

nomads People who move around in search of food; tribes of people who are not settled in any one particular location.

patron A financial supporter or sponsor.

samsara In Hinduism, a cycle of birth, death, and rebirth.

subcontinent A large portion of land that is a section of a continent; India is a subcontinent.

tribute A system of payment from one ruler to another ruler in return for protection.

Trimurti In Hinduism, the three major gods: Brahma, Vishnu, and Shiva.

Archaeological Survey of India
Janpath
New Delhi 110011
India
Website: http://asi.nic.in
The Archaeological Survey of India (ASI) is the premier organization for
the archaeological research and protection of the cultural heritage
of India. It is responsible for maintenance of ancient monuments,
archaeological sites, and remains of national importance.

Association of Ancient Historians
Department of History, Mercyhurst College
501 East 38th Street, Mailbox 165
Erie, PA 16546-0001
Website: http://associationofancienthistorians.org
The Association of Ancient Historians is the premier organization of
ancient history professionals in the United States and Canada. This
open-membership organization encourages scholarship of ancient
history.

National Council for History Education
13940 Cedar Road #393
Cleveland, OH 44118
(240) 696-6600
Website: http://www.nche.net
The National Council for History Education provides education, professional development opportunities, access to a wide range of
historical organizations, thought-provoking annual conferences,
publications, and information on critical national and local historical issues.

Society for Advancing the History of South Asia
Department of History
University of Victoria
P.O. Box 1700 STN CSC
Victoria, BC V8W 3P4
Canada
(718) 990-8187
Website: http://sahsa.uchicago.edu
This organization promotes scholarship on the history of South Asia.

WEBSITES

Because of the changing nature of Internet links, Rosen Publishing has developed an online list of websites related to the subject of this book. This site is updated regularly. Please use this link to access this list:

http://www.rosenlinks.com/SRFAC/icult/

FOR FURTHER READING

Ali, Daud. *Ancient India: Discover the Rich Heritage of the Indus Valley and the Mughal Empire*. Wigston, Leicestershire, England. Armadillo, 2014.

Bankston, John. *Ancient India: Maurya Empire*. Hockessin, DE: Mitchell Lane, 2012.

Buckley, A. M. *India*. Edina, MN: ABDO Publishing Company, 2012.

Holm, Kirsten. *Everyday Life in Ancient India*. New York, NY: PowerKids, 2012.

Lassieur, Allison. *Ancient India*. New York, NY: Children's Press, 2013.

Rowell, Rebecca. *Ancient India*. Minneapolis, MN: Essential Library, an imprint of ABDO Publishing, 2015.

Roxburgh, Ellis. *The Mauryan Empire of India*. New York, NY: Cavendish, 2015.

Sen Gupta, Subhadra. *A Children's History of India*. Illustrated by Priyankar Gupta. New Delhi, India: Red Turtle Publications, 2015.

Williams, Brian. *Daily Life in the Indus Valley Civilization*. Portsmouth, NH: Heinemann, 2015.

Wood, Alix. *Uncovering the Culture of Ancient India*. New York, NY: PowerKids, 2016.

Cunningham, Kevin. *Classical Civilization: India*. Greensboro, NC: Morgan Reynolds Publishing, 2014.

Dalal, Anita. *National Geographic Investigates: Ancient India: Archaeology Unlocks the Secrets of India's Past*. Washington, DC: National Geographic Books, 2007.

Lassieur, Allison. *Ancient India*. New York, NY: Children's Press, 2012.

New World Encyclopedia. "Indus Valley Civilization." http://www.newworldencyclopedia.org/entry/Indus_Valley_Civilization.

University of Washington. "Gupta Dynasty." https://depts.washington.edu/silkroad/exhibit/guptas/guptas.html.

Ushistory.org. "The Birth and Spread of Buddhism." *Ancient Civilizations Online Textbook*. http://www.ushistory.org/civ/8d.asp.

A

archaeologists, 8, 10, 12, 14
art, 28, 34, 38, 40
Ashoka, 18, 20, 22, 24, 30, 36
  edicts of, 22, 28
  pillars of, 22, 28, 32

B

Buddhism, 4, 20, 22, 24, 28, 34, 36

C

Chandragupta Maurya, 16, 26, 28
  death of, 18
Chandragupta II, 32, 34, 38, 40

E

economy, 12, 16
edicts, 22, 28, 32

F

faïence, 10, 12
farming, 6, 8
flooding, of Indus River, 12, 14, 16

G

Gupta Empire, 32, 38

H

Harappa, 8, 10, 12
Hinduism, 4, 36
houses, 8, 10

I

Indus River, 6, 12, 16
Indus Valley civilization, 6, 10, 12
  decline of, 14, 16
  religion of, 14

J

Jainism, 18, 34, 36

K

Kautilya, 16, 28

L

language, 4, 14, 28, 30
literature, 28, 34, 38

M

Maurya dynasty, 18, 22, 26, 32

Mohenjodaro, 8, 10, 12
music, 14, 34

R

religion, 4, 14, 18, 20, 22, 34, 36

S

Samudragupta, 30
  conquests of, 32
Sanskrit, 4, 28, 38
Shakas, 34
Shiva, 36
Silk Road, 26, 28

T

tribute, 32
Trimurti, 36

V

Vedas, 36
Vishnu, 36, 38

ABOUT THE AUTHOR

Susan Nichols lives and writes in Baltimore, Maryland. As a child, she read books set in colonial India by writers such as Rudyard Kipling. As she got older, she began to read more about the colonization of India by England, as well as about India's struggle for liberation. Currently, she enjoys reading novels by modern Indian and Indian American writers, such as Shashi Tharoor and Jhumpa Lahiri. Nichols has always been interested in ancient and medieval history, especially in cultures of the Middle East and Far East. She is the author of several biographies and history books for young adults.

PHOTO CREDITS